Now You Can Take Off Your Clothes:

Vignettes of an American Conductor Lost in Translation

Jon Ceander Mitchell

Riverhaven Books

www.RiverhavenBooks.com

Now You Can Take Off Your Clothes is a memoir. Names were not changed, places are actual, and events are recorded to the best of the author's ability. While this is not a historical document, it does capture the experiences of a conductor who chose to keep his clothes on.

Published in the United States by Riverhaven Books,
www.RiverhavenBooks.com

ISBN: 978-1-951854-06-5

Printed in the United States of America

Edited and designed by
Stephanie Lynn Blackman
Whitman, MA

Front and Back Artwork: Kurt Mitchell

Dedication

To Robert Grechesky,
who can tell a joke
much better than anybody else
and thus makes the world laugh with him.

Table of Contents

Jon Mitchell's account of his time in the UK in the 1980s brings back so many good memories - at the time I only knew half of what he was up to, and all the many things he would go on to do. This is such fascinating reading.
~Dr. Colin Matthews, OBE, Composer Emeritus, Halle Orchestra, Music Director of the Britten-Pears Foundation, former Managing Editor of G & I Holst, Ltd.

Acknowledgements

It was a couple of years ago, during a conference afterglow session of genial conviviality and imbibing, that a number of my friends and colleagues suggested that I should write a book containing many of the stories that they must have heard me relate more than once.

So many individuals have contributed to this book – some musically, some administratively, some doing proofreading, some offering suggestions, some offering moral support, some offering nothing but kindness, and still others by simply having the wherewithal to have lived through one or more of the adventures described herein. With all of these factors, I know that I'll forget to include someone; it is purely unintentional. Nevertheless…

I'd like to start off by thanking the soloists who shared one or more entire trips with me: Timothy McFarland, who was with me for what amounted to be the most outrageous journey to Istanbul and Bulgaria; Linnéa Bardarson, whose timely humor brought us through two recording sessions in the Czech Republic and beyond; Grigorios (Gregory) Zamparas, who was a great friend and colleague through the Rubinstein recording project sessions and so much more; Jeffrey Jacob, who invited me to be a part of his recording project in Hrádec Králove, Czech Republic, and world premiere concert in Prague. There were also fine musicians who assisted these soloists in other capacities: Orie Sato, Hans Gielge, and Z.Z.

There were a number of other soloists who were a joy to work with, in score study, rehearsal and performance: pianist Zofia Antes, soprano Aga Winska, and clarinetist Wojciech (Woytech) Mrozek (all in Wałbrzych, Poland), cellist Georg Stefan, and the Beethoven's 9th vocal soloists in Stara Zagora, Bulgaria: E. Barmova, D. Dkova, N. Mochov, and A. Radev. In addition, there were soloists within the Bohuslav Martinů Phiharmonic of Zlin, Czech Republic: timpanist Grigor Kruyer, flutist Jana Holaskova, bassoonist Zdenek Skrabel, and clarinetists Aleš Pavlorek and Jiří Kundl.

Administratively there were three people in particular who facilitated the European concerts and recordings: Tanya Tintner – to whom I owe a huge debt of gratitude – as well as Harry Hurvitz and Patricia Hitchcock of Symphonic Workshops. Administrative personnel who prepared for my well-being at concert and recording sites include Marek Obdrčalek and Tomáš Gregůrek, managers of the Bohuslav Martinů Philharmonic in Zlin, Mladen Stanev, choral conductor of the State Opera in Stara Zagora, and Josef Wilkomirski, conductor of the Filharmonie Sudecka in Wałbrzych. Two guides also deserve special mention: Natasha Uzunova, flutist with the Vratza, Bulgaria Philharmonic, and Julia Lewandowskaya, associated with the Filharmoni Chamber Orchestra of Arkhangelsk, Russia. Gennady Chernov also helped us a great deal upon our entry and exit from Russia.

The following assisted greatly in facilitating my research in England: Imogen Holst, Colin Matthews, Ursula Vaughan Williams, Major Roger Swift, and Lt. Col. Rodney Bashford. In facilitating research presentations on the continent: Wolfgang Suppan, Bernhard Habla, Doris Goldabend Schweinzer and most recently Damien Sagrillo. In facilitating for concerts and recordings: Tomaš Novotny, Dejan Pablov, Zbiegniew Bajek, Valeri Vatchev, and Kurt Mitchell.

While mentioning facilitators, I would be remiss not to mention the institutions of higher learning that awarded me at least partial internal funding toward many of these trips: University of Illinois, Hanover College, Carnegie Mellon University, University of Georgia, and University of Massachusetts Boston. And, involved on the technical side of things: Victor Sachse, Dan Cassins, Toby Mountain, Paul Griffith, Peter Janson, David Ackerman, Christo Pavlov, Hubert Geschwander, and Emil Nizmansky,

I have had many mentors, conducting and otherwise, throughout my career. Some are mentioned in various chapters of the book, though deserving of special mention are Harry Begian, Richard Colwell, Jonathan Sternberg, Victor Feldbrill, and Rostislav Hališka.

I consider most of the people I have met in my life as friends, including those mentioned above. Many other friends have contributed, in one way or another, to this book. First and foremost I have to mention compatriots Robert and Adrienne Grechesky, who provided me with a week's worth of the Merriest Olde England adventures imaginable. Also in England: Geoffrey Brand, Timothy Reynish, John Fowles, Rosamund Strode, Helen Lilley, Irene Giuffredi, Michael Short, Alan Gibbs, and Howard Skempton. On the European continent: Michael Dejnov, Erzebet and family, Dzidza and family. In the United States: Ricardo Averbach, Jeffrey Bell-Hanson, Paul D'Angelo, Elaine Baker D'Angelo, Emilian Badea, Paul Niemisto, Thomas Harris, and Daune Stevenson Sebastian.

Also Richard Fiske, David Whitwell, Valerie Traficante, Lauren Komack, Neal Hampton, Peter Cardarelli, Kile Smith, Joan Landry, David Mitchell, Gordon Jacob, John Bird, Mark Heron, Eric Banks, F. Vivian Dunn, Stephen Connock, Freda Burgher, James Mickel, Bernardo Adam Ferrero, Francis Pieters, William Johnson, Christard Janetsky, Mr. Sedlaczek, Agnetta, Oxana Chernov, Atanas Athanassov, Viechlav Novak, Georg Petrov, Vassilka Spassova, Dana Kruyerova, Pavel Mikeska, library personnel at the British Library, Westminster Central Library, Royal College of Music, Royal Academy of Music, Upper Norwood Library, Cambridge University, and last but not least, Nikolai the Woodcutter.

Prelude

"If I ever go looking for my heart's desire again,
I won't look any further than my own back yard.
Because if it isn't there, I never really lost it to begin with."
– L. Frank Baum, *The Wonderful Wizard of Oz* (1900)

This famous quote, read by millions of people and heard in the 1939 movie *The Wizard of Oz* by millions more, was spoken by eleven-year-old Dorothy Gale after her adventures in Oz. Not going further than her own back yard may have worked for Dorothy, but for many of us there is a certain personal fulfillment that requires us to get *out* of our own back yards again and again, to experience life in a very different setting.

For me, the journey toward personal fulfillment has followed many paths. One of them has involved travel. I've been to Europe more than fifty times. The first was at age thirty doing doctoral research, so my journeys haven't involved any youthful indiscretion, just occasional foolishness. The trips themselves can be broken down into four categories – research, conference, concert, and recording – yet few of these journeys fall into only one category; there is much overlap. At least twenty-three have involved conducting (either conducting concerts or recordings or both), another twenty-one "jawing" at conferences, and at least another seventeen doing research. A fifth category, being exclusively "vacation," has crept into my life since retirement, but it is beyond the scope of this book.

By profession I was a conductor and college professor for thirty-five years and a public school band director for seven years prior to that. Perhaps the professor in me has allowed me to observe more than I otherwise would have, and a lot of what I have observed really *is* funny. Victor Borge said in his book *My Favorite Comedies in Music* (1980) "…truth is not only stranger than fiction, but a whole lot funnier." This holds true for most of what I have observed, much of it being from cross-cultural miscommunication. There is no fiction here – I could not have possibly made this stuff up – though there may be some slight embellishing here and there. Yet not all of it is funny. Within comedy there is often a certain degree of drama and I hope that readers will not hold it against me for including some rather annoying episodes as well.

Now You Can Take Off Your Clothes: Vignettes of an American Conductor Lost in Translation, while written in the first person, is not meant to be strictly an autobiography. It does indeed contain memoirs, but is confined to a limited number of adventures abroad; most of these are humorous and all but one occurred in Europe. The book covers a thirty-five year period, from my first visit to England in January, 1980 through my latest recording venture in the Czech Republic during November of 2014. It is arranged more or less chronologically, though an exception is made for the three guest conducting stints in Wałbrzych, Poland, which fit together nicely as a group. For brevity's sake not all transatlantic trips are included, nor are all parts of each trip. For example, there have been very pleasant excursions to Ireland, Luxembourg, and Sweden, yet these were not of an adventurous nature.

Sources used in compiling this book include personal journals, ledgers, written correspondence, emails, phone conversations, documents, articles, CD liner notes, photographs, printed programs, posters, discussions with others involved, plus my own personal recollections. Though *Now You Can Take Off Your Clothes* is not an academic book *per se* (no footnotes or bibliography), an index is included for the reader's convenience.

It has been said that optimists look at their glass as being half full while pessimists see their glass as being half empty. Mine is at least half full, perhaps even ¾. Writing *NYCTOYC* and revisiting these adventures, both on and off the podium, has verified that for me. It has been a real joy, a true labor of love.

Enjoy!

JCM
Franklin, MA
Spring, 2020

A look back

at adventures abroad. . .

I. A Pie in the Sky

He looked me right in the eyes, shook his head, and said pompously, "Forget about going to London. It's a 'Pie in the Sky.'" These long, drawn-out words from one of the three professors on my thesis committee – the one who didn't bother to read my submitted chapters – were not encouraging. After all, nobody from the particular doctoral program I was enrolled in had ever received a University of Illinois Graduate College Dissertation Research Grant, let alone one that involved trans-Atlantic travel. Fortunately, I didn't listen to him and instead followed the advice of my well-connected principal advisor who valued my dissertation topic, "Gustav Holst: The Works for Military Band," and what I was attempting to do. Both he and the third member of my committee (my conducting mentor) encouraged me to "go for it," and a month later, sometime during the latter half of 1979, I received notification by mail that my grant request had been approved – every penny of it. "Pie in the Sky" became reality and changed my life forever.

* * *

$1,122 wasn't a whole lot of money, not even in January 1980, but it was all I had to get me back-and-forth to London, carry out my research, and survive there for three weeks. In certain ways I was prepared for it. For the past year and a half my wife of six years, our two infant daughters, and I had been surviving on roughly $3,000 a year – earned from my teaching assistantship and playing whatever gigs I could find. We lived in the university's married student housing at Orchard Downs and had temporarily embraced a lifestyle that included annual bus passes, driving as little as possible, buying generic groceries, and accepting assistance from the government's WIC program. These were not the best of times, yet, after six years of dealing with the intense pressures of being a high school band director – especially the public servant aspect (putting up with parents and having to perform in the stands at "other peoples'" games without any compensation) – there was a certain satisfaction in knowing that, somehow, better things lie ahead.

The flights to and from London had to be charter flights; the granted money did not allow for taking a major airline. On the way over, however, I lucked out with British Caledonian, known for their exquisite dining service (real silverware!) and, yes, I was able to eat a portion of apple "Pie in the Sky." This, however, was countered by the eight-hour return flight on Arrow Air – – not only was there no movie, but the obese woman seated next to me smelled really bad!

The British had just completed the Piccadilly Line Underground Railway connection from Heathrow Airport to central London, so my first view of London was not to see it at all for the first hour. I exited the Underground at Russell Square in Bloomsbury. This was the nearest "tube" station to the British Museum, which then housed The British Library, where I would do the bulk of my research. The station didn't have an escalator, but an elevator ("lift") instead, so the anticipation of that first view grew as I had to wait in a queue beneath the surface. When I was finally transported above ground, the view around Russell Square conjured up memories of the strangely American "Snob Hill" backgrounds painted for Walt Disney's *Lady and the Tramp.*

Friends familiar with London had recommended that I look for lodging in this Bloomsbury area, which was quite pleasant. These were the days before cell (mobile) phones and the internet, so everything had to be done by written correspondence, telephone, or simply showing up in person. These were also the days before most credit cards were universal, so there was a great deal of time spent in going to the American Express office on Haymarket Street to cash Traveler's Checks. The currency that I received was in British Pounds Sterling, of course.

The small hotel in the Cartwright Gardens crescent was about what I had expected: a charming townhouse serving professionals who had business in the Bloomsbury district. What I had not anticipated was the price per night: £8. I had expected it to be £6. Still, I thought I would give it a try. With my total daily budget at £13, it left me with £5 per day for meals and incidental expenses.

London was impressive; how could it not be? It was – – and still is –

– a great walking town. Foyle's, the largest independent English language bookstore in the world, was only a fifteen-minute walk, as was The English National Opera. It was there that I was able to see Mozart's *The Magic Flute* for the whopping student price of £1! The Bohemian neighborhood of Soho was another ten minutes west. This being early January, I often ended up walking in the dark. It was difficult to get accustomed to the mid-afternoon darkness, usually occurring before any thoughts of hunger set in. Most evenings I was back in Bloomsbury, ensconced at Russell's, a rather modern pub near the University of London. My work-study supervising professor, however, had recommended a different pub, Watney's Tap, and even had provided me with a £1 note to go there to have a "pint of bitters." It was supposed to be directly across the street from the entrance to the British Museum, but when I looked for that particular pub, I couldn't find it.

After three or four days of reasonably good living, I realized that I couldn't afford to stay in Russell Square any longer, so I consulted my 1976 *Nicolson's Guide* plus several newspapers to search for an alternative. I found it at a large white Victorian building with huge pillars located in the Bayswater District, not far from Paddington Station. Though billed as the Sussex Gardens International Students' Club in the telephone directory, I noticed when I got there that the place was now called the Welcome Inn. Though I had a private room, the "inn" was little more than a flop house; the unheated wedge-shaped fiberglass bathrooms were literally outside in an ascending three-story spiral ramp attached to the back of the building. Each wedge-shaped section contained either a sink, a toilet, or a shower. However cold these bathrooms were, at £5 per night this place allowed me to live like a king – – leaving a whopping £8 per day for meals and incidentals.

The stay in London was exceedingly busy. There were a number of people to see and manuscripts to be studied. My principal advisor had suggested that I see the people first, as people's schedules often changed on a whim. The first to be seen was Imogen Holst, daughter of Gustav Holst, composer of *The Planets* and the central focus of my doctoral dissertation. However, just prior to my arrival she had suffered a heart attack. Her physician advised her to have complete rest, which meant not having any personal interviews or even answering any personal questions. Dr. Colin Matthews, then managing editor of G. & I. Holst, Ltd. (named after the composer and his daughter), graciously helped me out here and at least I was able to have a couple of telephone conversations with Miss Holst. For both conversations I was in one of those wonderful red British phone booths. At that time calls cost a minimum of only two pence and one could insert either a 2p coin or a 5p coin. The UK had abandoned the shilling only nine years earlier. Their new 5p coin (similar in size to an American fifty-cent piece) was interchangeable with the shilling but their 10p coin was about the size of a silver dollar. The result was that everybody had very heavy pockets. British seamstresses must have had a field day mending them! I started by using up my 5p coins first. We were able to converse fairly well for about eight minutes until these ran out. Then I had to use the 2p coins, which interrupted our conversation about every five seconds. I remember Imogen Holst saying, "Oh, God!" as things became unmanageable. In spite of this, she (and Colin) opened the door for me to carry out my research, and for that I continue to be eternally grateful.

Contacts with other people resulted in varying degrees of help. One of the less productive visits was to see Arnold Bentley at University College in Reading, about forty miles west of London. If nothing else, it helped me learn about British punctuality and their then-precise railway service. I knew ahead of time that I would begin my journey sometime during mid-morning from Paddington Station but was flabbergasted when he wanted to know exactly when he had to be at the Reading station – 10:40, 10:50, or 10:55! At first I didn't know what to tell him, but decided on the 10:50 so that he would be only marginally upset if I were on one of the other two. Apparently he was not familiar with the legendary tardiness that characterizes Amtrak as well as various American Commuter Rail systems.

One of the nicest and least pretentious people I met was Geoffrey

Brand, chairman of the board of R. Smith & Co., the world's largest publisher of British brass band music. Geoffrey had a son, Michael, who was my age and, knowing that I missed my wife Ester and our three children, he and his wife Violet had me to dinner at their home near Watford. He had a very fatherly manner and earlier at his office he addressed me three or four times as "Young Jon." At the same time, however, he was very much a businessman and charged me for a copy of *Brass Bands in the Twentieth Century*, a book he had co-written with Violet.

Our initial interview was interrupted by a telephone call. As he was listening, Geoffrey looked quite concerned. He learned that his house had just been burglarized. The interview had to be cut short, of course. As we were about to leave, he maintained his composure, looked me directly in the eye and said twice, "Life goes on." What control!

Without a doubt the most fruitful visit on that first trip was to the highly esteemed Royal Military School of Music (RMSM). The school was then situated at Kneller Hall, on an estate located southwest of London, in Middlesex County, between the towns of Twickenham and Whitton. Originally the country residence of eighteenth-century court painter Godfrey Kneller, the building in its present form dates from 1849. The school itself had been located there since its founding in 1857. I had called the school ahead of time and they were expecting me. From what I could tell, the RMSM was run by the commandant and administered by the adjutant; both being entirely separate from the director of music. Upon my arrival, I was surprised to discover that the band from St. Olaf College in Northfield, Minnesota, was also visiting there. It was nice to get acquainted with the band's conductor, Miles Johnson, and his assistant, Paul Niemisto. Paul and I had both forgotten about this until, recounting our adventures to each other many years later, we discovered that due to this happenstance, we had actually known each other for many decades! We instantly became new old friends!

At Kneller Hall I was treated very well and given time to look at some of the manuscript musical scores in their student archives, a repository of arrangements done by army band directors when they were students at RMSM. Later that morning the commandant, Lt. Col. Rodney Bashford, OBE, gave me a grand tour of the grounds and I was invited (and honored) to have lunch with the officers. The Victorian Era dining room, the history, the tradition – all of this was somewhat overwhelming. The most memorable moment, however, had nothing to do with the normal pomp and circumstance of the place – or did it?

Before my departure, while still in the dining room, I overheard three or four of the officers discussing the lottery that was to be held during the next week. I asked them what all this was about. Rather sheepishly, one of them filled me in. It turned out that in the next few days Princess Anne was coming to visit and inspect the RMSM. This included a ceremonial dinner. Since she was a human being, it was expected that she would use the officers' toilet facilities nearby. The lottery was for ownership of the toilet seat used by her! As another officer put it, it was to be a memento of the Royal Ass!

The Kneller Hall visit was not my only contact with British military bands. I noticed that there was an event listed as "Guards Bands Spectacular" to be held at Royal Albert Hall, the enormous 5,600-seat concert hall located in South Kensington, near the Royal College of Music and Royal College of Organists. I eagerly bought the cheapest ticket available but didn't inquire about the layout of the place. My seat turned out to be the closest seat stage right on the highest level and looking directly down on the percussion. This was all fine and good until the last number on the program, Eckersberg's *The Battle of Waterloo*. The firing of the cannons just about blew my ears off!

In addition to doing my research work, I had plenty of time to explore London, as long as what I was exploring was free or nearly so. Walks in Hyde Park and along the Thames were frequent. Museums were also real winners. The British Museum had a lot to offer as did the great trio at South Kensington: Natural History, Science, and Victoria & Albert. Then there was one south of the river whose very existence wreaks of irony. The Imperial War Museum is most impressive; at that time it included exhibits from World War I through the then-very-recent Falkland Islands War. The museum is located in a building that once housed a psychiatric hospital, officially titled Bethlehem Hospital, later shortened to Bethlem, but it became best-known through its notorious nickname: Bedlam. Thus the building had undergone a transformation from housing one kind of insanity to housing another!

As time went on, the money began to run out. I was able to scrimp on meals, being satisfied with a 38-pence fish sandwich or 20-pence bowl of oxtail soup most of the time. The days of having a pint at a pub quickly became a thing of the past.

By my last day in London, I had enough money for the Underground ride back to Heathrow Airport but not enough to have lunch. Then I remembered that there was one person I had not yet contacted, a retired military band director. My conducting mentor had warned me about him. He had appeared as a guest conductor one day at my mentor's invitation and had alienated everybody, including the players in front of him, with his pompous nature and self-congratulatory tales. I had also heard much the same thing at Uxbridge from a Royal Air Force wing commander, who advised: "Don't go see him; he is a *colossal bore*."

Still, I was starving, so I made the call to the retired officer, who instantly invited me to have lunch with him at the Army and Navy Club at Grosvenor Square. What luck! However, it turned out to be one of the longest lunches of my life, listening to stories generating from his inflated ego for over an hour. Was it worth it? Well, he was generous – and I didn't starve…

During the remaining hours of this final day in London, by sheer accident I made a frustrating discovery – frustrating because it was too late to act upon it. In preparation for this trip, I had read dozens of journal articles, including one stating that St. Paul's Girls' School, the school where Gustav Holst had done the bulk of his teaching and composing, no longer existed. As I was walking around the Lancaster Gate area, however, I found a newspaper with a photograph of two students returning from break and *walking on the grounds of St. Paul's Girls'*

School. Indeed, it still existed, but I had only enough time to take a bus to Brook Green in Hammersmith to snap a picture of the outside!

* * *

About halfway through my doctoral coursework, eminent band historian David Whitwell visited the University of Illinois campus and mentioned to me that no one had written a dissertation on the band works of Gustav Holst. While most people don't enjoy going through the intense rigor of writing their doctoral dissertations, my own experience was an exception. I had expected my doctorate to propel me into a teaching position at the college level (it did, although one year later than expected), but I hadn't anticipated the amount of interest that my dissertation would generate within the profession. Correspondence from both the United Kingdom and the United States poured in, so much so that I decided to expand my thesis into a book – and in order to do that, I had to make at least one more sojourn to England.

By 1982 I held the title of Assistant Professor of Music at Hanover College in southern Indiana. Hanover, a small institution of higher learning with approximately 1,000 students, prided itself on being a "teaching" college, yet they had a small budget to assist the very few full-time faculty members who were interested in doing research. By this time our family had expanded to five and, with Hanover's extremely low pay, money was still very tight. It was my good fortune, however, to receive two grants from the research committee – sufficient for a pair of two-week return visits to England in June 1983 and July 1986. I was now conductor of two fledgling instrumental groups, the Hanover College Wind Ensemble and the Hanover College-Community Chamber Orchestra. Thus these research trips were also useful for finding new or unknown musical compositions for my groups to perform.

This trip (June 1983) the funding was sufficient for me to stay at the Georgian Hotel, a small bed-and-breakfast on Gower Street, without having to move to a cheaper and less attractive place. Once again confidence was high, and on the second day I walked down to Foyles'

Book Shop, then down Shaftesbury Avenue, from Bloomsbury toward Chinatown. All of London was my realm.

Unfortunately, *all* of London was right. As I was staring into a window somewhere in Chinatown, a middle-aged man accosted me, first shouting, "You bastards! You have destroyed our women and children." He then took two swipes at my head; the first one missed, but the second landed a solid blow. I then shouted "Help! Police!" at the top of my lungs and tried to run away from this guy. Shop owners stepped out to try to lend an assist, but the guy got away. A bobby who had come to the rescue asked me, "Are *you* okay?"

I answered, "Yes, I'm okay."

Then, referring to my attacker, he asked "Is *he* okay?"

I answered, "No, I don't think so," referring to his mental state. I was so shaken up by this incident that I went to bed at seven o'clock that evening and eight o'clock the next.

The following day I met Colin Matthews in person for the first time. Colin was managing editor of G. & I. Holst and, naturally, interested in my research. Both he and his older brother David were rising composers. Colin and his young family lived in a townhouse in Clapham, a neighborhood located in southwest London. Clapham, well-known for having the third-largest railway station in London, as well as a very large park (Clapham Common), had become increasingly gentrified over the years. Fellow composer Howard Skempton was also on hand. Howard lived nearby and at this point in his career was serving as Colin's editorial assistant. Howard cheerfully advised and accompanied me on a number of occasions during this trip; he also provided me with vital research information through later correspondence. The three of us laughed in recalling some of Gustav Holst's humor, an example of which follows:

Modern music is neither
a) modern
nor
b) music

I then related to them both about my having been accosted. They told me that this was extremely rare and would not happen again during my stay in London. It didn't. However…

A few days later, when I had just begun to recover my personal sense of security, I fell on the street while stupidly trying to jump onto the back of an already moving AEC Routemaster – one of those great red double-decker buses, the old type that had a pole running the height of its first story. I skinned my hands pretty badly and a Nigerian man came to my assistance. I thought he was a nice guy, but it turned out that he was too nice, first helping me up and then wanting to walk with me holding hands. I don't know whether or not this was some sort of cultural thing or if he was making some sort of advance. After emphatically shouting "No!" about five times, he finally got the hint that I was not of his persuasion – if that were the case.

In addition to calling on Colin Matthews, there were three other people I needed to see. Geoffrey Brand, whom I had met on my previous trip, had arranged for the two us to visit the BBC Written Archives Center in Reading to research the BBC Military Band. I was to meet him at 8:30 a.m. at the Moor Park railway station. Unfortunately, I slept through my alarm that morning. Scurrying like crazy, I quickly got dressed, ran outside, and was able to grab one of those legendary black London cabs for a quick ride to the Baker Street Underground station and, via one transfer, eventually arrived at Moor Park, somewhat later than I had wanted. Geoffrey was already there, nervously waiting for me. Of course we had a good laugh when I mentioned the ultraprecision expected from me on my arrival into Reading three years earlier. We then hurried over to the BBC Written Archives Center where we spent several hours. It was one of the most fruitful research days I have ever had. We even had a "mandatory" tea break served up in the finest English tradition.

The next day I was able to satisfy one particular item that was unfulfilled on my previous trip: a visit to St. Paul's Girls' School and conductor Hilary Davan-Wetton, then music director at the school. There I was able to see the Gustav Holst Music Wing, built in 1913, which allowed the composer his own large private office. The orchestra that Holst founded is still going strong there and, as a young Jane Primrose said on my way out, “It’s as if Holst’s spirit never left.”

There were a plethora of libraries to be visited during this trip. I had already been to many of them on my first trip, but there was always another stone to be unturned. The British Library, Upper Norwood Library near Crystal Palace Park, Central Music Library in Westminster, Royal College of Music, Royal Academy of Music, etc., all played an integral part in the scheme of things. The librarians were always efficient and kind yet self-deprecating.

One of the more interesting collections was at the Cecil Sharp House, home of the English Folk Dance and Song Society, located near Regent’s Park. This building, named for England’s most prolific collector of English folk songs, houses the Vaughan Williams Memorial Library, containing a huge collection. I went there to find the identities and various settings of folk songs used by Holst. I knew that Holst’s *Second Suite in F* started with “Glorishears,” but didn’t know the source. When I asked the librarian behind the counter about this, he said, “Oh Glorishears? It goes like this…” He hummed a few measures, but it wasn’t anything with which I was familiar. I shook my head. Then he hummed another, then another, then another. After going through about six of them, I hummed the tune that I knew back to him. He smiled and said rather loudly, “Oh, you mean the BAMPTON Glorishears!” It was a fortunate revelation for, by this time, other people in the library had begun to notice our rather comical “musical” conversation.

I had been warned about going to British military band concerts in the parks, but I didn’t listen. The curiosity element finally took hold. The British class system was still very much in evidence in 1983. The upper classes generally attended concerts by any one of London’s five professional orchestras, the ballet, performances by either the English National Opera, or the opera company at Covent Garden. The working classes (coal miners, shoe factory workers, etc.) attended (and often participated in) concerts by the more than 2,000 British brass bands. That left the middle classes (largely white-collar professionals) as the target audience for the military bands.

Eager to see what the military bands had to offer I scheduled myself to see two concerts for my last Sunday in London. At 3:00 in the afternoon I was at St. James Park, not far from Buckingham Palace, to hear the Irish Guards Band. Unfortunately, as a conductor, what I saw did not impress me. There were maybe one hundred spectators lounging in rented deck chairs, many entirely oblivious to the event at hand. The concert began with a christening of the new flat bandstand, with one of the players spilling champagne around its perimeter. Many of the gazebo bandstands, including this one's predecessor, had been replaced due to recent IRA bombings. After that ceremony, the concert was about one-third announcement, one-third joke telling, and maybe one-third music performance. The music was not of the stiff-upper-lip British military band tradition that I had expected. There may have been one or two marches and one or two selections from musicals, but the remainder was pablum. The performers were all quite capable but not respectful of the conductor, who appeared to be more interested in his own joke-telling skills than in conducting any type of meaningful musical performance. It was a most irritating afternoon for me, the result being that I decided not to attend the concert of the Band of the Royal Engineers at Regents Park later that evening.

Earlier on this trip I had gone to a performance by the Royal Philharmonic Orchestra, perhaps the best of the London orchestras then, at Royal Festival Hall on the south bank of the Thames. The concert opened with Beethoven's *Leonore Overture No. 3*, Op. 72b, one of the great overtures in the orchestral repertoire. The orchestra was warming up on the stage when the second bassoonist developed a look of panic on his face. Something was wrong with his instrument. He looked around and, taking his bassoon with him, ran off stage. Ten seconds later, one of the last-row cellists, seated stage left, discretely left the stage. Ten seconds after that, that cellist emerged from behind a curtain farther down the stage and sat down in the second bassoonist's chair. I was hopeful that the conductor had a "head's up" on the situation. He came out on stage, bowed to the audience, turned around, and conducted the overture without incident, with the interpolated cellist doing his best to imitate a bassoon. Following the overture, the second bassoonist reappeared on stage and the cellist took his usual seat, the emergency apparently solved. This was pure professionalism at its best.

One of the longer trips during this particular sojourn was a train ride to Manchester. Looking at the ticket prices, I was afraid that I couldn't afford it, but then I discovered the "Cheap Day Return" ticket if one left London's Euston Station after 9:30 a.m. – how convenient. The train arrived at Manchester's Piccadilly Station before noon and from there it was a short walk to the Royal Northern College of Music (RNCM) and an interview with Timothy Reynish. Tim, originally a horn player, was conductor of the Wind Orchestra at the RNCM. He had thick glasses and an inimitable gentlemanly approach. Tim and I had met during the previous year at a conference in Michigan. We talked about many things and, eventually, I mentioned that I was thirty-three years old, concerned that I had gotten into the conducting profession too late. Tim looked at me and burst out laughing. "Jon, you are spring chicken. Life begins at fifty!" It was only after I returned to the States that I found out that Tim was all of forty-five when he gave me that advice!

Afterwards Tim invited me to lunch and drove us north into the rural areas. We stopped at the old mill village of Withnell Fold to pick up his friend John Fowles. Fowles, who had made his fortune in road signs, had an expansive military band record collection dating back to ca. 1910. Much of it was on the already-by-then-ancient 78 r.p.m. disks; some of them were a quarter of an inch thick! He was very gracious and gave me two LPs of music compiled by the International Military Music Society (IMMS). One of them featured the BBC Military Band, key to my research. After a few minutes at his place, we drove further into the countryside to one of Tim's favorite pubs. The setting was precisely what one would have expected. Inside there was a tap featuring many different lagers and ales, and there were some men wearing tweed coats and Ivy League caps in heavy conversation while others were throwing darts. I was imagining all sorts of English pub fare – fish and chips, shepherd's pie, Yorkshire pudding, etc. – when Tim suggested we have the house specialty. Imagine my chagrin when it turned out to be pizza!

* * *

During the winter of 1985-86 I received a phone call from Robert Grechesky, band director at Butler University in Indianapolis, less than a two-hour drive from Hanover. Bob had shown a great deal of interest in composer Ralph Vaughan Williams, a life-long friend of Gustav Holst. Though I knew of him, Bob and I had never met in person so I invited him down to Hanover College to visit. I finished my last class of the day and walked home (a thirty-second walking commute from our back door) and found Bob already there, spread out in my favorite chair. His ebullient personality had already taken over our living room. From that very first instant we became close friends. In fact most people who have ever met Bob would also feel that way; he is that kind of guy. Bob told me of how he was going to London for two weeks in July to research Vaughan Williams. That was the impetus I needed to write another grant proposal and visit London for a third time.

Bob's second week in London coincided with my first, the result being that he and his wife Adrienne – Ad (pronounced "Aid") for short – carried me through the best jet-lag day that I ever had. I checked in to Hughes-Parry Hall, a dorm at University of London, and went to find Bob and Ad. We had to decide on somewhere to meet, and I recalled a pub that billed itself as "The Only Pub on Oxford Street" on the corner of Tottenham Court Road, but couldn't recall its name. This was in the day before we owned cellular phones, so we knew we were taking a chance on all being at the right place at the right time – trying for some sort of "Higgins-Pickering" meeting from George Bernard Shaw's *Pygmalion* (*My Fair Lady*). Throwing caution to the wind, we decided to meet at that particular pub. Fortunately, Bob and Ad found it without a problem and, of course, the pub's name turned out to be "The Tottenham!"

After downing a pint of bitters, we headed for a restaurant in London's East End, along the new wharf area beyond the Tower of London. I was still wearing my traveling clothes, which included a corduroy sports jacket. It turned out to be entirely inappropriate as London was experiencing a heat wave. When I mentioned to Bob and Ad that my room at Hughes-Parry was quite warm, they told me that they were staying in a private bed-and-breakfast house in the Fulham area that was owned and operated by a Mrs. Traube. Hoping that I, too, could stay at Mrs. Traube's, we took the Underground to her place only to find out that she was entirely booked. Mrs. Traube came to the rescue, however, and made a quick phone call to her friend who lived just around the corner. Her friend had room for me, and at only £6 per night.

Mrs. Irene Giuffredi was a seventy-four-year-old Italian immigrant widow who owned a two-story townhouse. There were three spotless guest rooms that were often rented out to English-speaking tourists, usually from South Africa. My room was located at the back of the second floor (Europeans would call it the first floor) with a rear window that looked over the fiberglass annex of a social club. There was some sound bleed on most nights from the London yuppies that frequented that establishment, but I didn't mind as I was always sufficiently tired enough to get a good night's sleep.

Mrs. Giuffredi was one of a kind. On the plump side, with dyed brown hair, and somewhat short, she usually could be found wearing some sort of sack dress with a floral pattern. Her usual jolly nature was complemented by a rather unique Italian-British accent. In the mornings she would often have breakfast with me. We would chat for a while and then, suddenly, almost on cue, she would turn to me and say quite loudly, "Off wich'ya now!" You always knew where you stood with her. She subscribed to *The Sun*. Why, I don't know. There were much better newspapers in London – *The Times*, *The Daily Telegraph*, etc. – but she read what was essentially a scandal sheet that always had a *Playboy*-type centerfold. For the next eleven years I stayed at Mrs. Giuffredi's whenever I went to London – not because it was financially a bargain, not because of the *Playboy*-type centerfolds, but because of her cheerful personality. Over the years she had become much more than just an acquaintance; she had become a friend and her place at the beginning of Quarrendon Road became my "home away from home" in London.

The first full day of this trip turned out to be one of great adventure. Bob had arranged for a visit to meet preeminent Ralph Vaughan Williams and Edward Elgar scholar Michael Kennedy in Cheltenham. Kennedy had some Vaughan Williams manuscripts that Bob (and I) wanted to see. Cheltenham, home of the Holst Birthplace Museum, is located about two hours northwest of London by train in a region known as the Cotswold Hills. I had been to Cheltenham once before – it's a beautiful small resort city, listed as Cheltenham Spa on railway signage – but this time getting there was going to be very different: we were going to *drive* there. Bob and Ad wanted to experience the countryside up close.

The first forty miles of our journey was by train. Knowing that London traffic was something that he didn't want to deal with, Bob had reserved a rental car in Reading. The agency was on a busy street – four lanes with a divider in the middle. After filling out the paperwork and getting the key, we piled into the tiniest of cars. Bob, the driver, was seated on the right and I on the left. Ad, much smaller than either one of us, had to sit in the back seat sideways since there was hardly any legroom. Bob started the car, pulled out of the parking lot and, just as every enthusiastic red-blooded American driver who had never before driven in the British Isles, *turned onto the wrong side of the divided street*! The three of us could have been killed! Fortunately, there was no oncoming traffic. Bob realized his mistake immediately and crossed to the other side at the first opportunity. The problems, however, were not quite over. Bob, still grappling with twenty years of left-side driving experience, overcompensated his position at the wheel and my side ended up hitting every curb, grate, gutter, and sewer cover that Reading had to offer! To Bob's credit, he adjusted quickly and, after we left Reading, the ride was much smoother.

Once in Cheltenham, we met Michael Kennedy at the hotel. He showed us the Vaughan Williams manuscripts and entrusted Bob with depositing them at the British Library. That afternoon the four of us went to the Holst Birthplace Museum. There we met the museum's curator, Lowinger Maddison, and Rosamund Strode, who had been Imogen Holst's assistant and was now with The Holst Foundation. Rosamund invited me to come to Aldeburgh, on the North Sea coast, to see the Holst archives and examine manuscript scores at the Britten-Pears Library. The impromptu gathering at the museum was a tremendous meeting of the minds, so to speak – Michael Kennedy, Lowinger Maddison, Rosamund Strode, and potentially Bob and myself. While still there, Bob commented about all of the knowledge that would be lost to the world had a bomb exploded at the Holst Birthplace Museum at that moment!

The drive back to Reading was a pleasant one through The Cotswolds. The area is characterized by its cottages of yellowish-gray brick. Ad had read about a particular town that had a model of itself in its town square. We found it and stopped there. Named Bourton-on-the-Water, to our young minds it naturally became known as Bourbon-on-Water.

The following day saw appointments with two people who lived south of the Thames – the first set up by me, the second by Bob. Colin Matthews, by now a prominent composer, had invited the three of us to his Clapham townhouse for a visit. Clapham had now become as fashionable as his new cappuccino machine which he eagerly demonstrated for us. Among other things, we discussed copyright clearances for Holst. We found out that at that point Holst, who had died in 1934, had now passed into public domain. (This would be rescinded in 1994 by future copyright laws).

From Colin's place, Bob, Ad and I took the Underground to Victoria Station. We then walked to a nearby pub where we met John Bird, the foremost living expert on composer/pianist Percy Grainger. We were in the midst of a great chat when, suddenly, a look of panic appeared on Bob's face; he noticed that his briefcase had disappeared. Bird immediately took us to the nearest police station where Bob reported the loss. While sympathetic, the officer in charge told us that pickpocketing and thievery were rampant around Victoria Station and that it was extremely doubtful that the briefcase would ever be recovered. After some thought, Bob remembered that this was his secondary briefcase, though it held his passport, plane tickets, and an expensive pipe that he had never smoked. Amazingly, he kept his composure throughout the entire process. The one bright spot was that the stolen briefcase was *not* the one containing the Vaughan Williams manuscripts entrusted to him by Michael Kennedy.

After this rather harrowing experience, John Bird took us on a walking tour of Percy Grainger's London. Born in Australia, Grainger had lived in London from 1901 until 1914. The tour was a great idea except that Bird was really tall. His crotch came up to my armpits. He also walked very fast. Bob was barely able to keep pace, but Ad and I were huffing and puffing a half block back. Still John Bird's tour was as unique as he was and, throughout Belgravia and Chelsea, we were introduced to a number of unconventionalities, from "This is the place where Percy first had sex, at the age of twenty with one Mrs. Lowery" to "This is the flat where Oscar Wilde was arrested."

Bird then invited us over to his apartment, located south of the river, near Battersea Park. The street of row houses caused one to ponder what life would have been like for London's working class a century earlier.

Upon entry, his place seemed to be very conventional, with no hint of the composer he had spent his life investigating. Further into the apartment, however, there was a noticeable change. Mounted on the slanted wall in back of the central stairway was a large charcoal portrait sketch of Grainger as he appeared in his early twenties. This rather imposing piece of artwork was drawn by none other than the American portrait artist John Singer Sargent! It was not a copy; it was the original, right here in John Bird's apartment in Battersea.

Bird then invited us into his bedroom. It was unlike any other bedroom I had seen. It was part library and part museum. On one wall was a bookcase housing dozens of wax cylinders, the same ones that Grainger took with him in 1905-06 when he recorded some 300 mostly-rural people singing English folk songs. On the other walls were shelves holding many of Grainger's music publications, and next to Bird's bed was a copy machine. He invited us to select anything we wanted, that he would make copies for us right there on the spot. So, of course, Bob and I had a field "night," sifting through as much music as we could. We stayed until well past midnight.

Bird was indeed eccentric, but thoroughly a gentleman. He was also kind and generous; in addition to the copied music, he gave us each an autographed copy of his 1976 book *Percy Grainger*. Today that book, currently in its third edition, is recognized as *the* Grainger biography.

Not quite as eccentric, but with a strong effervescent personality, was Ursula Vaughan Williams. We had tea with her the next day at her upscale townhouse in Gloucester Crescent, located on the north side of London between Regent's Park and Camden Town. A vivacious seventy-five year old with flaming red hair, she was seated in a tufted wing chair, smoking a stogie. Married to Ralph Vaughan Williams only during his final five years (1953-1958), she held the rights to all of his compositions. Thus it was essential that we visit her for copyright clearances. When she readily extended the clearances to us, Bob looked directly at me, smiled, and said softly but succinctly, "Bingo!"

One thing that Ursula Vaughan Williams didn't give us, but gladly showed us, was Beethoven's tuning fork, which had been passed down from composer to composer and had somehow ended up in the possession of her late husband. Six years after our visit, she donated the tuning fork to The British Library.

She was quite the conversationalist, joking about the various pageants for which her late husband over-composed. She then offered a stogie to each of us, but we declined since none of us smoked. Her eyes opened wide and she laughed out loud, declaring, "You Americans just don't know how to have a good time!"

Before we left, I had to clear up one item that I had been wondering about for years. At home, whenever a work of her late husband's was broadcast over the airwaves, announcers would pronounce his first name as either "Ralf" or "Rafe." I had to ask her which one it was. She looked me directly in the eye, laughed, and shouted, "Rafe! Rafe! It's always been Rafe!"

Okay. I never mispronounced his first name again.

That evening Bob convinced me to go with him and Ad to the Royal Tournament at Earl's Court. We knew from posted advertisements that there would be a competition among units from the four branches of the British military as well as a military band extravaganza. At £8.50, this was not a cheap ticket in 1986, but what it yielded was well worth the money spent. The Earl's Court Exhibition Hall was essentially an indoor soccer arena. We were seated in the rear stalls about fourteen rows up and could see the events unfold very well.

I don't know if we had had a little too much to drink, but the whole spectacle seemed to be delightfully strange. First were the competitions, which featured all sorts of Highland-type games, obstacle courses, cannon stoking, etc.; it was truly amazing to watch. Then there was a break in the action filled by a female radio personality leading the audience in singing the old pub song "Knees Up, Mother Brown…Under the Table You Must Go, E-I-E-I-E-I-O" etc. Everybody joined in except for us, of course, since we didn't know the words. Still, we managed to fake it in the midst of continuous laughter. It wouldn't be the first time that I would get caught up in the middle of thousands of Brits singing words that I didn't know. The same thing would happen to me later that same trip at the final Proms concert of the season in Royal Albert Hall. I did not know the words to "Land of Hope and Glory," which were paired with Edward Elgar's *Pomp & Circumstance No. 1*, a work that I had either played or conducted in countless graduation ceremonies, but I joined in anyway.

After "Knees Up, Mother Brown" came the military band event. The precision drill was something to behold as each band was as good as the next. Then, a giant disco ball suspended from the ceiling swirled as all four bands played a segment of Holst's "Jupiter" movement from *The Planets*. We assumed this to be the finale but, no, there was more. The Portuguese National Republican Guard Band, invited guests, performed on horseback. They were awe-inspiring, weaving in and out at various clips. We were spellbound until the band slowed down into a figure-eight pattern and began playing The Beatles' "Hey Jude." All sense of propriety seemed to go out the window; somehow it was too paradoxical. Yet there was more. The Constabulary Band of New Guinea was next – a marching band wearing sandals and skirts! The star of the band was its cymbal player; when the band stopped and assumed a concert position, he was front and center. His lively and flashy technique was incredible. It was amplified by his crashing the cymbals repeatedly between his legs. We were in awe, but also in constant fear for his manhood. It was all too weird for us and, in almost uncontrollable laughter, we nearly fell off the bleachers.

The following night we headed north to Hampstead Heath and a combined brass band concert at the Kenwood shell. Geoffrey Brand was conducting. Geoffrey's technique, certainly competent, was unusual in that instead of providing downbeats, his beats all went up. Security was tight; even Joseph Horovitz, the featured composer, could not get back stage. Many years earlier, I had been advised by the members of my thesis committee not to use the "Dr." title before my name in everyday life, lest I be confused with some physician. Apparently Bob had been told the same thing. However this was not a moment to be concerned about such modesty, so he told the guard, "We are Dr. Mitchell and Dr. Grechesky here to see Conductor Brand at his request." It worked – so well in fact that we were able to bring Horovitz backstage with us!

Afterwards Geoffrey and his wife Violet drove us back to Fulham in their Audi. He missed the turn-off twice; then Violet mentioned that it was right at a Montessori School where she had once taught. He glanced at her and shouted good-naturedly, "*Now* you tell me! *Now* you tell me!"

The following night they had all of us out to their place for dinner.

Soon thereafter Bob and Ad returned to the States, having been able to get new passports at the American Embassy. The friendship and occasional hilarity shared with them was absolutely golden. As Shakespeare called them, these were our "salad" days – never to be returned to (though we came close on numerous occasions), but never to be forgotten. The departure of the Grecheskys, however, didn't mean that the remainder of the trip was boring; quite the contrary.

Violet Brand, Adrienne Grechesky, Geoffrey Brand, and JCM in a rainy London, July 1986

Two days later I followed up on Rosamund Strode's suggestion and travelled north to Aldeburgh, a coastal town on the North Sea where the Britten-Pears Library was located. In addition, Aldeburgh (pronounced "All-bro") was home to the annual Aldeburgh Festival. It was also where Imogen Holst's cottage was located. Imogen had passed away two years earlier and her cottage was now serving as headquarters for The Holst Foundation, established to assist young composers. Rosamund, who had been amanuensis and assistant to composer Benjamin Britten as well as to Imogen Holst, was heavily involved with both The Holst Foundation (she was chair for some time) and the Aldeburgh Festival.

The journey to Aldeburgh was not difficult, but involved changing trains at Ipswich plus taking a taxi from Saxmundham, the closest railway stop. Once at Saxmundham I spotted a cab and, in all my eagerness, I jumped into the right side without thinking. Of course, I found myself facing the steering wheel. The cab driver was quick to comment saying, "So you want to drive, now?" Remembering Bob's experience with driving in Reading, I sheepishly declined. The cab driver then told me that this happened all the time and that he was always lying-in-wait for tourists from America and the European continent.

I was dropped off at Imogen Holst's cottage, a flat, modern single-story bungalow with face brick on the outside. There, Rosamund and her secretary Helen Lilley greeted me warmly and showed me to a desk that I could use in doing my research. My goal in coming to Aldeburgh was to study and possibly copy several Holst manuscripts at the Britten-Pears Library and then return to London. Rosamund's goal, however, was to *entertain* me. "When you go somewhere, you really have to *go* there," she said. She showed me all around Imogen's cottage; we then walked down to the main street (a replacement street for the original main street that had washed into the sea centuries ago) and looked around the 1500's Moot House which had provided an inspiration for Benjamin Britten's opera *Peter Grimes*. Following this we had lunch at Ye Olde Cross Keys pub, which did not disappoint. All the while I was thinking about the closing time of the Britten-Pears and if I would be able to get anything done. Finally we trekked the mile-and-a-half walk over hill and dale to Britten-Pears. After what seemed to be endless introductions to everybody there, I was finally able to study the manuscripts, but I had only about forty-five minutes before closing. I had never written so fast! Despite this awkward first visit, Rosamund became my rudder, my conscience, and quite the facilitator to many of my future Holst research efforts. She also became a very good friend, attending to the needs of Ester and each of our children on subsequent trips.

Back in London a few days later I was granted the privilege of perusing the library of the Band of the Coldstream Guards by its director, Major Roger Swift. One of the oldest bands of the British Army, the home of the band is in the Wellington Barracks, just off Birdcage Walk in St. James Park, maybe 1,000 feet from Buckingham Palace. I had been searching for one particular music manuscript which I thought might be at this location; I didn't find it, but discovered another – a set of parts to James Causley Windram's military band setting of some of Holst's *Choral Hymns from the Rig Veda* – which was actually more central to my research. I asked for permission to make photocopies of the manuscripts and it was granted. As I was finishing, I noticed a significant amount of activity outside. It was now 11:30 a.m. and I realized that I had stumbled onto something truly unique: first the assembly, then the marching, and then the music – I had an insider's view of the Changing of the Queen's Guard! The only disappointment was that the band was not playing a British march but instead Josef Friedrich Wagner's *Unter dem Doppeladler* (*Under the Double Eagle*) – *Austria*'s national march!

That same evening Holst biographer Michael Short and his wife Elaine met me at Mrs. Giuffredi's and took me out to eat just around the corner. I was totally bowled over with all the information Michael had on the tip of his tongue. The music history instructor at Kneller Hall and a trombonist, he had worked for many years with Imogen Holst, had two published books on Holst to that point, and was putting the finishing touches on his magnum opus, *Gustav Holst: The Man and His Music*. Indeed this had been quite a day.

The remainder of the trip was spent mostly in libraries, either locating suitable musical works for my ensembles to perform or quenching a thirst for more knowledge about Holst. There was one extraneous venture, however, that deserves mentioning. The Upper Norwood Library, located in southeast London, contained a book that was found nowhere else. London's Underground didn't go there, but the over ground railway did. The closest station was Crystal Palace, named after the great Victorian exhibition hall. Gustav Holst's *Second Suite in F for Military Band*, Op. 28, No. 2 [H106] and *Incidental Music for The Pageant of London* [H114] were performed on its grounds. The palace itself had burned down in 1936, but there remains a very sizeable park, replete with a maze, a track, and its most unique feature: Benjamin Waterhouse Hawkins' 1854 life-size sculptures of dinosaurs and extinct mammals. Subsequent paleontological research, however, has uncovered the fact that, to some degree or another, all of these dinosaur sculptures are incorrect. In retrospect, they must be judged as products of their time. Nevertheless, I photographed as many of these as I could for my then four-year-old son David, who was already heavily into dinosaurs. Decades later David and I would return to Crystal Palace Park, noting gleefully that these dinosaur "structures" are now included on the list of Heritage Protection's Grade I: buildings of exceptional interest.

A second extraneous tidbit happened while riding on the Underground about a week before I left. I got into a subway car that was occupied by quite a number of people, adults and children alike, dressed in purple and white formal attire. The men wore top hats. It occurred to me later that they were probably on their way to, or on their way from, Westminster Abbey and the ill-fated Royal Wedding of Prince Andrew and Lady Sarah Ferguson.

II. *Early IGEBs Plus a WASBE Thrown In*

It was Bob Grechesky who introduced me to the society that opened the door to so many adventures on the European continent. In early 1988 Bob told me he was going to be giving a speech at a conference in Europe that summer and suggested I might also be interested in doing the same. The Internationale Gesellschaft zur Erforschung und Förderung der Blasmusik (International Society for the Promotion and Research of Wind Music) – IGEB for short – was holding its 8th Kongress (biennial conference) that July.

Founded in 1974, the society was centered in Graz, Austria. For expediency's sake, Herr Professor Dr. Wolfgang Suppan, the society's "President for Life," nearly always held the conferences somewhere in the German-speaking area of Europe. This time, however, Suppan wanted to expand the society's reach farther east and have a conference in Sopron, Hungary. The attempt failed due to an economic crisis there as well as "red" tape. Therefore he relocated the conference to Oberschützen, a small town in Burgenland, the easternmost state of Austria. I applied to present a paper on Gustav Holst and it was accepted. Whether the conference was to occur in Hungary or in Austria made no difference to me; it was a great opportunity

Though membership was open to anyone doing wind instrument research, it felt like an honor just to belong to this organization. The conferences usually featured about thirty papers. At that time about three-quarters of them were presented in German (one of two official languages of the society) with the remainder in English (the other official language) or another major language such as Italian, Spanish, or French. These were presented by internationally respected scholars. Some were musicologists active in Europe; others were active in such diverse places as Mexico or Egypt. Still others were primarily conductors who hailed from such faraway locales as South Africa or Surinam. Presentations often resulted in articles being published in *Mitteilungsblatt*, the society's newsletter, or in *Alta Musica*, the society's prestigious hardbound journal. Occasionally entire monographs (books by a single author) were included as volumes in the *Alta Musica* series.

This was my first trip to the European continent, as my previous three trips had been exclusively to England. I was now Assistant Professor and Wind Ensemble Conductor at Carnegie Mellon University in Pittsburgh, Pennsylvania and received a small internal grant from that institution to speak at the IGEB conference. That grant, plus money saved up from my church choir and North Pittsburgh Civic Symphony conducting jobs, meant that, for the first time, my wife Ester was able to accompany me overseas. Our children were then ages six, ten, and twelve. We couldn't all afford to go, but through Ester's sister Rosario, a nun, we were able to hire a house sitter. Partly because Ester didn't want to leave our children again and partly due to ongoing financial considerations, this would be the last European trip she would accompany me on for more than a decade.

We spent the first three days of this trip in Vienna, the major city closest to Oberschützen. Our first impression was that we'd stepped into some sort of a dream world: a city that upheld its classical music traditions and had great chocolate, great coffee, and, of course, great food. We stayed at the Hotel Avis in the Josefstadt district just west of the city center. The Avis existed most of the year as a student dormitory – clean and safe, but that was about it. It served us well for our needs.

On our first evening in Vienna we met up with Steve and Kathy Miller. Steve was a professor and conductor at Case Western Reserve University in Cleveland at the time. A few months earlier I had driven over from Pittsburgh so that Steve and I could see Eric Leinsdorf conduct the Cleveland Orchestra in, among other things, Igor Stravinsky's *Concerto for Piano and Winds*. In Vienna the four of us went out to dinner at a restaurant on the Kärtnerstrasse that had salon music featuring a cimbalom; this was the first time I had witnessed one up close. I believe it was also here, at this restaurant that I began a wonderful hobby that would bring great joy to my life: collecting beer coasters. Today I have over 200 of them and can say without hesitation that I earned every one of them in the most honest way possible – by imbibing the liquid refreshment under which they were placed!

After that first evening splurge, Ester and I had to do Vienna on the cheap, though we did get to see the Kunsthistorisches Museum (Art History Museum) and Schönbrunn Palace. The rest of Vienna that we experienced either had nominal entrance fees, free admittance, or was simply outdoors. Within this framework, we went on a three-day tear, since we didn't know if we would ever be in Vienna again (fortunately, a wrong assumption). We saw Heiligenstadt, St. Stephen's Cathedral, the Zentralfriedhof (Central Cemetery – where many composers are buried), three Beethoven houses, Mozart's house, and Schubert's birthplace. There were also unplanned things: we practically ran into an Italian marching band in the Graben and, on the Ringstrasse, out of curiosity watched a middle-aged woman wander into a fountain, trying to retrieve a ball that was thrown in there by one of her grandchildren – or so it appeared.

We also made the classic American tourist mistake of not eating a large meal at noontime on a Sunday, only to discover that all that was available Sunday evening at any restaurant was ice cream and coffee! We were almost starving but then came across a würstel (sausage) stand near the Rathaus (City Hall) that had the best bratwurst and burenwurst this side of heaven! Now this – this was Vienna!

After our brief time in Vienna, we took a train and bus south to Bad Tatzmannsdorf, where we stayed at a very nice bed and breakfast. We saw no fellow conference attendees and learned a bit later that nearly all of them were staying in Pinkafeld, which was much closer to Oberschützen. Rather than take expensive taxi rides back and forth from Bad Tatzmannsdorf, we apologized to the owners and relocated.

When we got to the conference, the first person we saw was Bob Grechesky, who was beaming. He extolled Wolfgang Suppan's generosity. It turns out that Suppan had a great deal of clout with various entities, be it the Institute for Ethnomusicology in Graz (his home base) or various levels of the Austrian government. The result was that all of the lodging and all of the meals for this conference were free for those presenting papers! This amazing perk would continue at all successive IGEB conferences until 2002, when Suppan retired from the presidency.

I experienced Suppan's generosity first-hand when I met him at the conference. He shook my hand, smiled, and then spoke those wonderful golden words that every college professor fantasizes about: "You have written a book. We would like to publish it."

Shock! This was incredible! Three years earlier I had more-or-less completed my first book, *From Kneller Hall to Hammersmith: The Band Works of Gustav Holst*. I had actually made some three dozen Xerox copies of it and sold a number of them privately. But this – a real publication by a prestigious publishing firm in hard cover without any solicitation whatsoever on my part – was a dream. Suppan's word was good; indeed, two years later my book was published by Haus Hans Schneider in Tutzing, Germany as Band 11 (Volume 11) in IGEB's *Alta Musica* series. I have often told my students and my own children not to expect breaks to happen but to be sure sufficient groundwork has been done ahead of time if and when opportunity knocks.

The 1988 conference itself was a mixture of extreme interest and extreme boredom. It was quite formal: presenters and audience members dressed up. Presentations, grouped in fours (known as Sitzungen) were often quite stilted. The internet had not yet been invented and cellular phones were not common. This was also in the days before PowerPoint, and we counted ourselves fortunate if a speaker happened to have some transparencies for an overhead projector to display on the screen. Occasionally there would be audio examples, but these were few and far between.

Some of the topics were of universal interest, i.e. comparing the tones of different sized trumpets. Others were of local interest, i.e. biographies of Austrian or Prussian bandmasters. Still others were of such a trivial nature that they would be of interest to very few people – yet some of these would bring about the most heated of discussions. One of the fiercest was over the color of the stripe worn down the side of the pants on a particular 19th-century military band uniform. This went on for several minutes – and these people were completely serious!

For non-German speakers and those of us who spoke only a little bit of the language, many of the sessions in German were deadly. Leon Bly, a bilingual American living and teaching in Stuttgart, gave aural summaries after each presentation. Leon and his East German-born wife Ilona would become good friends of ours; later he would become president of WASBE (World Association of Symphonic Bands and Ensembles). Still, many of the sessions were difficult to sit through. One of the older professors, although he was respected and beloved, simply read in a monotone voice from his pocket-sized notebook. I had a small German-English dictionary that got passed around among the English speakers as we tried to glean what we could from what was being said. Before the internet and globalization I worked hard at learning German, though I never attained anything close to fluency. Mark Twain's quote about Spanish taking him thirty days to learn, French thirty weeks, and German thirty years rang true.

During the times when I was totally frustrated with my lack of language proficiency, I often mentally reviewed the scores of pieces (both band and orchestral) that I was currently conducting; sometimes I would think about the luncheons, dinners, and concerts to follow. Most of these concerts featured military or civilian bands whose directors usually exhibited perfunctory conducting styles. Chamber wind ensembles of varying sizes and degrees of musicality would often precede or accompany the meals – *harmoniemusik* as it was originally meant to be. Yet, at least as often, I would muse about the socializing that was to come at the end of the day – the *gemütlichkeit* for which Austria and southern Germany are famous.

At the end of one particular session I struck up a conversation with a German-speaking colleague – or at least I tried to. We were both having a difficult time as neither one of us spoke enough of each other's language. All of a sudden Bob walked up to me, laughed, and shook his head. "Jon, speaking English with a German accent doesn't help his comprehension." I had fallen into the trap of emulating the German accents from old movies and the *Hogan's Heroes* television series without realizing it!

IGEB 8th Kongress North American contingent on stage of the Haydnsaal at the Esterhazy Palace, Eisenstadt, Austria, 1988
1st row: Jon Piersol, Dennis Beck, Steven Miller, JCM
2nd row: Raoul Camus, Clyde Shive, Rik Hansen, Leon Bly, Robert Grechesky, Robert Gifford

IGEB conferences always have at least one excursion for the attendees; this conference had two. The first was the most memorable. We were bussed over to Eisenstadt, the capital of the state of Burgenland. The town is dominated by the Esterházy Palace, originally built in the 14th century. Substantially remodeled three centuries later, its façade is now painted in a glorious baroque yellow. Every musician knows that the Esterházy Palace is where Franz Josef Haydn, the "Father of the Symphony," did most of his work. We had the opportunity to tour the palace including the Haydnsaal, where Haydn's orchestra performed; the American contingent even had a group picture taken on the stage! Yet perhaps the most unforgettable part of this visit was the grand luncheon buffet served to us in one of the palace's dining rooms. It was a spread very typical of this part of the world – fruits, rolls, breads, cold cuts, eggs, pastries – yet it was so well presented. In the words of Harry Ellis Dickson it was a "sumptuous repast." This was something to write home about…and photograph!

The second day out we were taken to the birthplace of Franz Liszt. Most people know that Liszt was born in Hungary and that before 1990 Hungary was behind the Iron Curtain. In 1988 Hungary was still under fists of the communists. So how was it that we were allowed to visit this place? Over the centuries, the border had changed; today Liszt's birthplace is in *Austria*. One of the most impressive sights located there is an oversized cast of Liszt's hands.

That evening we were taken to a restaurant that was, from what I recall, owned by the governor of Burgenland. It set, literally, right up against the Hungarian border. It was a bit intimidating; from the restaurant we could see barbed wire fencing and a guard tower. The meal was served on wooden shingles and the wine flowed freely. It was a great party but when things became a bit too noisy, Suppan put an end to the gemütlichkeit and ushered us onto the bus. On the return trip to Pinkafelt, the bus made a pit stop and I learned what a *pissoir* was. The next morning, apparently to rouse us from our slumber (that is, primarily to get us up for the morning sessions), we were serenaded at dawn by one of the conferees playing a Swiss Alphorn outside! There was nothing ordinary about this conference.

At the conference's end, Ester and I hitched a ride with Herman Snijders of Surinam, and Doris Goldabend, Suppan's secretary, to the nearby city of Graz, where we stayed overnight. We had planned our exit from Europe carefully, taking one relatively short train ride each day for the next three days. On our westward progression we would spend one night each in Salzburg, Munich, and Stuttgart, from whence we would return home. We didn't have reservations anywhere, but it still worked like a charm. In Salzburg we saw Mozart's birthplace and had a marvelous stroll through the Getreidegasse. In Munich we went to the Hofbräuhaus (of course) and the Marshtallmuseum (carriages and sleighs) at Nymphenburg Palace. In Stuttgart we didn't do much; we were exhausted, but we did manage to have dinner at an outdoor restaurant in the city center's pedestrian zone. The menu was entirely in

German. I read "Fisch" and "Hollandaise" and figured that we couldn't go wrong. However, I was in horror when our order came – it looked like the fish was raw – but, in reality, the fish was pickled, and it was quite tasty.

Thus ended the first trip to an IGEB conference, a tremendously rewarding and enriching experience. Amazingly, through various in-house research grants and private funding, I was able to not only give a presentation at the next IGEB conference, but all subsequent ones – sixteen of them through 2018.

* * *

The 9th IGEB Kongress was held during the summer of 1990 at Toblach/Dobbiaco, a small town in the Italian Alps. This area, known for producing Italy's Olympic skiers and bobsled teams, was a part of the Austro-Hungarian Empire until the end of World War I, when it was ceded to Italy. Most of the area's residents speak German and Austrians still refer to this part of Italy as the Süd Tyrol. However, the people that live here are Italian citizens. Hence, many of the towns have two names and many landmarks and buildings have bilingual signage, such as the building where the IGEB lectures and presentations took place:

Grundschule
Scuola Elementare

It is a land where German and Italian, two languages not closely related, manage to coexist.

Two places I had always wanted to see, Schloss Neuschwanstein (Neuschwanstein Castle) and Venice, were each within an easy day's journey from Toblach/Dobbiaco, though in opposite directions. So, I decided to make the IGEB conference the center point of my trip. Wolfgang Suppan offered to show me his music collection at Pürgg after the conference. Since it and Toblach/Dobbiaco are closer to Venice, I decided to see Neuschwanstein Castle first.

I flew into Munich and then took two trains to get to the appropriately named town of Füssen, located in the foothills of the Alps. It is the closest town to the castle. There were tourist buses that made the four-kilometer trip up to Neuschwanstein, but I decided to walk it. The path was quite pleasant and very scenic – the Alps were in front of me. The way up was exhilarating, but the way down was a little bit nerve-wracking; it was near dusk and I had to walk through a graffiti-laden underpass. Right when I was walking through it, I was startled by a cacophony of bells. Coming out of the tunnel I was able to see that indeed there were dozens of cows adorned with cowbells; they were very noisy.

Neuschwanstein is the quintessential tourist poster castle. It is often considered *the* visual symbol of German romanticism. Ludwig II of Bavaria (1845-1886), known as "Mad Ludwig," was enthralled by the music of Richard Wagner and became the composer's patron. The king especially adored Wagner's operas *Tannhaüser*, *Lohengrin*, and *Parsifal* as they supported his own romanticized concept of what the Middle Ages should have been. He received Wagner at Hohenschwangau, the nearby castle that his father had built. When funds became available in the late 1860s, Ludwig started to build his own castle on top of the ruins of Schwanstein, a medieval castle. He called his castle Neuschwanstein. The reclusive Ludwig envisioned his "dream castle" to be a place where he could surround himself with the distant past yet still have late nineteenth-century conveniences (such as toilets that flushed). The inside is ornate; some of the rooms have murals depicting the search for the Holy Grail as well as scenes from the aforementioned operas. It is really something to see. While Ludwig enjoyed an occasional stay in the castle from 1884 onward, Wagner never set foot in it; he died in 1883.

The tour guide mentioned that when Ludwig died in 1886, at the age of forty-one, in a rather mysterious swimming accident, the exterior of the castle was finished but the inside was only thirty percent complete. Two middle-aged women, perhaps in their late fifties, were in line right behind me. One of them exclaimed how great it would be to die at forty-one while still having a hard body. I myself was forty-one at the time but couldn't break it to them that my body, while in reasonable physical shape, wasn't especially hard! At the time of my visit, the cost of the castle tour was only about $4. It was money well spent!

I stayed that evening in Füssen, relishing what I had just seen. The following day was a Sunday and, at the local parish church, a Dvořák Mass was being performed. Though not a Roman Catholic, I couldn't resist attending. There was a medium-sized choir supported by the organ and a small group of string players; they were upstairs. When the ushers weren't looking, I snuck in and walked up the narrow stairway to the choir loft, the result being that I had a firsthand view of the music-making. It was a wonderful experience, to say the least.

From Füssen I took a bus to Innsbruck, Austria and then two trains south through the picturesque Brenner Pass. The Eurozone had not yet been created so once we got there the first train stopped and everybody exited. An announcement came across the loudspeaker in three languages (German, Italian, and English) apologizing to everybody that the connecting train would be ten minutes late. *Ten minutes late!* This seemed incredible inconsequential to me, but it was not to the Europeans who expected their trains to be on time.

When the second train came, I climbed in and took a seat toward the front of the car. The train did not move for several minutes, and I sensed that something might be wrong. Suddenly two Italian guards equipped with weapons walked into the car. One walked right up to me; I didn't know what to expect. This was somewhat intimidating, his mustachioed mouth and heavy eyebrows adding to the mix. Then, all of a sudden, he smiled at me and asked: "Passaporto?"

What a relief! Happy to oblige! Any time!

There was one additional change at Franzensfeste/Fortezza and, after a very slow ride on an Alpine local, I arrived in Toblach/Dobbiaco. Once again, Wolfgang Suppan had chosen well. Toblach/Dobbiaco is known as the gateway to the Dolomites. These gorgeous thumb-shaped mountains change color, from grey to orange to purple, as the sun moves across the sky.

The theme of this IGEB Kongress was "Rundfunk und Blasmusik"

(The Radio and Wind Music). It was sponsored by RAI-Studio Bozen/Bolzano. All of our presentations were carried on Italian national radio. That Wolfgang Suppan was able to convince RAI of the importance of the conference was one thing, but this was nothing compared to the surprise awaiting Bob Grechesky and me while we were having a mid-afternoon beer in front of our hotel. Suppan walked up to us with a huge wad of cash in his hand. He gave us each the equivalency in Italian lira of about $130.00! He was all smiles as he said, "Ja, Ja, beer money!"

We both cheerfully accepted the money. I had never been paid, whether in "beer money" or other currency, for giving an academic lecture in my life – nor since, as far as that goes. I learned later during that week that Suppan had been able to gain financial support for the conference from both Austrian and Italian sources! Incredible!

There were a number of other things that made this conference memorable. One bus tour took us into the heart of the Dolomites, another to the town of Wiesen bei Sterzing and the Augustiner-Chorherrenstift Neustift Monastery, founded in 1142. Adding to the inherent beauty of the place was its winery. And in Toblach/Dobbiaco itself is Trenkerhof, the residential building where Gustav Mahler rented an apartment during his summer holidays from 1908 to 1910. Mahler didn't do his composing there but rather in a rustic cabin located a short walk away. It was in the vicinity of this cabin that composer Albert Mayr's *Echos* was performed for us at sunset. Several dozen instrumentalists were spread out over what seemed to be a quarter of a mile, with each playing as the evening's shadows were cast upon them. It was a remarkable event.

After the conference I went to Venice for a day as I wasn't sure if I would ever have that opportunity again. Venice has a real uniqueness. When one exits the train station and sees gondolas and vaporetti (water buses) in the canal, one knows that there is no other place on earth that fits this description. I didn't have a place to stay, so I got in a very long line at Tourist Information. While there, I was approached by a man who said he was representing the Hotel Mignon. I was skeptical, fearing that he might be some sort of hustler, but he wanted no money up front. Instead, he gave me a map and told me that he would call ahead to the hotel. After a ride on the Grand Canal and a short walk, I found the hotel; it had a small en suite room for me for about $54, a real bargain for Venice in the summer.

I spent the remainder of that day just walking around, making sure to include seeing St. Mark's Square and the Doge's Palace, of course. The only complaint that I had – and I had been warned about this by others – was that there seemed to be almost as many tourists as there were pigeons. After a late dinner I was a bit tired and decided to take a vaporetto back to the hotel. The vaporetto stops usually serve two routes. The signs for these stands resemble road signs, with two arrow-shaped directives adjoining a single pole. After consulting a map, I knew which vaporetto to take, saw the sign, and hopped on. The only problem was that this particular vaporetto was parked in front of the *wrong sign.* Within seconds I knew it, as the vaporetto didn't go into the Grand Canal, but instead sped across the open waters of the Canale della Giudecca! I got off at the first opportunity; I was now on the Isola della Giudecca; it was already after eleven o'clock at night, and very few vaporetti were still in operation. As I walked along the front street, I wasn't sure how I would get back, only that I needed to keep the lights of Venice proper in sight to my right. Then I saw a pontoon bridge about a quarter of a mile ahead of me miraculously connecting the island with the city. It turned out to be a temporary pontoon bridge set up only for a few weeks in July as a part of Venice's Redentore Celebrations. Talk about being in the right place at the right time!

After my all-too-brief stay in Venice, I took a train back into Austria and spent the night in the fairly sizeable town of Villach. One of the chamber maids at the small hotel where I was staying asked me in German where I was from. Though living in Pittsburgh, I responded with the city I was born in, Chicago. Immediately her arms grabbed a make-believe machine gun as she pretended to shoot me: "Al Capone! Rat-a-tat-a-tat-a-tat…"

I played along and pretended to be shot.

The next morning, with my gangster image clearly intact, I travelled to Stainach-Irdnung, the closest railway station to Pürgg, Wolfgang Suppan's home town. In Pürgg he showed me his barn full of music; it was an enormous collection but disappointing in that much of it was published music that was not of the best quality. Nonetheless, the day was not wasted by any means. Wolfgang and I walked down the mountain to Unterpürgg, where his cousin lived, and spent much of the afternoon eating peasant bread and drinking his cousin's homemade schnapps. I would liken it to moonshine, except that in Austria all citizens are legally allowed to make a certain amount per annum for their own consumption. That evening I stayed in Irdnung and got to watch several games of nine-pin bowling. The pins are set up in a diamond shape and small, almost croquet-sized, balls are used. The pace of the games complemented the schnapps, the result being that I slept very well that night.

The final night of this trip was spent in Salzburg. I had already seen much of the city with Ester two years earlier, so I walked a bit around the "new" city, across the river from the old. I was walking in the Mirabelgarten, not far from the Mozarteum, when I noticed some sort of social function going on inside the Mirabel Palace. My curiosity got the better of me and I walked up closer to the door to get a look. Perhaps because I was wearing a suit coat, one of the doormen motioned me inside. I was crashing the party! I had no idea what it was all about, or who "my" benefactor was, only that the food was spectacular and the music was first-rate.

* * *

To date, the 10th IGEB Kongress held in April 1992 was the only one not held during the summer months. As a result, there were fewer attendees, especially from this side of the Atlantic. In fact, there were only seven speeches given in English, and these included one by an Australian. This conference, while successful, didn't quite have the flair of the previous two. The setting, however, was fantastic. Wolfgang Suppan had selected the medieval town of Feldkirch as the site of the conference. This picturesque fairytale town is located on Austria's western frontier, on the border with Switzerland and Liechtenstein.

Time was a bit tight for this trip, so I flew into Zürich and immediately took the train to Feldkirch. By the time that I got there, the opening ceremony for the conference was already under way at the four-star hotel that Suppan had reserved for all speakers and presenters. The reception afterward continued until the wee hours of the night and I didn't get to bed until about 1:00 a.m. – fortunately without a trace of jet lag.

Impressive though this reception was, it didn't compare with the banquet held a few days later in the medieval Schattenburg Castle. We were dining inside a hall that had all sorts of medieval weapons – halberds, flails, shields, etc. – on its walls. When I got back to my hotel room that evening, I made the mistake of turning on the television. I couldn't understand the German all that well but saw that people were running in fear and anger all over the streets of Los Angeles. At first I thought it was an earthquake, but I later learned that it was the rioting over the Rodney King verdict. People were threatening, smashing and grabbing – unfortunately not too dissimilar from medieval warcraft, but without the weapons that I had just seen. Had the world not changed since the 1200s?

The conference day trip featured a bus ride through the Alps. While the snow was melting at this time of year, the roads were still snow packed in places, and the driver had to do some skillful maneuvering. At times he had to back up in order to make turns. I was seated toward the back of the bus next to a window and saw that, at one point, the bus had cleared the eve of a house's roof by about ¾ of an inch!

On another day, a group of us hired a taxi to take us to Vaduz, the capital city of the Principality of Liechtenstein, the sixth smallest country in the world and certainly the smallest I had ever been in. Much of it is essentially perched alongside a single mountain. Once there, we got our passports stamped. Since passports were never checked there, it was a thoroughly symbolic gesture by the Liechtenstein government, for which each of us paid the price of one Swiss franc.

After the conference I followed Ester's suggestion and traveled to Lucerne. She had been there before we were married and recommended it as one of the most beautiful places she had seen. She was not wrong; the lake, the wounded lion, the medieval bridges, and the city walls verified that. The one problem that I had was that the exchange rate between the dollar and Swiss franc at that time was not good for Americans. I went to Tourist Information and discovered that the only place I could afford to stay was a hostel on the north side of town. It turned out to be pretty good (after all, it was in Switzerland), though I had to share a room with three other men, all young Israelis. It was interesting to hear them address the situation in their home country, although they talked more enthusiastically about the new place they had visited the day before – Euro Disney!

* * *

Starting with the Fall 1992 semester, I was a music professor and conductor at what would be my final institution of higher learning. At my interview the previous spring at the University of Massachusetts Boston (commonly referred to as U Mass Boston or UMB), I was told that they wanted me to start some sort of instrumental ensemble. This was, of course, no problem as at this point in my life I had had significant amounts of both band and orchestral conducting experience. So, I was amazed to find out that in a university of some 9,500 students (which would eventually increase to over 16,000), they had a jazz band but no band (wind ensemble) or orchestra – and this was in Boston! As I was mulling things over in the dean's office of the College of Arts and Sciences, I glanced out the window and noticed a football field. I had to ask the obvious: "Does your university have a football team?"

The dean nodded.

Quickly I responded, "Then I am your *orchestra* conductor."

I was reluctant to take the job at first but knew that there was great potential in this place. Though my main charge was to resurrect a dormant music education program, at U Mass Boston I *was* the orchestra conductor. Nevertheless, most of my research up to that time had to do with band topics and I didn't want to refocus my efforts entirely. It turned out that I didn't have to; in the university's eyes, good research was good research, period. This was a boon as, during my tenure there, the university's focus shifted more and more toward research and scholarly activity.

At first U Mass Boston was willing to support me in trips that dealt primarily with delivering an address at an international conference that would result in getting an article published in a prestigious publication, such as IGEB's *Alta Musica* series. Later on they would also provide substantial funding for my overseas guest conducting and recording ventures. Thus, in the summer of 1993, this *orchestra* conductor received funding to do a presentation at a *band* conference.

WASBE (World Association of Symphonic Bands and Ensembles) is in many ways the performance counterpart to IGEB. Held in the odd-numbered years, WASBE conferences provide a showcase for the best bands and wind ensembles in the world. Each of their conferences also allow for a limited number of research presentations, though nothing approaching the scope of IGEB.

WASBE's 1993 conference was held in Valencia, Spain. The city was a great choice as it is one of the most musical cities in the world. There are some 600 bands there – not bad for a metropolitan area of approximately 1.6 million people. It also has great food, being the original home of the paella, a grand Spanish rice dish with various vegetables, meats, and/or seafood. Then there was the Sangria which, due to a favorable dollar-peseta exchange rate, cost roughly $.86 a bottle.

The conference was held in conjunction with Valencia's Certamen Internacional de Bandas de Música (International Wind Band Contest), featuring some 3,500 participants; it was held in the city's bullfight arena. The conference itself was held in the beautiful Palau de la Música, a modern building constructed on the shores of the Río Turia. Dozens of luminaries from the band world attended. Among them was Bernardo

Adam Ferrero, an esteemed conductor and composer I had met five years earlier at the IGEB conference in Oberschützen. I don't remember all the details, but he invited John Bourgeois, conductor of the United States Marine Band, Frank Byrne, the band's librarian, and me to his home by the bay for dinner one night. His wife Amparo made a tasty paella among other things, and we were treated like royalty.

Usually I joined a group of other delegates and we would eat at some outdoor local restaurant. I was seated at a table, sipping some Sangria, when I was called to help another table. Seated there were some German-speaking friends from IGEB. They were having a difficult time with the menu and asked me to translate for them. It was bilingual, in Spanish and Valenciano, the regional dialect which is essentially a variation of Catalan. Now I do pretty well with New World Spanish, a bit less with Castilian Spanish, nothing with Valenciano, and struggle mightily with German. Translating the Spanish menu into German was a real brain stretcher for me, but I did my best. Apparently it worked; I didn't hear any complaints from them when their food arrived.

The conference itself was impressive. On one particular evening the governor of the region sponsored a stand-up paella dinner for all of the delegates. This being Spain, the dinner started at about ten o'clock at night. There were six huge paellas (each in a circular pan approaching a meter in diameter) from which to choose: one had chicken, another rabbit, another octopus, etc. The colors in each were very different from each other. It was quite an event.

The concerts were excellent. Spanish bands are very large, many with over a hundred players, and most feature cellos and string basses. Two of the more fantastic concerts took place in the town of Cullera, on the coast just south of Valencia. A stage was erected in the center of the small plaza for the bands, with audience seating extending into one of the streets. The first concert started at 10:00 at night; the second started some time after 11:00. At the end of the second concert, well after midnight, those of us in the audience heard what sounded like loud clacking noises from above – the people who lived up there were opening their window shutters. The band then commenced playing *El Himno de la Comunidad Valencia* (*Regional Hymn of Valencia*). The people, including those above us, sang along with great enthusiasm. It went on five full minutes, ending with "¡Vixca Valencia! ¡Vixca! ¡Vixca! ¡Vixca!" ("Viva Valencia! Viva! Viva! Viva!"). There have been certain moments in my life when I knew that there was nowhere else on earth that I would rather be – and this was definitely one of them. It was nothing short of Grand Opera (there is no other way to describe it), and I was in the midst of it!

When the conference ended, Bernardo Adam Ferrero invited Scott Cohen and me to peruse his library in Lliria, located just north of Valencia. For a small town, Lliria had so much to offer, musically speaking – a conservatory of music, two fiercely competitive professional-level bands, and a symphony orchestra. It would be a great place for a musician to retire.

In the library, Scott and I sifted through hundreds of folders of music. I was mainly interested in looking at Spanish paso dobles for an article but, in the midst of my search, came across a folder with two marches by John Philip Sousa printed back-to-back by the Spanish Unión Músical: *El Capitan* and *Saludos a Ultramar*. I was familiar with the first one, of course, but drew a blank on the second. Thinking that I had uncovered an unknown Sousa march, I called Scott over to check it out. We started humming the tune and then realized that we should have known better: *Saludos a Ultramar* turned out to be *Hands Across the Sea*!

When I returned home, I wrote an article, "In Search of the Paso Doble." It was immediately accepted for publication in the forthcoming issue of the *Journal of the Conductors Guild.* At that point, the *Journal* was behind about a year and a half. Thus my article, for which I did research in 1993, was published during early 1994 in the Summer/Fall 1992 (Vol. XIII, No. 2) issue of the *Journal of the Conductors Guild*! Few people have ever accused me of being ahead of my time, but this would be written proof!

* * *

IGEB held its 11th Kongress in Abony (pronounced Ah-boyn), Hungary during the summer of 1994. Now that the Iron Curtain had fallen, Wolfgang Suppan had succeeded in securing a host on the eastern edge of what once had been the Austro-Hungarian Empire.

Thanks partially to another successful in-house grant, I was able to arrange for a two-week trip: four or five days in Hungary for IGEB, then train rides via Vienna to Bruges, an overnight ferry across the English Channel, and then several days of Holst research in England's Aldeburgh and London. The Euro was still five years in the future, so the currencies kept changing as I moved from country to country – Hungarian forint to Austrian schilling to German Deutschemark to Belgian franc to the United Kingdom's pound sterling – which meant that I had heavy pockets and a very colorful assortment of bills in my wallet.

My flight landed in Budapest, where I exchanged some of my dollars for Hungarian forints. From there I took a short train ride to Abony, a town of 16,000 in the center of the country. I was met at the train station by Szita, a sixteen-year-old girl who drove me in to the center of town. On our way we passed by a brand spanking new Toyota dealership, which I erroneously thought to be an indicator of a new Hungarian prosperity. Once in town I noticed that there were posters everywhere announcing the IGEB conference. These posters had cartoon paintings of brown tárogatós, single-reed folk instruments shaped like clarinets but essentially sounding and playing like wooden saxophones. A performance by a group playing on a number of tárogatós at the town hall was a featured part of the conference's opening ceremony.

As this was my first journey into a former Soviet-block country, I didn't know what to expect. The Hungarian government itself was only five years removed from communism. With its changeover to democracy and a Western economy, Hungary was going through a painful time. New items from the West were expensive and mechanical parts for old machinery were getting hard to find. The Russian Ladas, which had been the automobiles of choice, were suddenly getting very old. There were no hotels or pensions in Abony, so all of the speakers stayed with local families on this trip; in my case I was staying with the family of the local English teacher, Erzebet, who was very nice. While at her home, I noticed she was having trouble with her washing machine, which had a sideways drum; she referred to it as a problematic "socialist machine."

Some of what I witnessed in Abony was reminiscent of another century. At the center of town was an old-fashioned water pump. At first I thought that this was just a relic from the past, painted blue to give tourists a photo opportunity, but, no, it was perhaps the only source of water for hundreds of bicycle-riding babushkas who needed to fill their plastic bins. Outside of the center many streets were dirt, even those in what seemed to be newer neighborhoods. Then there was the town's synagogue which, due to the Holocaust, had been closed for more than a half century at that time.

The Hungarian language was incomprehensible to me. The letter "o" has more than a dozen pronunciations. The letter "s" sounds like "sh" unless it is followed by a "z" in which case it sounds "s" (think Franz Liszt). Hungarian isn't even an Indo-European language, but rather a Uralic one, sharing characteristics with Finnish and Estonian. I don't recall if it was at this particular IGEB conference or at another one that I found myself riding in a van with Kari Laitinen, a Finnish colleague, and László Marosi, a Hungarian one. I asked them if they could understand each other since their languages were from the same family. Kari responded, "Yes, we understand each other perfectly well – as long as we both speak English!"

These two were multi-lingual scholars, of course, but we couldn't take for granted that there would be a common language to communicate with our Hungarian hosts. Erzebet's husband, for example, spoke Hungarian and Russian. I spoke English, Spanish, and some German. All we could do was smile at each other, watch soccer together, and drink beer – which we both did very well. The one Hungarian word that we all learned, in fact could not avoid, was *Egészségedre*! (Cheers!).

It was in Abony that I first met Canadian conductor Keith Kinder. Keith, who was on the music faculty at Hamilton University, Hamilton, Ontario, conducted both the wind ensemble and chamber orchestra there. A fellow trombonist, his research interests lie largely in the music of Anton Bruckner, Franz Liszt, and Canadian composers. His program at Hamilton bore some similarity to mine at U Mass Boston and, ever since, we have shared ideas, repertoire lists, and music.

One of the features of every IGEB conference has been the day outing. At this particular conference we were all taken by bus to Kecskemét, first to view a fascinating folk instrument museum, then on to the Kodály Institute (a Mecca for many music educators), which unfortunately was closed. After that we were taken to a farm where we witnessed a stereotypical Hungarian whipping demonstration. The man who was showing off his whip cracking prowess had one of the women from our group step forward. He used her as his guinea pig, saying that whipping her wouldn't hurt her! It was all quite chauvinistic, even somewhat brutal, but I suppose he was right since our female "volunteer" didn't cry once.

Following this, we had a fish soup lunch on a boat cruise – well, almost. Since the boat was too small to accommodate all of us at once, the group was divided in half, with the second half waiting for an hour. I was in the second half. By the time we ate, there was plenty of bread, plenty of broth, but nothing else left in the soup. The first group had eaten all of the fish!

At the end of the conference the entire town of Abony threw us a closing celebration in their indoor sports center arena. It was quite an event. There was a long procession of pom-pom girls with multi-colored streamers followed by sixteen roasted pigs soon to be carved and served; each pig was carried on a silver platter by two very enthusiastic people. All of the carriers were dressed to the finest. (I tried hard not to look at the heads of the pigs, with fangs sticking out of their mouths, but to no avail). In addition to the food, there was plenty to drink, as well as music and fireworks. The town really knew how to throw a party.

The celebration continued very late, with no signs of letting up, and I was getting tired. I mentioned to fellow presenter Dianna Eiland that I was going to call it a night and walk back to Erzebet's house, which was about a kilometer or so out of town. Dianna said that I was lucky – her hosts were still at the party and she couldn't leave. So I gave her my condolences and started to walk in the direction of the house. Once I left the town center, there were no lights; it was pitch black except for one light far in the distance, which I assumed to be the house light. All I could think of was *What am I doing walking in the dark on a dirt road in the middle of Hungary at 11:00 at night?* After another fifteen minutes had passed, I was almost there, but then I noticed two lights coming in my direction. They turned out to be the headlights of the car belonging to Erzebet and her husband. When they saw me, they stopped and motioned for me to get into the car. I was being "kidnapped" and taken back to the celebration! All Dianna could do was laugh when she saw me return.

The next morning a large group of us took the train back to Budapest. I had only about three hours to kill before catching a train to Vienna. It was barely enough time to see either Buda (the castle and government center on a hill overlooking the Danube) or Pest (the commercial center), so I opted for Buda. I wanted to take the cog railway up the hill to get a great view of the city. Dianna, who decided to stay a few nights in Budapest, joined me. For her, it was a quick introduction to the city; for me it was the shortest amount of time I had ever spent in a city of such magnitude and splendor.

The trains have names on certain railway routes in Europe. Some are named after composers, others after trains from the golden age of rail travel. The Vienna-bound train I boarded was labeled the *Orient Express*; in reality it was just an ordinary InterCity Express, nothing resembling the opulent and exotic train from the past. Oh, well! At least I'd be able to tell my family and friends that I had ridden on a train with that name.

The journey started well but when we were about twenty-five minutes out of Budapest the train gradually came to a halt. The *Orient Express* had broken down. This engine failure also meant that the electrical/air conditioning system was also not working. Since it was a hot day, all of the passengers got off the train and waited outside. We were told that a replacement engine was being sent from Budapest.

After about a half hour, many of my fellow passengers started to get restless. Almost from out of nowhere a middle-aged man hopped into the engine cab and sounded the horn three times.

The tall black woman standing next to me asked, "Was bedeutet Dass?" ("What does that mean?")

At first the rest of us thought that this man was from the railway company, but, no; he was apparently just a fellow passenger trying to communicate to those in charge to hurry up, that he had had enough!

After a long wait, the replacement engine arrived and the journey continued. The *Orient Express* eventually limped into Vienna's Südbahnhof (South Station) nearly three hours late so I now had only one hour instead of four to catch the overnight train to Cologne (Köln). I'd been to Vienna before and had looked forward to paying that wonderful city a quick visit (similar to what I had just done in Budapest), but I reluctantly had to give up on that idea. Nonetheless, I was able to secure a top-level couchette bed, which meant that my nose was about six inches from the ceiling. I hoped that the ride wouldn't be bumpy; it wasn't, and I was able to get about five hours of sleep.

The next morning, after walking around in Cologne for a bit, I thought I had enough time to catch the train to Bruges (Brugge), Belgium. I got to the platform just in time, but the conductor wouldn't let me on. It was leaving at that instant, and he didn't want to accommodate me for fear that the train would depart even one second late. In some European stations one must plan ahead; being there in the nick of time doesn't count. I remember one conductor that I had in college who told us that if we showed up on time for a rehearsal, we were actually late. I took it to heart and later shared this concept with my own students. Missing the train turned out to be no big deal; within an hour I was able to catch the next one, and at least I didn't have to warm up an instrument beforehand.

Bruges was everything I had read about it: the best preserved medieval city in Western Europe. The city hall, the tower, and the boat ride on the canals all conjured up images of heraldry, knights in armor, and damsels in distress. After walking all over the town, I sat down in a park and watched the hares until late afternoon when it was time to board yet another train, this time to Zeebrugge, Bruges' port on the North Sea and – at that time – the southern terminus of P&O's ferry crossing to Felixstowe, England.

During that visit, there were two choices for the crossing: either take a five-hour ferry during the day or an eight-hour ferry over night. I chose the latter. The idea of sleeping overnight on a ferry was enticing. I could have saved money by riding in (and trying to sleep in) a chair on the main deck, but instead I opted to reserve a single bed in a very small double cabin. Was I ever glad that I did! It turns out that on that same ferry was the United States Collegiate Wind Band, an auditioned band of approximately eighty American high school-aged musicians. They were on their way back from a successful tour on the European continent. Their legendary conductor, Gladys Wright, one of the elites of the band world and founder of the Women Band Directors National Association, was on board with them, and we were able to have pleasant conversation. I felt sorry for the exhausted students though, as they had to try to sleep in the same chairs on the main deck that I had successfully avoided.

Before I retired for the night, I made an attempt to buy some casino chips by using an old UK £5 note. My last visit to the UK had been many years earlier and since that time their government had replaced the old bills with new ones that were more challenging to counterfeiters. So my £5 note was rejected, but right when it happened a Scotsman, who was standing in line right behind me, winked at me, smiled, and said rather loudly, "Aye, but in Scotland we'll take 'em!"

Once in England, I took two trains and a taxi to Aldeburgh, my second trip to that seacoast town and the first among many to do research there for my book which would eventually bear the title *Gustav Holst: A Comprehensive Biography*. It was my first visit to England in eight years, yet the warmth and friendship at the Holst Foundation displayed by Rosamund Strode and her secretary Helen Lilley made me feel as if I had never left. Over this visit and those of later years I grew to appreciate Aldeburgh as a very special place; it has so much offer: the beach and its lifeboat, the Martello Tower, Snape Maltings, the Aldeburgh Festival, the Parish Church where I saw a performance of Benjamin Britten's cantata *Saint Nicholas*, Maggi Hambling's *Scallop* sculpture (a tribute to Britten) on the beachfront just north of town, and of course the Aldeburgh Fish and Chips – the best I've ever tasted. The only shortcoming of the latter is that it is a carry out (British: take away) place and, although the pub owner across the street does not permit one to bring in food from the outside, he does allows one to carry the food to picnic tables in the back of his establishment. This is not as great as it first appears, for there is a constant battle not to share one's food with the omnipresent and overzealous seagulls! It gives a new meaning to the phrase "losing one's lunch."

It may have been on this visit that Rosamund permitted me to make dozens of Xeroxed copies of Holst's correspondence. She also gave me a copy of Imogen Holst's final book about her father's music, *The Music of Gustav Holst and Holst's Music Reconsidered.* We wrapped these items into a package so bulky that I did not relish having to take it back with me to Mrs. Giuffredi's place in London. So instead I went to the Aldeburgh post office and mailed it to myself c/o Mrs. Giuffredi, figuring that I would receive it some time in the next three days. About an hour later, I took a taxi to Saxmundam, where I boarded a train for the Liverpool Street Station, from whence I took London Bus No. 14 – the great red double decker that passes by St. Paul's Cathedral, Trafalgar Square, Westminster Abbey, Whitehall, and King's Road – to the corner of New King's Road and Quarrendon Road, where I crossed the street and walked about a hundred feet to Mrs. Giuffredi's. Imagine my surprise – and hers – to walk in the front door and see my package waiting for me! This was one instance where the phrase "postal service" did not add up to an oxymoron!

* * *

The 12th IGEB Kongress was held at the university in Mainz, Germany during the summer of 1996. From the happy coincidence of acquiring air miles and a grant, I was able to take our then seventeen-year-old younger daughter Lydia with me on this trip. We flew into London's Heathrow airport and went immediately to Waterloo Station. Due to a promotion, we each had a free round-trip ride on the then brand-new "Chunnel" train, passing through the tunnel connecting England and France. At that time, before England had finished its high-speed track work, the train left from that station. As a result of our good fortune, we decided to spend two nights in Paris on our way to Mainz and then another one there on the way back.

In Paris we had lodgings at the Henri IV hotel on the Ile de Cite, not far from the Cathedral of Notre Dame. The Henri IV was at that time a real budget bed-and-breakfast place, and we were fortunate in having a twin room, though it was on the fourth floor. The plumbing was not great and once, after flushing the toilet, it started to fill up to the point where it was going to overflow. We had no plunger and so I did the next best thing – I ran down two flights of stairs and, finding a chamber maid, gestured to her with both hands and shouted about the only two words I know in French: "Toilette! L'eau!" ("Toilet! The water!")

Conducting gestures (particularly for *crescendo*) came in handy. She immediately grabbed a plunger and ran with me back upstairs. She knew exactly what to do. Disaster averted!

I was a hero in the above circumstance but an anti-hero in another. Earlier, on our first jet-lagged day in Paris, we took the Metro subway. I gave the man in the booth a medium-size Franc note and he gave me two tickets and change – a combination of a note and coins. The problem is that I got distracted while I was putting my change in my pocket, and less than a second later could only feel the coins. I thought I'd been swindled and told him so. After being cussed out in French (I have no idea what he said), he gave me the note I had demanded. It was that evening that I discovered a hole in the lining of my jacket and, of course, the monetary note which had fallen through the hole. I felt really awful;

I hope that I didn't cost the man his job. I also knew that it would be useless to try to find him. Though it was just a small note, I recognized the fact that the money was not mine to keep and all I could do was to "pay it forward." So, at the end of our stay, I added it to the tip for the chamber maid who had saved us from a terrible bathroom flood.

Paris was wonderful but terribly expensive. I had just received tenure and promotion at U Mass Boston, so there was a little bit of wiggle room to do some touristy things. Thus Lydia and I saw what we could over the two days spent there: we climbed to the first level of the Eiffel Tower, climbed up to the bell tower at the Cathedral of Notre Dame, went to the Louvre, and saw part of the Paris Opera House. On the way back we took a sunset cruise on the Seine and had some escargot. Magnifique!

The next morning we had no problem finding the train for Mainz at the Gare du Nord. Once en route we noticed that there were several stops, but they were not announced and half the time it seemed the stations themselves had no visual identification. Mentally we were in the dark; at least we knew that eventually we would arrive in Mainz. All of this changed immediately upon crossing the German border. The conductor handed us "Ihr Fahrplan" ("Your trip plan"), a pamphlet with a detailed timetable listing all the stops. The impression that this rail journey gave was that the French were organized but they were not going to let you in on it while the Germans were also organized and they expected you to be organized too!

Mainz did not disappoint. Wolfgang Suppan arranged for us to attend a concert in the courtyard of Schott music publishers. There was also a visit to the gorgeous Zum Römischer Kaiser, the building housing the Gutenberg Museum, to see one of the surviving copies of the Gutenberg Bible. In addition, a group of us, including Raoul and Amy Camus and Charles Conrad, took a Rhine cruise from Mainz through the Lorelei to St. Goar. The castles and scenery are breathtaking.

Although steeped in hundreds of years of academic tradition, the physical aspects of the university in Mainz did not impress. Many universities in continental Europe are simply buildings within urban settings. At least this one had a bit of a campus atmosphere and, apparently, a very active student body. There were posters all around announcing various events. Needless to say we were not prepared for the following:

Masturbations-
Seminare
Bieten wir nicht an-
Aber wir haben 4500
Bücher, die dich
Befriedegen
Dürften.
Frauenbibliothek
Keller des Philosophicums
Raum 552
Nur für
FRAUEN

Now it doesn't take a German speaker to figure out the meaning of the first two lines. At least among the English speakers, these ubiquitous posters became the joke of the conference. I did my best to steer Lydia's attention away from these and apparently it worked. Fortunately she had always been somewhat of a bookworm and on this trip it seemed that she often had her head in some novel or another. About all that she remembers of the conference was watching *Star Trek* in German at our hotel.

Upon our return to England, I took Lydia to north to Aldeburgh to meet Rosamund Strode at The Holst Foundation. Once again, I was ending an IGEB trip with a few days of Gustav Holst research. In addition to writing a book, I was always on the lookout for new or different repertoire for my U Mass Boston Chamber Orchestra (UMBCO); the result was that we were playing more Holst than just about any other American college orchestra!

III. *An Old Rabbit and a Chocolate Steak*

Life begins at forty-seven! Timothy Reynish's prognostication was off by three years.

The winter of 1996-1997 was a fortuitous one for the faculty at University of Massachusetts Boston. As part of an agreement made between the administration and the faculty-staff union, all full-time faculty were given $1300 for research. This had no strings attached, but the university pointed us in the direction of spending these funds to buy a particular brand of computer for our offices. I wasn't particularly keen on the idea since I already had a reasonably functioning computer (which I used primarily as a latter-day typewriter, anyway). So, I decided to look for another place to invest these funds.

I didn't have to look very far. "Podium Notes," the newsletter of The Conductors Guild, carried an announcement on behalf of Symphonic Workshops, a Canadian firm headed by Harry Hurwitz. There was to be an international conducting workshop in Máriánské Lázně in the Czech Republic. I certainly had a solid background from my conducting mentor Harry Begian, and had been to many conducting workshops in the past featuring such esteemed conductors as H. Robert Reynolds, Elizabeth Green, Eugene Corporon, and Craig Kirchhoff. All of these workshops were excellent, but this one was different for three reasons: (1) it was entirely orchestral, (2) it was international, and (3) it was to be held on the European continent. Miraculously, the Máriánské Lázně workshop was held in mid-March, overlapping with UMB's spring break, and the cost was close enough to the $1300 that I knew what I needed to do.

I had not felt much support for the conducting aspect of my career for some time. True, I had achieved a measure of success in Pittsburgh, but at U Mass Boston (UMB), a commuter school, it was a different story. Any conductor would have struggled with the circumstances that prevailed there – a deplorable rehearsal space and no budget to speak of. Though I had achieved early tenure (which, in addition to job security, also meant my family's well-being), I felt that I needed to re-validate my own position in the conducting world. I had to see how I measured up.

To this point in my life I had made two great decisions: 1) asking the woman I fell in love with to marry me, and 2) getting my doctorate. Deciding to put UMB's $1300 gift toward an international conducting workshop was indeed the third. Had I done what the university's administration suggested instead, there would now be a decades-old UMB computer once used by me sitting in a landfill somewhere!

So, it was off to Prague. I would visit that great city after the workshop, but my immediate objective was to go directly from the airport to the train station to catch a train to Máriánské Lázně. Once I arrived at the airport, I did as the guidebooks suggested, changing money to Czech crowns ($1=ca. 25 CŠK) and then taking Bus No. 119 to the Dejvická subway stop, which was the one closest to the airport. So far, so good. I knew that I had to change trains at the Muzeum stop and then continue one stop farther to the main train station.

My first impression on the subway was that, for once, the Soviets (who had built the system) did something right; it was relatively fast and modern, though utilitarian. At each stop, bells played the main theme from Bedrich Smetana's symphonic poem *The Moldau*. What a great introduction to the Czech Republic! This sense of glee was short lived, however. When I exited the train at the Muzeum stop and started to look at the signs, I got totally confused. So, I got out my Czech phrase book, walked up to a well-dressed middle-aged man, and tried to speak a phrase in a language I had never even heard: "Hlavní nádraží?" ("Main train station?")

All I got was a blank stare. Czech is a guttural Slavic language; my pronunciation was atrocious. I walked up to another middle-aged man, asked him the same question and received the following: "Ne." ("No.")

Of course, this person thought I was asking if this happened to be the stop for the main station. Finally, I asked a younger person in English for directions and had no problem. My ego was bruised a bit but, on the positive side of things, this experience made me work harder on my Czech pronunciation.

Máriánské Lázně is a spa town with an interesting history. It is located on the western fringes of the Czech Republic in an area formerly known as the Sudetenland. This area, in spite of the fact that it was German-speaking, was incorporated into the newly formed Czechoslovakia in 1918. Twenty years later it was ceded to Hitler, then in 1945 ceded back to Czechoslovakia. German and most English speakers still refer to the town as Marienbad (as will I from this point forward), although there are very few German speakers in the region today. Much of the town is made up of beautiful nineteenth century "opulent age" buildings surrounded by hills and forests. The Casino, Colonnade, and Cure Park hearken back to a time when the middle and upper classes afforded themselves the pleasure of these peaceful surroundings. Many notables, such as Johann Wolfgang Goethe, Frydryk Chopin, Mark Twain, and Winston Churchill spent leisure time here. The 1961 surrealistic French black-and-white movie *Last Year in Marienbad*, which marginally heightened the spa's fame for a while, was not shot there and therefore not at all representative of the town's ambience.

The workshop was a ten-day affair, led by clinician Victor Feldbrill. In his early seventies by this time, he had many credentials, including the conductorship of the Winnipeg Symphony Orchestra and Toronto Symphony. More important than that, however, he was a teacher par excellence who emphasized the importance of baton technique. The orchestra on hand was the Western Bohemia Symphony Orchestra, conducted by Rostislav Hališka; he served as the second clinician. Dr. Tomaš Novotny of Ostrava was the workshop coordinator.

The orchestra had some labor issues; string players would appear and disappear – under the old communist system (still intact) there was a system of rotation and everybody had to be used. A couple of the players – the ponytailed grey-haired principal cellist (whom we called the "ringleader") and the principal trumpeter – were quite arrogant while the competency level of some the woodwind players was questionable. All of this bothered Victor a great deal and, while some of us lost sleep over jet lag, he lost sleep worrying about the situation and about Tomaš, who often seemed to be overworked. Victor was also concerned about the level of musicianship within the orchestra. While comprised entirely of professionals, many performers were somewhat lazy and not at all playing up to expectations. For this reason he cut one of the pieces, the "Love Scene" movement from Hector Berlioz' huge choral symphony *Romeo et Juliette*.

My own initial lack of sleep was tempered somewhat by a couple of late-night score memorization sessions with Richard Fiske, who was auditing the workshop. Dick, as he is known, was a slightly older conductor from Mt. Shasta, California. He and his Polish-born wife, Stasha, were in Marienbad on their second honeymoon. When I still woke up in the middle of the night, usually from about 3:00 until 5:00, I either did some conducting exercises or studied my scores. Fellow workshop participant Joan Landry, whose room was directly below mine, would always comment the following morning about when I would get up and where I would move around.

Some fourteen conductors from five different countries participated in the workshop. All were sincere individuals and most were established conductors, or at least well on their way. Among them were David Stockton (who had conducted a professional opera company in Boston), Jeffrey Bell-Hanson (then at Michigan Tech), Joan Landry (an ambitious but likable twenty-six year old), Christard Janetzky (a Polish-born German pianist-conductor), Tai-wai Li (from Hong Kong), and Leo Najar, conductor of the Saginaw Symphony. Leo and I had actually met fifteen years earlier when I played under his direction as part of the buccina chorus in Ottorino Respighi's *Pines of Rome*.

The Casino served as the rehearsal hall as well as the site of the first concert, though the private conducting sessions as well as nighttime entertainment were held elsewhere. Such entertainment included Federico Fellini's satirical 1978 film *Orchestra Rehearsal* and a midnight showing of a Leonard Bernstein "Young People's Concert" episode featuring the finale of Brahms' *Symphony No. 4 in E minor*. The latter was dubbed into Czech, naturally.

The housing was good but not up to Marienbad's standards. We stayed in a pension built by the Soviets and the guard there was one of those old school communists. He never smiled and did as little as possible outside the confines of his immediate job. All of our rooms were on the upper floors, which meant taking the elevator. The elevator was small but functional; it was also very narrow. It held three persons, not sideways but in a single file, front-to-back. At least it worked.

All conductors were given a list of the pieces to prepare weeks ahead of time. Conducting assignments, based on this list, were posted on a board the night preceding the first session with the orchestra. The sessions began reasonably well for most of the conductors. Some, including myself, started to address the orchestra in German, but the musicians did not want to hear the language of their conquerors, even though more than half a century had passed since the end of World War II. Many of the conductors used English, and Tomaš, who spoke eight languages, served as interpreter. What I did, however, and still do, was to write out a crib sheet full of numbers, phrases, nouns, prepositions, etc. in the dominant language of those in front of me – anything that would help in getting one's points across. That plus "musician's Italian" usually works fairly well, but not always. During one of the first rehearsals, on a particular spot in the "Cathedral" movement of Robert Schumann's *Symphony No. 3 in E flat* ("Rhenish"), I asked for more woodwind, or so I thought. I looked at the woodwind section and, giving an ascending palm up, said the Czech word that I found for wind: "Vitry." The woodwind section unexpectedly broke out in laughter. Later, Tomaš told me that the combination of my hand gestures and choice of word meant stomach gas!

At least my gaff was not serious. Early on, Victor told us that one of the best ways to restart the orchestra in the middle of a piece was to identify the nearest rehearsal letter, and since the letters are pronounced differently in Czech, it would be helpful to identify them by calling out composers' names that started with them, for example "D: Debussy," or "E: Elgar." One of the conductors whose native language was not

English didn't quite pick up on this. While on the podium, he wanted to restart at letter H, so he called out "H: Hitler" – just the thing a central European orchestra wanted to hear! The players were greatly offended and scowled at him. The rest of us gasped, and the embarrassed conductor – well, he eventually recovered from his monumental error and made it through to the end of the conference.

After the first few days, things settled into a groove and Victor announced that he would soon make final decisions about the two scheduled concerts. Each concert was to feature seven participants conducting either one single-movement stand-alone piece or one movement of a symphony. The first concert, scheduled two days before the second, was to feature the more seasoned conductors and had Brahms *Symphony No. 4 in E minor* as its cornerstone. I had hoped to be chosen for the first concert, and there were hints along the way that that would be the case. In the meantime, for the next go-around I was assigned the finale of Mozart *Symphony No. 25 in G minor*, a piece I had conducted many years earlier. I initially felt bad about the assignment, that I may have disappointed earlier, but Victor told me later that he just wanted to see me conduct in my chamber orchestra domain. It worked, and from that point on I had no more jet lag. After the rehearsal, one of the younger German-speaking conductors called me an "Old Rabbit," which was meant to be complementary!

There was much more to the workshop than conducting the orchestra. The individual sessions with the clinicians were invaluable. Victor was a supreme technician, quick to point out correctable deficiencies in one's conducting. Rostislav Hališka was quite different – a "heart-on-his-sleeve" romantic. He and I spoke nothing of each other's language, so we tried communicating in German. I'd had one semester of college German taught by a native German speaker. This meant that I had good pronunciation, but it could get me into real trouble. Hališka's German was not much better, but somehow we understood each other. We did not need a common language; we had music. While music in itself is not the "universal language" as some would say (try telling somebody to pick up a spoon using only music), it is symbolic of the human experience. The three private sessions with Hališka confirmed this; they were absolutely golden.

The next day all of the workshop participants were allowed to conduct whatever they wanted from the workshop repertoire. I chose Wagner's *Siegfried Idyll*, a warm romantic work. Two of the others had chosen to conduct the same piece; they preceded me. By the time I stepped on the podium, I knew what I wanted from the orchestra and they responded very well – we had totally connected aesthetically and the final moments were of unmatched sensual beauty. Victor told me that it was far too slow, but nevertheless great, and that the orchestra was totally focused. Tatiana, the concertmaster, also sensed this. Then Hališka congratulated me. He walked up to me almost laughing, but also almost crying, and uttered the only words I ever heard him speak in English: "It is a miracle."

Wow!

That evening Victor's "day of decision" finally arrived and I was shocked and honored not only to be chosen to conduct on the first concert, but also to conduct the first movement of the Brahms – a real plum. I asked Victor later in a private session about his decision and he said, "I saw something there. I knew that you were the person who could pull off the Brahms 4th first movement." At that moment I felt re-validated as a conductor. It also meant that a lot of the pressure was off.

With four different conductors, the Brahms symphony became a real team effort. It became known as "Brahms-by-committee" or, as Leo Najar jokingly referred to it, "The Peoples' Brahms." Leo conducted the finale, Jeffrey Bell-Hanson conducted the second movement, and Beat (pronounced "Bay-aht") Santini, from Switzerland, conducted the third movement. Beat usually conducted things on the fast side and when he showed up at the dress rehearsal with a cup of the local tar-laden coffee in his hand, Victor broke out in laughter and promptly took it away from him.

The orchestra had the following day (Tuesday) off, and so did we.

Christard Janetsky offered to drive Joan and me to Bayreuth, Germany, the final home of arch-romantic composer Richard Wagner. Bayreuth, previously in West Germany, was an hour and forty-five minutes away. What an opportunity! We had no trouble locating various places associated with the composer and immediately went to the Festspielhaus, built to Wagner's specifications to house his *Ring Cycle* operatic quadrilogy. Unfortunately it was closed. At least the three of us were able to walk around the grounds. However, Wanntrieb, Wagner's last house and now the Richard Wagner Museum, was open and did not disappoint. Completed in 1874, it contains Wagner's library, dioramas, and the piano used for the 1876 premiere of the *Ring Cycle*. Wagner may have been a great composer, but he was also one of the most egocentric, evil, and abusive persons the world has known. The chill one feels while touring this place confirms this. His second wife, Cosima, for whom he composed *Siegfried Idyll*, was far too good for him.

The next day (Wednesday) featured a 40-minute rehearsal of each of the pieces chosen for the first concert; it was the first time that the orchestra and I played the Brahms together. They did reasonably well for me. We had one additional rehearsal the following day, the day of the concert. All of the conductors knew their scores thoroughly. That afternoon I wandered around town, trying to relax. It snowed all day, but it melted instantly, giving a shimmering glow to this elegant locale.

The concert that evening went quite well, beyond Victor's expectations. We all celebrated at Charlie's, one of a dozen or so restaurants in Marienbad. As our entourage entered, there was loud music playing and Victor told the management to turn off the music or we would not eat there because we needed to preserve the afterglow of the performance. Victor's demand was effective; it impressed me so much so that I subsequently have insisted on the very same thing at many restaurants on many occasions. Charlie's was one of the larger establishments in town. Many, such as Mes Amis (the usual hangout), were very small and all were quite inexpensive – a $4 lunch, a $6 dinner – a gastronomic fantasy world! How any of the restaurants made a profit was open to speculation – was it the favorable US dollar-CZK exchange rate – or mafia ties, perhaps?

The funniest eating experience happened early on. Jeffrey Bell-Hanson and I usually ate at Filip, a tiny restaurant having only three tables, but one night we thought we would live it up and dine at Charlie's. The menu was only in Czech and none of the wait staff spoke any English. One of the items listed on the menu was "čokoláda biftek." We figured that it couldn't possibly be what the words looked like, and Jeff, being the eternal experimenter (and optimist) ordered one. What arrived was a steak smothered in chocolate sauce! Jeff ate it, of course, but said that it was perhaps the weirdest main course he had ever had. Sometimes foreign words are exactly what they appear to be.

The pressure was now off; the second concert was to be held on Saturday, but mine was now history. Friday's rehearsals took place in the Marienbad opera theatre, a small hall seating about 300 people. Unfortunately, the acoustics were dead. I attended the morning sessions then headed to the town's music store. The favorable currency exchange rate meant that buying music was a bargain. I bought a complete set (score and parts) of the 4th through 6th symphonies of Czech classical composer Jiři Benda for around $9 (about $3 per symphony)!

The following day, Saturday, I wandered around Marienbad's spa area in the morning, visiting the Goethe museum, where one could see two pictures of one of his mistresses – twenty years apart! I also went to the Kolonáda (Colonnade) to sample the waters from Marienbad's famous underground springs. I bought a small decorative drinking vessel and tried the waters from three different faucets:

No. 1: This one tasted like hot, rotten eggs.

No. 2: This one was also hot but salty.

No. 3: This one was cold and indescribable.

Apparently the soothing effect of the spring waters applied to the body, not to the taste buds. What did appeal to the taste buds were the enormous wafer cookies (about nine inches in diameter) that are somewhat unique to Marienbad. I readily bought several boxes of these to have as gifts for family and friends. Some of my colleagues got massages as well, but I passed. Instead, I headed to the bus station where I bought a one-way ticket to Prague for the following day (Sunday) that cost about $3.50. For some reason the 8:20 a.m. bus sounded a lot better than the 6:53 a.m. train.

The Saturday evening concert was held at Františkovy Lázně (Franzenbad), another spa town located near the Czech-German border. Beethoven and other such luminaries had visited this place. Visually, the most remarkable thing about the town was that nearly all of the buildings were painted some shade of yellow, conjuring up thoughts of the land of the Winkies from L. Frank Baum's book *The Wonderful Wizard of Oz*. Franzenbad's theatre was beautiful and ornate, a fitting place for the final concert and the end of the workshop.

The "Last Dinner at Marienbad," after the final 1997 Symphonic Workshops concert at Marianske Lazne. Victor Feldbrill, is fourth from the right

The next morning Tomaš arranged for an early breakfast for the people taking the bus to Prague. There were six of us: Dick Fiske, his wife Stasha, Joan Landry, Rei-Li Chang (originally from Taiwan), Victor, and myself. About halfway through the journey the bus made a quick stop at Plzeň (Pilsen), home of Pilsner Urquell. Victor jokingly requested a beer break – at 9:30 on a Sunday morning!

Once we got to Prague, Victor went on to a Best Western hotel while the rest of us stayed at Penzion Balbin, which had been highly recommended by Tomaš. It had a somewhat decrepit entrance with floor tiles spelling out "1887" (presumably the date of the building's construction), two sets of steep stairs, and a telephone-booth-sized elevator. Not knowing what to expect, I gingerly pushed the 4th floor button and it ascended without a hitch. As the elevator door opened on the 4th floor, I could instantly see why Tomaš had recommended this place. We had arrived at Shangri-la! Penzion Balbin was quite modern – almost brand new, in fact. I was assigned a room on the top floor that had four beds, a full bath, and a skylight – all for about $32.

Prague itself was magnificent. It was spared the strategic Allied carpet bombing that decimated so many European cities toward the end of World War II. True, it had suffered four decades of communism, but the lasting effects were not felt as deeply as in Bulgaria or Romania. Now, seven years after the fall of the communist state, most of the center of the city was freshly painted, providing a truly colorful Old Worldliness. As soon as we received our room assignments and dropped off our luggage, the five of us headed to nearby Wenceslas Square, where Soviet tanks had quashed a nascent rebellion during the Prague Spring of 1968. We then ate in a typical Czech place with terrible service but great beer; we also tried, but did not succeed, in getting opera tickets for Dvořák's *Rusalka*. After lunch we took in the sights: Wenceslas Square, Karlov Most (Charles Bridge), the Vltava (Moldau) River, the Golden Mile, Prague Castle and, within its walls, the St. Vitus Cathedral. The walk was strenuous, but the view was well worth the effort. To top off the trip, that evening we attended a performance of the Mozart *Requiem* performed on original instruments at the Jan Huis church.

I returned home thoroughly refreshed and greatly encouraged. I had been depressed since leaving Pittsburgh six years earlier, but sometimes doors close so that others open. Though I did not yet realize the full impact of what I had experienced, I knew that I had rediscovered my inner conducting self during this ten-day period and that it was good.

IV. A Gunshot and when "Yes" means "No"

In many ways, the first of the 1998 trips was the most colorful of any of them. But before elaborating, some background information:

During the 1997 Marienbad workshop I learned that three of the participants had been conducting concerts with professional orchestras in Eastern Europe. Those concerts had been arranged through the same organization that sponsored the Marienbad workshop: Symphonic Workshops, Inc. A fee was charged, but the exposure for the conductors was well worth it. What I found encouraging was that none of these three conductors were stars yet; all were decent hard-working human beings trying to establish a foothold in the profession.

So, in the weeks following the workshop, I contacted Harry Hurwitz, head of Symphonic Workshops and asked about the possibility of having my own concert in Eastern Europe. He replied that since I did well under Victor Feldbrill that there would be no problem. He then put me in touch with Tanya Tintner, wife of Halifax Synphony conductor Georg Tintner, who handled such things. Tanya then set me up to guest conduct the Vratza (also spelled Vratsa and Vratca) State Philharmonic Orchestra in Bulgaria the following March. She then requested me to propose three programs; each would consist of an overture, a concerto, and a symphony. The host orchestra would then choose one from each of the categories. Vratza chose an all-Beethoven program: *Coriolan Overture*, Op. 62, *Piano Concerto No. 4 in G*, Op. 58, and *Symphony No. 8 in F*, Op. 93. As fate would have it, the concert would occur on March 26, the 171st anniversary of the composer's death.

The Beethoven 4th Piano Concerto had always been one of my favorites, serenely spanning both the classical and romantic eras. It was also a favorite of my U Mass Boston colleague Timothy McFarland. Tim was head of the piano faculty and a good friend. We had previously collaborated on Mozart's *Piano Concerto No. 23 in A*, K. 488 at UMB, on the same composer's *Piano Concerto No. 21 in C*, K. 467 with The Belmont Orchestra, and on Liszt's *Totentanz* with the Waltham

Philharmonic. These were not professional orchestras, but they did provide us with solid performances. Thus it was only fitting and logical that I invited Tim to be the featured soloist on the Vratza concert.

Direct flights to Sofia were not cheap, but I was able to find a relatively inexpensive alternative: a $484 airfare to Istanbul. This was on British Airways with one change in London. Since Bulgaria is next to Turkey, I figured that we could then take a train or bus from Istanbul to Sofia. Tim readily agreed, though, as in the case of most pianists, he was concerned about maintaining the feel of a piano's touch during the time when he would not be able to practice. Correctly anticipating that Istanbul would have few pianos available to him, Tim brought along a dummy piano keyboard; it made no sound, but provided a suitable amount of resistance when one depressed its keys. Musically, Tim was well-prepared for this trip.

What Tim was not prepared for was the same thing that I was not prepared for: this was Tim's first trip overseas. By this point, having been to Europe at least a dozen times, I was a seasoned international traveler. I had done my homework: securing bank card clearances, acquiring the necessary phrase books, and getting an idea of what to expect through reading various guidebooks, particularly Fodor's and Frommer's. Long before we left the States I had secured lodging for us in Istanbul at the Empress Zoe Hotel, in the Sultanahmet District, very close to the Aya Sofia, Blue Mosque and Topkapi Palace. We would also visit that city on the return from Sofia.

The major drawback of traveling through Turkey was paying $46 for the required visa. This colorful visa ended up looking very nice on my passport; maybe it was worth $5, but not $46. Another drawback was the lopsided currency. The Turkish monetary unit, the lira, was experiencing an incredible slide. At our time of travel, 330,000 Turkish lira equaled one U.S. dollar – foreshadowing Howard Stern's "Who wants to be a Turkish millionaire?" Indeed we became Turkish millionaires several times over, yet often had difficulty negotiating all of the zeroes on the bills. On one occasion we left a tip at a coffeehouse of a 50,000 lira coin, only to realize later that its value was only about sixteen cents.

I had planned things out in great detail, or so I thought. In step with the guidebooks, after deplaning we would take a trolley to a certain point within sight of the Sultanahmet District, then walk across a field (some would call it a plaza) to the street where the Empress Zoe Hotel was located. It was to be the start of two days of joyful tourism before heading to Bulgaria. We couldn't go wrong. However…

One of the guidebooks had a particular warning for those staying in the Sultanahmet District: Once you get off the trolley and start to walk across the field, you might acquire a new "friend" or two. This "friend" would actually be an employee of the notorious Ali Baba Hotel, which at that time had the reputation for being little more than a front for an aggressive rug selling business. Once you enter the Ali Baba, you would not escape without buying a rug.

Sure enough, as we soon as we exited the trolley and headed toward the Sultanahmet, we were joined by a young Turk who enthusiastically spoke those words that I had hoped not to hear: "Hello, my friends."

He immediately started up a conversation in his perfect English and asked the two of us where we were going to spend the night. I responded quickly that we had reservations to stay at a hotel nearby but did not divulge its name. He then asked, "Where?" Tim, not having read the guidebook, immediately told him that we were staying at the Empress Zoe. The Turk responded that he represented a much better place, and that we should stay there. Tim asked him where that was and the Turk's response sent shivers up and down my spine: "The Ali Baba."

It turned out that the Ali Baba was on the same street as our hotel, which was okay except that we had to pass by it before getting to the Empress Zoe. As we got closer, our "friend" invited us in to the Ali Baba for some tea and cakes. An alarm rang loudly in my head. I had read about something called the "Turkish knock-out," whereby an unsuspecting tourist would be invited into a place for refreshments, only to be drugged and later awaken penniless in a dark alley somewhere.

As we walked, the Ali Baba was on the right, as was our "friend." Tim was to the left of him; I was to the left of both of them. To my horror, the Turk convinced Tim to follow him into the Ali Baba. Tim later told me that he seemed to be a nice guy. All I could do was follow the two of them inside, hoping that we would find some way to escape.

The Ali Baba was a relatively small hotel. Its lobby was what I had been led to expect: some Middle Eastern decorations, a small circular staircase leading to the upper floors, a beautiful Turkish rug on the floor and, of course, additional rugs rolled up against the walls. We stood in the middle of the room while our "friend" arranged for some refreshments to be brought to us. All of a sudden we were joined by his uncle, then a cousin, then another cousin, then another. We were surrounded. I had grown increasingly uncomfortable with the situation and quietly told Tim that we had to go. Tim didn't hear me, but one of the "cousins" caught wind of this and told me that I was the very first American tourist who wanted to leave before the refreshments arrived. Sure…

As the refreshments came, I recalled what I could from my college German 101 and said assertively, "Tim, Wir gehen jetzt!" ("Tim, we go now!"). Naturally one of the Turks spoke German, so that didn't work. I don't know why, but all of a sudden the Pig-Latin of my childhood flashed through my mind and, looking Tim right in the eye, I said even more assertively: "Eway avehay otay ogay ownay!"

That was all it took. Tim understood perfectly; the Turks had no clue. We bolted out of the place, with our lives – and our wallets – intact. Normally this would have been the end of such an episode, but no, not in Istanbul. The next morning, upon leaving the Empress Zoe, there was our friend, down the block. He looked at us and waved.

"Hello, my friends."

We waved back and then made sure that we walked quickly in the opposite direction.

The Empress Zoe did not disappoint; quite the opposite. It provided us safe lodging in an exotic setting of Turkish decor – spiral staircases, urns, all sorts of pottery, tapestries, and sumptuous breakfasts consisting urns, all sorts of pottery, tapestries, and sumptuous breakfasts consisting of a wide variety of breads, fruits, cheeses, and olives. The view provided from the terrace was absolutely breathtaking – Sea of Marmara, Aya Sofia, Blue Mosque, the Cystern, etc. This alone made our first "Turkey leg" of the journey worthwhile. Istanbul was truly a fascinating place.

Unfortunately the city was in the clutches of a cold snap. We expected temperatures in the mid-fifties (ca. twelve degrees centigrade) but instead experienced the mid-forties. This made touring unheated buildings such as the Aya Sofia a bit uncomfortable. Still, the weather did not kill our enthusiasm and after two relatively uneventful days of sightseeing, Tim and I needed to make our way to Sofia, Bulgaria. We thought about taking the train, but I had read that since the original railway construction crews were paid by the kilometer, the tracks had been laid in a zigzag manner in order to guarantee as large a payoff as possible. Thus a ride on the train would take much longer than expected. We also heard from the manager and others staying at the Empress Zoe that passengers were regularly robbed on this train route. We also considered going by bus but Ali, the sympathetic bartender at the Empress Zoe, warned against it; he told us that the buses made frequent unannounced stops in order to accommodate predatory salesmen eagerly awaiting the opportunity to get passengers to spend their money. So, after hearing this, we realized that the only reliable mode of transportation for us was by air.

During this time of visit, Bulgaria had been free for only about seven or eight years. Its airlines, Balkan Air and Hemus Air, had fleets consisting largely of aging Soviet-built aircraft. The airplanes were strictly utilitarian in nature and the passenger compartments offered little or no comfort. Still, we figured that we could deal with minor discomfort in a flight lasting less than an hour and a half. Naturally, sufficient leg room would have been a real luxury. Neither Tim nor I are tall people, yet when we sat down, our knees touched the seat backs of the row in front of us. To make matters worse, Tim's seat was broken and kept reclining into the row in back of him. This annoyed the man sitting behind him and he kept punching Tim's seat with his fist.

To our surprise, lunch was served on the flight. This normally would have been a good thing, but the rows were so close together that instead of lowering to a flat position, the trays attached to the seat backs in front of us only descended to about a 45 degree angle, hitting us in the middle of our chests! When we were handed our food trays, we had to surround them with our left arms so that they wouldn't fall, and when the drinks arrived, the whole thing became a precarious balancing act. Still, it could have been worse. Across the aisle were the members of the Nigerian soccer team, all very tall individuals, balancing their food trays between their necks and their knees, which were touching their chests!

After deplaning in Sofia, we discovered to our chagrin that we needed visas and statistical cards to enter Bulgaria. This was no big deal as we were able to purchase them without any hassle at the airport. The cost: $23, exactly half the price of our Turkish visas. Was this a coincidence? We never found out. At any rate, the Bulgarian visa was a disappointment; it merely amounted to a stamped entry in our passports. Perhaps it was worth only half of the beautiful Turkish one. As the saying goes, you get what you pay for.

Bulgarian currency was another matter. At that time, the non-convertible Bulgarian lev was tied to the German Deutsche mark, with a rate of 1,000 lev equaling 1 mark (about 60 US cents). Thus, just as in Turkey, there were a lot of zeroes to contend with, though not quite as many. To our delight, we found the exchange rate to be exceedingly beneficial and, when all was taken into account, most items cost only about a third of what one would expect to pay for them in the United States. We were no longer jet-lagged, but it still hurt our heads to calculate ca. 1700 lev equaling one dollar.

An additional challenge awaited us in Bulgaria: the Cyrillic alphabet. In Sofia there are statues of Cyril and Methodius, the ninth-century saints who invented this alphabet as a vehicle for bringing Christianity to Bulgaria. Cyrillic is similar to Russian and is used in various countries in Eastern Europe. For those accustomed to the Latin alphabet (used by all Western European languages), there are certain mental adjustments to be made to the instant glance of familiar letters: "H" is "N," "P" is "R," "B" is "V," "C" is "S," and "X" is "H." Thus, the ubiquitous "PECTOPAHT" is "Restaurant." And that's just the beginning: a backwards "N" is "I," and the number "3" is "Z." Add to this letters borrowed from the Greek ("Φ" is F" and "Γ" is "G."), a cadre of digraph symbols, a very different set of lower-case letters and, well, it takes a bit of time to even begin to pronounce what one sees, let alone *know* the Bulgarian language. Still, the Bulgarians exhibited a great deal of patience and understanding with our attempts.

After checking into the Hotel Niky (more on that in a moment), we set out for an afternoon of sightseeing with Tim's contact person, Agnetta, who turned out to be an excellent guide. A woman maybe in her early sixties, she knew exactly what we should see in Sofia. The city was not yet set up for tourists the way that Istanbul was: it was a real mishmash of late nineteenth century architecture, rather stark communist-built government buildings, and scattered Roman ruins. The statues of Saints Methodius and Cyril were impressive, as was the Alexander Nevsky Cathedral, named for the thirteenth-century Russian prince and military leader. Planned to honor the Russian soldiers who helped liberate Bulgaria from five centuries of Ottoman rule in 1878, it is perhaps the most stunningly beautiful building in all of Sofia. On its grounds and in a nearby park were all sorts of vendors. A number of them were selling Eastern Orthodox wooden icons which, until just shortly before, had been hidden away by the communists. Beautifully painted, many of these icons dated from centuries ago. A young woman approached me about buying one for $20US. $20! I declined as I had already exchanged my American money for Bulgarian currency, though I could have borrowed the $20 from Tim. Today, I am still kicking myself for this missed opportunity!

We thanked Agnetta, bid her farewell, and then headed over to a bar/restaurant near the impressive but drab monolithic Palace of Culture. There we met up with Valeri Vatchev, conductor of the Vratza State

Philharmonic Orchestra, which I was to guest conduct. Valeri (emphasis one the second syllable) was very young for a professional orchestra conductor, only thirty-five but, musically speaking, was experienced far beyond his years. In addition to his native Bulgarian, he spoke many languages – Russian and German in particular – but, having grown up in the Soviet-dominated communist system of Eastern Europe, he spoke no English. I, on the other hand, spoke no Bulgarian or Russian and my German was rudimentary at best. I do speak reasonable new-world Spanish, but that didn't help here. Tim knew some Spanish and German. So, Valeri, Tim, and I tried to converse in German, but were not entirely successful. Again some "musicians' Italian" helped a great deal when sprinkled in. Miraculously we came to an understanding that Valeri would meet us at the train station the next morning and would help us get tickets and board the train bound for Vratza.

The Hotel Niky, located on a side street one block from the main road to Mt. Vitosha, was highly recommended in one of the guidebooks as a small, reasonably priced hotel (ca. $40) in a nice neighborhood. Its few rooms were Spartan but clean, and each had "en suite" facilities. Tim's room and mine were right next to each other. The rooms themselves opened up into a relatively small lobby area. Breakfast was provided and, rather than being served in a restaurant area, was brought directly to each room. This rather unassuming setting provided the location for the most exciting adventure we were to experience thus far.

Tim and I retired to our rooms about 11:00 that night. I was totally exhausted from what had been a very busy day and fell asleep almost immediately. I was in deep slumber when I was aroused by the sound of a gunshot and then heard Tim's desperate cry through the wall: "Jon…help!"

Was this a dream or reality? The answer came immediately as I heard Tim cry out again: "Jon…help!"

I quickly put my pants on and ran out my door. Tim's door was open and I looked in. There I saw Tim with a not unattractive young woman in his room. She was maybe in her late teens, with hair dyed "Balkan

Red." Both of them were fully clothed. Tim was holding a handgun and his right leg was bleeding slightly. There was also a $20 bill on the floor. What was I to think? Was this gamine a lady of the evening? I had known Tim for six years at this point. He had a fetchingly beautiful wife at home and never gave the slightest hint that he would ever be looking for a prostitute. There had to be more to this, and there was. Tim recounted the events leading up to this tableau in great detail.

The American humorist Samuel Clemens (Mark Twain) once wrote "Giving up smoking is the easiest thing in the world. I know because I've done it thousands of times." Tim had given up smoking many times too, but during this trip he was at it again. Unable to sleep, Tim got up, walked outside the hotel with the intentions of smoking a cigarette and, realizing that he needed a light, walked into the first bar that he saw in order to get one. While there he was approached by the young woman who told him a hard luck story in English. He listened to her talk while he finished his cigarette, but he wasn't at all convinced of the tale she was spinning. He then headed back to the hotel.

To his horror, the woman followed him through the doorway of the hotel and into his room. To his *greater* horror, she then pulled a gun on him and asked for his money. Tim quickly pulled out a $20 bill and offered it to her. She grabbed it, threw it on the floor, and said emphatically: "I don't want that. Now show me the *real* money!"

Sensing imminent danger, Tim wrestled the gun from her. As he did so, it went off, grazing him in the right leg. Fortunately it resulted in just a superficial wound. At that point he called for my help.

I remained standing in Tim's doorway, effectively blocking it. There was no physical contact with the young woman as my presence there was enough to deter her from leaving. At first I had wanted to call the police but then had second thoughts. The fact that we were in a foreign country – particularly a former Eastern bloc country – meant that we didn't know if we had any rights. After nixing the possibility of contacting the police, Tim suggested that I call Valeri Vatchev and cancel our concert. I wanted no such thing, of course. There was too much at stake here. I had been studying the conductor's scores to the selected Beethoven works for months and had put a great deal of time, effort, and money into the planning of this trip. No, I was not about to let anything like this get in the way of doing this concert. Had Tim backed out, I still would have gone by myself to Vratza, even if that meant modifying the program by substituting a second Beethoven symphony for the concerto. Thus calling Vatchev late at night was not an option. Still, we had to do *something*. After taking a couple of deep breaths, we decided to call the hotel manager. He responded immediately.

The manager was very angry at first and threatened to throw us out. Tim surrendered the firearm to him forthwith. I then pointed out to the manager that we stayed at the Niky solely based on a guidebook's recommendation and that as soon as I got back to the States I would contact all the guidebook writers and tell them to withdraw their recommendations. I don't know whether it was because of my bluff or because he happened to look directly at the young woman that he quickly changed his tune. Full of remorse, he then looked at us and said rather sullenly: "This is not *your* problem. This is *my* problem."

He then left. So did the young woman. Tim and I were puzzled; we didn't know what he meant, but we were both glad that the incident was over. However, the next morning…

About 8:00 a.m. there was a knock at my door. I opened the door and there was my eagerly anticipated breakfast had arrived breakfast tray held by the same young woman who had tried to rob Tim only a few hours earlier!

So what had we come across? A prostitution ring run out of the hotel? A prostitution ring run by forces outside the hotel? An independent prostitute? Or was it simply a sympathetic hotel manager trying to help out a wayward girl by giving her a job? We never found out, of course. At that point all that we wanted to be concerned with was checking out of the hotel and being on our way.

Later that morning we met Vatchev at the train station. He helped us buy tickets and set us on the train to Vratza. The ride was only about an hour and a half, a piece of cake, so we thought. We even had our own compartment. Still, we were not in complete control of the situation. Having been repressed for so many decades, first by the Ottomans and then by the communists, the Bulgarians eagerly sought all things Western. This sometimes meant launching headfirst into material items without thinking things through. Thus we had a good sound system in our compartment, but it had the same nine-minute tape of popular songs looping over and over. For two classical musicians preparing for a concert, this was pure hell. We even tried putting our coats over the speaker to absorb the sound, but it was positioned too high. Perhaps appropriate to the situation we had just been through, one of the three selections on the tape was The Animal's version of "House of the Rising Sun," a very good 1960's rock song – but we were forced to listen to it at least nine times during that train ride!

There is a house in New Orleans
They call The Rising Sun.
And it's been the ruin of many a poor boy
And God I know I'm one.

We didn't know what to expect when we arrived at Vratza, only that we would be met by somebody connected with the orchestra who would serve as our guide and translator. As we exited the train a cheerfully flamboyant woman in her late thirties with hair dyed "Balkan Red" (though slightly lighter than the gamine's) approached us and introduced herself, enthusiastically exclaiming in English with a husky Bulgarian accent: "Hello. My name is Natasha. I am *yours* for the *week*!"

In Vratza, Bulgaria, 1998: Our guide, Natasha Uzunova with Timothy McFarland

Initially, all Tim and I could do was glance at each other and laugh as "House of the Rising Sun" was still fresh on our minds. However, Natasha Usunova, a flutist in the Vratza State Philharmonic, was and is a very sincere person. She became a real godsend to us, taking us everywhere and introducing us to what seemed to be everybody that she knew. We soon became good friends, to the extent that she and the orchestra's principal clarinetist, Mikael Dejnov, came to the States two years later and performed as soloists with my U Mass Boston Chamber Orchestra (UMBCO) at St. Paul's Episcopal Church in Brookline, MA. Natasha was a brunette on that occasion.

During their stay we met Mikael's daughter Deya Dejnova, who was a fine cellist. News about Natasha and Mikael's appearance with us got around, the result being that it seemed as if half of Boston's Bulgarian community came to our concert.

I met up with Natasha again in Bulgaria about eleven years later. Her hair was now a very light brown, almost blonde. I garnered up enough courage to ask what her real hair color was. She gave me a Mona Lisa smile and said, "Jon, you'll never know." That was good enough for me.

Back to Vratza: Natasha took us immediately to our lodgings, which happened to be owned by the orchestra. It was the apartment of a string bass player who had recently passed away. As is the custom in Bulgaria, there was a sheet of paper tacked onto the front door. Printed on it was a death notice containing a picture of the deceased. We saw these everywhere, tacked onto outside walls and even stapled onto trees. The apartment itself contained two bedrooms at opposite ends, separated by a kitchenette and a bathroom. There was a library of books in Cyrillic and one of the bedrooms had an old fashioned non-electric Singer sewing machine that was operated by a steel mesh foot pedal. It was the same type of machine that my maternal grandmother had used more than half a century earlier. It turns out that these early Singers were ubiquitous in Bulgaria. The bathroom was simple and functional, with a shower fixture attached to the wall; there was no separate shower stall nor a tub beneath it – just a drain. This setup was very commonplace in Bulgaria.

After our experience at the Niky, it was great to have so much space and so much privacy. There was one drawback: the water ran for only eight hours a day. To compensate for this, we filled three enormous plastic bins which we found in the bathroom every day as soon as the water returned. Thus, in spite of the fact that we had to plan ahead for scheduling showers, we never ran out of water.

Vratza is a town of about 70,000 people located on the edge of the Vranchanska Planina mountain range. Though the town has somewhat of an Alpine feel, most of it is actually lower in altitude than Sofia. It was beautiful to our eyes but should have been more so. The construction of utilitarian communist-era buildings put a real blight on the true beauty of the region. Nevertheless, the Hristo Botev monument and the medieval Tower of the Meshchtii are quite impressive. There is also an outstanding historical museum housing various riches of antiquity, including the Rogozen Treasure and all sorts of Thracian gold. The area's best-known natural wonder, Ledenika, Cave, was still closed for the season, but the local beer named for it was always readily available. Packaged into relatively large bottles (the equivalent of about 22 oz.) and having a high alcoholic content, the brew packs a real wallop.

The weather left a lot to be desired. The same cold spell that we had experienced in Istanbul was stubbornly hanging on in Bulgaria. It even snowed one morning. The cold permeated our coats, but Natasha saw to it that we got suitable sweaters. There were, of course, other ways to beat the cold. One of the best was presented to us at Mikael's home. In addition to being a fine clarinetist, Mikael was also a physician. One of his hobbies was making rakija in his basement. Rakija is a clear fruit brandy from either plum or grape; many Bulgarians consider it to be their national drink. Mikael told us that we could drink as much of it as we wanted to without suffering a hangover the next morning. Fortunately we found this to be true, at least in respect to this particular batch.

Natasha took us everywhere. We ate in some of Vratza's best restaurants and, with the exchange rate being so favorable, we were happy to pay for her meals. One day while Tim was practicing, Natasha took me to see Nikolai the Woodcutter. Natasha told me that it was the established practice for guest conductors of the Vratza State

Philharmonic to receive custom-made batons from Nikolai. His shop was itself wooden and somewhat primitive, evoking thoughts of Gepetto's workshop in Walt Disney's *Pinocchio*. Nikolai asked about the type of baton that I wanted, so I indicated the desired length and weight. Two days later we returned and he presented me with a beautiful wooden baton with a cork handle. When I asked him how much it cost, he laughed and flipped a stotinki coin at me. One hundred stotinki equal one Bulgarian lev. Since 1700 lev equaled one U.S. dollar, this meant I owed him approximately 1/1700th of a cent! It was a great bargain, one he never collected.

One evening Natasha invited us to dinner at her place in a "suburb." It turned out that she lived on the outskirts of town in a very small apartment. The large white building housing the apartment was itself part of a sizeable subdivision. Western Europeans derisively refer to such buildings as "dirty sugar cubes" and to such subdivisions as "Stalin towns." These are ubiquitous throughout Eastern Europe and Russia. The apartments are very cramped. I learned years later from a reliable source that Josef Stalin had planned these with the idea of a minimum of only ten square meters of living space per person! While Natasha cooked, Tim and I watched a Bulgarian version of *Wheel of Fortune* on the television in her small living room. We suddenly came to the realization that this room doubled as her bedroom, with a Murphy bed arrangement. Her kitchen was the size of a small bathroom and her bathroom was of similar size. The place, in essence, was a very small studio apartment. But the dinner featuring, among other things, peppers, cucumbers, Bulgarian (Feta) cheese, and, of course, Natasha's companionship, was one of the most enjoyable that we had during the entire trip.

The Vratza State Philharmonic was savvy to the benefits of receiving media coverage. Tim and I were interviewed by the local television station outdoors in front of the concert hall. We were interviewed in English, but I felt that I had to say *something* in Bulgarian. Since I didn't speak the language, I pieced together what I thought would make sense: "Dober Den, Vratza."

It worked. When our interview was telecast, it was entirely voiced over in Bulgarian except for my above greeting, which means, "Hello, Vratza," or, literally, "Good day, Vratza." The broadcasters pronounced my name correctly, but not Tim's. He acquired a new last name: McKaufermann, which stuck with him from time to time.

In addition to the television interview, we received a good-sized article on the back page of the local newspaper, *Shans*. I could make out my name in the article's heading, but not what followed, so I asked Natasha to translate. She smiled and answered triumphantly: "Jon Mitchell, a Professional Conductor." The article contained the expected biographical and concert information. It also mentioned that I liked Ledenika beer, which must have been important to the local journalists!

The Vratza State Philharmonic is one of a dozen or so professional orchestras in Bulgaria. Its concert hall, though sufficient, was built by the Soviets and has no real personality. At the time of our visit, the orchestra had about fifty-two players. I was told to expect a contingency of two flutes, two oboes, two clarinets, two bassoons, two horns, two trumpets, one person playing timpani, and strings. This is what I had to work with, which was fine, though I learned later that the orchestra also had some additional players, including trombones. They were not needed for this particular concert. Bulgaria was and still is a relatively poor country and some of the instruments were in need of repair. Mikael's clarinet, for example had a couple of rubber bands serving as temporary replacements for springs that were on order. In spite of such physical limitations, the orchestra, Tim, and I worked well together, forming a bond almost immediately. We had about twelve hours of rehearsal time spread out over four days; it was adequate for the program.

During breaks, most of the players headed to a rather sizeable room downstairs. I joined them on several occasions, just to get to know them better. As a bonus for my being sociable, they helped me learn the Cyrillic alphabet and tolerated my awkward attempts at spelling people's names. One of the woodwind players told me that she had relatives in the United States and asked if I would take a couple of the orchestra's records with me so that I could forward them to her relatives when I got back home. I was happy to oblige. I had learned quickly that mailing within the European continent was inexpensive, but that intercontinental mailing was quite the opposite.

The one bad thing about being downstairs during breaks – and this was prevalent in Eastern Europe at the time – was that just about everybody smoked. I don't know how many years of my life were lost just by being downstairs during that week. I semi-joked about this with a group of the players and told them that smoking was really bad for their health. They all laughed, saying that due to the Soviets, the air quality was so bad that they already had years taken off their lives; so it didn't matter to them!

The concert day finally arrived. The orchestra, Tim, and I were well-prepared for the performance, though I was taken aback by an incident that occurred at the very start of the concert – actually extending back before then. I had wanted to make a video recording of the concert and had my VHS-C camcorder with me. I had started to set it up in the recording booth, when the 2nd bassoonist in the orchestra offered to help. Having other things to attend to, I readily accepted his offer and went backstage to give some final thoughts to Beethoven's *Coriolan Overture*, the piece which would open the concert and one of the composer's more romantic works.

The orchestra assembled onstage and then, as customary, the concertmaster walked onstage and signaled for the principal oboe player to give three concert A's. This having been accomplished, I walked onstage, shook hands with the concertmaster, had the orchestra stand, bowed to the audience, ascended the podium, faced the orchestra, and then, to my horror, discovered that there was an empty chair where the 2nd bassoonist should have been sitting! He had not yet made it back from the recording booth!

Now *Coriolan Overture* has a passage in the development section, about halfway through the piece, where there is an essential second bassoon part; the second bassoon plays sustained tones underneath the violins' rapid broken chords. Since the 1st bassoonist does not play in this passage, I looked at him to see if he could cover the part. We both knew what needed to be done. I nodded to him and then he nodded to me. I started the piece and all was fine until we got to that passage. At that point, the violins played their part, but there was no bassoonist playing!

So what happened? I had fallen into a cross-cultural trap: a nodding of the head, especially in an upward motion, means "No," in Bulgaria, while a shaking of the head from side-to-side means "Yes!" The 1st bassoonist and I were so caught up in the emergency of the moment, that we interpreted each other's nod from our own cultural perspectives. Would this have happened in another country? Probably not, as this motioning of the head is reportedly uniquely Bulgarian.

The second bassoonist took his place on stage at the end of the overture and the remainder of the concert went off without a hitch; the performance of Beethoven's *Symphony No. 8* was particularly well received. After the concert Natasha invited Tim and me to a party at the house of a friend. I don't remember the name of her friend, but do recall those of her pets; they were named after movie stars. Her dog was "Julia Roberts" and her cat "Charlie Chaplin." Tim and I were in a state of post-concert relaxation, nibbling away at snacks when suddenly her friend started to place certain items on the table – items that we had not yet seen in Bulgaria – Avon products! Our initial response was to break out laughing. We expected to hear a sales pitch, but that didn't happen. We don't know if she wanted us to buy anything or if she was just proudly displaying her wares. At any rate, Western capitalism had infused itself into the personal lives of the Bulgarian populace!

The following day we bade farewell to Natasha and boarded a train that was headed back to Sofia. The train was full and, although we had seats, many people had to stand. Neither Tim nor I wanted to return to the Hotel Niky and, as we discussed the matter, a young Bulgarian from Plovdiv offered us some advice. He had recently stayed at the Grand Hotel Bulgaria and recommended it to us. Understanding that the hotel was near the Alexander Nevsky Cathedral, which was not too far from the train station, we followed his suggestion.

The Grand Hotel Bulgaria at that time was far different from what it is today. The building was one of the more ornate structures in Sofia, giving the impression of a yellow turn-of-the-twentieth-century three-story wedding cake. Tim and I were awestruck by its outward appearance, that is, until we walked inside. Here we were in a different world, one in which we felt very uncomfortable. After the communists ceded the Bulgarian government a few years earlier, the mafia filled the void, and we sensed that perhaps we were in one of their hotels. Our imaginations may have been running wild. Still, there were well-dressed men with thick necks, looking like NFL prospects, at some of the doors. There were also white circular universal traffic signs posted in the lobby, the type that are rimmed in red with a red slash marking across the diameter. On the road these might indicate no entry or, with a silhouette of a truck in the center, no trucks. Here, however, were silhouettes of handguns and cell phones in the center of these signs. What had we walked into?

We asked for and got a room with two single beds. The man behind the counter insisted that we let a bellboy take our luggage up to our room. We weren't accustomed to this but grudgingly followed his advice. When we arrived at the room, we tipped the bellboy, who winked at us and said in a husky voice:

"You want I should bring two Bulgarian girls up to your room?"

Tim and I were astounded. We explained to the bellboy that we were both married to two attractive women.

His response was not what we expected: "So…you want I should bring two Bulgarian girls up to your room?"

We burst out laughing, of course, though he did not; his business on the side was foiled. At least that was what we thought. He could also have been working for a pimp, or even been a pimp himself. We'll never know.

The next morning we returned to the Sofia airport to catch our return flight to Istanbul. The airport had not yet been modernized and we had to wait in an outer hall. The departure schedule took up most of the wall in front of us, and we located the black strip containing the number and destination of our flight. We couldn't proceed yet as we had to wait for the yellow bulb next to the strip to light up. Thoughts of Orwell's *1984* and H. G. Wells' *The Time Machine* flashed through our minds.

The flight back to Istanbul was uneventful as was our walk from the tram to the Sultanahmet District. This time we were able to stay at the Empress Zoe Hotel but only on the second night, so we spent the first night at the Hotel Alp. It was a boutique hotel, very nice but, temperature-wise, very cold.

On this return trip to Istanbul we saw Topkapi Palace with its harem. On our way to the palace, a Turk stopped us and pointed to a coin on the pavement. He asked: "Is this your penny?"

The idea was when the tourist would bend over to look at it, the guy would grab the tourist's wallet. We didn't fall for it.

On our way back from the palace, we were baffled by a young Turkish boy who, holding some sort of guidebook, jumped out in front of us. He looked Tim right in the eye and declared: "If you do not buy this book, you will go to jail!"

We ignored him, of course, though once we passed him we broke out laughing. Tim shook his head and asked quietly, "Is everybody in this country on the take?" We laughed again, but the worst was yet to come.

Standing in the plaza in front of the Aya Sofia, we decided to go see the Blue Mosque and pulled out our map to confirm directions. Almost immediately we were approached by a young man who said he knew a short cut and to follow him. I politely said no, that we knew the way, and pointed to the Blue Mosque, which was visible, but off in the distance. He persisted. I again said no, a little more assertively. He persisted a third time and by then I had had enough. I waved my arms up and down and said, "No. We know where the Blue Mosque is and we certainly are not going to follow *you*!" Suddenly a slightly older man came out of nowhere and confronted me, shouting: "What is this? We speak with our *mouths*.

You come to my country and you speak with your *hands*!"

I was terrified. Decades of conducting made using my hands to emphasize speech a natural thing. People were starting to gather around. This time, however, it was *Tim* who would rescue *me*. Seeing a touring group nearby, Tim motioned to me that we should take a few steps to the left and pretend to be part of the group. This we did and it worked. The two seedy bastards disappeared, though after this encounter neither of us had any inclination to visit the Blue Mosque.

Instead we returned to the Empress Zoe and relaxed at the bar, sharing our escapades with Ali the bartender. Just being in Istanbul would have been an adventure in itself. It was and is an alluring city, and we had not seen nearly enough – but by this time we were worn out.

* * *

Tim and I returned to Boston where the temperature was in the upper eighties – very hot for late March; there were no leaves on the trees yet. I returned to UMB just long enough to conduct one rehearsal and teach two classes. Three days later I traveled to Manchester, England alone to serve as a clinician and conductor at the BASBWE (British Association of Symphonic Bands and Wind Ensembles) conference at the Royal Northern College of Music. It was spring there, about sixty-five degrees, with the trees in full bloom. Thus it was that in a remarkable four days I experienced three different seasons, at least in regard to outdoor temperature – from winter to summer to spring!

It was wonderful to spend some time with Timothy Reynish again and get better acquainted with fellow conductor John Boyd. While there, I guest conducted The Wirral Band in my edition of George Smith's military band transcription of Gustav Holst's "Country Song" from *Two Songs without Words,* Op. 22. Smith is perhaps best known for having arranged "Mars" and "Jupiter" from Holst's orchestral magnum opus *The Planets*, Op. 32. Smith was bandmaster of the regimental band of the Sherwood Foresters back in the 1930s – Were they a group of Merry Men? His transcription of "Country Song," however, was made during the previous decade, while he was a student in the Bandmasters Course at the Royal Military School of Music at Kneller Hall.

I had discovered Smith's manuscript more than a decade earlier in the Student Archives there and edited it for modern wind band a few years later. The publishing firm Novello, eager to have anything by Holst in their catalog, published it without my first having had a chance to try it out, in order to make any necessary corrections. In retrospect, perhaps I was to blame. Still, this being my first music publication, I was very proud of it until…

When the Wirral Band and I rehearsed it, the players discovered mistakes in their parts – one by one they politely raised their hands to let me know of these; it was a slow and agonizing process. Novello later promised me that there would be an errata list inserted into the publication. I'm not sure that ever happened. They also promised me £300, which I never saw. Oh, well! At least it's out there in print – somewhere.

* * *

That summer my son David, then sixteen, joined me on a trip that eventually led us to Banská Bystrica, Slovakia and the XIII IGEB Kongress. To get there, we travelled through Vienna. It had been a decade since Ester and I had visited that great city, so I didn't mind it at all. David and I stayed at a pension on the north end of the city center. Just as Ester and I had experienced before, this one was a converted university dormitory – not the greatest place, but a good jumping off point. To satisfy David's curiosity, we went to the Wiener Naturhistorisches Museum (Vienna Natural History Museum) to look at the dinosaur bones and the coelacanth, thought to have been extinct, but rediscovered in 1938 off the South African coast. It was by far the ugliest fish I had ever seen. We also went to the impressive Tiergarten (Zoo), where we were nearly attacked by a giant anteater; fortunately, there was a glass barrier between it and us that did not break.

The next day we took the 1½ hour train ride from Vienna to Slovakia's capital, Bratislava. We stayed overnight there at the apartment of Peter Cardarelli, who had been the saxophone instructor at U Mass Boston, but was now carving out a living for himself as a jazz performer. He was actually becoming well known throughout central Europe. Peter directed us to a particular restaurant in the center of the city. As we were ordering the food, the waiter asked us if we wanted some potato pancakes as an appetizer. I was remembering some of the Eastern European potato specialties I had eaten in Chicago and so readily agreed. Imagine our disappointment when the promised potato pancakes turned out to be – Tater Tots!

The IGEB conference itself did not disappoint. Banská Bystrica, Slovakia's fifth largest city, is located in in the center of the country. It has a beautiful town square. The only drawback to the conference was that our free lodging was in a university dormitory. Meals served there were also free, but they were not served on the weekends. So that Saturday morning David and I walked to the town square, looking for a place to get breakfast. None of the restaurants were open yet, but we did find a deli. On the way in, we nearly bumped into a man walking out with a large beer and a shrimp salad sandwich, and this was at nine in the morning!

In spite of the dormitory setting, the IGEB delegation managed to entertain itself. Leena Heikkilä, from Finland, did not present a paper this time around, though her dog Sergei provided us with much to watch during some of the duller speeches. And Australian trombonist extraordinaire Gregory van der Struik always kept us rolling with his "down under" jokes.

As usual, Wolfgang Suppan planned some interesting entertainment for the delegates. The first daytrip involved visiting the Artikular Church in Hronsek, a Lutheran Church built entirely of wood (including the nails) which had to be constructed just outside the city limits because it was not Roman.Catholic. We also saw the historical center of Kremnica with a sword-fighting demonstration and then a concert inside its 13th century castle. Unfortunately it rained that day. A few days later, in the town square of Banská Bystrica, there were performances by a seemingly never-ending variety of bands and folklore groups.

The second daytrip outdid the first. It was actually a day-night excursion into the Lower Tatra mountain range. First we saw the winter ski resort of Tále (which didn't overly impress in the summer) and then we were taken to the village of Čierny Balog, one of the jumping-off points for the Čierny Hron historic forest railway. Its gauge was quite narrow, only 2½ feet wide. As we waited, none of us quite knew what to expect. Eventually an engine appeared all by itself. Diminutive in appearance (only about as tall as the average person), it didn't look at all powerful. Soon after that some wooden open-air cars that seemed to be too wide for the gauge were attached; one had to wonder about the possibility of these tipping over in transit. We need not have worried; the train moved along at only about ten miles per hour.

As the train ascended through the foothills, we were serenaded by a trio of gypsy musicians who were placed toward the front of the second car. These musicians were authentic; they were singing songs based on the gypsy scales, sometimes matching the harmonies that their instruments produced, sometimes not. I remember well the string bass player who pounded the strings with his fist. He was missing about two-thirds of his teeth, but that didn't stop him from joyfully wailing away. It was a different aesthetic, one that was new to me.

After about an hour, the train stopped at our destination: a small clearing. There was a fire going and food cooking, but the sun was setting and there was nothing, absolutely nothing, around us except forest. Just being there was an adventure, but it was also a bit intimidating. We could have been beaten, robbed, or even killed, and nobody would have known for days. This, fortunately, did not happen.

I thought that this would be our only adventure concerning a different sized railway gauge, but it was not. On our way back, as we were enjoying the comradery of Hoosiers Charlie and Anne Conrad, the train suddenly came to a halt. We all had to get out with our luggage and walk to another train. It was not all that easy. Thankfully David was able to help a great deal.

A few days before the end of the conference, several of the delegates who were passing through Vienna on their way home decided to meet for a farewell gathering at the Riesenrad (Giant Ferris Wheel) in The Prater. The wheel is over two hundred feet tall and has enclosed cars that hold at least a dozen people. Taking a ride on this was one of the things I had wanted to do ten years earlier but time (as well as Ester's reluctance) prevented me from doing so. However, this time David, Gregory van der Struik, and the others were up for it, and the ride was a great way to end the trip.

V. From Kidnapped to Freedom

The spring 1999 trip had a dual focus: four days of research in England, primarily on my "magnum opus" *Gustav Holst: An American Perspective* (original title), followed by a week of guest conducting in Wałbrzych, Poland. I was on sabbatical that semester and therefore this became one of my longer trips. It was also one of the strangest – not strange in that there was anything particularly earthshattering – just strange in the sense that there were a number of weird and funny incidents along the way.

That having been said, the first part of the journey wasn't strange at all; England had become a second home, and I felt very comfortable there. However, right from the start it offered something I hadn't experienced before: the new British Library. Soon after deplaning at London's Heathrow Airport, I took the Piccadilly "tube" line to the Kings Cross/St. Pancras Station stop and then walked through all sorts of construction to the new British Library, a nice looking but, from what others have told me, a horribly expensive building. I know that they needed the space, but I actually preferred the library's old location inside the British Museum; the wonders of gazing at the Rosetta stone, the huge Chinese bells and/or the Elgin Marbles always seemed to ameliorate the drudgery of filling out cards and then sitting and waiting *ad nauseam* for items to be delivered.

I also learned quickly that just because the library was new didn't mean it was any better. Delays caused by the computer being "down" wasted three valuable hours of my life! And then one of my requested scores could not be obtained because it had been sent out to be rebound. Aargh! In spite of all that, I was able to accomplish most of my research goals there.

It was during this period of research at The British Library that I made a discovery that would eventually have a direct bearing on one of my future conducting/recording projects. I had read in Imogen Holst's *A Thematic Catalogue of Gustav Holst's Music* (referred to by Colin

Matthews as "The Bible") that there was a 1905 collaborative work, *Pan's Anniversary*, featuring music by both Ralph Vaughan Williams and Gustav Holst. Vaughan Williams composed the introduction, hymns, and arranged some of the incidental music; Holst arranged the folk tunes and dances for orchestra, a total of seven short movements. Imogen Holst indicated there would be nine pages of what her father had contributed, implying that what the library had was incomplete. She was right, of course, but when I was studying Vaughan Williams' contributions to *Pan's Anniversary* later on that same day, I found the missing Holst pages among them – they had simply been misfiled. What a find! My enthusiasm bubbled over. *Pan's Anniversary* is not a great work, but it is a good one, displaying a solid collaborative effort on the parts of two major composers. I immediately called a library staff member over to my desk who – surprisingly – was rather defensive about the pages having been misfiled and did not share in my joy of discovery!

Another find at The British Library (I cannot claim it as a discovery) were the horn parts to Holst's *Greeting*. Transcribed from his own original for violin and piano, *Greeting* is his earliest published orchestral work. I had a set of the published parts, but the set did not include horns. Imogen Holst indicated in *A Thematic Catalogue* that there were two horn parts and indeed there are. Although they double other parts, they add considerably to the romantic character of the piece. So I copied out the horn parts at The British Library by hand. These two works, *Dances from Pan's Anniversary* and Holst's orchestral setting of *Greeting*, would later form the backbone of my CD *Gustav Holst: Composer as Arranger*.

Following this bountiful research session I went to the Liverpool St. Station and caught the train bound for Saxmundham, the closest British Rail stop to Aldeburgh. Rosamund Strode met me there later that afternoon and took me to my bed & breakfast place – the Burrow Residence, located halfway (¾ of a mile) between the center of town and the Britten-Pears Library, which has some of the composer's musical manuscripts The next three days were spent at that library and at The

Holst Foundation, the little cottage where Imogen Holst, the composer's daughter, had lived. To say that Rosamund took care of me well would be an understatement; in addition to securing my lodgings and reserving a table for me at Britten-Pears, she hosted me for three dinners: one on The Holst Foundation, one on her at the "152" restaurant, and one at her place.

Aldeburgh's climate is cool and windy. This day was no exception. On my way into Britten-Pears. I bumped into Philip Reed, one of the librarians, and asked him if there were any really warm days in Aldeburgh during the summer. He looked somewhat perplexed and answered, "This *is* a really warm day!" Also at the library I met Jonathan (whose last name escapes me), a young television camera operator and producer who was working on a documentary about Benjamin Britten. We had an invigorating lunch together at Ye Olde Cross Keys. It's always great to meet and share experiences with creative, but not crazy, people; it stirs the senses.

After three days of research and escapism in Aldeburgh, it was time to leave England. I had a choice: either go back through London and fly to Poland or avoid London altogether and cross the North Sea by ferry from Harwich to Hamburg, Germany and then take trains to Berlin and Poland. I was in no hurry so I decided on the latter. Besides, the idea of traversing the North Sea on an overnight ship fascinated me. So I took the train from Saxmundham to Ipswich and then another to the Harwich International train station, which was right on the ferry docks. At about 3:30 that afternoon I boarded the *Prince of Scandinavia* (of Scandinavian Seaways), or at least I think I did, for the passenger area on the dock is set up in such a way that one never actually sees the ship.

The *Prince of Scandinavia* is quite a vessel. With a capacity of 1,600 passengers – six lifeboats on each side – it is the largest ferry ever built for European service. This being early May, there were only about 300 fellow passengers on this nineteen-hour journey. My cabin, which could have slept four, was on the seventh of nine decks. Strolling around the ship I noticed three open restaurants, a small casino, a corridor with additional slot machines, three bars, and a nightclub. The restaurants had hardly anybody in them; high prices took care of that. The nightclub, however, was free, so I checked it out. The entertainment was a real hoot – a middle-aged Danish female singer backed up by a Bulgarian rock band. This was unusual in itself, but the band had a young diminuitive female keyboard player who on certain songs ran out in front of the group and doubled as a tap dancer! What entertainment! It was fun, but I gave up after about forty-five minutes and headed to my cabin for a good night's sleep.

By the time I woke up in the morning, the *Prince of Scandinavia* was already in the estuary of the Elbe River and by 1:00 p.m. it had docked at Hamburg. Long before this trip I had decided to skip Hamburg, though the city has many worthwhile places to visit. My main interest would have been the birthplace of Johannes Brahms, but the building was destroyed during World War II. After clearing customs, I took a bus to the train station and barely made the 3:08 train to Berlin. The train ride was an easy journey and I was well-rested by the time I checked into Berlin's Hotel Crystal around 6:00. I then had dinner at a German restaurant on the Kurfürstendamm (known by the locals as the Ku-damm), the main street of what used to be West Berlin.

I would do some sightseeing in Berlin on the return journey, but in this direction my focus had to be on getting to Wałbrzych, Poland. The next morning I caught the 9:23 train for Wrocław from the Berlin Zoo station (honest – the station is named for the zoo which borders it). Shortly after the train ride was underway, I noticed that much of East Berlin appeared to be under construction or, perhaps, re-construction; it was trying to catch up with the West. In fact most of East Germany doesn't look as prosperous as the West; forty-five years of communism didn't help. Poland was still poorer in appearance. First Hitler, then the nefarious Soviet strongman Josef Stalin just about destroyed it, the result being that the Polish economy lagged far behind the West, at about a 2:1 ratio. The two-and-a-half-hour journey from Hamburg to Berlin on a German Inter-City train cost about $55, while the five-hour ride on a

Polish Inter-City train from Berlin to Wrocław cost only about $42.

Most of what I saw out the window on that second train reminded me of the Midwest – not particularly scenic. But was I seeing the real Poland? The answer was no, at least not over the past two and a half centuries. What I was seeing was Silesia, the eastern part of pre-1945 Germany but with Polish adornment, if one could call it that. At the end of the war, the German-Poland border was moved west, to the Oder and Neisse rivers, meaning that a huge area of Germany was ceded to the Poles. On the surface this appears to have been a reasonable post-war settlement but the truth, however, was that it was the result of a land grab. Immediately after the war, Stalin seized the silver mines of eastern Poland for himself and forced the people living in those areas to relocate to Silesia. The vast majority of Germans who had been living there were expelled. Therefore Breslau, Germany became Wrocław (pronounced Vrot-swav), Poland and Waldenburg became Wałbrzych (pronounced Vowb-zsik), which was my destination.

On this leg of the journey I was seated in a compartment with a distinguished looking South African college professor. We started up a conversation when he surprised me by saying: "Zwei studiert Musik?" ("Two studying music?")

He then pointed to the young woman next to me. Her name was Marta, and it turned out she was a public school music teacher in Poland. She was reading a Polish book on children's music. Now, whenever the train made a stop, the bells would ring a descending major triad: Sol-Mi-Do. So, naturally from the point when we introduced ourselves, every time the train made a stop, we would look at each other, laugh, and sing in unison with the bells, "Sol-Mi-Do!"

Rather than arrive in the wee hours at Wałbrzych, I decided to spend the night in Wrocław, a city of about 600,000. To save money, I stayed at a hotel literally stacked on top of the bus station. It wasn't bad, a Motel 6 of sorts, and cost about $25. It was located conveniently across from the train station, providing a quick get-away in the morning. Since there were a few daylight hours remaining, I decided to go into the center of

Wrocław. One of the guidebooks suggested taking Tram No. 0, which would run a circuitous route in and out of the center. Wrong! I got onto Tram No. 0 and ended up at the end of the line in some industrial area, far from the city's center. So I had to pay another fare (a whopping twenty-four cents) in order to travel in the opposite direction to get the center. Once there, I saw the Rynek (town square), the Cathedral complex, and some type of May Day celebration in a nearby park.

Polish is one tough language for non-native speakers. The good news is that the Latin alphabet is used, although there are some exceptions, such as the "ł", which has the sound of a "w." I never did get the hang of it and only mastered about a dozen words. Fortunately, for rehearsal purposes, numbers are similar to, but not necessarily the same, as those in other Slavic languages. It is still very easy to get confused as a little bit of knowledge could be a dangerous thing. For example "tak" in Swedish means "thank you" while "tak" in Polish means "yes." Also, many words have a preponderance of consonants. There were times when I wanted to ask *Wheel of Fortune*'s Pat Sajak if I could "buy a vowel." Sajak, himself of Polish descent, grew up in Chicago only a few miles from where I did.

It was in downtown Wrocław at a fast food joint that I first tried to communicate in Polish. There were three menus listed on the signs behind the counter. I wanted to order Menu #3, but with beer instead of Coke. I thought the girl behind the counter understood as I pronounced the words for three (trzy) and beer (pivo) correctly. I even pointed to the sign, but instead of bringing me Menu #3, she brought me three *beers*! I laughed and shook my head. I thought that everything was straightened out, that I wanted Menu #3 – but this time she thought that I wanted *three* meals with *three* beers! Composer Georg Friedrich Händel was said to have placed such a triple order frequently in London – and then eat it all by himself. Finally we got it straight and everybody in the place had a good laugh.

The next morning I rode first class (which had been recommended to me) on an Inter-City train to Wałbrzych, a journey of about an hour and a half; it cost about $5. I got off at the Wałbrzych Miasto (Wałbrzych Town) station, itself a landmark building. It is essentially a single-story corner structure, shaved off in the front at 135-degree angles and featuring four prominent columns; its curved roof looks either like some sort of inverted tulip or a deer hunter's hat worn by Sherlock Holmes. From the station I could see the Hotel Sudety, where the Filharmonia Sudecka had arranged for me to stay. It was what one would expect from the former Soviet bloc – a big impersonal communist block structure probably built in the 1960s. It was the only hotel in this city of 138,000 – reasonably priced and quite boring.

Wałbrzych was at that time (and probably still is) a dirty graffiti-laden industrial town that used to be a coal mining center. The last of the mines had closed in 1996, resulting in high unemployment. Many young people had left the area. There was still plenty of industry, however, meaning that the air was quite polluted. A lot of the neighborhoods looked like the sets used in old World War II movies – unpainted trim, fallen plaster, cement holes, etc. Poverty was everywhere and one wonders how people could live in these conditions. Yet I never felt threatened in any way; in most cases, I think the people there were quite honest and just thankful for what little they had. In spite of its distressed outward appearance, Wałbrzych was a regional cultural center; in addition to the orchestra, it also had a theatre for live performance and a museum with a fine porcelain exhibit.

There were no rehearsals for the orchestra during my first two days in Wałbrzych. May 2nd was a Sunday and May 3rd was a holiday, so I spent a lot of time walking around; the city center was about 1¼ miles from the hotel – a 25-minute walk. The Rynek (town square) was getting a facelift; there was construction everywhere. Nearby there is a second square situated in front of the Town Hall. This building is one of the most unique in Wałbrzych, and its twin turrets on opposite ends of its front façade give it the appearance of a fairy tale castle. On J. Słowackiego, one of the streets that directly connects the Hotel Sudety to the Rynek, I found the Filharmonia Sudecka's building. I knocked on the door and was greeted by a very nice custodian who spoke only Polish. At first he wouldn't let me in. I then pointed to the poster in the outside glass case, the one that advertised the upcoming concert. When I tried to tell him that I was the guest conductor whose name appeared on it, he thought that I was trying to *see* that conductor and told me that he wasn't there yet! This was cleared up when I took out my wallet and showed him my driver's license!

That evening I couldn't find an open restaurant and resolved myself to starve when I saw a "Burger King 2 min." sign. The last place that I wanted to eat while in Europe was at an American fast-food chain restaurant, but on a Sunday evening there was no choice. I figured that the "2 min." on the sign meant driving time for vehicles, of course, but even that would have been a stretch. So, I walked for twenty-five minutes from the town center back to the hotel, then another forty minutes north on some broken sidewalks and through some bad intersections before getting there. At least it was open – but then I had to walk back!

Tuesday, May 4th finally came and I had my first rehearsal with the orchestra. Josef Wilkomirski, the founder, manager, and regular conductor of the orchestra was in the hospital, so there was no opportunity to meet him on this trip. From all accounts he was a wonderful man who had done so much for this region of Poland with his orchestra. I knew that I had to write to him as soon as I returned to the States.

I was given my own room backstage on the first floor (second floor to Americans). It faced the street and had a piano. What luxury!

The Filharmonia Sudecka was the finest orchestra that I had conducted up to this point in my career. There were about sixty-one players for my concert. Of these, about fifteen spoke *some* German and about five spoke *some* English. The German speakers and I were able to converse to *some* extent as I spoke *some* German. The tuba player, Zbiegniew Bajek, a distinguished looking man in his fifties, was also the equipment manager. He was an enormous help. He spoke fluent German, and the two of us were able to converse reasonably well. Contact with most of the other players was through facial expression, head nods, single words from my Polish cheat sheet and, of course, a lot of musicians' Italian, which usually worked.

Rehearsals on the first day were generally very good. The programming was to the orchestra's liking: Felix Mendelssohn's Overture to *Ruy Blas*, Sergei Rachmaninoff's *Piano Concerto No. 2 in C minor*, and Ludwig van Beethoven's *Symphony No. 5 in C minor*. The orchestra knew the Beethoven blindfolded, which actually made it more difficult for me put my own stamp on the performance of that work. The Mendelssohn was an entirely different matter, however, since the orchestra had never played it. The musicians were very open to suggestions. The really hard piece was the Rachmaninoff. The orchestra had performed it a number of times with different soloists. The orchestral parts are not extremely difficult, but the jobs of the conductor and piano soloist are. When I mentioned that I was conducting this work to Jonathan Sternberg, a score study mentor and former conductor of the Royal Tunbridge Wells Ballet, he exclaimed, "The Rachmaninoff *Second Piano Concerto* is a real *conductor's* piece!"

The concert hall was modern and had just been renovated. It seats about 350. Unfortunately, the renovation didn't include an on-stage acoustical shell or the removal of a steel horizontal ceiling beam which, had it been on the floor, would have bisected the orchestra front to back. That ceiling beam caused an acoustical nightmare and made (1) the woodwinds difficult to hear, (2) the horns' sound spread all over, and (3) difficulties in hearing the solo piano at times – the combination of the piano's open lid and the horizontal beam pushed the sound away from the stage and didn't allow for the orchestra or the conductor to hear enough of the solo part. When the hall filled with people, it was even worse because the sound on stage was live, that over the audience was dead – and we had a sell-out crowd!

Rehearsals on the second day also went well. Zofia Antes, the piano soloist for the Rachmaninoff, arrived that evening. I was supposed to meet her at the concert hall but was "kidnapped" by a family – Dzidza, who worked for the Filharmonie, her husband Andrzej, and their English-speaking seventeen-year-old son Arek. They took me to one of their favorite places in the Sudeten mountains – all the way to the Czech border. We didn't cross it, but we were right there. What a view! However, in addition to the scenery we saw something else, something which was heartbreaking: two Kosovo refugees who were going through customs. Poland had recently become a member of NATO, which was good in that there was no anti-American sentiment there; however, I wasn't sure about the Polish sentiment toward these refugees. Afterwards, still way up in the mountains, we had a Bar-B-Q with chicken, bread, the obligatory beer, and the even more obligatory kielbasa. I already had tasted a number of beers in Poland – Zwiebiec and EB come quickly to mind – and while in that country I picked up a number of beer coasters for my continuously expanding collection.

On the way back we stopped at Krzeszów Abbey, the enormous monastery with a hotel where, prior to 1946, a plethora of Mozart and Beethoven manuscripts, including the latter's *Piano Concerto No. 3 in C minor*, had been housed. It was quite a place. We left the monastery via a back road through a heavily forested area. The car suddenly stopped in the middle of the woods. I was taken aback. Why did this happen? Without discussion, the other three people exited the car, each walking several meters in different directions. I did too as it dawned on me that this was a pit stop for each of us to take care of nature's business!

Back at the Hotel Sudety I finally met Zofia Antes. She was a twenty-six-year-old brunette who had graduated the year before from Warsaw Conservatory with the equivalency of a Master's degree. I was surprised and somewhat relieved to learn that she had already played the Rachmaninoff concerto three times. Her husband, Pavel, was also a concert pianist. They had been to the States three times, in particular to Washington State, California, New York City, Miami, and Hawaii. Aside from Arek, Zofia was the only person I met in Wałbrzych who was fluent in English. She and I studied the Rachmaninoff score together until about midnight – we would have only two rehearsals together before the concert – not nearly enough time. I asked Zofia if there were one concerto that she had not played yet, but would love to do, and she said the Mozart *Piano Concerto No. 24 in C minor*, K. 491. We mused that perhaps we could team up together to perform this piece somewhere in the future. I did conduct it several years later, but Yoko Hagino was the solo pianist.

The rehearsal on the following morning began at 9:00. Zofia was not yet on stage when I described her to the orchestra using three words from my Polish phrase book – a "beautiful young woman." One of the violists raised his eyebrows in a lascivious manner and everyone started laughing until I explained to them that we were each happily married, although not to each other, and that I was old enough to be her father! Ouch! Things settled down after that.

The beginning of the second movement of the Rachmaninoff is quite challenging. All parts have beat subdivisions that add up to twelve, but the solo piano has three four-note clusters versus the conductor's four three-note clusters. This can be confusing to the principal flutist, who enters after hearing and seeing these contradictions. So, I decided to dismiss the orchestra a bit early before the break and sat down with the principal flutist Iwona Leroch, a wonderful player. We worked out everything; she never had any later difficulties with the passage.

After the orchestra rehearsal Zofia and I had lunch together at a restaurant located in the basement of a building down the street. The pizza that I selected had spinach over the entire top and was quite good. While there, we discussed the program order. Mendelssohn's overture to *Ruy Blas* was naturally slated to be performed first, then the Rachmaninoff *Second Piano Concerto*, and then after intermission, Beethoven's *Symphony No. 5*. I mentioned that it was fine with me if Zofia preferred putting the Beethoven second in the concert and ending with the concerto so that she could share in the final applause. I recalled performing in an all-Beethoven concert with the Elgin Symphony Orchestra when the conductor, Margaret Hillis, placed Beethoven's 5th before the intermission and then ending with the 4th piano concerto and the *Choral Fantasia*.

Zofia's answer was swift and compelling: "No, absolutely not. Don't you know what this symphony means to these people? It means *freedom*!"

I nodded my head. I knew this also. There was no argument to be made. One of my long-term goals had been to conduct Beethoven's 5th before my fiftieth birthday. I would succeed in doing so, but only at this moment was I beginning to realize the inherent responsibility that went along with conducting this masterpiece.

As we left the restaurant, I noticed a dozen or so wood reliefs of horses' heads that were for sale. These had been carved out of single blocks of wood that were originally about two inches thick. Zofia found out that they were carved by an older gentleman whose work was sold only by this restaurant. I was quite impressed with the artistry involved and, knowing that one of the smaller ones (about 8" X 18") would fit into my suitcase, bought it for about $16. This didn't quite make up for my having passed on purchasing an original icon in Sofia the year before, but it came close. This "Polish horse" still graces one of the walls of our dining room at home. After lunch, Zofia and I returned to the concert hall for a much-needed private rehearsal.

I was all set to return to the hotel and do some serious score study when once again I was "kidnapped" by what had now become my favorite Polish family. This time they took me a few kilometers north of town to the Książ (pronounced something like Kshantz), one of the largest castles in Eastern Europe. Formerly known as Fürstenberg, then Fürstenstein, it was begun in the 1290s and gradually expanded over the centuries to have more than 400 rooms! It was too late to see the inside, but the outside, which included various terraces, was very imposing and quite eclectic in style – renaissance, baroque, and early twentieth century. The accompanying buildings – gatehouse, annexes, and various garages – added to the grandeur of the estate. For many centuries the castle was owned by the Hochberg family and they were responsible for much of the construction.

My “kidnappers” wanted to take me to see several other places, but I insisted and persisted with them that I needed to be back by 6:00 in order to do more score study. They had other plans, however, and took me to their house where they treated me to a home cooked meal of very delicious, though unpronounceable, food. While there, they showed me Arek’s room; the walls were plastered top to bottom with Filharmonia posters! They finally took me back to the hotel at about 7:15 – an hour and fifteen minutes after I wanted to return, but the meal was definitely worth it.

Concert day had finally arrived and the morning dress rehearsal went well. Zofia and I again had lunch together at the same restaurant. As we left, she noticed a violinist playing alone on the street with an open case at his feet. She gave him some coins and mentioned that she always tried to help out the musicians. I followed suit; it was something to remember and to consider for the future. I then headed back to my hotel room where I slept for a little more than an hour. In the meantime, at the Filharmonia, Zofia was given the office I had been using because it had a piano. Consequently, I was given the director’s room upstairs, which afforded me some time to collect myself. Josef Wilkomirski had quite an impressive literary collection in his office – books in Polish, German, and English, plus Chinese calendars.

Overall the concert that evening went very well. The orchestra did a fantastic job on the Mendelssohn – sensitive, majestic, and clean. There was nothing within it that I wanted to take back, so to speak. In many ways it was perhaps the best ten minutes of my conducting career to that point; the videotape bears this out. The Rachmaninoff was next and the first movement went reasonably well. The second movement had some minor problems, largely due to the acoustics. That awful horizontal ceiling beam played havoc in a couple of instances: whenever the horns accompanied the solo piano, their sounds swallowed up that of the piano to the extent that I couldn’t hear Zofia very well at those points. There were some scary moments, but we pulled it off and the audience certainly enjoyed it. The third movement, the one that I had worried about the most, came off without any problems. Zofia, of course, was absolutely brilliant.

Beethoven's 5th went well with two exceptions. At the very beginning a couple of old communist "party members" seated at the back of the second violin section came in on my anacrusis (upbeat)! Nobody in the audience would have caught this, but I sure did. I preceded onward. Perhaps because of this the adrenaline really kicked in and the first movement was a bit on the faster side, yet vigorous and clean. The second movement was fine except for an early viola entrance in a very delicate spot toward the end. It was one of those errors that is so easy to make. In the break before the third movement, I looked at him as if to say that I should have helped more in that particular place. He looked at me with remorse, shaking his head ever so slightly and placed both hands over his heart as if to say, "No, maestro; it was *my* fault." It was a tender moment of complete empathy and mutual respect, one to be cherished forever. The third and fourth movements, which are connected, went superbly, with conductor and orchestra melded into a single entity, sharing in the exhilaration created by a composer who was a total genius. And, yes, the unbridled joy released in the performance of these two movements even eclipsed the feeling I had experienced earlier in the concert on *Ruy Blas*. The full house applauded our efforts with great enthusiasm and gave us three curtain calls! I made sure to thank as many of the orchestra members individually as possible; something really special was created that evening.

Unfortunately, Zofia had to leave immediately after the performance. I was all set to return to the hotel for a good night's sleep when, for a third time, I was "kidnapped" by my favorite family and taken to an after-concert party in a restaurant – free beer and pizza this time.

The day after the concert is nearly always anti-climactic for any conductor, and this day was no exception. I was glad to leave the poverty of Wałbrzych behind but thrilled with what I had experienced there. I dragged myself out of bed and headed over to the Wałbrzych Miasto railway station. I tried to purchase a first-class ticket for the ride back to

Wrocław but didn't succeed. The woman at the counter spoke neither English nor German. I kept holding one finger up, trying English, then German ("erste Klasse"), then Polish ("pierwszej klasy") but each time she said "nie" and eventually handed me a second-class ticket, which I reluctantly accepted. I then joined what seemed to be hundreds of other people waiting on the platform for the train to Wrocław. When the train finally arrived I realized what the situation was with the woman at the ticket office: the train was a graffiti-laden local that had no first class. It looked awful. To make matters worse, the train was more than overcrowded when I boarded.

The car that I entered was set up the way most railway cars are: entryway – main cabin – entryway. Doors separated the three compartments. Since there were neither seats nor standing room in the main cabin, I had to stand in the entryway with my luggage at my feet. Ten other people, most of whom smoked, also had to stand there. The compartment was maybe 6' x 9' (fifty-four square feet), so there was no extra space. I thought that things could not possibly get worse, but they did!

At the first stop, an elderly woman got on. At the second stop a young mother with an infant in a baby carriage got on. Nobody had exited yet, so the space got tighter; I had to put my suitcase in an upright position between my legs. We were packed in like sardines. There was absolutely no room now, and I was hoping that everyone in the compartment was honest since I didn't even have enough room to feel my wallet, which was in my hip pocket. The discomfort wasn't even at full force yet: the epitome was reached at a later stop when a soldier got on with his bicycle! The whole thing was pure Marx Brothers – the ship cabin scene from their 1935 classic *A Night at the Opera*!

The following train ride from Wrocław back to Berlin was much better except for the fact that the people in my compartment smoked. When the conductor came to collect tickets, I pointed to the "no smoking" sign. His response was not what I had expected: he showed me their tickets, which said "smoking." It didn't make sense to me but, rather than raise a fuss, I spent about half of the five-hour ride standing in the narrow hall outside the compartment, conversing with a German businessman who was returning from doing some work in Krakow. He told me not to miss Krakow on my next trip, that it was the *real* Poland.

I arrived at Hotel Crystal at about 7:00 p.m. It was fortunate that the hotel's concierge had reserved a room for my return journey as the hotel was fully booked. That evening I ate at the Aschinger Gasthaus-Brauerei on the Ku-damm. Aschinger brews its own beer and has a rip-roaring, though not terrifying, atmosphere, with wenches serving steins of beer on paddles; the food was all German and outstanding. I really slept well that night.

The next day was dedicated to touring Berlin. I bought a one-day transportation pass and immediately headed for the Brandenburg Gate to get a glimpse of the Berlin Wall. At that specific location there is no more wall, except in one room the Stille Raum (The Room of Silence). In that room are two items: a small black tapestry and one triangular chunk of the wall that measures approximately 10" x 12" x 18." This wall remnant, as well as a line of about twenty-five white crosses honoring the people who were gunned down while trying to escape East Berlin, were poignant reminders of the Cold War. All of this, coupled with the fact that I had just conducted Beethoven's 5th – the World War II "V for Victory" symphony – was overwhelming. Zofia's words stayed with me; it is impossible for me to further describe either intellectually or emotionally what went through my mind during those minutes.

Later that morning I saw the Reichstag, the building that Hitler burned, now rebuilt as the new center of German government. I hoped that they would get it right his time. Tours were being given of the inside, but the line to get in was very long and I wanted to see other things. Early that afternoon I walked into East Berlin and saw the Lutheran Cathedral and a huge flea market that had mostly books and antiques. Prices were still cheaper than in West Berlin, though there is no longer any formal separation of the two halves. Later I went to Schloss Charlottenburg, the huge Prussian palace of Frederick the Great. It was magnificent, but in the light of everything I had experienced on this trip, seeing this palace merely amounted to an afterthought.

* * *

In 2002 I had a return engagement in Wałbrzych. Conducting-wise so many things – good things – had happened since my first trip there and any return engagement would seem at first glance to be anticlimactic. It wasn't, for three reasons: (1) the quality of the orchestra and featured soloist, (2) budding friendships and (3) the music itself. It turned out that this was the first of four trips to Europe that year that involved either research or conducting or both:

1. This concert.
2. A recording session with Jeffrey Jacob and Maria Stäblein in Hrádec Králove in the Czech Republic followed by a concert with that same orchestra in Prague.
3. Presentation of a research paper at the IGEB conference in Lana, Italy, and
4. A recording session with Linnéa Bardarson in Zlin, Czech Republic.

This time I decided to approach Wałbrzych from the southwest, a great excuse for wearing off jet lag in Prague. That great city has two venues for professional opera. This time I went to the Prague State Opera theatre to see Giuseppe Verdi's *Nabucco*. The "Chorus of the Hebrew Slaves" was absolutely riveting.

After a day in Prague, I took a direct Inter-City train that took about four hours. The first stop for Wałbrzych was the Wałbrzych Główny (Wałbrzych Main) station on the far south end of town. While the freight yard saw significant use, the station itself appeared abandoned, with broken windows, etc., an instant reminder of how economically depressed the area was. Still, people entered and exited the train here, appearing to be more-or-less oblivious to the station's condition. Fortunately, I didn't have to exit there; I got off at the Wałbrzych Miasto station, across from the Hotel Sudety, where once again I was staying.

On this trip I finally met Josef Wilkomirski, the permanent conductor of the Filharmonia Sudecka, at the concert hall. An older gentleman, though not quite elderly, he was very accommodating. I noticed the word "Kobiet" on top of the poster advertising my concert and asked him what this meant. He said "women." The date of the concert, March 8th, was International Women's Day and fittingly the featured soloist was female vocalist Aga Winska. She would be featured on the *Concerto for Soprano and Orchestra* by Soviet composer Mikhail Zherbin (1911-2004). The other works on the program were Carl Maria von Weber's Overture to *Oberon*, and Robert Schumann's *Symphony No. 4 in D minor*, Op. 120.

On my way out of the building I saw Zdizda, the matriarch of my favorite family of "kidnappers." We talked – she in Polish, I in English – so each of us had very little comprehension of what the other person was saying. However one item was clear: I asked her about her son Arek and she indicated that he was away studying at a university.

The Filharmonia Sudecka was a very busy orchestra with many engagements and many guest conductors. On my walk from the hotel to the hall before the first rehearsal I wondered if anyone would even remember me. I needn't have been concerned. As I was making some adjustments to my stand onstage before the rehearsal, Marek Badach, one of the horn players, smiled at me and shouted "Jon Mitchell! Beethoven's 5th!" Everything was going to be fine – and it was.

Rehearsals on the Weber and Schumann pieces went well. I had played Weber's overture to *Oberon* no fewer than three times, so it was totally audiated within me. The orchestra had also performed it a number of times, though not recently. So the framework was firmly in place and working on it was more-or-less a matter of fine tuning. The Schumann, however, required more work. While a work in the core orchestral repertoire, it proved to be challenging, especially in the links between movements. Also, Schumann's orchestration was very thick, with winds often doubling the strings. Thus clarity is an issue in this symphony, particularly in the first movement. So I tried something rather bold. I asked the strings to play through the exposition alone and for the winds to follow along in their parts. Then I asked for the reverse, with the strings listening to the winds. It resulted in the desired effect; the players responded well with a beautifully blended tone color on each line. Not every professional orchestra would work with a guest conductor in this way. I was very fortunate indeed and, in a way, so was Schumann.

The Zherbin was a very different story; it was refreshing to perform a work by a then-living composer, but it was quite unfamiliar. I had previously conducted a number of works for soprano and orchestra – Mozart's *Exsultate Jubilate*, Beethoven's *Ah! Perfido*, and a few other concert arias – but this one was different: it was a *vocalise* concerto and therefore had no text. The piece was late Romantic in style, quite reminiscent of Rachmaninoff, and parts of it sounded very Russian. The score and parts were Xerox copies of Zherbin's manuscript, which made them slightly difficult to read. For the first two days of rehearsal the orchestra and I were willing participants but, not yet having heard the solo line, we were at an interpretive disadvantage; I could only guess at some of the nuances that the soloist would make.

This was a lonelier trip as I ended up eating alone much of the time. This was nobody's fault; it just happened that way. One evening I thought I would give the local Chinese restaurant a chance. My waitress was Polish and the location of the table at which I was seated allowed me to glance into the kitchen now and then. I saw two Polish cooks, but no Asian in sight! Perhaps that person stepped out. I don't know. It didn't matter; the food was very good.

Polish soprano Aga Winska arrived on the third day. She was an attractive thirty-something brunette who already had made significant inroads into establishing her career. She had her young daughter with her and, as a result, was not quite as free for socializing as Zofia Antes had been three years earlier. Nevertheless Aga and I found significant time for score study and rehearsal. She was professional in every way and was thrilled at the opportunity to perform the Zerbin – and what a voice! Once she started rehearsing with the orchestra, the Zherbin made perfect sense and we clicked. The horizontal ceiling beam that had played havoc with the piano on the Rachmaninoff three years earlier was still there, but had little or no effect on the conductor's ability to hear a vocalist.

The concert was a total success; once again I had three curtain calls. Afterwards Josef Wilkomirski asked me if I had gotten what I wanted to out of his orchestra. I wasn't sure if he expected me to comment on one or two places that could have gone better, but I took the high road and simply responded "yes" as any minor blemish was cancelled out by the high degree of musicianship and overall sense of well-being conveyed by the orchestra and the music.

* * *

In 2005 I was thrilled to be able to return for a third engagement with the Filharmonia Sudecka. Tanya Tintner told me that being brought back a third time was a real rarity, that the orchestra appreciated my work, and that I should be grateful. Indeed I was. This trip was far different from the other two, for Ester was able to accompany me.

We started the trip with two days in Prague where we stayed in a private apartment across the street from the Prague National Theatre (Národní divadlo). Naturally we decided to go to the opera and saw the world premiere of *La Conquista*, also known as *Montezuma*, by contemporary Italian composer Lorenzo Ferrero. It was trilingual: most of the opera was in Aztec (!), a sizable amount was in Spanish, and a very small portion of the second act was in English. We did well with the Spanish and English, since Spanish is Ester's native language, but our non-comprehension of the Aztec was not helped by the Czech supertitles! Still, it was impressive.

The train that I had taken three years earlier from Prague to Wałbrzych had been curtailed, so we took the same direct train (3½ hours) from Prague as far as it would go – to Mezimisti, on the Czech/Polish border. Ester and I then had to exit the train and cross the border on foot. We were greatly relieved when, once in Poland, we were greeted by a middle-aged man and his young daughter, the owners of the Pensjonat Wanda in the Wałbrzych suburb of Szczawno Zdroj; they were now the official caretakers of guest conductors for the Filharmonia.· We had previously arranged for them to drive the 25 km. across the border to meet us and drive us to Wałbrzych. They were really nice. Gas was quite expensive in Poland at that time, and we were more than happy to pay $40 US ($20 each way). We also paid about $6 each day for them to take us back and forth to the Filharmonia for rehearsals. This was fine but was made even better as the orchestra picked up the cost of my lodging! We had to pay for Ester's stay there, of course, but all the meals we chose to eat there were specially prepared for us and cost us nothing! It turns out that the old communist Hotel Sudety, which used to house the guest conductors, went bankrupt, since visitors to Wałbrzych generally preferred to stay in the more picturesque guest houses in the surrounding areas.

Wanda is located just outside of Szczawno-Zdrój (pronounced something like ShChawvno Zdrewy – try saying that quickly three times in a row!). Wanda is a beautiful place, a modern two-story detached building that had everything we could have wanted in a B & B: a nice bedroom with en suite shower, a pretty breakfast room with paintings of spa buildings on the wall, and a bar room in the basement where I could study scores. I was also able to store Zywiec beer on an outside window ledge in the snow.

At Pensjonat Wanda, the best way to study scores in Poland!

Zywiec + score study = a perfect Polish combination.

In addition to breakfast, we were also served dinner there, which always turned out to be a culinary delight. I remember very well the homemade mushroom soup served in a bread bowl. Good-bye to pizza and Chinese – Hello authentic Polish cuisine!

The town itself is an interesting place. Located about three kilometers northwest of Wałbrzych, Szczawno-Zdrój (known as Bad Salzbrunn before 1945 and Ober Salzbrunn before 1935) is a spa town of about 6,000 inhabitants. It has neither the reputation nor presence of Marienbad, yet people are still drawn to it for its mineral waters. As in the case of the entire region, the town had seen better days, though parts of it were quite picturesque. Still, the town as a whole had a rather quaint feel to it. At first sight Ester coyly mentioned to me, "I guess we're not in Kansas anymore."

This was mid-March and Wałbrzych was in the throes of a difficult winter. Three years earlier I had been there in early March and there had been no snow to speak of. This time, however, there must have been about eighteen inches on the ground. Daytime temperatures were above freezing and nighttime temperatures were below, the result being that there was a great deal of ice everywhere. Apparently Wałbrzych had very limited snowplow service and Szczawno-Zdrój seemed to have none, for all of the side streets had deep ruts where people drove their vehicles. Just being in the car while our hosts maneuvered their vehicle through the ice and snow was quite an adventure in itself.

On tap for this concert was Aaron Copland's *Clarinet Concerto*, Krzesimir Dębski's *Krajobraz* (2000) (*Landscape*), Nicolai Rimsky-Korsakov's *Russian Easter Overture*, Op. 36, and Ludwig van Beethoven's *Symphony No. 6 in F*, Op. 68 "Pastorale." The soloist for this concert was Wojciech Mrozek, by reputation "the best clarinetist in Poland." I had been studying the scores for months. The Dębski, for clarinet and orchestra, was not difficult to learn; it reminded me of some of Lucas Foss' music. Dębski himself is of my generation, and I welcomed the opportunity to conduct the work of an esteemed contemporary in his homeland. The Copland was another matter; even though the orchestral accompaniment was only scored for strings, its inherent difficulties meant that it required the greatest amount of score study. Even though the Beethoven was the most substantial piece on the program, the Copland absorbed more of my time.

There was a bit of confusion, however, regarding programming. The first evening at the Pensjonat Wanda I was handed a score to Claude Debussy's *Premiere Rhapsody* for clarinet and orchestra. It turns out that the parts for the Copland *Clarinet Concerto* were somewhere in Brazil! Wojciech Mrozek had just completed a tour of Brazil and Argentina, and his satchel containing various parts and scores had not arrived yet. So, he requested that the Debussy be substituted for the Copland. I had heard the piece a couple of times and faintly knew it, but I'd never really studied it. This was the first time I had been put into this position. Still, I readily accepted the change in program – and the challenge. This meant that I had only about twenty-four hours to learn the Debussy; it's an enjoyable work, and thankfully I'm a relatively fast learner. Wanda's empty basement bar room and some cooled-in-the-window-by-snowdrift Zywiec beers greatly assisted me in accomplishing the task.

There was another glitch. I had expected to conduct Rimsky-Korsakov's *Russian Easter Overture*, as agreed upon in writing in July. Somehow the orchestra, perhaps meaning Josef Wilkomirski and/or his manager, had forgotten this, and he was quite surprised when I asked him about it. His office was well-organized and they had all of the email correspondence in hard copy verifying the agreement. He apologized. Understanding that I make all sorts of mistakes too, and that in the greater scheme of things this was minor, I adjusted, but I really would have liked to have conducted the piece there.

As before, the first two rehearsals were without the soloist, thus I concentrated mostly on the Beethoven. Beethoven was truly a great composer, but sometimes his hearing loss affected his sense of timbral balance. There are parts of the "Pastorale" where, to me, two horns are insufficient. The third and fourth horn players were delighted when I asked for them to double the first and second horns in certain passages. The new balance worked very well in the Filharmonia concert hall.

Wojciech Mrozek arrived the next day. Wojtech, as he called himself, was a young man, probably in his early thirties. He was cordial, professional, and wonderful to work with. The rehearsals involving him went very smoothly, especially considering the change of program.

It was during the evening of one of these rehearsals that Dzidza and her husband Andrij "kidnapped" Ester, Wojtech, and me. They drove us to the nearby city of Jelenia Góra ("Deer Mountain"). Ester remembers that the ride over there was a very eerie experience, with the sun setting over the deep snow while dense fog was moving in. Once at Jelenia Góra, we entered an old downtown building and descended a narrow staircase to a small eating establishment that was in the basement. The restaurant was remarkable, almost paradoxical, in that it was a Jewish restaurant in Poland! Either it was founded centuries ago or (more than likely) sometime after World War II. Sausages of all shapes and kinds dangled from poles placed parallel to the ceiling. The young yamaka-wearing owner greeted us and, right in front of our eyes, set up a table with a cross section of a tree on it that served as a cutting board. Then he took one of the sausages down, chopped it up with a cleaver, and gave it to us to eat. It was one of the most delicious sausages that I had ever tasted. I can't imagine that many other tourists (if any) in Poland had the same dining experience that we did that night.

The dress rehearsal on the following day went well. The orchestra and I had become old friends over the past six years and there was a strong sense of unity of purpose. I expressed a concern to Wojtech that the first half of the concert might be too short. The original first half, featuring the Rimsky-Korsakov, Dębski, and Copland, would have been about forty-one minutes, a good length considering that the Beethoven on the second half was about forty-two minutes. The Debussy, however, is a much shorter piece than the Copland, with the result being that the first half now had only seventeen minutes of music. Wojciech told me not to worry, that he had a plan. I said okay, that I trusted him on this.

In rehearsal with clarinetist Wojciech Mrozek and the Filharmonia Sudecka in Wałbrzych, Poland, 2005

After this final rehearsal Arek, my third "kidnapper" and now fully an adult at age twenty-three, took Ester, Wojteck, and me to lunch at the Pod Gospoda Wieza, a tavern in downtown Szczawno-Zdrój.

The concert that evening was outstanding but also most unusual. The Dębski, though modern "frozen" music, was well received. The Debussy was beautiful; the harp and horns really came through. Wojteck, of course, was fantastic on these pieces. Then the time-stretcher happened. With the orchestra and myself still onstage, Wojteck went into a series of unaccompanied solo improvisations which stretched the possibilities of his instrument. He continued this for about six minutes. Audience, orchestra, and conductor were enthralled. The applause went on and on. After the concert Wojteck invited me to conduct at a festival in the Ukraine in September! I wanted to do this, but my duties at U Mass Boston at the beginning of that academic year prevented me from doing so.

The second half of the concert featured the Filhamonia's beautiful rendition of Beethoven's *Pastoral Symphony*. The orchestra was with me all the way. The performance was excellent (only a brief let-down in the difficult bassoon-cello unison soli toward the end of the last movement). Three of the four horns of the Filharmonia were out with illness, so they imported three players from the Wrocław opera – and did they ever play! I doubled the horns in the Storm Scene and various parts of the Finale; they were wonderful – and returned the compliment! It was certainly an evening to treasure.

Following the concert Dzidza took us all to a party that was held in a room right across from the concert hall. It was a joyful occasion, the highlight of which was one of the violinists doing his impression of a chicken! His facial expressions and quick turns of the neck were right on target. In another life he would have made it as a nightclub comedian. His rendition alone would have made the entire trip to Poland – in fact all three trips – worthwhile.

The next day Ester and I had planned to take a streetcar or two from Szczawno-Zdrój up to the Książ Castle but were elated when the older of the Wanda owner's two daughters offered to drive us there. This was very fortunate, for time-wise we would never have made it. In spite of the fact that it was already early afternoon by the time we left, we were still able to see the interior of the castle. A lot of care must have gone into the restoration; many of the rooms that we saw were magnificent – Maximilian's room which featured balconies for the court musicians, the hunters' hall, knights' hall, etc. There was, however one thing lacking: there was hardly any original furniture. Hitler cleaned out a lot of what was there as plans were being made (but ultimately unrealized) for the castle to be used by the Nazis as one of their headquarters; to make matters worse, the Red Army was also there in the months immediately after the war. Thus most of the furniture pieces we saw were recent additions, though tastefully incorporated into the style of the architecture of each room.

Ester and I totally enjoyed walking around inside the castle, so much so that we lost track of time. Apparently, it was after the 5:00 p.m., closing time, when we made our way to the front exit. We discovered with horror that it was locked! There was nobody around. I suppose we could have hollered, but there was no guarantee that anyone would have heard us. So, we turned around and walked quite a distance through several halls to a side entrance that we had passed earlier. Fortunately, it was not locked. As we walked out onto the terrace, we realized that this "side" entrance was actually about ¾ of the way to the back of the castle. We also discovered that none of the outside terraces of the castle had been cleared of snow. So there we were, having to trudge through eighteen inches of very heavy melting snow all the way to the front of the castle; neither one of us were wearing boots. Fortunately we didn't get sick from this misadventure, and seeing the interior of this enormous castle was well worth the effort.

VI: A Magnanimous Gesture and Becoming a Hero

Late in 1999 a "Recording Fest" was advertised in the Conductors Guild's "Conducting Opportunities" bulletin. It would take place the following March. The Moravian Philharmonic, an excellent regional professional orchestra located in Olumouc, Czech Republic, would be the host ensemble and a recording company would be present. Qualified conductors were given the option of buying blocks of recording time with the orchestra. There was no contract with any company to produce CDs, but even so, conductors could follow this up on their own if they felt that the recorded takes were to their liking.

Before this, I had made two recordings that had involved concert performances by amateur ensembles. Good as these recordings may have been, they did not approach a professional level, either in quality of performance or in quality of recording. By this time, I had had some experience working with professional orchestras, so participation in the Moravian Philharmonic Recording Fest seemed to be a logical choice. I had also reached the dreaded age of fifty and didn't know how many more opportunities like this one would be available. It was expensive but not out of reach. I had saved up some money from teaching extra courses during summer sessions. Still, this money was not an extravagant amount, so it was imperative that I figure out the best way to utilize these meager funds. But how?

I knew that I wanted to make a promotional CD from the recordings, one that would last between fifty minutes and an hour. The idea was to record musical works from different periods of music: one baroque, one classical, and one from either the romantic period or the twentieth century. Most professional recordings are made with a minimum ratio of 12:1, a ratio of twelve minutes of recording time to one minute of finished product. I didn't have enough money to buy twelve hours (six two-hour blocks) of recording time, but I was able to buy six hours (three two-hour blocks). I wasn't sure that it would suffice, but thought that somehow, maybe, it could.

Then it dawned on me: to get the most out of the recording blocks, I should choose musical works having a lot of repeats. The best take of each repeated section could then be used twice for the final product. So I chose to do the best symphony that I could find which, at least in its original version, had the most repeats. The answer was Mozart's *Symphony No. 35 in D*, K. 385 (1782), "Haffner." The "Haffner" runs about eighteen minutes without repeats, but a little over twenty-seven minutes with them. Good; that left me with filling in the remaining twenty-five or so minutes with a concerto and another piece. The Johann Sebastian Bach *Keyboard Concerto No. 1 in D minor*, BWV1052, lasts about twenty-five minutes and also has a number of sections that, while not having repeat markings, do repeat themselves.

Linnéa Bardarson, a pianist colleague in the music department at University of Massachusetts Boston, had performed the aforementioned concerto with the UMB Chamber Orchestra (UMBCO) under my direction during the previous fall semester. She was a Nordic blonde in her late thirties, quite attractive in appearance and somewhat statuesque. Linnéa also had the perfect touch for the Bach: delicate, yet strong when needed. She and I had collaborated a number of times prior to this, including two do-it-yourself *Messiah*s at the church where she was employed and the Carl Philipp Emmanuel Bach *Double Concerto in E flat*, again with UMBCO. It took Linnéa only a day or so to commit to the project. She asked if she could have her then-husband Bruce Millard along for moral support. Of course the answer was yes – the more the merrier. Bruce was well-known as a jazz mandolin player in the Boston area, and he brought two of his instruments on this trip.

The third piece chosen was Gustav Holst's *Gavotte* from 1933. It was originally the second movement of *Brook Green Suite* [H191], a work he had written for the St. Paul's Girls' School Junior Orchestra. In rehearsal, Holst thought the movement too difficult for the group and excised it. *Gavotte* had never been recorded in its original form and, having obtained permission from the copyright holders, I had a potential world premiere recording on my hands, even if it was only two minutes long!

Thus the plan was set and the three of us headed to the Czech Republic in early March. The best way for us to get to Olumouc was through Prague, and that is where we spent the first two nights. In that great city Linnéa, Bruce and I lodged at Penzion Balbin, the same place near Wenceslas Square that I had stayed three years earlier. It hadn't changed a bit – still modern and very accommodating. On that first evening we walked into central Prague and ate at a traditional restaurant in a cellar. Linnéa remembers that we sat on animal skins – on stools, of course.

The next morning was a bit of a surprise. We ate in Penzion Balbin's breakfast room, which featured the usual tasty mid-European buffet. Among other items, there was a pop-up toaster that had a way of rebelling when longer-than-usual slices of bread were shoved into it! One of Bruce's French bread slices was expelled half-way across the room, and we were laughing boisterously when I noticed esteemed conductor Jonathan Sternberg eating at another table. He was then in his early eighties. Twice, two and three years earlier, I had gone to the maestro's home in Philadelphia for score study sessions. He remembered me well, and it was great to renew ties with this mentor of mentors.

That afternoon Linnéa, Bruce and I walked through Wenceslas Square to the outdoor Havel Market (named for the former president). There were bargains to be had everywhere. The Czech koruna at that time was worth about four US cents, yet each koruna would buy about eight cents' worth. Linnéa spotted what was certainly the best bargain in this market: large calendars of the current year featuring different sepia-toned photos of gargoyles, cornices, and other decorative moldings for each month. These calendars went for a whopping fifteen cents apiece! I bought ten. I gave away nine to friends and relatives. The tenth hung in my office for many years. I didn't care how out-of-date it became; I just liked looking at it.

After scoring great finds in the marketplace, we walked by the Prague National Theatre, noticed that there was an opera to be performed that evening, and that there were tickets available. We didn't buy them then. Instead, we took Tram No. 22 (known to locals as the "Pick-pocket

Express") across the Moldau River to the Mala Strana. There we spotted the Capriccio music store and exited the tram immediately. The bargains continued. At Capriccio I found a concerto for piano and strings (score and parts) by contemporary Czech composer Ivo Jirásek for about $1.12 and another for about twice that much. The real find, however, was a complete set of score and parts to the Robert Schumann *Cello Concerto*, a major work in the core cello repertoire, for less than $9.00! I used this set a few years later when cellist Priscilla Taylor soloed with UMBCO.

That evening we decided to take in the opera at the Prague National Theatre (Národní Divadlo). Before we went, I made the magnanimous gesture of offering to treat everybody on our floor at Penzion Balbin to the opera and had five takers in addition to the three of us. The whole thing cost me somewhere around $16! These were cheap, last-minute seats in the uppermost balcony – "nosebleed seats" – but they did give us a clear unobstructed view of the stage and the orchestra pit. To get there, all we had to do was walk up eight relatively short flights of stairs. The opera was Bohuslav Martinů's *Julietta*, or *The Key of Dreams)*, written in 1937 while the composer was in Paris. The co-production was a joint effort between the National Theatre Opera Prague and Opera North of Leeds, England. It was sung in the English translation done by David Pountney. Anglophiles would normally expect this to be a good thing, but opera sung in English is often difficult to understand. We expected that the supertitles would help – and we were in prime position to read them – but, to our dismay, these supertitles were in Czech (of course)!

The following morning we took the train to Olumouc. Prague is in Bohemia, known for its beer, while Olumouc, about four hours to the east, is in Moravia, known for its wines. Olumouc is a beautiful town. Its main square has the towering Holy Trinity column and an impressive town hall with an outdoor astronomical clock. Rebuilt after World War II in 1946, it features communist proletariats instead of saints or Habsburgers circling around on the hour. There are also several fountains with Greek mythological gods; Poseidon with his trident is especially impressive. A scale model of the old town itself in bronze sits nearby. The only other place I had seen a scale model of a town in its square was in Bourton-on-Water near Cheltenham, England. Another square, almost attached to the main one, is more triangular in nature and has a formidable plague column. The food in Olumouc was wonderful, though on one occasion Linnéa and I were hard pressed to identify a green mystery sauce that covered our plates. It tasted good and, fortunately, neither one of us suffered food poisoning.

We stayed at Penzion Best with some of the other Recording Fest conductors. While there we befriended a young Asian conductor named Ilo, who had developed a tremendous crush on the owner's daughter. We more-or-less took Ilo under our wing and he was often a part of our small entourage. Penzion Best treated us like royalty and, as we departed, the matron there gave us each a small brown ceramic plaque featuring the outlines of Olumouc's notable old town buildings.

One afternoon, while Linnéa, Bruce, and I were walking around the old town, we came across Jazz Tibet, a night club. Jazz saxophonist Peter Cardarelli, the former UMB colleague that David and I had stayed with two years earlier in Bratislava, performed occasionally in Moravia. Linnéa and I wondered if we might run into him. Jazz Tibet was closed, but we noticed a door inscribed with the signatures of various performers who had played there. Lo and behold! There it was: Peter Cardarelli's signature. Never to miss a cue, Linnéa smiled and exclaimed, "Jon, we have just *seen* 'Peter Cardarelli!'"

The Recording Fest was held at Moravian Philharmonic Hall, a beautiful three-story yellow baroque building on the main square. As we entered the building for the first time, we went upstairs and met with the person in charge of things, a friendly businessman whose only fault was that he referred to *everything* as somebody's "cup of tea." It was apparent that English was not his first language, yet his attempt at using an English colloquialism seemed funnier every time we heard him speak it. Yet I should talk; I have made plenty of mistakes myself in learning other languages. In Puerto Rico when I was first learning Spanish, I ordered a plate full of trucks (camiones) instead of shrimp (camarones)!

Moravian Philharmonic Hall was to be remodeled in the following year, but the acoustics were still very acceptable; the more-than-sufficient stage area was entirely wooden and had microphones suspended from above. Outside of the hall, however, conditions surrounding the Recording Fest were far from ideal; work was being done on the building next door and the sound of jackhammers filled the hall on occasion. Fortunately the jackhammers were not in operation during the recording sessions or, if they were, the microphones didn't pick up their sounds.

Most of the Recording Fest conductors recorded works that required a very large orchestra. There was probably more Gustav Mahler recorded that week than any other composer. This week-long diet of heavy post-romantic music was very taxing for the orchestra, so when it came time for us to record baroque and classical music, the orchestra was more than willing. Linnéa suggested that we were supplying "comic relief." One of the other conductors chided me, saying that I was not taking full advantage of the sonorities that the orchestra had to offer. Perhaps not, but my goal was to obtain a performance of professional quality on the works that I had chosen, not to have a merely passable performance of an enormous work.

The recording of single movement works or single movements of multi-movement works are done in segments, say from rehearsal letter "A" to rehearsal letter "B," with some overlap to avoid obvious splicing. Each segment is then recorded three times:

> 1). The first time through is rough. The notes are there, but the music is not. In general nothing is usable from this take. On occasion the first time through might yield the best recording of a single note or even a single phrase, but that is extremely rare.
>
> 2). The second time through is much better, with notes and expression quite acceptable, but the musical sensitivity is not quite at its peak. Often these second takes supply good material for

patching over certain places that may not have been the best in the third take.

3) The third time through is usually the "charm," with the proper energy and focus yielding the best product. Both orchestra and conductor are as one.

4) Sometimes there is a need for a fourth time. More often than not, though, this results in overreach, as the orchestra has now become somewhat complacent.

Our segments of recording time were spread out over two days: two hours on the first day and four hours on the next. For the Bach concerto, we used only twenty-five players: six 1st violins, six 2nd violins, four violas, four cellos, three basses, one bassoon, and a harpsichordist. Bach would have performed the solo part on harpsichord in the 1730s and, on most occasions, would have had a second harpsichordist in the orchestra. The solo instrument available to us was a Petrof piano. Its clear bass tones were very suitable for the Bach. Linnéa performed the solo part on this piano, and for additional tone color we had a harpsichordist (a superb player) in the orchestra. From the experience of having performed this concerto four months earlier, Linnéa and I were able to cruise through the recording sessions with complete trust and admiration for each other's talents. The only concerns we could have had involved two extraneous noises. One was a bow drop in a critical place; the other was a workman, possibly next door, shouting something. We didn't hear either of these as we were recording; we were totally immersed in making music. Much later, while "supervising" the editing being done in Boston, we noticed them. Unfortunately, these extraneous noises showed up on our best takes.

Recording Fest with the Moravian Philharmonic in Olumouc, Czech Republic, 2000

For the Mozart, I used a slightly larger contingency – eight first violins, seven second violins, six violas, five cellos, four basses, as well as pairs of flutes, oboes, clarinets, bassoons, horns, trumpets, and timpani – a total of forty-three in all. To this we added a harpsichordist since Mozart would have conducted from the either a harpsichord or fortepiano, whichever was available. For the Holst, I kept the same string component, plus one each of the woodwind instruments. The brevity of that piece (2'16") allowed for several takes to be done over a span of only about twenty minutes. The orchestra worked well with me through all three of the recording sessions, especially when I tried to communicate by using phrases from my "Czech" list. It didn't matter, as there was a special kind of an ESP among all of us, allowing for that relaxed state of concentration that Timothy Gallwey addresses in *The Inner Game of Tennis*.

Linz flautist, teacher, and composer Han Gielge happened to be at the Recording Fest and gave us some additional moral support, turning pages for Linnéa. He, his wife, and Ilo joined us for a celebration dinner on the final night. The next morning Linnéa, Bruce, Ilo, and I returned by train to Prague, where Bill Tribilsi, a friend of Linnéa's, joined us. Bill was quite entertaining. Of Lebanese descent, he exclaimed about Tony Shalloub's presence on the television series *Wings*, "We now have a face!" He was a good companion, offering his own satirical (and unrepeatable) theories about the names of some of the city's landmarks.

In retrospect the Recording Fest was successful, though it was just the start. We brought with us sufficient DAT tapes (then the industry standard) to record the entire length of our sessions – over five hours' worth. Once we returned to the States, our UMB colleague Peter Janson transferred the DAT tapes to CD. We initially started the editing process with a suburban Boston firm. It turned out that the company owed the editor a huge amount of back pay, so he left town, but not before he sabotaged the machines! As a result, one day's worth of editing was irretrievably lost, stuck inside one of the machines. The owners of the company wanted us to stay with them but we quickly withdrew. At least we still had the original DAT tapes and were able to begin the editing process anew. In the grand scheme of things, it turned out to be just a minor hiccup. Within weeks Linnéa found us another (and better) editor: David Ackerman of Harvard University. He did the editing at his apartment, with Linnéa and me at his side. A short while later Toby Mountain of Northeastern Digital did the final editing and mastering. I went to Toby, a master of editing (to use a play on words), for the vast majority of final edits on the CDs that were to come.

Once the master was completed, Linnéa and I proceeded with getting the CDs made – 300 in all. We formed a non-existent company, JUMBL (Jon, U Mass Boston, Linnéa), assigned a catalog number (JUMBL-001), and came up with a title: "Preteritions" – things of significance often left out. The Bach and Mozart, at least, are great works preformed too infrequently while Holst's excision of "Gavotte" from his *Brook Green Suite* made it a real preterition. I wrote all of the accompanying notes (as I have done for all of my CDs) and for the CD cover we used a photo that Bruce had taken of Prague's St. Vitus Cathedral. We had taken quite a chance – anything could have gone wrong over the span of the entire process – yet it was all worth it at the very end: within a year we had a contract with Centaur Records to record some Beethoven.

* * *

Only two short months had passed since the Recording Fest in Olumouc, yet the itch to conduct in Europe persisted. Thus another engagement was set up, one that involved a return trip to Bulgaria. This time I would be guest conducting in Pazardjik, a city of about 80,000 people, on June 1st. The repertoire would include three works: Carl Maria von Weber's Overture to *Der Freischutz*, Ludwig van Beethoven's *Piano Concerto No. 5 in E flat*, Op. 73, "The Emperor," and Johannes Brahms' *Symphony No. 2 in D*, Op. 73.

I flew in to Sofia on a Friday – this time not via Istanbul, thank you – and even at the airport found the situation in Bulgaria to be much improved over what Timothy McFarland and I had experienced only two years earlier. To my delight, there was no more required visa, no more statistical card, and no more border tax! This meant that I had roughly $23 extra money to spend. The Bulgarians had also modernized their currency, lopping off three zeroes, thus 1,000 old lev=1 new lev, which was worth about fifty cents – much easier on the brain than before.

Valeri Vatchev, who now had a firm control of the English language, met me at the airport. He also had become a raging capitalist as he was serving as the go-to person for many of the guest conductors in Bulgaria. We visited, reminiscing over my guest-conducting of his orchestra in Vratza, while awaiting the arrival of two other Americans on British Airways. One of them, Michael Krausz, would be conducting the orchestra in Pleven. On his program was Beethoven's *Piano Concerto No. 4 in G,* Op. 58 – the same work on which Timothy McFarland and I had collaborated in Vratza. Michael taught Philosophy of Music at Bryn Mawr College in Pennsylvania. He was accompanied by his friend Roy Fitzgerald, a fellow psychologist whose wife was Provost at Swarthmore College. We all hit it off very well and enjoyed our brief time together.

Valeri took us to Hotel Maya, a private third-floor hotel located in central Sofia near the Sheraton. The Maya would supply bookend lodgings for this trip. It had only three rooms and had no air conditioning, but it was quite accommodating, especially after a long flight. It was also cheap – about $30 for the night. Michael, Roy, and I ate at an open-air Bulgarian restaurant nearby before hearing a concert by the Sofia Philharmonic Orchestra. Though it was very warm that evening, it was a wonderful start to the trip.

The next morning Valeri accompanied me to the train station. Though I would be conducting in Pazardjik, my instructions were to ride beyond the Pazardjik stop to Plovdiv, Bulgaria's second largest city, where I would be staying. I bought a first-class ticket, which only cost 4.90 levs (a little less than $3.00) – a real bargain for a 2½ hour ride. At the Plovdiv station I was met by Dmitr, a young man who went by the nickname of Mitko. He would be my interpreter for the week. Mitko, a student at the Sofia Conservatory, played timpani in the Pazardjik Philharmonic. He was also a taxicab driver. It was interesting to see him plaster a role of black-and-white checkered duct tape to the sides of his car whenever he was serving in that capacity and to remove it when he wasn't. This must have happened four or five times during the week.

Mitko drove me over to Old Plovdiv, primarily an eighteenth-century neighborhood north of the downtown area. It was certainly the most picturesque area I had seen in Bulgaria. Many of the buildings were of the timbered architecture so well-known throughout parts of Europe. What made many of them unique was the fact that their second and third stories progressively protruded out, perhaps eight feet, beyond the level immediately beneath them. Thus, when these buildings are across the street from one another, the distance between their second and third stories are progressively much smaller than the distance between their ground floors. Someone explained to me that the reason for this had to do with property taxes based upon the size of the ground floors, but not on what was above. The city-owned building that I stayed in was not one of these but was nevertheless built in the eighteenth century. I had a room on the ground floor facing the courtyard. It was very rustic, with modern conveniences, but no television or telephone – great for score study. It was almost across the street from a small park that has some ancient Greek ruins – broken columns about six feet tall which, unfortunately, were covered with graffiti. I felt the same sense of rage when I saw vandalism on Lookout Rock on the King Philip Trail, one of the most beautiful vantage points in central Massachusetts.

I had dinner that night at what I originally thought was a Greek restaurant, Phillippo. The food was not Greek, but it was still very good. Later that evening I met Dejan Pablov, conductor of the Pazardjik Philharmonic. He was also assistant conductor of the State Opera – Plovdiv Symphony Orchestra. Dejan was young (thirty-six), strong-willed, and opinionated, but after the first couple of days, we overcame any minor differences that we may have had and became friends.

The following day was Sunday and Mitko and his girlfriend took me to see Bachkovo, the second-largest monastery in Bulgaria. Located south of Plovdiv, it is a real tourist attraction. During the five centuries when Bulgaria was under Ottoman rule, Christianity (in this case Eastern Orthodoxy) was suppressed and, as a result, much of the populace had to retreat to the mountains to practice their faith. The striking architecture, chapels, and frescoes bear witness to a combination of Bulgarian, Byzantine, Armenian, and Georgian cultures. Even for a country filled with so much history, this is truly a special place.

That evening I walked through Old Plovdiv and into the downtown area. Old Plovdiv is a very difficult place to walk in with any speed. The streets are made up of huge, rounded cobblestones that don't quite fit the feet, and in the center of most of the streets is a drain. The setup is very hard on the ankles. I had read that Plovdiv was filled with ancient ruins. The first one that I came across, in front of the Academy of Music, was by far the most impressive: a Roman amphitheater still in use! It was built about 90 AD under the rein of the Emperor Domitian. The theatre was locked and, with vision through the gate very limited, I didn't get to see much of it this time around. I walked further into downtown and saw a mosque and part of a Roman stadium. Only one end of this Circus Maximus-type stadium, a 180-degree curve, is visible; a restaurant overlooks it. The remainder of the stadium is underground, directly below Plovdiv's main street, so it will never be entirely excavated. Farther down the main street was a central fountain area and a stage where Bulgarian folk music and dances were to be performed all month. It was still very hot, so I returned to Old Plovdiv where I saw the ruins of a medieval castle before having dinner at Panorama Restaurant which, as its name implies, had a great view.

The next day was Monday and my first rehearsal at Pazardjik. I was up at 6:00 a.m., full of anticipation and enthusiasm. Mitko and Dejan took me to breakfast at Scorpino before heading to Pazardjik. The distance from Plovdiv to Pazardjik is about twenty-three miles (thirty-six kilometers). It was not that long a ride. On the way we stopped to pick up Kat, a string bass player who regularly played in the Plovdiv orchestra. It was while on this road connecting the two cities that I first noticed signs of the Gypsy (Roma) population; they comprise about four percent of the Bulgarian populace. From the distance I noticed a building that looked like a square vanilla cake with enormous white mushrooms protruding from its sides. It was actually an apartment building full of television satellite disks leaning out of the windows. Mitko told me that that was one way of identifying a building that was inhabited by Gypsies and that the Pazardjik area had a high concentration of them. I then innocently asked Dejan if there were any Gypsies in the Pazardjik Philharmonic and was taken aback when he frowned and shouted "No!" at me. Apparently what I had read was true: the Roma were despised throughout Europe, at least in this part of Europe.

All rehearsals took place in the Sala T. Amanasov, the home of the Pazardjik Philharmonic Orchestra. The rehearsal that morning was a bit rough, but overall it went well; I still may have had a bit of jet lag and also had some lingering nervousness from the mini encounter I had just had with Dejan. Regardless, the orchestra members liked the selections. The four horn players were especially enthusiastic about the Weber, which features a horn quartet, one of the best-known in all of the orchestral repertoire.

After the rehearsal, the hall's custodian approached me and asked me something in Bulgarian. Of course I had no idea what he was saying. So, as I had done previously in other places, I went into a series of questions to determine if there was a language, or part of a language, in which we could communicate. My own language proficiencies formed a series of rapidly diminishing returns: English (native), then Spanish (able to get by), then German (significantly less), then help – find a dictionary! I wasn't expecting that the custodian would know any language other than his native Bulgarian, but I asked: "Do you speak English?"

"Neh" ("No")

"¿Habla español?"

"¡Sí!"

What was this? A custodian in the middle of Bulgaria who spoke

Spanish?! Indeed he had spent a good amount of time in Spain. All he was asking about was if the chair placement was to my liking. He was a very sincere fellow and we conversed about many other things over the next few days.

Early that afternoon we returned to Plovdiv and this time I was actually able to get in to see the ancient amphitheater. It was a sight to behold. The audience area is built in the shape of a horseshoe of twenty-eight rows; it seats about 5,000. There are ancient markings on the marble steps indicating where people from the various neighborhoods of ancient Philloppo were assigned to sit. Green all-weather pillows (that are not too comfortable) are scattered around these stone "bleachers" for modern-day patrons.

The stage is immense, with approaches and scaenae frons adorned with statues in front. The orchestra pit is also very large. Perhaps the most amazing thing about the theater, however, is that nobody knew of its existence until the 1970s, when a landslide uncovered a good-sized chunk of it.

That evening Dejan took me to dinner at an authentic Bulgarian restaurant where we had an absorbing discussion about the music of Dvořák, Spohr, Mendelssohn, and Richard Strauss.

I had only about four hours of sleep that night but, in spite of this – or maybe because of it, the rehearsal on the following day went much better. Dejan congratulated me on it. It was during this rehearsal that I met the piano soloist who would collaborate with me more often than any other: Grigorios Zamparas. Gregory, as he called himself in English, was only twenty-four at the time (the same age as my elder daughter Monica). He hailed from Lamia, Greece and was already being noticed throughout the classical music world. He had previously performed a number of piano concertos that are staples of the repertoire – Bach *D minor* (BWV1052), Mozart *No. 23 in A* (K. 488), Beethoven No. *4 in G* (Op. 58), Brahms *No. 1 in D minor* (Op. 15) – and he would perform the Liszt *No. 1 in E flat* at Indiana University in the fall. A graduate student there, he was very fluent in English which helped greatly since my Greek is non-existent. We were a generation apart but, as in the case of Haydn and Mozart, it made no difference in our ability to connect either intellectually or musically. Gregory was (and still is) a musical genius – almost a savant, yet very much a part of the real world.

Our first rehearsal on the "Emperor" concerto was a breeze. The orchestra had performed it earlier in the season but without much success. This time they knew – and we knew – that it would be different. What a thrill it was to collaborate with Gregory and the orchestra on this work! We all knew the piece backwards and forwards; all we had to do was to pool our own musical resources together, to meld with Beethoven. The Weber and Brahms also went much better at this rehearsal, coming along *poco a poco*, as they say in musicians' Italian. That evening Gregory and I walked around Plovdiv and had dinner at a Chinese restaurant where the portions were about the size of footballs!

The following day, Wednesday, I had breakfast again with Mitko and Dejan, this time chomping on Bulgarian "empanadillos." The rehearsal was very good, though I was concerned that all of us needed to maintain focus. Through Mitko I told the orchestra of a recent performance of the "Emperor" concerto by the MIT (Massachusetts Institute of technology) orchestra that was thrown off kilter by a baby's sudden outburst. Following that story, everything was fine in our own rehearsal until the principal flutist made an entrance in the wrong key. I stopped the orchestra but before I could address this one of the violinists exclaimed "Bebe!" ("Baby!). The place went up for grabs. We all had one enormous laugh and I knew at that instant that I had the orchestra in the palm of my hand; the concert would be great.

Trombone and tuba reinforcements from the State Opera – Plovdiv Symphony Orchestra started to rehearse with us on that same day. There was now an impressive depth of strength and power on the Weber and Brahms that had not been heard previously. I thought from here on in everything would go along on automatic pilot, but then I encountered some interference. The first movement of the Brahms symphony has a repeat of the exposition (the first part) that is indicated by the composer.

I nearly always take repeats for three reasons:

1. It is what the composer wrote,
2. For the same amount of rehearsal time, you get twice the amount of music, and
3. It always goes better the second time.

Dejan told me not to take the repeat. At six minutes it is one of the longest expositions in the orchestral repertoire and he was thinking about the orchestra's wherewithal, the fatigue factor. I told him that I would think about it. The concert was quite substantial, about ninety minutes of actual music, and this was an important factor in my decision. What really convinced me not to take the repeat, however, was when one of the older violinists came to me after rehearsal and pleaded with me not to take it. The choice was simple: I could be absolutely right and be an ass or I could compromise and be a hero. I chose to be a hero.

The rehearsal ended with the Beethoven "Emperor" Concerto. In the coda of the last movement the composer inserted a cadenza (duet) for the piano soloist and the timpanist. Beethoven had done this once before, in the first movement cadenza written for the piano version of his violin concerto, but here it is an integral part of the musical flow of the entire work – the music slows down around it. Unexpectedly Mitko was having trouble coordinating his part with Gregory's. Had he not heard recordings of this? The rest of the orchestra was visibly aggravated; a couple of the players turned around and sang his part to him. With apologies to Gregory, I finally decided that I should conduct every beat of this passage so that Mitko would get it right. It worked well. Mitko watched like a hawk and the passage came off beautifully in the concert.

Early that evening Gregory and I were going to attend a piano recital held at the Academy of Music. We got there too late but were able to meet up with Georg Petrov, head of the piano faculty. He had heard Gregory play four years earlier and remembered not only him but also everything that he played on that particular program! He enthusiastically referred to Gregory as an absolute genius. Petrov spoke Bulgarian and

French. Gregory speaks Greek and English but also has a passing understanding of the romance languages. So, Petrov's comments were understood by Gregory and, since he was talking about music, I could understand about 50% of his French. Petrov then invited us to meet him as well as his colleagues the next evening, after our concert. We looked forward to what promised to be a memorable occasion.

Later that evening Dejan invited Gregory and me to attend the dress rehearsal of Verdi's *Othello* at the Roman Amphitheater. During the summers, the Plovdiv opera gives open-air performances here at night. I was very fortunate that my conductor credentials allowed me in to see this ancient place in action. Wow! The orchestra was in attendance, the entire chorus was involved, and it was thrilling to see dozens of singers practice rushing onto the stage and off again. I was able to videotape some of this. Afterwards, we ate at Phillippo, the same quasi-Greek restaurant I had eaten at earlier. Gregory told me that Plovdiv was also called Philippopolis by the Greeks; it was named after Philippos II, the father of Alexander the Great. Still, the food was more Bulgarian than Greek.

Thursday was the day of the concert. I spent the morning studying scores and walking around Old Plovdiv. At 2:00 Mitko met me to help move my things. I had to relocate; the city had reserved my quarters for somebody else, starting with that evening. So the orchestra arranged for me to spend my last night in Plovdiv at the R & S Hotel, which was closer to the modern town center. Gregory would also stay there that night. The R & S was the epitome of the concept of the boutique hotel. It was extremely narrow (maybe twelve feet wide), was three stories tall, had an elevator, and had only one room on each floor. It was modern, however, and had *en suite* facilities. After settling in, Mitko drove us to Pazardjik. I don't know if it was just me, but the road seemed to have much more side activity than I recalled seeing earlier: shepherds, Gypsies with their horse-drawn wagons full of junk, and prostitutes wanting to be picked up by truckers. Perhaps it was that dealing with great music all week had given me a heightened sense of awareness; I don't know.

At 3:30 we had a dress rehearsal, going over the more difficult passages and fine-tuning bits and pieces. This lasted until 5:10, when Gregory and I were whisked into a side room for an interview. We then had about an hour to relax and get into our formal attire. Gregory had some difficulty with his tie, but it was a very minor thing. The concert started at 6:30. I videotaped the entire program; the Weber and Brahms were done from an offstage stationary speaker's podium. One of the horn players convinced me that the Beethoven could be better recorded if he held the camera. While the Weber and Brahms used four horns, the Beethoven required only two, so he was free to record. I reluctantly agreed, not knowing what the final product would be. It turned out that he did very well, albeit from a horn player's perspective, which meant that the sound was a bit out-of-balance; it was recorded on the side of the orchestra facing the bells of the horns. Thus, the "horn fifths" passage in the first movement exposition turned out to be a featured close-up.

The Weber and Beethoven were on the first half; the Brahms on the second. Both halves created a furor. The audience applauded wildly, the orchestra members were very happy, and so, of course, were Gregory and I. A reporter met us backstage and told us that he would write a great review for the local newspaper, *Zname*. It appeared two days later, with our pictures. Later, I received a letter from Dejan thanking me for my "exiting" music – I'm sure he meant "exciting" music. At any rate I am pleased and honored to have it. I have certainly had worse nights! And this one wasn't over yet…

When we got back to Plovdiv we went to Georg Petrov's place. We were met at the door by his fifteen-year-old daughter, who told us that he wasn't there but that he would meet us at the fountain in the center of town at 10:50. It was already well after 9:00 and most of the restaurants were closed, so Gregory and I ate at a Greek take-out. Gyros under the stars in the most aesthetically pleasing city in Bulgaria while wearing formal attire – fantastic!

At the appointed hour, Gregory and I met Petrov, his wife, and one of their colleagues at the fountain. We then walked over to Club 6, frequented by the local musicians and artists. Once inside, we grabbed a large round table and had five different languages going on at the same time. It reminded me of an old *I Love Lucy* episode, where people were lined up, with each speaking two and only two languages, understanding the language of the person in back, then relaying what that person had said, but in another language, to the person in front, etc. So we sat in a configuration that allowed all of us to be able to understand at least most of what each other was saying:

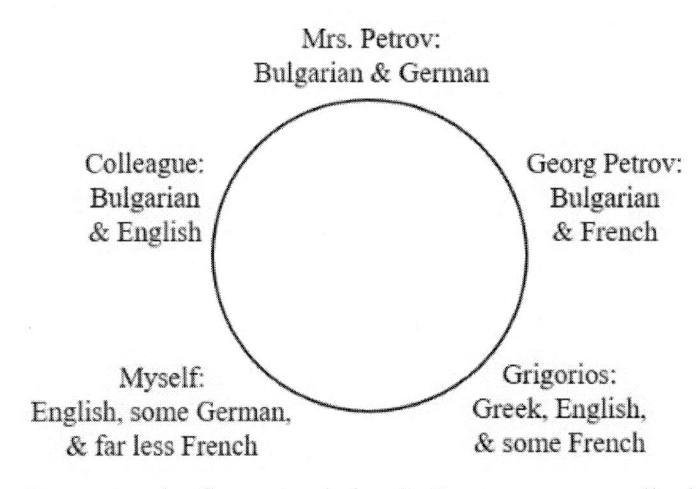

Mrs. Petrov spoke fluent (and clear!) German, so we talked quite a bit and drank quite a bit. So did the others. Then, all of a sudden and with great alacrity, Georg Petrov and Gregory took turns running over to the Russian piano in the corner of the room, trading off on various Chopin Etudes and other short pieces. It was like a classical version of dueling banjos. This went on for over two hours! I can't remember ever either witnessing or being involved in anything quite like this. This "gemütlicheit" at Club 6 was the crowning point to one of those great days that, with luck, one experiences once every ten years or so. None of us wanted it to end. I finally got to bed at about 1:30, too full of exuberance to sleep very much.

At 11:00 the next morning we met the same people at the Academy of Music. There we also met Professor Vassilka Spassova, widow of Ivan Spassov, the former conductor of the Pazardjik Philharmonic, and Professor Emil Yanev, conductor at the Academy, who invited us to perform there next winter and/or summer. Yanev was particularly interested in twentieth-century American chamber orchestra music. Gregory also mentioned the possibility of my conducting in Greece. Neither of these gigs came to fruition, but – wow, so many other things did. Following this brief get-together, we took Georg Petrov to lunch and he took us to his favorite coffee shop in Old Plovdiv for the best baklava I have ever tasted. Fabulous!

A few hours later I boarded a bus back to Sofia with a bit of melancholy. Pazardjik and Plovdiv had provided me with such great memories, yet I didn't know if I would ever renew friendships with any of these people again.

Valeri Vatchev met me at the bus station and took me back to the Hotel Maya. I expected to spend a lonely quiet evening, but that was not the case. Mark Hooper, an Australian pianist, was also lodging at the Maya. He had just appeared as the featured soloist on the Beethoven *Piano Concerto No. 4* in Plevin, on the very same concert conducted by Michael Krausz! Mark was living in Oxford, England at that time and had a Masters in Clinical Psychology. The two of us had much to discuss – another melding of musical minds. To continue further discussion, we took Valeri to dinner that evening.

The next morning, Mark and I spent some time at the market in downtown Sofia. Then it was off to the airport and going home in an exhaustive state of fulfillment.

VII. 2002: My Favorite Year

The first trip of 2002, my second conducting engagement in Wałbrzych, Poland, is detailed in Chapter V. However, the next trip that year differed from all others for the following reasons:

1. It began with a chance encounter at my home university, University of Massachusetts Boston;
2. It involved a recording session of a new work featuring the composer as a soloist; there was also a follow-up concert in Prague featuring the world premiere of that work;
3. The composer of the work invited me to be the conductor for both of the above.

During Fall Semester, 2001, David Patterson, head of music theory at U Mass Boston, invited pianist/composer Jeffrey Jacob to give a performance and lecture in the university's Muriel S. Snowden Auditorium. Jeff was Chair of the Piano Division, Artist-in-Residence, and Professor of Music at Saint Mary's College, Notre Dame, Indiana. Already known as an accomplished performing artist (among his credentials: recording the complete piano output of George Crumb), as well as for his own compositions, he bowled us over with his great musicianship and remarkable dexterity. We were very fortunate to have him, even if only for a day.

Imagine my surprise when, weeks later, I received an email from Tanya Tintner saying that Jeff had requested my services as conductor for a recording that he was going to make in Hrádec Králové, Czech Republic. The work at hand was his double piano concerto *In Memoriam*. There would also be a follow-up concert in Prague featuring the world premiere of that work as well as an overture and a symphony of my choosing! Wow, this was quite an honor! I accepted immediately, of course, in spite of the fact (or maybe because of it) that I already had a very busy guest conducting year. 2002 had become my "year of the four Jeffs" – Jeffrey Mitchell (principal flautist in my U Mass Boston Chamber Orchestra), Jeffrey Bell-Hanson (then conductor at Michigan

Technological University in Houghton, Michigan, with whom I had a podium exchange), Jeffrey Rink (who invited me to guest conduct his Longy School of Music Chamber Orchestra), and now Jeffrey Jacob.

Our recording of *In Memoriam* would eventually be released on the *Orchestra Music of Jeffrey Jacob* CD, itself a part of the *Vienna Modern Masters 2004 Series: Music from Six Continents* (VMM 3057). Although not printed on the CD booklet, this was actually Volume 2; *Orchestra Music of Jeffrey Jacob*. Volume 1 had been released some time earlier by Centaur Records. The recording sessions and concert were set for late June, sandwiched in between the guest conducting stints at Michigan Tech and Longy.

Even without counting the works involved with this project, the period from March to July 2002 was quite a busy one as I conducted a good assortment of repertoire:

Beethoven: *Piano Concerto in D*, Op. 61
Beethoven: *Symphony No. 6 in F*, Op. 68 "Pastorale"
Beethoven: *Symphony No. 7 in A*, Op. 92
N. Barber: *A Reply* [to Charles Ives' *The Unanswered Question*] (2002)
Mendelssohn: *Symphony No. 4 in A*, Op. 90 "Italian"
Schumann: *Overture, Scherzo, and Finale*, Op. 52
Schumann: *Symphony No. 4 in D minor*, Op. 120
Weber: Overture to *Oberon*
Żerbin: *Concerto for Soprano and Orchestra* (1960)

Jeffrey Jacob was still composing *In Memoriam* when I was contacted. The work is dedicated to the children of the Middle East. He comments:

> On one particular day in early 2002, I read of the deaths of two small children, one Israeli, one Palestinian, victims of Middle East violence. I wanted to write a meditative, thoughtful work in their honor, a piece without harshness and rhetoric, but simple commemoration and love.

The work itself is in three movements ("Elegy," "Children's Games," and "Legacy") and lasts about twenty-seven minutes. The orchestration generally supports the two pianos, though it features particularly important solos for the clarinet in the second movement and violoncello in the third. There is also very effective use of percussion, particularly the wind chimes. For both the recording sessions and the concert, Jeff played the first piano part and Maria Stäblein, then a member of the piano faculty of Notre Dame University in South Bend, Indiana (very near Saint Mary's College), played the second.

The orchestra at hand was the Philharmony Hrádec Králové, and the recording would take place in the orchestra's rehearsal hall. Hrádec Králové is a small city (population: 93,000) located about an hour east of Prague by train. It is just south of a region known as "Czech Wonderland" by the locals for its magnificent scenery of rolling hills and mountains. The city itself has a splendid old-world market square (its beauty unfortunately compromised by its use as a parking lot during the day) as well as a thriving "New City" built in the late 1800s and located just west of the old. Hrádec Králové is also the home of Petrof, one of the largest piano manufacturers in Europe. We spent part of an afternoon there, trying out the best of what Petrof had to offer.

Jeff and Maria had been able to practice together sufficiently to ensure that their sounds blended well. For me, however, it was a different story. Time was of the essence. Jeff had sent me a full score minus the piano parts a month or so ahead of time, but I only had a couple of weeks to study the complete product. So I continuously felt on edge during the recording sessions, not that that was a bad thing in itself. The acoustics were difficult to negotiate and at certain points I could barely hear the orchestra over the pianos; one had its lid open with the long stick and the other had its lid off entirely. Still, the end result was very acceptable, though I had no input as to the editing of the takes.

Then there were the bells. I thought that it would be great to stay in the old town center and thus arranged to stay at a pension right on the square. The problem was that my room was on the side of the building facing the town's clock. Not only did the clock strike every hour, but also every quarter, half, and three-quarters of an hour. So, in bed I always knew exactly what time it was when I tried to get to sleep; sometimes that knowledge even entered my dreams! Needless to say, I didn't get much uninterrupted sleep during those days.

In addition to the recording sessions, I had two full rehearsals and part of a third on the two other pieces slated for the Prague concert: Bedrich Smetana's Overture to *The Bartered Bride* and Antonin Dvořák's *Symphony No. 8 in G major*, Op. 88, sometimes referred to by its misnomer, "The English." I have conducted maybe sixty overtures and can honestly say that Smetana's is one of the most difficult ones due to its phrasing irregularities and delayed melodic entrances. The Dvořák symphony, the second of his last great trilogy, is deceptive; at first glance it appears to be not too difficult, but in reality it is very demanding. Again, time was of the essence, even though I had been studying these scores for months.

In the midst of all this hard work there were many moments of levity. We were quite fortunate in that we were able to use the regular conductor's office. Most of the furniture there was quite modern, including a white sequined sofa and a black ergonomic chair that soothed any back pain (whether real or imagined). It was a great place to relax. Then there was the sculpture: a two-foot-high polished wooden phallic symbol which looked very much like what we imagined it to be. We didn't know whether this was a visual commentary on the meanness of old school conductors or something else, but its very existence became the center for much discussion – and provided us with some particularly bawdy humor!

Hrádec Králové itself offered its own share of diversion. One afternoon I took a stroll through the town and on a side street came across a small plaza and a "Punch and Judy" show. There were many children gathered around, such joy in their hearts. I noticed the orchestra's principal clarinetist among the crowd. He greeted me with playing his second movement "Children's Games" solo on an air clarinet – one of those delightful moments that defies further commentary.

With the end of the recording sessions, the center of our musical activity shifted to Prague. Jeff, Maria, and I took up lodgings there while the Philharmony Hrádec Králové personnel were presumably in the city just for the day. Prague is divided in half by the Vltava (Moldau) River, with the old town center (Staré Město) on the east bank and the Prague Castle and lesser town (Malá Strana) on the west. The site of the dress rehearsal and concert was the principal music hall of the Academy of Performing Arts in Prague. This beautiful venue had been revamped in 1991. Named for Czech composer Bohuslav Martinů (1890-1959), the hall is on the first floor (second floor to Americans) of the Lichtenstein (Liechtenstein) Palace, just off the central square of the Malá Strana. It is important for one to specify that location of the palace to avoid confusion, for there is another Lichtenstein (Liechtenstein) Palace in Prague. That one is located in close proximity to the other, at water's edge on Kampa Island, still considered to be in the Malá Strana.

Jeffrey Jacob on the Karlov Most (Charles Bridge) in Prague, Czech Republic, 2002

After the dress rehearsal Jeff and I walked across the Charles Bridge and had lunch in the Old Town. On our way back, we experienced something that would have been quite out of the ordinary to us, except that we were in Prague, one of the world's great musical centers.

It is commonplace in the larger cities of Europe for hired hands to be advertising concerts on the streets by passing out leaflets. Hawkers in eighteenth-century dress, for example, are notorious for targeting tourists in Vienna on behalf of Mozart concerts of questionable quality. Prague was no exception. Jeff and I should not have been surprised when, as we returned to the Malá Strana via the Charles Bridge, two young men in modern dress approached us. Each was distributing flyers for *our* concert! We decided to have a little bit of fun with them.

Taking one of the flyers, Jeff read it and asked, "What can you tell me about this composer, Jeffrey Jacob?"

"Oh, he is a great American composer, the very best."

"And is he a fine pianist?"

"The very best!"

Next I got into the act: "What about the conductor?"

"A great conductor. He is very famous in America."

"I have never heard of him."

"You will soon. He is the very best."

Fantastic! This was exactly the type of publicity we could use. We played along as much as we could, never letting on that we were the performing artists, though as soon as we were beyond earshot, we doubled over with laughter!

The flyers that were being handed out served in two capacities, as concert posters and as the printed programs. In addition to the printed information, including the listing of Dvořák's 8th as "The English," there was a color photo of an empty Bohuslav Martinů Hall, taken from the back of the auditorium. Looking at one of these a second time, Jeff shook his head and said, "They've done it again. They've added an "s" to my last name." This brought out the curiosity in me and I asked about the origins of his last name. He commented that it was German and that he was brought up in the rigid Missouri Synod of the Lutheran church, where congregants never smiled. I laughed, revealing that half my heritage was Swedish, that I too was raised Lutheran, but in the

Augustana Synod (later merged into the Lutheran Church in America). The big difference was that we were allowed to smile – occasionally.

The size of the audience for the concert, about a hundred people or so, was a bit disappointing. Nevertheless the orchestra played masterfully on all three pieces. At the close of the concert, after the Dvořák symphony, I exited the stage after the second curtain call, ready to relax. Feverishly, the stage manager came after me, saying emphatically, "You *must* go back; it is *expected*." And so I did. Even though the audience was small, it was very appreciative.

After a post-concert celebration with Jeff at a nearby restaurant, I headed back to my lodgings at Penzion Balbin and switched on the television. Imagine my surprise when I discovered that the Tom Cruise film *Mission Impossible* (1996) was airing at that very moment. Much of the movie had been shot in Prague. As I watched the film, I noticed that the "American Embassy" looked quite familiar. There it was: The Lichtenstein Palace – the *other* one, not the one that I had just conducted in, but the one on Kampa Island, the one that I passed by every time I walked to the Lichtenstein Palace housing the Bohuslav Martinů Hall. This amounted to a near miss, but it was still quite a coincidence!

* * *

A few weeks later, I made my third jaunt to Europe that year to speak at the 15th IGEB conference in Lana, Italy. As in the case of Toblach/Dobbiaco, Lana, a beautiful scenic town, is located not far from Bozen/Bolzano in the bilingual northern part of Italy that was a part of Austria before it was ceded to Italy at the end of World War I. The conference went on as expected: scholarly presentations, serious gemütlicheit, and a day trip to the Dolomites. By this time Wolfgang Suppan had ceded the presidency of the society to his protégé Bernhard Habla. Though lacking Suppan's ability to secure outside funding, Bernhard had excellent organizational skills and a terrific sense of humor that ensured the continued quality and comraderies for which IGEB had become known.

On the third day of the conference it was announced that there would be a rail strike, one that would interrupt service for those of us returning to Austria or Germany. This meant that many of us would have to leave the conference a day early. Strikes in Italy and elsewhere in Europe are quite commonplace, but at least they are announced ahead of time. So Johann Buis, a South African musicologist whom I had met during my one year appointment at University of Georgia, and I took the train together from Bozen/Bolzano to Innsbruck, Austria. He had already arranged for lodgings at a Pension there. Unfortunately the place was full and I had to seek lodging elsewhere. I found it to be what I thought was a reasonable place until later that evening when I was propositioned by a young woman in the men's bathroom! It meant nothing to me as I had been happily married for more than twenty-eight years at that point. At first I thought about reporting it to the manager, but decided that I didn't need the hassle of (a) filling out a complaint, (b) dealing with the manager and the police, and (c) probably having to find another place to sleep. Besides, I had a private room which I could lock.

Earlier that evening Johann and I had met for dinner and had taken a stroll through Innsbruck's old town. As we were walking, we saw an advertisement for a performance of the Beethoven *Septet in E flat*, Op. 20 that very evening at a nearby church. By the time we arrived, the church was nearly full, except for some spaces in the center of the first pew. Too bad! We grabbed these "box seats" and had a truly memorable musical experience.

* * *

The final 2002 trip was the first to have as its source a recording contract with Centaur Records, Inc., one of the largest classical recording labels. Earlier that year Centaur had sent out a call for performing artists' proposals. Centaur didn't just accept anybody, nor did they approve many of the projects presented to them. As part of the application process I sent them a copy of *Preteritions*, the CD that Linnéa Bardarson and I had put together from the 2000 Recording Fest, as well as a proposal for recording the Beethoven *Piano Concerto No. 2 in B flat*, Op. 19, with both its initial (*Rondo in B flat*, WoO 6) and final endings. A short while later I received a phone call from Victor Sachse, owner of Centaur, who lamented that there were too many recordings of that particular concerto and asked if I could record something else for them.

This was almost too good to be true and, after doing some serious contemplation, I came to the realization that there were very few available recordings of Beethoven's own piano version of his *Violin Concerto in D*, Op. 61. Beethoven wrote no cadenzas for the violin soloist, but for the piano version, put together one year later, he composed four – one for the first movement that features the timpani along with the soloist, one for the end of the second movement, and one each for two different places in the third movement (including one that is almost never heard). If we were to include all four of these, then ours would be the first recording to do so.

The concerto lasts about forty-five minutes, so in order to fill up the CD I needed another work lasting about a quarter of an hour, but what else of Beethoven's had not been recorded very much? I then remembered the *Piano Concerto Movement in D*, K. Anh 7, a spurious work that had been attributed to Beethoven in the past until a publication surfaced that had it as the first movement of a concerto written by Hungarian/Bohemian composer Johann Josef Rösler. No copy in Beethoven's hand has ever surfaced. Musical piracy was prevalent in the early nineteenth century, however, so there is still sufficient doubt about the true composer's identity.

With the selections decided, I submitted a proposal to Centaur to record these two works. It was readily accepted and I received a contract from them in short order. The next item on the agenda was to secure the services of a professional orchestra. Recording costs on this side of the Atlantic and in Western Europe were prohibitive, so I was looking to record in Eastern Europe. Patricia Hitchcock of Symphonic Workshops recommended the Bohuslav Martinů Philharmonic Orchestra of Zlin, Czech Republic and, with the help of a U Mass Boston faculty grant, I was able to meet the financial terms of the orchestra. The orchestra had some free time in late October, and the recording sessions were set to take place then.

My colleague Linnéa Bardarson, who had been the piano soloist for the J.S. Bach *Keyboard Concerto in D minor* on the *Preteritions* CD, agreed to share her talents once again for this Beethoven CD. We met a number of times before making the trip in order to discuss the necessary musical nuances that would make our recording unique. The spurious *Piano Concerto Movement in D* had no acceptable written cadenza, so I composed one, all the while checking with Linnéa for her approval. As for Beethoven's piano version of the *Violin Concerto in D*, Op. 61, we had to figure out where in the third movement to insert the fourth cadenza. We also made the decision to use the lower octave choices in Muzio Clementi's 1807 publication that limit the piano to a 5½ octave range, which was the norm for that time. Fortunately, we had the opportunity to test these choices that spring by performing Op. 61 at the next U Mass Boston Chamber Orchestra concert, one in which I shared the podium with Jeffrey Bell-Hanson.

Zlin is located in Moravia, about three and a half hours east of Prague by train, but also about two and a half hours straight north of Vienna. Both of those cities are wonderful to visit for musicians, but ultimately I opted for Vienna because the flight connections were better and because it was closer to Zlin. Besides, I had been to Prague twice earlier in the year – in connection with Jeffrey Jacob's project and my second trip to Poland.

When Linnéa and I arrived in Vienna, we immediately headed to the Hotel Fürstenhof where I had arranged for us to have two single rooms. The Fürstenhof is a comfortable yet dark relic from the days of the Austro-Hungarian Empire. It features a staircase with an open mesh covered elevator, one that conjures up thoughts of every spy movie ever made. Also, many of its rooms in the center of the building, including the ones we stayed in, have no windows. With a buffet breakfast included and relatively inexpensive rates, it offers the tourist a chance to experience Old Vienna, aka old-world Vienna, without dealing with the high cost of accommodation in the city center. Its location across the street from the Westbahnhof, at that time the most important train station in Vienna, was paramount in our decision to stay there.

After we got settled, I was happy to assume the role of tour guide since I had been to Vienna twice previously. The first thing that I wanted to do was to show Linnéa the city and its environs from the best possible viewpoint that I knew – the top of the Riesenrad, the giant Ferris wheel located in the Prater amusement park. When my son David and I had ridden it four years earlier, it cost about $3.50. Now, with a small museum attached, it cost more than twice that much. It didn't matter; it was still worth it. When the wheel started its rotation and our car ascended, I immediately walked over to the windows and started to point out various things. Arriving at the top, I referred to the famous "Orson Welles-*Third Man*" view looking almost straight downward. It was only then that I realized that Linnéa was not looking through the window, but was seated on the bench located in the car's center. She then told me that she had acrophobia! Wow, acrophobia plus jet lag! What a trooper! Had I known that, we never would have taken the ride. Fortunately, she did not get sick.

That evening we attended a concert of the Vienna Philharmonic at the Musikverein. I was fortunate in getting us seats that were actually on the stage, near the basses. Miraculously, on the first half of the program was Beethoven's *Violin Concerto in D*, Op. 61 – the exact same piece (except with violin soloist) that we were going to record in Zlin! Not missing a beat, Linnéa said, "Just think about it. We are appearing on stage at the Musikverein!" That was good enough for me. The second half of the program featured Franz Schubert's *Symphony No. 9 in C Major*, D. 944 ("The Great C Major"). Robert Schumann described the hour-long work as a "symphony of heavenly length." That was fine and good, but Linnéa and I bailed. Our jet-lagged bodies needed "sleeps of heavenly length."

The next morning, to ward off any remaining jet lag, Linnéa and I rode the trolley to Schönbrunn Palace where we took a tour and then had a brisk walk up to the Gloriette, the small celebratory monument located on the opposite end of the grounds. This is a good distance and uphill, but at fifty-three I was actually in reasonable physical shape and Linnéa, well, she was running 5K and 10K races in Boston, so it was absolutely no problem for her.

Following this, we started out for one of my favorite spots in Vienna – the Zentralfriedhof (Central Cemetery). Its name is a misnomer; there is nothing central about its location since it lies south of the city. To get there, we had to take the U-Bahn (subway) to Karlsplatz, and then walk through the long underground station corridor to a stairway leading up to the Ringstrasse where we could catch Tram No. 71. As we walked, we stumbled across something I had not seen before; it was a place that had to be the focal point of all tourists wanting to relieve themselves in Vienna – the Opera Toilet! The doorway, with lanterns on each side, was clearly marked with a red and yellow sign. There was an antechamber with Johann Strauss' *Blue Danube* waltz blaring away while attendants carried out their work. Branching out from there were doors leading to separate facilities for men and women; each had booths colorfully decorated to resemble opera stalls. Linnéa and I compared notes, of course, and joked about the Opera Toilet being the highlight of our entire trip!

The Zentralfriedhof is a place unlike any other. It is said that many people of the Viennese middle and upper classes save for an entire lifetime in order to have the most lavish monument created to their own narcissism. This city must be a great place to be a stone cutter; one could spend days, possibly weeks, admiring the artistry involved. During the late nineteenth century, the remains of many of Vienna's greatest composers were relocated to a dedicated area not far from the cemetery's main entrance. There visitors can stand in the midst of the final resting places of Beethoven, Schubert, Brahms, Johann Strauss, and many others to just contemplate the greatness surrounding them. It is an exhilarating yet humbling experience.

For our second evening in Vienna I wanted for us to dine somewhere special. I had previously imbibed at a number of Vienna's heurigen (wineries) in Heilengenstadt, the town north of Vienna where Beethoven wrote his famous testament. I thought about us going there but had just read a guidebook saying that one particular huerig in Floridsdorf, on the other side of the Danube, was not to be missed. So, Linnéa and I took a long but easy trip on the U-Bahn to a distant (and rural) station in Floridsdorf. The problem was that when we got there, we had no inkling about which way to turn. This being late October, the sun set around 5:30 (17:30 to Europeans) and the area was rather poorly lit. It was a real crap shoot. We had to go *some* way. So, we walked to the left where, after ten minutes, we naturally found ourselves across from an open field. Slightly disheartened, we turned around and after walking another fifteen minutes found the huerig touted in the guidebook – but it was closed! I was beside myself; we could have been enjoying a nice meal in Vienna. However, after walking about a block, we found a smaller huerig run by a cheerful couple which turned out to have great food. All was not lost.

The next day we took the train from Vienna to Zlin, which doesn't go directly to the latter; it requires a change at the small town of Otrakovice. From there one takes a commuter rail train which makes every stop in and around Zlin. Our stop, Zlin Štred, was about the eighth one on that line. We were initially concerned about the four-minute change that we had to make at Otrakovice, but it wasn't an issue; we just had to join the crowd walking across the tracks to the awaiting commuter train.

Once at Zlin Štred, we walked across a busy street, under a viaduct, and halfway up a rather large hill to the Hotel Moskva (Moscow), a monolithic nine-story holdover from communist days. The hotel had three different ethnic restaurants (Mexican, Greek and Chinese) on the ground floor. These were open at different times from each other on different days of the week, which made us wonder if the same chefs were doing the cooking for all three. The very acceptable rooms at the hotel were not large, but all had vestibules, probably to block out sounds from the hallways.

Hotel Moskva was the largest of the buildings in the immediate area.

Right next to it was Tomáš Batá University, named for the entrepreneur and shoe magnate who employed much of the town. Nearly all of the university buildings, the earliest dating from the 1920s, were laid out parallel to each other – reflecting Batá's socialist vision – and sideways on the slope of the hill. Each was of the same size and architecture, perhaps intended to look like shoe boxes, but in reality they have more the appearance of orange-colored Kit-Kat bars. At the top of the hill was the glass-fronted Dům Uméni (House of Arts) which was then the home of the Bohuslav Martinů Philharmonic. The twice-daily strenuous treks up the hill from the Hotel Moskva to Dům Uméni were both invigorating and exhausting.

Marek Obdržalek, a middle-aged man who was then manager of the orchestra, was there to greet us on the first day. He was very business-like, but not unfriendly. We discussed particulars of the recording sessions – where our offices were, the length of each session, etc. – and when our discussion veered to other things, in particular the Kit-Kat architecture, Marek said wistfully but directly, "Zlin is not a historic town." I read later that it didn't amount to much until 1894, the year that Tomáš Batá opened his shoe factory. Nearly all of the town's buildings were constructed after that date.

Early on we met Dana Kruyerová, the concertmaster for our recording sessions. She and I discussed violin bowings and other things. She was quite friendly but also very business-like. When I told her that I thought things would go very well, she responded, "Of course. That is our job."

With Linnéa Bardarson and Marek Obdržalek on the Dům Uméni stage, Zlin, Czech Republic, 2002

Though she had the music memorized, Linnéa did not want to take a chance on anything going wrong and requested that she have a page turner. Orie Sato, a former student of hers then living in Germany, did the job remarkably; she met up with us in Zlin. A young Japanese chain smoker who was fluent in both English and German, she turned out to be a lot of fun.

In addition to the three restaurants heretofore mentioned, on its third floor the Hotel Moskva had a snack shop and a two-lane bowling alley incorporated right into the same room. This was not the nine pins game that I had witnessed in Austria, but a regular ten-pin setup played with standard sized bowling balls. On one of the evenings the three of us decided to have dinner there. Orie and I bowled while Linnéa, wisely protective of her fingers, sat out. I remember bowling one of my better games – then Linnéa quipped, "Jon Mitchell is a good bowler." This of course jinxed the second game, which turned out to be one of my worst!

The ratio of recording time to finished project is often difficult to determine. It depends on the difficulty of the music, the preparedness of the artists, and the quality of the orchestra. While many professional recordings are done on a 15:1 or even an 18:1 ratio, I figured that we could do 12:1 since the orchestra knew the accompaniment of Op. 61 and since I knew that Linnéa was rock solid. So, I paid for twelve hours' worth. The recording sessions were set up to take place over two days. Each day had three hours in the morning and three in the afternoon, and there were breaks built into each session. Right after the break during one of the afternoon sessions, on what had already been a long day, some of the orchestra members were a bit slow to return to the stage. One of the violinists then stood up and, in a declamatory manner, shouted something in Czech. Linnéa looked at me, smiled, and said rather mischievously, "I think he said, 'Get your asses on stage!'"

All in all, the recording sessions went very well. While the conductor is responsible for all things musical, the sound engineers essentially determine the pace, signaling "Next" or "Okay" to move on. "Wait" indicates problems occur of a technical nature or when extraneous sounds occur. Sometimes these happen in the middle of a take; and are not noticed by the conductor who is wrapped up in the music – a creaking chair, a cough, a dropped mute, etc. Even a change in the conductor's weight distribution on the podium can create unwanted noise.

At Dům Uméni there were a couple of other particulars that had a slightly negative bearing over what we were hoping to achieve. For one thing, the Steinway piano was brand new, meaning that its action was a bit stiff; Linnéa had to get used to it – and did so with stamina and grace. The other thing had to do with acoustics. The performance hall inside Dům Uméni had eight two-foot wide support columns. This is not unusual for European concert halls, but four of these columns were situated right on the stage. The sound bounced off them. The players were used to dealing with this this, but I was not. So, at every opportunity, I ran back to the recording engineers who were set up in a room backstage, in order to check out the balance, etc.

The first movement of Op. 61 went off without a hitch, with the orchestra reading my mind during the sublime *meno mosso* "lone sentry trumpet" passage (although two trumpets actually play it in octaves). I also took a slower tempo than most conductors for the second movement because of the inherent beauty of the left hand accompanying figures found in certain passages; these do not exist in the violin version. Likewise, there is one staccato "music box" passage that requires a tremendous amount of clarity which is not fulfilled if the tempo is taken too fast. I was after a subtlety of expression that I not yet achieved anywhere else, and this orchestra was up to the task. After we had recorded that movement, I singled out the clarinetists who had such a remarkable sense of phrasing (and stability). The other members of the orchestra applauded them. Later on, I was surprised to find out that many in the orchestra were familiar with the spurious *Piano Concerto Movement in D* and was delighted with how well it fit together.

I dismissed the orchestra after eleven hours; they had performed superbly, having been well on task throughout the sessions. The twelfth hour was set aside for Linnéa to record the cadenzas. This is commonplace in recording concertos. The five-minute-long first movement cadenza in Op. 61, the one for piano and timpani, was recorded first. Grigor Kruyer, the orchestra's regular timpanist and Dana's husband, was the timpani soloist. He did such a fine job that we credited him on the CD booklet.

As soon as the last recording session was over, Linnéa, Orie, and I headed for the train station. Once again Linnéa and I decided to carry the DAT tapes back with us. We then settled in for a relaxing train ride back to Vienna with Orie and planned for a final dinner at the Mayerhof, the heurig in Heilengenstadt where Beethoven once lived. Our plans went awry when the two-and-a-half-hour train ride ended up taking nearly twice that long; high winds incurred halfway through the journey interrupted travel for more than two hours. We didn't know it at the time, but this was a harbinger of things to come. We finally reached Vienna without further incident and the three of us did have dinner, though not at the Mayerhof, but instead at a restaurant near the Hotel Fürstenhof.

Upon arrival at Vienna's Schwechat Airport the following morning, we learned that our flight was delayed by an hour due to heavy winds, possibly the remnants from the windstorm that had affected our train ride the night before. A one-hour delay was not the end of the world, and we figured that we still had sufficient time to make our connecting flight at London's Heathrow Airport. Once we got to Heathrow, however, we noticed that something was terribly wrong. There was a line of people extending from the gates through the waiting areas that seemed to be a half-mile long. Most of the people looked exhausted and many were seated up against the walls. As we started to walk in the direction of our gate, one man looked at us and uttered a well-known quote from the 1986 remake of the movie *The Fly*: "Be afraid. Be *very* afraid."

What was this? Why were all of these people sitting around? It turned out to be that windstorm "Jeanette" had shut down all Trans-Atlantic flights from Heathrow. We learned that our flight back to Boston had been cancelled. Then we were told to go to the back of the line and wait. So we did. Unbeknownst to me, Ester's niece Anita, then a professor at Salem State College, was also in that line – it was so long and winding that we didn't see each other!

After a few hours Linnéa and I learned that the windstorm had subsided and we expected that we would be put onto the first available flight. This did not happen. To add insult to injury, a flight to Boston that had been scheduled *after* ours was leaving on time. It was full, of course, except for one space, which neither one of us would take. Heathrow had let us down; they could have sent all of the people scheduled to be on our original flight onto that one, but they did not. It looked like we would be stuck at the airport overnight when Linnéa approached the counter at the gate of a flight headed for New York's JFK airport and singlehandedly used what she jokingly referred to as her "feminine wiles" and was able to get us seats. So, at about 10:00 (22:00) that night, we boarded the aircraft, unsure of what lie ahead. At least sleep came easy on that flight.

It was after midnight Eastern Time when we landed at JFK. New York is about two hundred miles, or a four-hour drive, from Boston. We didn't really want to take a flight in the middle of the night to Boston's Logan – I'm not sure that we could have found one – so we exited the building. It appeared that we were facing the prospect of having to take a cab into Manhattan and then journeying to Boston from there, but we didn't know the train or bus schedules. However, we learned from others that were in the same predicament that there were jitney cab drivers available at the airport who would be willing to drive us to Boston. Unbeknownst to their employers, these are cab drivers who were working under the radar in order to earn extra money. Fortunately, we found such a driver willing to take us to Boston without charging us an arm and a leg.

What we didn't know from the start was that the driver was dead tired. He had just completed an eight-hour shift. His driving got progressively worse as we moved along, to the point where he was starting to weave all over the interstate. I was getting sick, so we stopped and I took a seat right next to him in the front. Linnéa, who remained seated behind him, spoke to him the whole rest of the way on a variety of topics in order to keep him awake. I also chimed into the conversation from time to time. At that time I lived about eighteen miles off the direct route from New York to Boston, but the driver did not want to veer from the route that he knew. So, I was let out at Boston's South Station, where I had to wait until 6:00 a.m. to get a commuter train back home. It was a very difficult finale to what had been an outstanding trip.

VIII. The Family von Trapp

After the flurry of activity during the previous year, 2003 would have been a bit of a letdown except that in that year I was promoted to the rank of full professor at my home institution, University of Massachusetts Boston. Armed with a renewed sense of confidence, I set out on my next adventure, conducting the Bohuslav Martinů Philharmonic Orchestra of Zlin, Czech Republic in a concert at Luhačovice Spa. By this time, the orchestra and I knew each other somewhat – the result of the October, 2002 recording sessions with pianist Linnéa Bardarson – so there was no initial apprehension associated with guest conducting this orchestra.

Earlier that summer I had addressed the biennial conference of the World Association of Symphonic Bands and Ensembles (WASBE) in Jonköpping, Sweden. Ester and our son David were with me. It was an exhausting trip. We flew into Copenhagen, took the train over the bridge to Sweden, saw cousins, went to the conference, did sightseeing in Lund and Stockholm – and dealt with car rental procedures as well as two different currencies. Thus, when it came time for this conducting venture, I wanted to simplify things. Rather than go through Vienna again, I decided to pass through Prague, thereby confining myself to a single country and a single currency. It was also a solo trip for me.

By the time of this, my second European trip that particular summer, all of central Europe was in the throes of a heat wave. Prague, of course, was no exception. Initially I tried to escape the city's heat by confining my sightseeing (which included the Jewish quarter and Kafka's hangouts) to mornings, but the heat was oppressive even in those early hours. Then I tried an out-of-town train trip from the Staropramen Brewery area to Karlstajn (Karlstein) Castle, one of the very best preserved in Europe. Having the appearance of something constructed by a giant who had an ancient set of Legos, the castle and its courtyard resemble those found in fairy tales. Still, the heat was unbearable and I returned to Prague.

Back in Prague I thought of a way to beat the heat. The Tesco department store located in the new city had a supermarket occupying its ground floor and basement. Once inside, I immediately took the escalator down to the store's basement, where the frozen foods were. It provided a bit of a relief from the heat, but it was also extremely crowded. There must have been seventy-five people down there, and I was certain that all of them couldn't have been buying frozen fish! Apparently word had spread that this was the coolest place in town!

Zlin turned out to be just as hot, but at least I was able to focus on the music. Although this was to be a spa concert, the music chosen was certainly suitable for a full-length concert in a performance hall. On this winning docket was Ludwig van Beethoven's *Overture to Leonore No. 3*, Op. 72b, Franz Krommer's *Concerto for Two Clarinets in E flat,* Op. 35, and Felix Mendelssohn's *Symphony No. 3 in A minor*, Op. 56, "Scottish." Beethoven's great overture is the only work of the three that offers any real conducting problems. The *Presto* start of the coda, with its irregular descending eighth note patterns, is very tricky and requires a lot of study, unless one fakes it – which I never do. The Krommer is an absolute classical delight. The two clarinetists who performed so well on the slow movement of our recording of Beethoven's *Piano Concerto in D*, Op. 61, Aleš Pavlorek (a fine composer in his own right) and Jiří Kundl, were the featured soloists. Krommer was Czech; his real name was František Vincenc Kramář, and the orchestra was more than happy to play the music of their countryman, regardless of when it had been written. The Mendelssohn symphony is a favorite of orchestra members and audiences alike, though the coda of the last movement has been a stumbling block to many. Most conductors take it too fast, which doesn't reflect the grandeur established by the composer. The orchestra had no problem going along with my interpretation of it.

Rehearsals were held at the Dům Uméni, the orchestra's home. During one of the breaks, I was walking around backstage and noticed a posting of the players' salaries. I was horrified to find out that most of them were making only about $7,200 a year. The American dollar did go about twice as far in the Czech Republic, but still the $7,200 here would mean only about $14,400 in the USA, not enough for a family to live on. I learned later that there had been a degree of labor unrest among the members of the orchestra. It eventually boiled over to the point that it cost the orchestra manager, Marek Obdržalek, his job. Fortunately he was able to secure an education administration position in the nearby town of Otrakovice.

On the day of the concert, Marek and his wife, a flute player in the orchestra, drove me over to Luhačovice Spa, a picturesque little town a few kilometers southeast of Zlin. As is the case with other spa towns in central Europe, Luhačovice has its share of buildings decked out in baroque yellow. There is a park in the center with carefully manicured trees providing some welcome shade. Surrounded by forest and well-known for its mineral waters, it is exactly the type of place where one would go to spend a few days in total relaxation. Well-known Czech composers such as Leoš Janaček and Josef Suk spent considerable time there.

The orchestra performed at the Spoléčenskŷ Dům, a rather nondescript yellow building that had an outside stage, which jutted out from the building, at its center. . At the rear of the stage was a mural of a small gazebo; the sides of the stage were glass, with each containing an exit door. There were also two onstage support columns similar to those in the Dům Uméni. These were annoyingly placed at center stage, which of course meant right in the middle of the orchestra.

We had one very hot dress rehearsal at the Spoléčenskŷ Dům. With consideration for the players, I tried to make it just a run-through and they were appreciative. When we got to the Beethoven *Leonore No. 3*, however, a formula for disaster awaited us. In order to provide the audience with a foretaste of the drama that was to come in the actual opera, the composer inserted an offstage trumpet call. The offstage trumpet is in addition to the two trumpets onstage. Most of the larger orchestras carry three trumpet players, so the third player assumes this role. However, for smaller orchestras or for those not carrying a third trumpet player for a particular concert, the second trumpet player sneaks off the stage and plays the trumpet call.

Well, I ended up having to rehearse this passage three times, starting with the chord progression leading up to the trumpet call:

- The first time, the second trumpet player got up, walked through the door stage left, and then shut the door! Nothing happened. Obviously the trumpet player had been taught correctly to always shut the door behind him. We weren't sure whether or not he could hear the orchestra through the outside wall; if he did play, we didn't hear him.
- The second time, the same thing happened! This evoked memories of that spot towards the end of Rodgers and Hammerstein's *The Sound of Music* when "The Family Von Trapp" is announced twice – but nobody is there. By this time all of the players were laughing.
- The third time was the charm. This time the first trumpet player accompanied the second trumpet player to the door and made certain that the door stayed open. Finally, the offstage trumpet call was heard loud and clear!

Fortunately during the concert the second trumpet player remembered to leave the door open and the trumpet call came through in all its glory. Unfortunately there were few people – maybe seventy-five or so – that heard it. The heat was extreme and nearly all of the audience members grouped themselves under the well-manicured trees described above. This was too bad, for the orchestra put forth a heartfelt effort with excellent results.

On my way back through Prague, I made a point to have dinner at U Fleků, founded in 1499 and purportedly the oldest brewery in world. By this time my beer coaster collection had expanded to nearly a hundred, and I was eager to have one from there. U Fleků is enormous; it has eight different halls and seats some 1,200 people. I ate in one of the smaller halls. I eventually needed to relieve myself and said to a waiter one of the few Czech words that I had learned: "*Toalety*?" ("Toilets?")

He nodded his head and pointed somewhere down the side of the hall. I then proceeded in that direction but, with so many passages and angles, almost immediately got lost.

Down one of the darker hallways I walked into a room that I had imagined might be an antechamber of a bathroom. It was not. This small room had been somebody's office at one time or another; it quite possibly had belonged to a former manager. There was a sizeable desk and on the walls were many hundred-year-old photographs of horses and – to complement them – many hundred-year-old photographs of naked women! I was initially surprised, but then realized that I had been set up, for the same waiter came running down the hall, laughing. He pointed at the pictures and chortled in German: "Ja, Er liebte Bier, Pferde – und Frauen!" ("Yes, he loved beer, horses, – and women!")

* * *

Most music history books tell us that Ludwig van Beethoven composed five piano concertos. The truth of the matter is that he composed seven. The early unnumbered one, *Piano Concerto in E Flat*, WoO 4, dates from sometime between 1783 and 1785, during Beethoven's early teenage years. As such, it was his earliest orchestral work. The other unnumbered concerto is the composer's own 1807 piano version of his *Violin Concerto in D*, Op. 61. This neglected version, known as *Piano Concerto in D*, Op. 61, along with the spurious *Piano Concerto Movement in D*, K. Anh 7, was recorded by Linnéa Bardarson and me during the autumn of 2002.

The early *Piano Concerto in E Flat*, WoO 4 became a pet project of mine, a labor of love, so to speak. There is a bit of a mystery surrounding it: only the solo fortepiano part and some corrections in Beethoven's hand have survived. Found among the composer's possessions after his death, it contains a condensed two-line soloist's score with orchestral tutti sections written in whenever the soloist is *not* playing. These sections contain occasional cues for flutes, horns, and strings. What this means is that whenever the soloist *is* playing, the orchestra accompaniment is *not* indicated; therefore it is anybody's guess as to what the orchestra has, or even if the orchestra has anything at all. There have been some conductors and musicologists, in particular Willi Hess, who have done their own realizations (arrangements) of what the piece could have sounded like. Hess, however, missed a number of opportunities in the scoring and also flagrantly committed two crimes in changing the endings of both the second and third movements. Not being satisfied with what Hess had done, I decided to do my own realization of the score. Most of this work was done during 2002-2003. I showed it to my orchestration students at U Mass Boston as my work progressed, though I didn't solicit any advice from them.

The *Piano Concerto in E Flat*, WoO 4 lasts about thirty-five minutes, depending on the tempi taken and the length of the cadenzas; Beethoven himself wrote no cadenzas for this work, so these would have to be composed. Looking toward recording the concerto, I knew that at least another twenty minutes of music would be needed for a CD of reasonable length. One work that fit into the scheme of things very well was Beethoven's *Romance Cantabile*, H 13, probably the middle movement of a sinfonia concertante or triple concerto. Dating from about 1786, it is scored for a solo trio consisting of flute, bassoon, and keyboard plus an orchestral accompaniment of strings and oboes. Set in E minor, its music provides a rather relaxing effect, perhaps eliciting thoughts of sitting in a cottage before a fire in an easy chair with an afghan blanket, a hot toddy, and, of course, a Saint Bernard at one's feet.

At the bottom of the first page of *Romance Cantabile* are four empty staves; each is marked *tacet*. This indicates that more instruments (possibly flutes, horns, trumpets, and timpani) were needed in the orchestra for the preceding movement. *Romance Cantabile* is itself a fragment, though it was a finished movement at one time. The main section (and the longer of the two) is complete, but only the first four measures of the E major trio section survive – maybe someone was carrying the music and dropped a part of it at some point. It was not difficult for me to supply some complementary material for this section. This was not my first completion. Years earlier, to the vexation of some purists, I had completed an unfinished wind septet movement of Gustav Holst.

The length of *Romance Cantabile*, about eight minutes, still left the CD short of time, so I added one additional early Beethoven work, the *Ritterballet*, WoO 1 (1790-91). This work was composed for a costume ball held at the palace of Count Ferdinand Ernst Gabriel von Waldstein, who had passed it off as his own work. Beethoven apparently held nothing against him later, for in 1804 he dedicated his well-known *Piano Sonata No. 21 in C*, Op. 53 to Waldstein. *Ritterballet* is in several brief movements, a number of them recalling events with which eighteenth century socialites would have been familiar: "March," "Hunting Song," "Serenade," "War Song," "Drinking Song," "German Song (Waltz)" and "Coda." These are connected by a "Deutsche Gesang" ("German Song"), reprised after each of the first six movements. Clocking in at about fifteen minutes, *Ritterballet* was of perfect length to round out the CD.

Sometime during 2003, I pitched the concept of a CD of little-known early Beethoven to Centaur Records and it was readily accepted. Next I approached the Bohuslav Martinů Philharmonic and, in the wake of the success yielded by my prior recording with them, as well as the concert of the previous summer, we were able to come to terms very quickly. They had three days in early February 2004 that they were able to dedicate to recording the CD; it turned out to be the third time in two years that I conducted them. By this time, they were used to me and I was used to them. We couldn't miss. However, there was only one major problem: I had no piano soloist yet!

Linnéa Bardarson, who had played the solo piano part on the previous two CDs, was unavailable. There were two professional concert pianists with whom I had previously worked with in Europe: Zofia Antes and Grigorios Zamparas. Both had been marvelous collaborators. I don't recall the particulars, but somehow or another I found out that Grigorios was working on his doctorate at the Frost School of Music of the

University of Miami in Coral Gables, Florida. This made my decision easy, as he was not difficult to reach. Grigorios had been teamed with me four years earlier in Pazardjik, Bulgaria on Beethoven's *Piano Concerto No. 5 in E flat*, Op. 73, the composer's last, and he was eager to see what was on the opposite end of Beethoven's concerto spectrum. He accepted my offer almost immediately. The dates of the recording coincided with the starts of our respective semesters, so there was no problem with the timing.

Grigorios (Gregory, as he called himself) flew into Boston and spent two days at our home in Franklin. We had a great time going over the music at the kitchen table as well as working out ornamentation consistency and other musical things on the Adam Schaaf baby grand I'd inherited from my father. It was a great time. I showed him my completion of the *Romance Cantabile* as well as the cadenzas that I had written out for WoO 4. Each cadenza was limited to the five-octave fortepiano range that Beethoven had at his disposal during his early years. Gregory added a couple of personal touches to the cadenza for the first movement and for this I gave him shared credit in the CD booklet. For the second movement cadenza, I transposed some of Beethoven's discarded material and inserted it between my own contributions. For the brief third movement cadenza there was almost nothing to be done. Beethoven himself discarded some material that worked in beautifully – unaltered!

Studying scores with Grigorios Zamparas at home, 2004

We flew into Vienna, stayed one night at the Starliten Suites across from the Stadtpark, and then took the train north to Zlin. This time the Bohuslav Martinů Philharmonic arranged for us to stay at the Hotel Garni, which was significantly closer to the Dům Umění than the Hotel Moscow, which made the uphill climb a whole lot easier. The concert hall's Steinway grand piano, which had slightly stiff action a year and a half earlier, was now broken in and magnificent in all respects. We had twelve hours of recording time spread out over three days to record the twelve separate movements. Eight of them were the very short ones in *Ritterballet* so, with careful planning, there was no rush. Much of the available time, however, was used to establish the intense focus required in bringing out the tenderness of the concerto's middle movement.

Two of the orchestra's principal woodwind players, flutist Jana Holaskova and bassoonist Zdenek Skrabal, gave freely of their time and energy to form, with Gregory, the featured solo trio in the *Romance Cantabile*. For an actual performance they would have been seated in front of the piano, but for the recording sessions, with microphones strategically placed, they were seated between the conductor and pianist. As a result, the sightlines were excellent and this helped achieve a tight, well-balanced sound.

The *Ritterballet* was more difficult to record than I had first imagined. Most of the short movements had double repeats, but nearly all of them had to have the correct acoustical lead-in to the "Deutscher Gesang," which was interpolated between all of them. I had imagined that these reprises would help reduce the amount of time needed in recording the work, but in reality they only added to it. Thus, counting all of the lead-ins, we needed to record more takes for the "Deutscher Gesang" than for any other movement.

The following May, three months after the recording sessions, I flew down to Miami to have the takes edited. Gregory was "house-sitting" for a lawyer friend in Coral Gables. It was an upscale home full of modern conveniences, including some magnificent landscaping and an outdoor pool with speakers connected to the indoor sound system. On the walls were many masques and shelves full of pottery as well as knick-knacks from around the world. Gregory and his friend Megan also took me out to dinner at Coconut Grove and gave me a tour of the South Beach area. I felt as if I were spending time with the "haves."

Gregory had arranged for Paul Griffith at The University of Miami to edit the takes. Beforehand I had developed an editing plan – use Take "A" up to a certain time, then switch to Take "B," etc. With Gregory and me at his side, Paul did marvelous work, and I joked about his "Grammy Award-saving" edits. The evening that followed the conclusion of Paul's work, Gregory and I were relaxing in the lawyer's pool under the stars, sipping drinks and listening to the final edits of our own hard work via the outdoor speakers. Wow! I imagined that there were very few people on the face of the earth who would have ever done this same thing – certainly not at that moment in time. With the exception of being with my wife, it was one of perhaps a half dozen or so moments in time when I wouldn't have wanted to be anywhere else doing anything else.

A few months later the project was submitted to Centaur Records under the title of "The Youthful Beethoven." For the cover I chose a silhouette that Joseph Neeson had made of the composer around 1786. The CD was released almost immediately by Centaur as CRC2725 and selections from it have been broadcast by classical radio stations ever since. But that wasn't all. Gregory came up to Boston the following year and we gave the world premiere performance of my realization of WoO 4 at a UMB "Concertos" concert held at St. Paul's Episcopal Church in Brookline. We reprised this three years later in "Reconstructing Early Beethoven," a concert given with my Boston Neo-politan Chamber Orchestra at The New School of Music in Cambridge. Then there was the interview by a reporter from *The Boston Globe* who wrote an article "Professor Finishes what Beethoven Started" and, a few years later, my critical edition (including full score and notes) of *Beethoven: Early Piano Concerto in E Flat. WoO 4* was published by A-R Editions. The project indeed was a labor of love that bore many fruits!

* * *

Later that same year I received a blanket email from Patricia Hitchcock of Symphonic Workshops announcing the availability of the Philharmonia Bulgarica, an orchestra consisting of up to sixty musicians, to record CDs in Sofia's "state of the art Bulgarian National Radio recording studios." The fees were to include one-night's accommodation, breakfast, and transportation to and from the airport.

The Philharmonia Bulgarica was fully professional; many of the players were also performing in the city's radio orchestra. Valeri Vatchev would be the producer. I jumped at the opportunity. The cost of recording in the Czech Republic was rising rapidly as the Czech crown was gaining significantly against the dollar. Once again I received a small grant from U Mass Boston and knew that the money received from it would stretch further in Bulgaria than in the Czech Republic.

The Youthful Beethoven project had left me in a state of both exhilaration and exhaustion. Encouraged, I was all set to do another CD, one that would be an extension of my Gustav Holst research, featuring works by the composer that, to my knowledge, had never been recorded. This project began through correspondence with The Holst Foundation and the British Library. Gustav Holst officially went out of copyright at the end of 2004 (he died in 1934), although not all of the manuscripts under the auspices of The Holst Foundation did. Two of the works that I wanted to record, *Dances from Pan's Anniversary* (1905) and *Incidental Music for the Pageant of St. Martin-in-the-Fields* (1921), were in manuscript. A third, the single-movement *Greeting* (1904), had an almost complete set of published parts (without horns), but no conductor's score. Fortunately I found the missing horn parts at The British Library and therefore was able to construct a score.

The seven movements for *Pan's Anniversary* are divided into three sections. The first, "Entry of the Maskers," uses the sixteenth-century dance "Rogero." The second, "The Mein Dance," consists of "Pavan" (the sixteenth-century dance "Mal Sims") and "Galliard" ("Spagnoletta"). The third, "The Stratford Revels," consists of "Sellinger's Round" plus three English folk tunes – "The Lost Lady," "Maria Marten," and "All on Spurn Point." The *Incidental Music for the Pageant of St. Martin-in-the-Fields* consists of five movements: "Funeral March," "Kings' March" ("Rogero" and "Lord Willoughby"), "The Crusaders' Hymn" ("On This Day Earth Shall Ring"), "St. Francis' Hymn," and "Shepherd's Hey." In spite of having a combined total of thirteen movements, the timing for all three of these works put together is only about twenty-four minutes. Something else had to be added to the mix. As it turned out, I didn't have to look very far.

Holst edited three suites of baroque incidental music for his own student orchestra at Morley College for Working Men and Women in London. Each of these suites, from the pen of English Baroque composer Henry Purcell (1659-1695), features an overture plus several dance movements. Holst's chief contribution was to add non-obtrusive parts for winds and percussion (two flutes, two oboes, two clarinets, one bassoon, two horns, two trumpets, and timpani) to Purcell's strings. All three of Holst's Purcell arrangements were published in the 1920s. One of them, *The Gordian Knot Unty'd* (1922), was still in print. It was divided into two parts, either by Holst or the publishers, and thus was available for purchase as two separate suites. However, the other two publications, *The Virtuous Wife* (1925) and *The Married Beau* (1928), were not to be found in current publishers' catalogues. There was also a fourth suite, *The Old Bachelor*, which Holst wrote about having started.

I began my search for these in Aldeburgh at the Britten-Pears Library during January of 2005. I didn't find the two completed Holst arrangements, but when I looked at the collected works of Henry Purcell, I found that *The Old Bachelor* had some scribbles for additional instrumentation; these were far from complete and written only into the first three movements. For some reason, Holst had given up on it.

Two days later, back in London, I went to the antiquarian music firm of Travis & Emery, located on Cecil Court, the pedestrian street full of antique bookstores near St. Martin-in-the Fields. After a computer search of everything in their vast collection, the shopkeepers found that they had one sole copy of each of the published full scores to Holst's arrangements of *The Virtuous Wife* and *The Married Beau*. These were small (octavo size) but in very good condition. I willingly paid for them. With the exception of a very few libraries, these may have been the only extant copies around. There were no individual parts, however, so at home I had to rewrite the scores into my computer, extract the parts, edit them, and print them.

Each of these suites was of significant length. Both published suites of *The Gordian Knot Unty'd* together had eight movements, *The Virtuous Wife* had five, and *The Married Beau* had eight. The latter had one additional movement, "Aire," which Holst intended to include as the sixth movement but, for reasons unknown, was omitted by the publishers. I reinstated it. Thus, these suites had a total of twenty-two movements and added about forty-six minutes to the length of the CD. Taking into account the other pieces, this added up to a total of thirty-five separate tracks to be recorded! The project was approved by Centaur that fall.

By this time Valeri Vatchev and I knew each other. He recommended that fifteen hours be set aside for the recording. However, taking into consideration the moderate level of difficulty of the pieces and the ubiquitous repeats, I knew that the recording could be done in six hours and this was agreed upon. We also agreed upon the size of the orchestra. In 1921 Holst had about fifty players in his Morley College ensemble; with considerations for tonal balance, we decided upon fifty-two. Holst's situation, with working commuter students, was not much different from what I had at U Mass Boston and, in a way, I wanted to record a CD that would more-or-less "glorify" what music-making could be in both situations. Thus I decided early on that, in regard to the baroque suites, the final product should represent Holst more than Purcell. This meant no double-dotting of the notes in the slow introductions of Purcell's overtures.

January 16, 2006 was the big day, and early in the morning Valeri picked me up at my hotel, the Rotasar, located halfway between the airport and the center of town. I had become somewhat familiar with Sofia and knew the downtown area, but not the destination that he drove us to: a semi-industrial area on the northwest side of the city that conjured up memories of old gangster and detective movies. The building housing the recording studio looked like it had seen better days, and I was a bit hesitant. What had I gotten into? Was this the "state of the art Bulgarian National Radio recording studio" that was advertised?

Valeri assured me that much of the current recording in Bulgaria was done there. Alright – I had no choice but to trust him; the orchestra was already there. The OKI Nadeshda Auditorium was indeed a well-worn facility but the acoustics were good, the recording equipment was new, and the recording engineer, Christo Pavlov, was fully competent.

My plan was to record the easier movements first, beginning with the dances from the Purcell suites, then moving to the overtures, and then on to the Holst originals. As we became totally immersed in the music-making, I knew early on that the orchestra and I had something special. Very few people would have been familiar with *Greeting* and nobody alive would have actually heard *Pan's Anniversary* or the *Incidental Music from the Pageant of St. Martin-in-the-Fields*. Valeri really gushed over *Greeting* and "Maria Marten" from *Pan's Anniversary*.

Unfortunately, in the midst of the wonderment, there was a dark side to the recording process. I was expecting the same efficiency that I had experienced when recording with the Bohuslav Martinů Filharmonie in Zlin, but that was not the case here. While the orchestra was fully on task, we had to halt the recording process a number of times on account of technical problems. Then there was the pacing. We had to record each of the thirty-five individual movements at least three times. Furthermore *Greeting* and the overtures had to be recorded in small segments and each of those also had to be recorded at least three times. So, all in all, we recorded an amazing 158 takes that day! I could have done it in six hours, but Valeri, who controlled the pacing, was a bit slow at times, perhaps deliberately so, and by the end of the allotted time we were not quite finished. We still had yet to record *Greeting*, "St. Francis' Hymn," "All on Spurn Point," and "Shepherd's Hey."

Valeri and I then talked. This was my one shot to record all of the pieces in the same place with the same orchestra, and I did not want to blow the opportunity. So, I reluctantly offered to pay for another hour's worth of recording time; this cost me an extra $1,000. Valeri spoke to the orchestra and they agreed to stay. He paid them on the spot. I had my suspicions that Valeri had planned all along to get more money out of me, but I pocketed those thoughts; it was better to work with him than against him. Unfortunately the slower-than-it-should-have-been pacing controlled by him turned out to be a bellwether. My next two conducting trips to Eastern Europe, a concert in Romania and another recording session in Bulgaria, featured hosts whose actions were – how can I say it? – less than honorable.

Was the Holst CD worth the extra money? Undeniably so. Valeri, Christo, and I celebrated that evening in Sofia. The following day Valeri had a rehearsal in Vratza, where I had guest conducted eight years earlier. He invited me to ride up there with him and so I did. It was great to see clarinetist Mikael Dejnov again and, of course, to sample his current batch of rakija. Flutist and guide Natasha Uzunova was on tour, so I did not get to see her on that occasion.

Back home, during February and March, I worked on the CD booklet notes and constructed a seven-page "edit plan" from the 158 takes for Christo – editing and mastering were included in the cost. In late March he edited the recordings according to my plan (he did a beautiful job!) and shipped off copies of the master both to Centaur and to me. Within a year *Gustav Holst: Composer as Arranger* was released. On the whole, it is perhaps the cleanest CD of mine to date. Regardless, it is without question the most successful: selections from it continue to be broadcast over the airwaves.

IX. "Now You Can Take Off Your Clothes"

The Cold War was raging when I was a child. The arms race was in full throttle, and we were all afraid of nuclear war. At school we had air-raid drills lest we be unprepared for a bombing from the east. Soviet Union Premier Nikita Khrushchev shouted, "We will bury you!" to Western diplomats and later banged his shoe on his desk in protest to a Filipino's speech at the United Nations. Then there was the Cuban missile crisis. Things were very tense. Russia was, in the minds of many Westerners, an angry, forbidding country out to destroy the rest of the world.

It was no wonder then that after the fall of the Soviet Union I jumped at the opportunity to conduct in Russia. In March 2006 two concerts were promised me with the Filarmoni Chamber Orchestra, a fully professional string ensemble centered in Arkhangelsk, a city far to the north of St. Petersburg. The first was scheduled to take place at Severodvinsk, a major military shipyard center located about thirty-five kilometers west of Arkhangelsk; the second in Arkhangelsk itself. I was told that this orchestra could play just about anything so, with one exception, I selected a program of reasonably difficult repertoire: Felix Mendelssohn's *String Symphony No. 5 in B flat,* Ralph Vaughan Williams' *Fantasia on a Theme by Thomas Tallis*, Antonin Dvořák's *Serenade for Strings, Op. 22,* and the original version of Aaron Copland's *Appalachian Spring*, featuring strings, flute, clarinet, bassoon, and piano. In case this program ended up being too much for them, I brought with me a somewhat easier work that could be used as a substitute: Gustav Holst's string version of his own brass band masterpiece *A Moorside Suite*. The University of Massachusetts Boston Chamber Orchestra (UMBCO) and I had premiered this string version way back in 1994.

Ester was eager to come with me, and the two of us planned things out in great detail for an eighteen-day trip. I was once again on sabbatical, planning to do some research in England for my latest book, *Ralph Vaughan Williams' Wind Works*, so it was only natural that we would use London as our "home" base. After a couple of days there, we would travel to St. Petersburg, and from there on to Arkhangelsk. Afterwards, we would once again spend some days in St. Petersburg and in London. The whole trip would have a musical arch form to it:

London – St. Petersburg – Arkhangelsk – St. Petersburg – London
(A) (B) (C) (B') (A')

In spite of careful planning, the Russia part of our journey almost didn't materialize. We had applied through the mail for the visas necessary to visit Russia, but got nervous when, with less than a week to go, they still hadn't arrived. So we drove four hours down to the Russian Consulate in New York City to see if there was any problem. It turns out that there wasn't – just "red" tape – and we got our visas, though I often shudder to think about what might have happened had we *not* been within driving distance of the consulate.

The first London part of our trip started off extraordinarily well. We checked in to the Westpoint Hotel on Sussex Gardens, not far from Paddington Station, and a sense of *déjà vu* instantly set in. The hotel is located in the same block as the former Welcome Inn, where I had stayed for much of the time on my first London trip. We had a very small room in front of the elevator which kept us from getting much sleep.

After an attempted nap, the first thing we did was go to the University of London Senate Building cafeteria to have lunch with fellow Holst researchers Alan Gibbs and Raymond Head. We spoke enthusiastically of all things Holst, though afterward Ester mentioned that it was difficult to handle their very pronounced British accents while still experiencing jetlag. After spending some time at the British Museum, we walked down to The National Portrait Gallery, which we had never seen – all in an attempt to ward off any lingering jetlag.

The next day was spent mostly researching Vaughan Williams at The British Library. Still, Ester and I had time that day to do a couple of things that were quintessentially British – eating lunch in an Indian hole-in-the-wall restaurant on Shaftesbury Avenue, then attending the

Evensong service at Westminster Abbey. It was a fitting end to the first English leg of our trip.

The flight from London to St. Petersburg is not a particularly a long one, even though the latter lies three time zones ahead of Greenwich Mean Time. The shorter-than-expected length of the flight is due to the narrow time zone widths so far north. At the time of our Russian visit, all international flights arriving at St. Petersburg landed at Pulkovo II – the international airport. Our contact, Gennady Chernov, was there to meet us and took us to the apartment where we would stay that night as well as three additional nights upon our return from Arkhangelsk.

The apartment, on the fifth floor of a large building, was very good, much roomier than what we had at London's Westpoint Hotel, and it was centrally located, just three blocks west of the Mariinsky Theatre. The key was multi-functional; it was used to gain access to the building's courtyard (where the residents parked their cars), the building itself, and the apartment. The apartment had a large living room where we slept (on a futon), a bedroom with a desk and piano, a kitchen with a separate drinking-water tap, a toilet closet with a toilet paper holder that kept falling apart, and a bathroom that contained a sink, tub and shower, and a clothes washer. Showers, however, had to be quick – when the hot water ran out, one had to wait another twenty minutes for the hot water to replenish itself (shades of the apartment in Vratza, Bulgaria, where Timothy McFarland and I had stayed eight years earlier). The clothes washer was also a real experience as the directions were entirely in Russian. Oxana, Gennady's wife, came by to show us how to use it. Gennady also showed us where there was a nearby grocery store.

So far, so good, but then things suddenly took a dramatic shift downwards. Gennady told us that the conductor of the Filarmoni Chamber Orchestra had tried repeatedly to email me but had heard nothing from me. Of course he hadn't since I hadn't received any of his emails! This turned out to be very minor, however, in comparison with what we were about to experience.

We were really taken aback when Gennady demanded cash for the apartment as well as for the Aeroflot Airlines tickets. The apartment was €40 per night, the airline tickets $362 US apiece ($724). Nothing like this had happened anyplace we had ever been. We had $480 in cash (correctly anticipating the food and incidentals budget during our twelve-day stay in Russia), so I was able to pay Gennady $200 (to cover the €160) for our four-night stay in the apartment. As I look back, Gennady's initial handling of the situation may simply have been his lack of experience in hosting Westerners coming to his country for the first time.

Gennady then took us to an ATM cash machine near the Mariinsky Theatre so that we could withdraw money for the airline tickets. Something was wrong as the machine rejected both my credit card and my bank card. Uh-oh. A sense of doom started to set in. Gennady then took us to another ATM near St. Isaac's Cathedral and the same thing happened. Throughout the evening all attempts to secure cash via both of my cards failed; this was extremely stressful. Ester had identical cards but we decided, wisely it turned out, not to try hers. Aargh! We certainly didn't want our first night in Russia to be like this. Ester and I discussed in Spanish the prospect of returning to London immediately but, before making that decision, I first needed to let our hosts know how we felt.

When we got back to the apartment, I sternly told Gennady that we were not prepared for this demand for cash, and that this was not our fault as we had not been warned to bring so much cash ahead of time. While I am not proud of my conduct, my statements did underline the stress that he had placed upon us. Gennady understood and, to his credit, a complete turnaround took place. He and Oxana then invited us to their previously planned engagement, a birthday party on the other side of the river for their five-year-old daughter Natasha (who already spoke a lot of English) attended by Gennady's parents. It was at a restaurant called the Barricuda, and the food was tasty (also moderately priced). Within hours, we all transitioned from what had been a tense unwelcoming situation to a warm and caring relationship.

The next morning Gennady called. He had read on the internet that on March 8th (the day of our arrival) Citibank had frozen all cash withdrawals in Canada, the UK, and Russia due to a very deep month's-long security breach. This explained the credit card problem. I was able to use it once again in London. As far as the bank card problem, well it turns out that our own bank put a hold (freeze) on my card when I attempted to withdraw the same amount of money from the second cash machine as from the first. According to their records, the first machine that we tried – the one at Mariinsky Theatre – was not functioning correctly and so, when a similar withdrawal was attempted from another machine, they stopped my card temporarily for security reasons – all "for my protection." My bank card still did not work on our return to London, although Ester's did. It is very fortunate that we did not try Ester's card in St. Petersburg or we would have had cash problems in London as well.

Now, totally aware of our predicament, Gennady and Oxana did a very noble thing. In order to allow us to continue to Arkhangelsk, they lent us 16,600 rubles plus €100 (roughly $800 total) to cover the cost of the airline tickets plus the Hotel in Arkhangelsk. Ester and I were really touched by their generosity; it made all the difference to our well-being for the remainder of the trip. When we got home I remembered the title of Bob Hope's best-selling 1963 book, *I Owe Russia $1200*, and immediately wired the money to Gennady's account.

After a good night's rest, Ester and I ventured into what seemed to be the world's most crowded grocery store for breakfast and lunch supplies. The bread aisle was about two feet wide and was located right at the turnstile, which made it difficult to turn back for other items. At least the prices were right: a loaf of really good Russian brown bread cost 8.92 Rubles (about thirty-five cents).

There were two choices of transportation from St. Petersburg to Arkhangelsk: a cheap twenty-eight-hour train ride or an expensive one-hour-and-forty-minute plane ride. This was a no-brainer as we didn't want to spend over a day riding on a very slow train. At the time of our visit St. Petersburg had two airports, one for international travel (Pulkovo II) and one for domestic travel (Pulkovo I).

Because of our luggage and lack of a subway station nearby, we took a taxi to Pulkovo I, probably my least favorite of all the airports I have ever been in. One couldn't even enter the building without a ticket and (for foreigners) a passport; the screening was right there. We were "greeted" by a stone-faced armed security guard, a real personification of what Westerners perceive the Soviet side to have been during the Cold War. He was intimidating, to say the least. He looked at our passports from every possible angle then stared at our boarding passes. He scowled at each of us as he indicated for Ester to place her baggage on the conveyor belt next to him. Then he looked her right in the eye and gruffly shouted those immortal words in English:

"Okay! Now you can take off your clothes!"

What?! Of course, what he meant was for her to take off her *coat*, but it was irretrievably funny. We were both laughing so hard internally that every rib hurt. We dared not even look at each other for fear that we would have burst out laughing, not to mention the possibility of enticing the guard to pull out his weapon. Ester almost couldn't remove her coat; I too was in a nearly incapacitated state, but we had to hold it in – at least until we had cleared security. And then we had one of the best laughs of our lives. Once we were through security though, it wasn't much better. Pulkovo I was very similar to the old Sofia airport, with an Orwellian "Big Brother" green light blinking when one was to move through the ticket lines.

As to the Aeroflot plane – it was small, only four seats across, but at least it was a jet. Our flight was announced, but since we had not yet mastered the pushing-shoving technique of the Russians, we were the last two people to get on the plane. We noticed two seats together in the second row at the front of tourist class and wondered why nobody had taken them. Ester noticed that some of the people were chuckling as we sat down. We soon learned why. When the plane was being de-iced the fuselage leaked almost a steady stream of water onto the backs of the seats in front of us, spraying us for most of the trip. We were able to fend off some of this by holding up our magazines. Then we looked around.

It turned out that we weren't the only ones getting wet; the leakage occurred almost everywhere. As if to confirm the situation, a female flight attendant entered our part of the cabin with a towel wrapped around her arm. She then wiped the fuselage's ceiling in a nonchalant manner; it was undoubtedly just a part of her job.

Deplaning at Arkhangelsk's Talagi airport was unusual in that all passengers stepped off the plane into ten-degree Fahrenheit weather and then walked over to a gate where dozens of well-wishers greeted them – outside the airport proper. All then left the field and walked the length of the terminal building outside before re-entering the terminal to retrieve the checked-in luggage. Confusing? Yes, but we just followed the crowd. This was no backwoods airport – but we knew that we were in a very different and remote place.

As we walked through the gate, we were greeted warmly by Julia Lewandowskaya, a dark-haired woman, probably in her late thirties. An Arkhangelsk native, she was an independent English instructor employed by the orchestra as a staff member. Her English was impeccable, much better than mine, and she spoke with a British accent. We learned a lot about Julia over the next several days; most of it was very good, though some of it was tragic. She had a seventeen-year-old son and was divorced – her alcoholic ex-husband had beaten her. In spite of the latter, she possessed a very positive outlook on life. She was also a Jew who had converted to Russian Orthodox Christianity.

Julia and her helper Boris then walked with us along the terminal building and then back inside to collect our luggage. After this had been accomplished, they drove us from the airport directly to our hotel, the Artelecom, located about a fifteen-minute walk from the Academy of Fine Arts, where the rehearsals were to be held. The hotel, probably of post-communist era construction, was very good, clean, and modern. Our room, on the second floor, was sizable but difficult to walk in – since the floor was on two different levels about two inches apart, we kept stumbling on our way to and from the bathroom. Still, it was a good bargain, costing us about $58 US per night, including breakfast. A real bonus was that our room overlooked an open end of the hockey stadium that was across the street. We would often see the grounds crew cleaning the icy surface and could even watch the teams play. The type of hockey we saw here was *bandy*; it resembled American field hockey, with players using a curved stick to hit a ball instead of a puck.

After we got settled, Julia and Boris took us to Arkhangelsk's best grocery store, which was reasonably large. Julia exchanged money for us there. The personnel in the store didn't want our American dollars but a colorful figure (an older man who was probably a holdover from the black-market era) exchanged them at a reasonable rate!

Julia told us: "In Russia there is always a problem, but there is always a solution to the problem."

Okay…

Breakfasts at the Artelecom were really weird. We were always given yogurt, Russian brown bread, and some type of roll, plus a second course. The first day that second course consisted of a medium-rare ground beef patty with mashed potato; the second day it was some type of coleslaw, and on the third day it was a strange type of chocolate-covered ice cream bar – dessert for breakfast! We never did figure out whether these second courses were leftovers from the night before or that the hotel's concept of breakfast was radically different from ours. All of the breakfasts were eaten in the hotel's rather plush café. A major deterrent to pleasant conversation there was the 52-inch television monitor with its volume always set too high. Apparently this was to satisfy the wait staff who were fixated on a particular soap opera that aired in the morning.

In mid-March, Arkhangelsk is still in the dead of winter, averaging about fifteen degrees Fahrenheit, with snow-packed sidewalks and streets. Located only about forty kilometers from the White Sea (itself a part of the Arctic Ocean), Arkhangelsk is the largest city (about 400,000 inhabitants) that far north in the entire world! The climate is similar to that of Fairbanks, Alaska, except that Arkhangelsk is somewhat warmer in the winter and cooler in the summer. At least the days at this time of year are about twelve hours long. Scarves, hats, and boots are a necessity.

There is good bus service in Arkhangelsk. The buses were squatty looking vehicles – the width was normal, but the length was only half of what one would expect. A ride on one of them was a real bargain at eight rubles (about thirty-two cents), and the buses were almost always full. Most people walked, however. Although the snow and ice were packed down, walking from one place to another took nearly twice as long as what we anticipated; we often had to lean forward and take very small steps, as if we were crippled in some way. It was not easy, especially when carrying a heavy briefcase. We were not alone in this. Young women could be seen struggling to push old-fashioned baby carriages through the snow.

The city itself is not particularly attractive – mostly communist-era dirty sugar cube buildings with an occasional pre-revolution wooden boarding house thrown into the mix. Away from the city center it was difficult, sometimes impossible, to figure out what was in the stores, since nearly all of them were in similar nondescript communist structures with very small windows. One evening Ester and I were trudging through a minor snowstorm, looking for a restaurant. All of the buildings looked the same to us and we were about to give up when, finally, we found a young man on the street and asked him. He pointed to a building about 100 feet away that we had just passed. It turned out to be a night club-restaurant with a very small dance floor. There were also two Karaoke singers, one of whom came off as a Russian Julio Iglesias wannabe! At least the food was good.

Advertisement for a curtain company in Arkhangelsk, or so we were told!

All around the city were posters advertising our upcoming concert on the 16th. These were in Russian, of course, and seeing one's name in bold Cyrillic letters is always mind-boggling for a Westerner. The poster that really caught my eye, however, was one that was even more prevalent. It featured a photo of the backside of a naked young woman sitting down on the floor with her legs crossed and playing the tuba! She hadn't a stitch of clothing on except for a cloth covering her behind. Someone explained to me that it was an advertisement for a curtain company. Okay.

The heart of the city is, surprisingly, Lenin Square, featuring an enormous monument to Vladimir Lenin, the communist revolutionary. Dating from 1988, it was the last of dozens of such monuments to be constructed in the former Soviet Union and in other countries behind the Iron Curtain. I asked Julia about why it still existed. She said that, while nobody liked what Lenin did, the monument was a commissioned artwork and is respected as such; it also serves as a reminder of the past. What Julia said could pertain to the Confederate monuments found in the southern United States, not that the situations are parallel.

In front of the Lenin monument, Arkhangelsk

The embankment of the Northern Dvina River is really impressive. The river itself, appearing to be about as wide as the St. Lawrence at Montréal, was totally frozen over, and we could see hundreds of cross-country skiers on the ice. Stalin had destroyed the city's historic churches and it was good to see that the Assumption Church, located on the embankment, had just been rebuilt. The city's Cathedral of the Archangel Michael was scheduled to be next; it was in the process of reconstruction while we were there.

One thing really significant about Arkhangelsk is that the people there have a real zest for life; they embrace the cold weather. This was never more evident than when Julia and some of her friends took us to an outdoor museum. In addition to the three of us, the entourage included Nina (a corporate lawyer who worked with Americans at Polarlite) and Julia's former students Masha and Ludmilla, who had gone with her to Prague a few years earlier. They lent us some cold weather hats, which were greatly appreciated. Giving the impression of something like Lincoln's New Salem in Illinois or Sturbridge Village in Massachusetts, Malye Karely is a vast outdoor museum of wooden architecture, perhaps the largest in Europe. It features as many as fifty 18th and 19th-century houses, windmills, stores, and churches. There are also swings, one-horse-open sleigh rides, sleds, and a "Russian Mountain" (ice roller coaster), in addition to singing and dancing demonstrations. It was an invigorating and thoroughly enjoyable afternoon – the sun was out, though it was still quite cold. To save money at the entry gate, Julia passed us off as Russian citizens, instructing us to "Keep quiet and remember, Russians don't smile."

We followed her advice and it worked. We didn't know it at the time, but Russia has a two-tiered system of fees for Russian citizens and foreigners.

Julia and her friends were very kind to Ester and me. She had us over to her apartment for a dinner party one evening. Her professor friend Stanislaus was also there. Julia was an excellent cook and made borsht among other things. There was also some tasty orange-colored caviar. At the dinner table Julia served Ester a ladle of borsht, then another ladle, then another…until Ester finally realized that Julia was waiting for her to give some signal to stop! The dinner ended with some excellent Russian vodka, of course.

Julia also took us to the Arkhangelsk Regional Folk Art Museum, a real treasure in this part of the world. Russian Orthodox icons, bone carvings, costume, and decorative arts were features of this outstanding museum. Toward the end of our stay we met up with Julia and her friends at the Arkhangelsk town library, where they presented us with a Malye Karely shot glass and mug (both of which are still in use).

The Filarmoni Chamber Orchestra itself was very small – only four 1st violins, four 2nd violins, two violas, two cellos, and one bass – but the players were very professional and had a tremendous work ethic. Some in the orchestra spoke a little bit of English, and I did have a Russian guidebook with a small dictionary, but these only complemented the musical ESP that we had among us from the very start. The orchestra was mostly women, including the regular conductor's wife, Lena, who played principal viola. There were only three men. Of the women, four were named Olga!

All rehearsals, with the exception of the dress rehearsal, were held at the Academy of Music. It occupied a typical communist block building set back from the street. The third-floor rehearsal room doubled as a lecture hall, with four rows of fixed seating facing a central performance area. Placed high upon one of the walls was a beautiful mural of inlaid wood art celebrating Arkhangelsk's 400th anniversary. It featured the city's embankment and skyline.

On the very first day of rehearsals, Ester and I discovered that the Academy of Music did not have any toilet paper in any of the bathrooms! When we asked about this, we were told that this commodity was no longer stocked in public buildings since it was stolen all the time. Fortunately we discovered a small grocery store on the way from our hotel to the Academy. The store was reasonably stocked, though it was very crowded, with aisles that were only about three feet wide. It did have toilet paper. Local people brought their own toilet paper with them wherever they went – so we did too!

Julia attended all of the first rehearsal so that I was able to give the orchestra some background information about the pieces. They had performed the Dvořák *Serenade for Strings* a couple of years earlier, but the other works on the program were new to them. They enjoyed the early Mendelssohn string symphony; its twelve-year-old composer's Bach-like approach kept everybody more than a little bit busy. The Vaughan Williams *Fantasia on a Theme by Thomas Tallis* they absolutely adored, although at first they found it puzzling. I almost sacked it because there were three fewer players than I was expecting, therefore requiring that the music be cross-cued in a number of cases (though none of the sound was changed). It soon became the favorite. In one of the early rehearsals we sightread *A Moorside Suite* by Holst, considering it as a possible replacement, but the players told me that they greatly preferred the Vaughan Williams and that they would ultimately be up to the task.

The Copland *Appalachian Spring* was the most difficult piece, but this orchestra was more than ready for it. Of course we did the original chamber orchestra version that the composer wrote for Martha Graham in 1943. Though rehearsals started on Friday, the winds and piano required on this piece were not available until Sunday. The flute and bassoon players were highly-skilled professional musicians from St. Petersburg. Andrev, the bassoonist, who was fluent in English, told me that he had taken the train from St. Petersburg. I asked him how he was able to cope with the twenty-eight hour ride. He told me that it was something that the locals simply dealt with; he read and slept. It was no problem for him.

The pianist did not sight read all that well, but she really worked hard on the music and did well on the final concert. The clarinetist, though very sincere in his approach, was not up to the level of the other players. It turned out he was a Russian Navy bandsman from Severodvinsk – and he had to miss two rehearsals because of his military commitments. This badly compromised the first concert – we couldn't play the Copland – but not the final one.

The first day's rehearsal ended around 1:00 (13:00) and we celebrated by taking Julia out for lunch. She led us into downtown Arkhangelsk to a place located in the basement of a large building. "Cantina" was a cafeteria of the old type, stark in appearance and featuring traditional Russian food – blini (Russian pancakes), cabbage casseroles, shepherd's pie variants, fish, potatoes, stews, etc. This, we felt, was the essence of Russia. One could assemble a large plateful of food for about $2. It was a real bargain for us, but not for the vast majority of the people sitting around us. Nevertheless, it was the best food that they could afford.

Though we made "Cantina" our go-to place for lunch, the center of Arkhangelsk had a number of other restaurants offering a good variety of food. The simply labelled "Kafe" was located near the concert hall and had good open-face sandwiches. Many Pomorsky State University students ate there. The "Beer" restaurant, owned by a friend of Julia, was the most expensive. We took Andrev the bassoonist there one night. It cost about as much as a middle-class restaurant in the United States. Then there was the "Kafe 64th Parallel" (yes, Arkhangelsk is that far north), where we went with Julia after the final concert. When we entered the place there was a loud Ukrainian Karaoke singer who conveniently left right after we were seated.

On another day, following one of the rehearsals, Ester and I checked out the hall where the final concert was to take place. The building itself had been constructed as the Lutheran Church of St. Catherine in 1768; there were many Finns living in Arkhangelsk at the time. After the revolution the communists turned the church into a gymnasium. Later it was remodeled into a concert hall with a decent stage and great acoustics. Today it remains a concert hall, but Lutheran church services are once again happening there on Sunday mornings. We found this situation to be true in St. Petersburg as well: a lot of the churches that had been taken away from the people and used as museums there had now been returned to the people for their original use. Anyway, when the concert hall manager found out who we were, he gave us free tickets to an organ recital happening later that evening. He then showed us the guest artist room and the private washroom, which was up four floors and within sight of the belfry. Afterwards we checked out the auditorium by ourselves and went out to dinner.

When we returned for the organ recital the manager enthusiastically greeted us at the door and cheerfully exclaimed,

"Now you can go downstairs and take off your clothes."

This time we totally lost it – We couldn't stop laughing! These same words spoken by the airport security guard were still fresh on our minds. Was this mere coincidence? Was there was a Russian-English phrasebook that translated "coats" for "clothes?" Or was it just a Russian colloquialism? We never found out.

Both Ester and I were interviewed by reporters from the local television stations. Julia was there to interpret, of course. My interview went off well; I was happy to do it. It was more-or-less what I had come to expect. Ester's interview, however, was quite different. The agenda-driven "journalist" questioned Ester about modern American women. She was really thrown for a loop when Ester told her that she was a Puerto Rican who had grown up on a tropical island; she was thrown for a second loop when Ester said that she actually enjoyed traveling with her husband!

The following morning we saw one of the two-minute spot news clips on the television. It opened with a camera view focusing solely on my hands (!) and gradually expanded its scope, moving through the orchestra during the opening section of Copland's *Appalachian Spring*. I was even dubbed into Russian! PBS and other networks could learn a lot from the Russians about advertising and advocating for conductors, bands, and orchestras in America!

In concert with the Arkhangelsk Chamber Orchestra, 2006

The concerts turned out to be different from what I had expected. The Severodvinsk concert was cancelled due to the auditorium there being used for some sort of military event. This is probably what the orchestra's regular conductor wanted to convey to me in the emails that were never received. Apparently the cancellation of concerts in Severodvinsk had happened before; no one was surprised by it. This concert was replaced by a fraction of a concert plus one full concert. The "fraction" was a performance of the first movement of the Mendelssohn *String Symphony No. 5* at the Arkhangelsk region's Arts Awards Ceremony held at the Arkhangelsk Concert Hall. Although we were featured on stage, there were no chairs; so we performed standing up. We were just one part of the show. All sorts of groups performed – singers, dancers, balalaika players, and an organist playing Khachaturian's "Sabre Dance." The official "replacement" concert for the one lost at Severodvinsk turned out to be one for the students at the Academy of Music on the 15th. It was not well attended. It also felt a little bit strange to be doing it wearing formal attire in the same room in which we had just been rehearsing.

The concert on the 16th was an entirely different matter – well advertised, it drew a near capacity audience at the Arkhangelsk Concert Hall. For once, there had been enough rehearsal time to do justice to the material. At that point, it was one of the most satisfying and fulfilling concerts in my career. We opened with the Mendelssohn, and then proceeded with the Vaughan Williams and the Dvořák. The Copland occupied the second half and the orchestra poured everything they had into it. Everything went smoothly.

After the concert, the orchestra's librarian asked if he could make copies of all the music since Russia does not adhere to international copyright laws. He assured me that I would get the music back before leaving Arkhangelsk. I was reluctant, though I understood how little money the orchestra had for buying complete sets of parts. I hung onto the scores, but allowed him to copy the parts, or so I thought. I never saw those parts again.

When we left Arkhangelsk, we had a sense of longing – for the people. They really have a hard life. We had been treated very well and the music–making was superb. The artistic struggle toward perfection among people living in such economic misery and in such an uncompromising climate is something that I'll never forget. Taking into account what had happened during the first Russian leg of our trip, it was not without certain misgivings that we boarded the plane for St. Petersburg. Still, we were going to be spending three nights and two full days in one of the world's great cities.

Gennady very kindly had arranged for us to have a free private car from the airport. I walked over to the man holding the large card bearing my name but then had to reenter through security just to get our luggage! Upon our return to St. Petersburg, we found the city to be a real mess; the snow and ice had begun to thaw, resulting in what seemed to be an inordinate number of flooded sidewalks. Ponds were everywhere. We quickly found out why. Many of the buildings in St. Petersburg have enormous drainpipes, not quite a foot in diameter. We were standing very close to the side of a building, maybe about three feet away from one of these drainpipes, when we heard a very loud "Whoosh!" and a torrent of water came down. It was very fortunate that we were not standing in front of it!

On the first full day back from Arkhangelsk we visited The Hermitage, which houses one of the four greatest art collections in the world. We paid 350 rubles (about $14 US) to enter; that amount was on a par with what the Boston Museum of Fine Arts was charging at that time. This was fine for something world-class, though I found out later that the Russians pay only about 15 rubles (about 60 cents). As we entered The Hermitage, we were approached by a well-dressed English-speaking man who wanted to show us the highlights of the museum for a fee. I had a St. Petersburg guidebook in my hand with a floor plan of The Hermitage as well as what to see there, so I turned him down. He was persistent, but so was I. By the way that he spoke and moved around I could tell that he was not hired by the museum. Entrepreneurs such as he are plentiful in the tourist areas. Ultimately he did guide a small group of people through the museum's highlights. We know this because we ran into him everywhere!

The Hermitage is truly amazing for its decorative features as well as for the tremendous collections of art on display. In about four hours we saw, among other things, the Jordan Staircase, Alexander Nevsky's sarcophagus, the Spanish collection, and the Impressionist collection, stolen by the Nazis and then re-stolen after World War II by the Russians.

Later that afternoon we headed over to Theatre Square, where the Nicolai Rimsky-Korsakov Conservatory and Mariinsky Theatre are located. The conservatory, founded by Anton Rubinstein in 1862, has an impressive statue of Rimsky-Korsakov on its premises. That same evening we attended the performance of the Kirov Ballet at the Mariinsky Theatre. We had ordered our tickets online before we left the United States, hence we had no problem with overpaying. For roughly

$24 apiece we had dress circle box seats in the tier above the main floor. The music was Ludwig Minkus' *Don Quixote*, a ballet which is well-known in Russia, but relatively unknown elsewhere. The dancing was traditional yet superb in every way. The scenery was what one might expect for a Neopolitan opera, not the colored sheets that have destroyed the scenario of many a ballet performance on both sides of the Atlantic. The whole thing was a real treat for the senses. All people who don't like ballet should see one of the Kirov's performances: great scenery, great orchestra, and dance steps that actually make sense.

The next day Ester and I walked over to the Church on the Spilled Blood and intended to go inside it, as well as the Russian Museum and the Russian Ethnological Museum. Each of these places wanted 300 rubles ($12) apiece. By this time I had had it with the two-tiered "soak the tourists" system. Out of principle, I refused, partially because of the two-tiered system, but also because America's Smithsonian Museums are free to all people regardless of nationality; so are the United Kingdom's national museums. Another reason was that we owed Gennady and Oxana a great deal of money and I wanted to return at least some of it before we left.

We decided instead to attend an afternoon concert given by the Akademisch, St. Petersburg's second professional orchestra. On the program were Maurice Ravel's *Mother Goose Suite* and *Piano Concerto in G*, as well as Gabriel Faure's *Requiem*. Andrev, the bassoonist who performed on the Copland in Arkhangelsk, played in that orchestra. When I inquired at the box office, the woman behind the counter smiled and showed me the tourist price on her calculator: 700 rubles per ticket (about $28). I was quite angry, showed her my U Mass Boston faculty I.D. card, and said very loudly, "This is outrageous. I am a music professor and a conductor!" I am not certain which of these turned the key, but all of a sudden, still smiling, she showed me a new price of 200 rubles (about $8) on her calculator. So, we went to the concert – and had good seats, too!

The next day, as the plane lifted off the runway at St. Petersburg, a number of the passengers applauded. I would have been one of them, but the wonderful experience in Arkhangelsk (even though my music was not returned) more than made up for any of the troubles that we had experienced in St. Petersburg. Russia had been a real experience, one that I would not have missed, yet it turned out that we were there at just the right time. Relations between the United States and Russia were still reasonable. Vladimir Putin was in his second term and had not yet become, well, Putin!

We returned to London's Westpoint Hotel and this time got a better room, away from the noise of the elevators. We both had a sense of relief. That evening Ester stayed at the hotel to relax while I took the tube to Cadogan Hall at Sloane Square where I met Alan Gibbs for the James Allen's Girls' School spring concert. Alan had arranged to get free tickets for us, and the seats were perfect – right in the center. Being Holst researchers, we were treated like celebrities since Gustav Holst had taught at James Allen's Girls' School (JAGS) from 1904 to 1920 and was the founder of their orchestra. We were also treated to a special reception during the intermission that had some outstanding white wine. The orchestra and chorus were both excellent, even though I had to endure the Faure *Requiem* for a second straight night.

The next day Ester and I took the train to the university town of Cambridge. The Cambridge University Library had a number of Vaughan Williams musical manuscripts that I wanted to see. So, after having lunch and enjoying the environs – Cambridge reminded us of Harvard Square with its many bookstores but without traffic – Ester and I walked over to the library. Now librarians are usually very pleasant people, thankful to be in a job with relatively little stress. The same could be said of most library guards. This time, however, I was met by the grumpiest, meanest library guard that I had ever come across! A woman perhaps in her fifties, she gave me a hard time, requiring me to produce all sorts of documents and such. That she would not allow Ester to enter into the library with me was no surprise, but her gruffness was something I'll remember the rest of my life. It was a blotch on an otherwise pleasant day's outing.

Back in London, Ester and I ate at a Thai buffet in Camden Town before heading over to The Barbican Centre to hear the Orchestra of the Age of Enlightenment perform Beethoven's 8th and Rossini's *Stabat Mater*. It was a truly inspired performance.

On our final day we did some sightseeing in the morning and I was able to do some more Vaughan Williams research. Rosamund Strode, who had been so gracious in facilitating much of my Holst research, came down from Aldeburgh and met us for lunch at The British Library. It was so great to see her again. Unfortunately it was the last opportunity to see her; she died two years later at age eighty-one. At the time of this trip, however, she was as lively as ever and her cheerfulness added to the joy we experienced on the flip side of this trip.

Later that afternoon we went to the apartment of Stephen Connock, President of the RVW (Ralph Vaughan Williams) Society. Stephen had recently resigned from being the People Manager of Easy Jet. A very generous person, he gave me an autographed copy of *There Was a Time…*, the book that he and Ursula Vaughan Williams had compiled about her time with Ralph Vaughan Williams. He then invited us to afternoon tea at the Winter Garden restaurant in the Landmark Hotel on Marylebone Road. Ester and I found out how "the other half" lives, admiring the eight-story atrium with its palm trees, listening to flute and harp chamber music, and noshing on the most scrumptious cakes and other culinary delights imaginable. Stephen and Em Marshall, who also met us there, were keen on my proposal to conduct a CD's worth of Ralph Vaughan Williams' early orchestral works; I had been studying these at the British Library and at other places. Unfortunately, Stephen stepped down from his presidency shortly thereafter and the project came to naught. Still, just the planning of it all was invigorating and helped obliquely on other things.

Sometimes one is in the right place at the right time to witness a particular performance. Four years earlier Linnéa Bardarson and I were in Vienna to hear Beethoven's *Violin Concerto*, Op. 61, which we were about to record in the composer's own transcription for piano and orchestra. This time, Ester and I were able to purchase £10 balcony tickets at the London Coliseum for the English National Opera's performance of Vaughan Williams' 1928 four-act opera *Sir John in Love*. It was the first time that it had been staged since 1958. The title character is Shakespeare's Sir John Falstaff and, even though the stage director dared move the setting (a pet peeve of mine) from Shakespearean times to the Victorian era, the performance was stellar in every respect. Two folk songs presented in this opera – "Greensleeves," featured prominently, and "Lovely Joan," sung offstage – were assembled under the composer's watchful eye by Ralph Greaves to form the well-known chamber orchestra piece, *Fantasia on Greensleeves* (1934). Watching *Sir John in Love* and hearing these two songs as Vaughan Williams originally set them in the opera added up to a wonderful way to end what was a very special trip.

X. Exasperation No. 1 and Exhilaration

The first part of this chapter is not for the faint-hearted. Unfortunately, not all of my guest conducting experiences have been pleasant. Most of this one was irritating. I thought about excising any mention of it since the circumstances surrounding the performance still evoke feelings of anger and, to an extent, betrayal. I can name the country, Romania, but since I believe the host, soloist, and orchestra are still active, *names are left out to protect the guilty*.

Though I don't see him as often now, one of my closest friends is Dr. Emilian Badea, a professional bassoonist and accordionist who taught at U Mass Boston and played in both my orchestras. Emilian, a Romanian immigrant, knew of my conducting ventures in Eastern Europe and wondered if I would ever conduct in his home country. As it was, I found an advertisement for a guest conducting opportunity in Romania; included with this was a one-person workshop in the techniques of the Zen Buddhism-inspired conductor Sergiu Celibidache (1912-1996). I knew very little about Celibidache's transcendental approaches to music-making, so I eagerly signed on to what I thought would be a positive, enlightening experience.

The works to be performed on the concert were Gustav Holst's *Greeting*, which I had recorded one year earlier but had not yet performed in concert, the *Violoncello Concerto No. 1 in A minor*, Op. 33 by Camille Saint-Saëns, and the anchor piece, *Symphony No. 3 in E flat*, Op. 55 "Eroica," by Ludwig van Beethoven. I went into this knowing that the orchestra, with a string contingent of six 1st violins, five 2nd violins, four violas, three cellos, and two string basses, would be "bare bones" for the *Eroica*. One month earlier I had conducted the U Mass Boston Chamber Orchestra in Beethoven's *Symphony No. 4 in B flat*, Op. 60 with similar-sized forces, but the *Eroica* was larger in concept and scope. Not taking chances, I paid for four additional performers – three extra violinists plus the all-important third horn for the *Eroica*. That would have given me eight first violins and six seconds; with professional players, a reasonable performance would have been within reach.

I knew that this would be a different situation from any of my previous ones when I received a request at home to bring an extra $100 for gas and tourism. I was rather dumbfounded as I had nearly always taken public transit from the respective airport to my lodgings and had taken care of my own tourism. It was also requested that I bring with me certain on-the-shelf medicines for the host's wife. She had breast cancer and needed medicine that, while reasonably priced in the United States, was very expensive in Romania. I was more than happy to comply, filling about a third of a piece of carry-on luggage with pills. On my way I looked forward to seeing the gracious satisfaction that it would bring to my host. This, however, did not materialize.

My host was very, very tall (maybe 6'7"), foul-mouthed, and intimidating. He met me at the Bucharest airport. Instead of the friendly "Welcome to Romania, Jon" that I had expected, my host very bluntly and gruffly demanded, "Where is the medicine?" He almost shook me down, so to speak. He didn't care who I was, as long as I brought the medicine.

We got into his car and he started to complain loudly about global warming and the air being bad – and that it was all the fault of President Bush (#43) for not signing the Kyoto climate accord. I didn't want to discuss politics; I just wanted to make music, so I ignored him. After a minute of silence he brought up the same topic. This time I let him have it, raising my voice and vociferously telling him that (a) we Americans have our own strict anti-pollution laws and (b) that ninety years of communist rule on his side of the Atlantic was responsible for much of the climate change and the poor air quality in Eurasia. He looked at me and said, "Good. This is the type of emotion you need to show in front of the orchestra tomorrow." Who did he think I was? Some twenty-three-year-old graduate student? I later learned that he was really hurting. In addition to his wife's cancer, his mother-in-law who had dementia lived with him, and his own mother had died a couple of months before my visit. Still, that didn't excuse his excessive profanity and abusive behavior.

After the political assault he told me many things. I could·say very little. Every other word he spoke was a four-letter word, and most of those were "F" bombs. I looked at him and told him that most educated people don't speak that way. I then asked him where he learned English. He answered, "From watching American movies."

♫ Hooray for Hollywood! ♫

He drove like a maniac through the streets of downtown Bucharest. While catching my breath at the traffic lights, I noticed that I had no trouble reading signs; they were, of course, in Romanian. Two years of high school Latin as well as my Spanish helped me out a great deal. Here, in the midst of the Slavic countries of Eastern Europe, many of which used the Cyrillic alphabet, was an island of modern-day Latin. I could even understand a good portion of what people were saying, though I didn't know enough of word endings or inflections to be able to answer them.

We continued on to my lodging, a Spartan yet clean room in a pension. The place was located in the middle of a communist hell – six-story dirty sugar cube apartment blocks as far as the eye could see in either direction. These eyesores stand as witnesses to the "Romanian Systemization" which, under the directive of former dictator Nicolae Ceauşescu, destroyed so much of the country's traditional architecture. I was essentially deposited at this place for a day and a half. There was a monsoon on the second day, so I couldn't really go anywhere except to the grocery store and internet café across the street. By this time I had already had enough of "modern" Bucharest, but at least I had time to do some serious score study.

The first rehearsal with the orchestra was terrible. I knew at once that I had been deceived. I expected a fully professional ensemble, such as I had worked with in other parts of Europe. Instead, I had in front of me a private initiative, an orchestra that hadn't played together in four months!

This group was really no better than what I had at U Mass Boston. The string bass players were substitutes for the permanent ones who were at some sort of competition; they were typical "jazz band" bassists, and they *couldn't count*! Neither could the last-minute replacement clarinetist. This wasted a great deal of time. As to the four extra players that I had paid for: the horn player was excellent but the three extra violinists never did materialize. And one of the regular second violinists showed up only for the first rehearsal. Then there were substitutes in the second rehearsal. Clearly, I had expected better; I was overmatched for the group.

Just before this rehearsal I was introduced to the cello soloist for the Saint-Saëns. He was a sixteen-year-old student, a very talented musician who used a wide vibrato in his playing. He was darker skinned than the others, and my host explained to me that he was of a class of "reformed gypsies" (Roma) who had entered the Romanian mainstream.

My host and I had marked philosophical differences about the soloist's role in a concerto. I had always worked along *with* soloists, not *for* them. We'd sit down and discuss things in a mutually respectful manner, doing what we thought was best for soloist, conductor, performers, and composer – taking into account so many factors. During this first rehearsal, at the beginning of the Saint-Saëns my host pointed to the soloist and said loudly before the entire orchestra, "He is the boss!"

Like hell! I thought; my host had just insulted me. I was not going to be at the mercy of an adolescent. The youth was very bright, but he was no Mozart. None of this set well with me, but for the purposes of good will I played the game. Needless to say, I felt that this rehearsal had been hijacked from me. Prior to the Saint-Saëns, the orchestra and I had done some practicable first-day work on the Beethoven, but now we had to spend so much time on the concerto that we never did get around to rehearsing the Holst.

The second day of rehearsal was a mixed bag; the *Eroica* went better, but the concerto did not. My host told me to have the soloist play the same passages that he was having trouble with "one hundred times" for me during the fifteen-minute break that followed. Right. The soloist and I certainly could have gone over everything beforehand had my host arranged for the soloist (and possibly his teacher as well) to meet me during that first rainy day when I was unceremoniously dumped at my lodging. Needless to say, I felt that this rehearsal too had been hijacked from me. At least we got to the Holst this time. Finally, in the morning of the day of the concert (Sunday), the cello soloist, the host, and I worked out the difficult passages in my hotel room.

The location for the concert was the Palatul Cercului Militar National (Palace of the National Military Center), one of the more attractive buildings in downtown Bucharest. The 1914 edifice has been described as "an architectural jewel." There are many gorgeous halls and galleries within. Unfortunately the Performance Hall, beautiful though it may be, is quite small and so is the stage. The acoustics are dead, and the thirty-four-piece orchestra barely fit; it was like playing in a shoebox stuffed with paper towels.

The 6:30 p.m. concert as a whole went about as expected. Holst's *Greeting*, a relatively simple piece, was performed reasonably well. The Saint-Saëns went better than I had expected, though there was a problem with the soloist's concert etiquette. At the end of the piece, I got off the podium and shook hands with the soloist. He bowed, and then we bowed together. We exited the stage and then I sent him back for a solo bow. He bowed again and, instead of acknowledging the orchestra, he just stood there, staring at the audience and waiting for them to stop applauding! Then he played a solo encore! Both my host and I were infuriated by this, but at least I was able to cool down during the intermission. The *Eroica* performance that followed was marred instantly by the timpanist coming in on the *second* beat instead of the first, and then that last-minute clarinetist did not follow my cue to enter during the first time on the second theme! This was almost compensated for by the fact that the principal cellist was also a last-minute substitute, but he was from the Bucharest Philharmonic and greatly improved the sound of the lower strings. The audience received the concert well.

At the end of the concert, I was surprised to be approached by two of Emilian Badea's friends who had been in the audience. They presented me with two beautifully painted terra cotta bowls. I thanked them very kindly and was careful not to tell them of any of the troubles I had with the engagement. For some reason, however, they expressed embarrassment over the situation and said that I deserved better. Oh, yes – and now I felt vindicated!

So what happened with the Celibidache workshop? Well, it didn't amount to much. I had expected physically to be on a podium, conducting and receiving some kinesthetic pointers about how Celibidache would have put things together. Instead, during a free time, my host came to my hotel room with what looked like his own student notes. For about two hours, he sat in a chair discussing Celibidache's philosophy and patterns while I sat on my bed, taking notes. I was unable to get a word in edgewise. It was like pushing the button on an automatic hand dryer and then not being able to shut it off. Still, I did get some good notes, so all was not lost.

And what happened to the tourism? Well, I did walk around downtown Bucharest early one evening and saw the Antim Church. Some of the orchestra members told me where I could get a good Romanian meal, and I did get to the Ateneul Român to hear the George Enescu Philharmonic play some Schumann. The only real tourism that my host provided was when we were in his car on the way to meeting his wife (who was very nice) and his son at an indoor mall. He pointed out the building that all Romanians hate: The Palace of the Parliament, formerly known as The People's Palace. Ceauşescu destroyed much of the southwest end of Bucharest to make way for it. It was built in the mid 1980s, a particularly brutal time for the destruction of many of Romania's architectural landmarks. I had heard earlier that Ceauşescu thought that he was erecting the largest building in the world in terms of cubic space; the only problem was that he forgot about the Pentagon and probably several others.

Eventually the excesses caught up with Ceauşescu; he and his wife were later executed – everything adding up to nothing. The people had suffered greatly under that egomaniac, and some were suffering still. I had read about the lost children of Bucharest and it left a bad taste in my mouth. Interestingly, as I waited at the airport for my flight back home, I saw a beer vending machine. Any four-year-old child could have purchased a can of beer from it.

I did spend the part of one good evening with my host, his wife, and his son, eating dinner and buying some souvenirs, but it didn't quite make up for the abuse I had experienced earlier. I still feel ripped off. Gasoline is more expensive in Romania than in the United States, but what was used on my behalf was nowhere close to $100 worth. This, however, was miniscule in comparison to the cost of the four extra players, three of whom never appeared. Eventually I did get my money back for those three phantom players, but I would rather have had them show up. The concert was not a disaster, but this was by far the worst conducting experience I had had in Europe to this point. I did write to my host, however, thanked him and invited him to co-author an article on Celibidachian techniques for the new *CODA (College Orchestra Directors Association) Journal*, of which I was editor. He never responded.

When I recounted this trip to Ester, she suggested that I could have a better conducting experience in Boston by forming my own professional per-service orchestra for a fraction of the cost. I had already started on this venture. Boston was brimming with professional musicians. The Boston Neo-politan Chamber Orchestra had its premiere concert less than three months later.

* * *

That June, Ester and I travelled to Glasgow, Scotland for the BASBWE (British Association of Symphonic Bands and Wind Ensembles) International Wind Festival held at the Royal Scottish Academy of Music and Drama (now the Royal Conservatoire of Scotland). There I did a lecture/conducting demonstration titled "Holst's

'Warm-ups' for *Hammersmith*." In late 1927 Gustav Holst had been approached by the British Broadcasting Corporation to compose a twelve-to-fifteen minute work for their Wireless Military Band. The work that would eventually be composed for the commission was *Hammersmith*, Op. 52. However Holst, having not composed for military band for quite some time, asked if he could first arrange some shorter piece for the medium. The BBC agreed and Holst actually did three such arrangements: *Bach's Fugue a la Gigue* and two of his own pieces, "Marching Song" from *Two Songs without Words*, Op. 22 and an incomplete military band version of *A Moorside Suite* (only the "Scherzo" movement was finished). The clinic ensemble was The Glasgow Wind Band, a fully professional organization that was right on task. I felt honored to conduct them, even in these three short pieces. It was a real joy, especially in the wake of the way I had been treated in Romania.

After the conference we took the train north to Oban, a thriving metropolis of 8,000 on Scotland's west coast. There we saw some authentic Scottish dancing and ate some authentic Scottish food, which meant haggis for me. We stayed in a bed-and-breakfast run by two former Michiganders who gave us a nice upstairs room with a great view of the coastal islands. I thought that I would try to capture a photo of the sun's first rays shining on the islands and so set our alarm for 4:00 a.m. When it rang, I got up immediately with great enthusiasm, took a look outside, and was instantly dismayed to find that the islands were already in broad daylight. I forgot how far north we actually were!

The main reason for going to Oban was to take in what was truthfully advertised as the "Three Isle Tour." It began with a ferryboat ride from Oban to Craignure, on the Isle of Mull, then an extensive bus ride down a single-lane road on the Ross of Mull to Fionnphort, on the far corner of the island. More than once the bus driver yielded to sheep, as required by Scottish law. From Fionnphort, we took a very short ferry across to the island of Iona, of historical and religious significance, where we visited the Abbey and the ruins of its Bishop's House and Nunnery.

We had been warned that the Three Isle Tour might turn out to be a Two Isle Tour if the weather was bad. On this day, however, the weather was reasonable and we were able to ride in a much smaller boat to the uninhabited island of Staffa. With its unusual hexagonal pencil shaped columns, Staffa is considered the northern complement to The Giant's Causeway of Northern Ireland. Staffa has many caves, the most famous of which is Fingal's Cave, visited by Felix Mendelssohn in 1829. We had a choice: either look at the puffin colony on top of the cliffs on the opposite side of the island or visit Fingal's Cave. Of course, we chose the latter. To get to the cave, one has to grab onto a cable that is hammered into the rock and then inch one's way toward the mouth of the cave. If not, you slip into the sea. Ester opted out of this, but there was nothing on this earth that would have prevented me from continuing onward.

The cave is magnificent! The hexagonal columns continue into it. The cabled path only goes about a fourth of the way into the cave, but one can nonetheless get a full appreciation of the cave's beauty and power. The cave itself is about the size of a cathedral and with the water rushing back and forth one can imagine (and some can internally hear) the agitated parts of Mendelssohn's *The Hebrides* overture. What an exhilarating experience! Now I have seen Niagara Falls and the Grand Canyon, but Fingal's Cave is a special place that every musician – and every non-musician – should visit at least once in a lifetime!

XI. *Exasperation No. 2: "Fool Me Twice"*

Sometime during 2007 I made three proposals to Centaur Records, Inc.:

1. another early Beethoven CD,
2. an early Richard Strauss CD, and
3. all five of Anton Rubinstein's piano concertos.

All three proposals were accepted, though Centaur president Victor Sachse really liked the third idea. The concertos of Anton Rubinstein (1829-1894) are seen as forerunners of those by Piotr Tchaikovsky and Sergei Rachmaninoff and therefore occupy an important position in the history of Russian classical music. No. 4, considered his masterpiece in the genre, is still performed occasionally, but the others have fallen out of the core repertoire. While all of the Rubinstein concertos had been recorded at one time or another, all five had never been recorded by the same pianist-conductor team. At that time there were a few recordings currently available of *Piano Concerto No. 4 in D minor*, Op. 70 (1864), one of *Piano Concerto No. 3 in G*, Op. 45 (1853-54), one of *Piano Concerto No. 5 in E flat*, Op. 94 (1874), and none of the two earlier ones.

One of the available recordings of No. 4 was performed by pianist Josef Hofmann (1876-1957) in 1942. Hofmann was a student of Rubinstein during the composer's latter years and, thus, his recording provided an authentic link back to the composer. The available recording of No. 3, paired with the single-movement *Caprice Russe*, Op. 102, was fairly new; it featured pianist Valerie Traficante with José Serebrier conducting the Rheinische Philharmonie. I was able to make contact with Valerie and gained some additional insight from her.

I asked pianist Grigorios (Gregory) Zamparas, who had worked with me previously on *The Youthful Beethoven* CD if he would be interested in the project and he said, "Why not?" Since I had a relatively low budget to work with, I contacted Valeri Vatchev in Sofia to act as producer. Though I was not happy with having to pay for an extra hour of recording time the year before, the Philharmonia Bulgarica was a good orchestra and his engineer, Christo, did provide me with a fine finished product. This time we were to record at the Lyubomir Pipkov National School of Music in Sofia.

Early the following year (2008) I decided that we would record Nos. 3 and 4 first, since these two were in print and readily available. Each lasts about thirty-three minutes and the two of them fit together very well onto a single CD. There was another reason for starting with these two, however, and that had to do with Rubinstein himself: they are the most musical of the five. If, for any reason, the Rubinstein concerto project had to be curtailed, then at least we would have recorded these two. No. 3 is one the few concertos that is cyclical in nature; it is an experiment in form. The rolling, nautical themes from the first movement as well as the contemplative themes from the second show up in the third movement cadenzas – one for the piano and one for clarinet plus orchestra! The coda of that third movement is a musical thrill ride for both pianist and orchestra. No. 4 is composed along more traditional lines, but the melodies, among Rubinstein's finest, are quite memorable as is his skill in motivic development. The orchestration for all of the Rubinstein piano concertos follows along the conservative leads of Mendelssohn and Schumann: two flutes, two oboes, two clarinets, two bassoons, two horns, two trumpets, timpani, and strings. There is one exception: the orchestration for the satirically demonic finale of No. 4 is enhanced by the addition of a piccolo. Here was a composer who knew – and got – exactly what he wanted.

When the music arrived I noticed that No. 3 was okay, but the printed parts to No. 4 were of such poor quality that I had to draw in nearly all of the note stems, and that took considerable time. I also noticed some mistakes in the parts and corrected those. Then too there was one bogus clarinet passage; it belonged to the trumpet, so I edited that. This was all yeoman's work, but it had to be done. Rubinstein wrote so much music and used so many different publishers that the expected quality control was sometimes lacking.

The trip began auspiciously. The plane ride on that September 9th was one of the most beautiful that I remember. The aircraft flew over Nice and then Sardinia, where the mountains almost appear to go into the sea. A dot of red appeared; it gradually changed to an orange ball as it rose over the clouds and the Mediterranean. Such a wonderful sight!

When I arrived in Sofia, I immediately went to the place where we would stay. I was there alone at first; Gregory, now Assistant Professor of Music at the University of Tampa, would arrive the following day. He had made arrangements for us to stay in a two-bedroom apartment on Vrabcha Street, pretty much in the center of the city. The place was owned by his friends, Tony and Anglicka Ivancheva, two Greek nationals living on nearby Rakovsky Street. Anglicka's sister, Ivelina, a professor at Professor Pantcho Vladigerov Academy of Music, was married to Atanas Athanassov, dean at the same school. The Academy of Music, however, is not the same as the National School of Music, which is for younger (high school) students. The location of the latter, next to the British Consulate and near the National Library, was an easy walk from the apartment.

I grabbed the single bed that was in a separate bedroom. Early in the morning of the next day I woke up facing the dome of Sofia's landmark Alexander Nevsky Cathedral. The stone part of the structure was lit up. The sky above it changed from black to navy to light blue, highlighting the dome in different hues. This certainly complemented what I had seen on the airplane the previous morning. Gregory arrived from Florida later that afternoon but, in addition to being jet-lagged, he was frazzled. Alitalia had lost his luggage and, to make matters worse, the pants he was wearing got discolored when he sat on a plastic bag. Fortunately the apartment had a washing machine, though we had to go out to buy detergent. There was a heat wave in Sofia and, by necessity, for the next three evenings we ate at some good Bulgarian outdoor restaurants.

The next morning we headed to an indoor market where we stocked up on some Greek foods. Gregory's clothes finally arrived that afternoon. Yurgos Manessis, his former piano teacher in Greece, also arrived that day. Yurgos was very much a gentleman. He was also a guru and slept on two very thin mattresses placed on the floor. Later that afternoon Valeri Vatchev, who would once again be the producer, and Christo Pavlov, the sound engineer, visited us at the apartment to confirm things.

The timing of the Holst CD was about seventy-two minutes; that of the Rubinstein Nos. 3 and 4 CD would be about sixty-six minutes. However, Rubinstein's concertos were much more complex than the Holst and Purcell pieces that I had recorded with Valeri and Christo two years earlier; they also had no repeats. Therefore I asked for twelve hours of recording time: three hours on Friday evening, six hours on Saturday, and three on Sunday. Later that evening I worked out a recording order and determined that we should start with the first movement of No. 4, as that might be the easiest for pianist, conductor, and the orchestra to grasp at the onset. Gregory agreed.

Thursday morning marked our first visit to the National School of Music. My first impression that it was not a bad place and that the hall was fair. It was smaller than I had expected but would hold the pianist, conductor, and fifty-four players reasonably well. (I would record in a barn if I thought that the players were comfortable and the acoustics were good.)

Valeri had promised earlier that we would be recording with the best piano at the school. There were two pianos there. Gregory tried out both of them but didn't want to use either one. Neither did I. The Bösendorfer, kept in a storage area in back of the stage, was newer, but it buzzed. The Steinway on stage was old and not in the best of shape. It was obvious that Valeri didn't check them out ahead of time. Gregory was very nervous and upset as was I. We tried to borrow a piano from the Academy of Music, but they were unable to lend us one.

That afternoon we went over to Tony and Anglicka's apartment. Ivelyna was also there and she derided the situation. She argued that the hall was not worthy of us, let alone the pianos. The five of us plus Atanas ate dinner that evening at a very good outdoor restaurant. While there, Atanas phoned Valeri and spoke with him about the situation. I don't speak Bulgarian, but I could tell that the conversation was very serious.

The next day started with a bad omen: the shower in the apartment flooded. What followed was aggravating. The plan was for the piano technician, Z. Z., to meet us at the National School of Music at noon. The school's director, Mrs. Mikeva, said that the hall would be empty, but it was not. It turned out that a band rehearsal had been scheduled. I listened to most of it; the ensemble was actually quite good. I had to force myself to keep from laughing, however, when the group started to work on F. W. Meacham's *American Patrol*. It was not what I was expecting to hear in Bulgaria. Z. Z. returned at 1:30 to work on the pianos. I hung around a while longer, but Gregory and Yurgos returned to the apartment to rest up before the first recording session, which was scheduled for 18:00 (6:00 p.m.). It was also best for me to be alone at the moment. Things were quite tense. I kept thinking about the three T's that my chiropractor said are best avoided: toxins, traumas, and (negative) thoughts.

The first recording session proved to be the most difficult I have ever had. The promised piano was indeed a Steinway but, according to Z. Z., it was twenty years old. Valeri was told by someone at the school that it was a new piano; it may have been new to the school but that was all. It had many problems: continuously falling out of tune, uneven action, worn pins, and some rusty strings. This was coupled by the heat wave and, of course, the hall was not air conditioned. Fortunately Z. Z. was right at hand through all of the recording sessions. We had to stop often because of the piano's inability to hold pitch. It was especially aggravating when we would have to stop in the midst of some truly great music making. All-in-all the constant interruptions for retuning, etc. probably cost us twenty-five to thirty minutes' time, not to mention focus! It was Valeri's responsibility to have overseen the piano situation properly, and this meant his having to have done so personally.

The piano situation almost caused the whole project to be cancelled. It also caused friction between Gregory and myself that otherwise would not have been there. We both were and are absolute perfectionists. The conductor in me wanted to get on task, to get things done. The pianist in Gregory wanted to have his say about whether the instrument in front of him was of sufficient quality in order to continue. At one point he was ready to walk out (and I likewise), but then we remembered that the problem was not of our own making. We both took a deep breath and then Gregory smiled and said, "Let's make music."

That was all it took. We knew that we could rise above the situation. It was maddening that we had to fret over the condition of the piano rather than put our energies into some additional, last minute, careful interpretive study.

The orchestra was very good, but it also had its problems. Both flute players on Friday were superb. The flute thirds in the second movement of No. 4 came off very well. Unfortunately, a substitute flutist, whose tone was inferior, replaced one of them for the Saturday and Sunday sessions. This caused significant intonation difficulties, especially in the slow movement of No. 3 – difficulties that had to be dealt with on the spot as we were recording. I asked Valeri about why we had to deal with this change of personnel, why the original 2nd flute player wasn't there. He simply responded with, "Oh, he couldn't make it." Couldn't make it?! So why not hire someone who could make all the sessions in the first place? Sofia must be crazy with professional-level flutists!

Also, I had asked for three string bass players; Valeri brought in four. This normally would have been a good thing, but the fourth player had intonation problems and kept making counting errors, thus causing us to have to record many passages over and over. We would have been better off having just the other three. Aside from this, the string section as a whole was excellent.

Then there was the wrong note. In one of the fast passages in the Rubinstein 4th concerto there was a wrong note somewhere. Gregory heard it first; then I heard it. I wanted to remove it through the usual process of pulling the orchestration apart – taking the passage section by section (brass, then woodwinds, upper strings, lower strings, etc.) but we were rapidly running out of time. Months later, during the editing process with Toby Mountain, I easily identified the wrong note; it was in the 2nd clarinet, and I had it removed.

The strain of everything took its toll and we needed to have an additional hour in order to record everything. The early pacing had been very slow. This was all too familiar; I had experienced it two years earlier when recording *Gustav Holst: Composer as Arranger*. There may also have been a red herring: Valeri was videotaping our sessions. Were we part of a documentary? I don't know about that, but we were set up. The need for an additional hour was planned by Valeri from the start. Had the piano been the world's greatest instrument, he still would have found a way to squeeze another hour's worth ($1,000!) from me. It brought to mind the old adage, *Fool me once, shame on you. Fool me twice, shame on me.*

But I was not fooled. The situation was also obvious to Gregory, who said, "Don't you know he is toying with you?" Yes, I knew it, but I wanted to finish the recording, so there was really no choice to be made at the moment. To return in order to record missing parts of the CD would have meant another plane trip plus additional expense that would have been far greater than paying for one additional hour. So, I purposefully took it on the chin. Sometimes it is better to allow some slack on the surface. At my age, with a number of positive European connections, I wasn't about to burn any bridges. I only knew that I could never have Valeri Vatchev as a recording producer again. The piano situation alone was enough to solidify that, let alone the flute fiasco and forced extra hour.

After the final recording session on Sunday, Valeri and Christo took us to the Happy Bar and Grill, Bulgaria's version of Hooters. Even though we had an enjoyable time, it did not make up for what we had been through. As for the resultant CD? It was fine.

Recording session with Grigorios Zamparas, Sofia, Bulgaria 2008

XII. No Umlauts!

It is not unusual to have professional goals. One of mine was to conduct Beethoven's 5th by the time I was fifty. Another was to conduct Beethoven's 9th by the time I was sixty. Both goals were easily met, though the latter did not quite happen the way that I had anticipated.

By this time in my career I had conducted all of Beethoven's other symphonies, some more than once. The *Symphony No. 9 in D minor*, Op. 125, however, is quite different in its demands. Its finale features Beethoven's setting of the German poet Friedrich Schiller's 1785 *An die Freude* (*Ode to Joy*). Thus, in addition to an orchestra of at least sixty players, the symphony requires four professional-level vocal soloists (soprano, alto, tenor, and bass) and a sizable four-part chorus. At about seventy minutes, the 9th is twice the length of most symphonies. It is also the only one from Beethoven's third creative period. Therefore the responsibility factor in conducting the 9th exceeds that of the others.

The 9th also requires a balanced approach on the conductor's part. There have been too many instances where the first three movements have been given pedestrian treatment in order to get to the finale. On the other hand, there have been performances where the first three movements were very musical, but the finale was noticeably under-rehearsed.

Then there is the fact that the main theme of the last movement is a relatively simple one: everybody knows it – whether from church, car commercials, or the 1965 Beatles movie *Help!* Beethoven presents it in many guises and it is the conductor's job to delineate its uniqueness in each. But that is just the theme. The last movement as a whole has also been the recipient of all sorts of abuse. The worst, on a global scale, came as Seiji Ozawa was conducting it at the opening of the 2000 Olympic Games in Sydney, Australia. CBS cut halfway through it for a commercial! To add to the mortification, the announcer couldn't even pronounce Ozawa's name correctly!

Taking all of this and more into account, I still jumped when I had the opportunity to conduct the work at the Stara Zagora, Bulgaria State Opera. Ester had never been to Bulgaria; she did not need to be talked into accompanying me on this trip. Before leaving I contacted the opera's choral director Mladen Stanev via email with some particulars. He was very gracious. His English at that time was halting, but it was infinitely better than my non-existent Bulgarian.

With Ricardo Averbach in Sofia, Bulgaria 2009

The first leg of our journey involved flying into Sofia and then taking a bus to the center of the city where we were staying. As we exited the bus, the handle came off one of our carry-ons, which contributed to the difficulty of transporting it. In retrospect this appears to have been some sort of foreshadowing. Things did not go perfectly on this trip; however, many things went well. We stayed at The Red House, a pension with large rooms. It was there that we met up with Ricardo Averbach, a friend whom I knew through CODA (College Orchestra Directors Association). A native of Brazil, he had studied in Bulgaria alongside Valeri Vatchev. Always a very generous person, Ricardo had two tickets available for us to hear the Sofia Philharmonic Orchestra that evening. We looked forward to it but made the mistake of taking a nap on our jetlag day and accidentally slept right through the time of the performance – one of life's embarrassing moments!

Stara Zagora is located in the center of Bulgaria and, as far as we knew, there was no direct way to get there on public transportation. So we decided to take a bus to the historic hub of Plovdiv, Bulgaria's second-largest city, and from there we would take a train. I wanted Ester to experience Old Plovdiv, so we stayed at a very rustic hostel there. The ancient Roman amphitheatre and partially excavated coliseum, were nearby and not to be missed.

The next day we walked to the train station where we saw several large posters with a painting of a voluptuous young Latin woman advertising "caffe Porto Rico." Being from Puerto Rico, Ester was at first taken aback. In the years immediately following the Spanish-American War, the Americans established many businesses on the island, often misspelling "Puerto Rico" as "Porto Rico." One of the permanent legacies from this period appears on manhole covers scattered throughout the island and stamped with "Porto Rico Ironworks." Puerto Rico is tropical and the island does have several coffee growing areas, resulting in a number of brands: "Café Adjuntas," "Café Yauco," etc. As we studied the posters more carefully, we laughed as we noticed two small Italian flags placed on each side at the top and realized that while the "caffe Porto Rico" product may have originated in Puerto Rico, it had passed through Italy on its way to Bulgaria!

The train ride from Plovdiv to Stara Zagora was quick and pleasant. Shortly after our arrival, we walked over to the Hotel Vereya, located in the center of town. The Vereya, named after one of the city's ancient appellations, was very good – clean and modern. The television in our room had over a hundred channels, mostly overdubbed in Bulgarian.

After we checked into the hotel, I called Mladen Stanev and he met us there the next morning. I was surprised at his youth; he was only thirty-four at the time. Mladen was very nice and walked us over to the opera theatre. En route we passed through the Augusta Trajana Roman ruins of what once was an impressive amphitheatre and forum. We also passed by a large beautifully ornate building that looked like a pink wedding cake. This edifice turned out to be the former state opera house. Constructed in 1925, it is the earliest Bulgarian theatre to be built for that specific purpose. Mladen explained to me regretfully that there had been a fire in the new opera house. While the orchestra rehearsed in a room that had been repaired and renovated, the building's main hall was undergoing extensive renovation – primarily for the removal of asbestos material. All of this meant that the concert would have to take place in the old opera house. What? Trade in a performance in the rather bleak utilitarian communist structure for the older, more beautiful one? Anytime, anytime!

During our spare time, Ester and I were able to do some sightseeing in Stara Zagora. The city has been described as underestimated in regard to tourism, and we found this to be quite true. Stara Zagora, with about 150,000 inhabitants, is rich in history; its seven name changes reflect that. We started out by visiting the tourist office and then headed over to the Regional History Museum. It holds a myriad of artifacts, but the most interesting thing is its excavated Roman street, located on the lowest level. After seeing the museum we took a bus to the outlying Neolithic Dwelling museum where, in addition to hundreds of artifacts, we saw the foundation of an 8,000-year-old house!

Modern Stara Zagora left an entirely different impression. With its entry into the European Union, Bulgaria received a large sum of money to get on its feet, so to speak. Though the mafia seemed to have infiltrated their government, the people here didn't seem to be as oppressed as those in Russia; they also seemed to be more in control of their own destiny. However, while the Czechs used their European Union money to build concert halls, the Bulgarians built casinos. Stara Zagora had a lot of them. There appeared to have been more casinos than restaurants, yet more bars than the restaurants and casinos put together. Gigantic outdoor televisions and flashing lights gave a Las Vegas type appearance to the main street at night. One almost expected to see a disillusioned Jimmy Stewart wander through the main streets here as he did in the "Pottersville" segment of the 1946 film *It's a Wonderful Life*. And during the day there seemed to be hundreds of well-fed cats holding court on the downtown streets and in the Roman ruins.

On one of our walks through town we noticed a poster advertising everything that was presented in the performing arts – plays, concerts, and operas – for the entire month of March. Ours, occurring on the 19th, was about halfway down the list. Of interest was the order of the listing: the soloists on the last movement were listed on top, then the conductor, then the orchestra, and then the chorus. I really didn't mind; at least I was listed. It brought to mind an incident that had occurred in Boston about two months earlier. A famous Russian conductor bowed out of a Boston Symphony Orchestra performance in a huff because the cello soloist Lynn Harrell was listed before his name was!

Mladen told me that the Stara Zagora orchestra was nervous about doing this concert for two reasons: (1) the music was more difficult than what the players were accustomed to; the orchestra had not performed Beethoven's 9th previously, and (2) they were used to performing in the orchestra pit, accompanying the operas, and not out in the open on stage where everybody could see them. He then provided me with a generous rehearsal schedule (twenty hours), written according to the traditional European twenty-four-hour clock:

Monday, 16.03 (March 16th)		
11-13	Orchestra	hall (rehearsal room)
14-15	Chorus	hall
16-19	Orchestra	hall
Tuesday, 17.03		
11-13	Orchestra	hall
16-19	Orchestra and Chorus	hall
Wednesday, 18.03		
11-13	Orchestra	hall
15-16	Soloists and Piano	small hall
16-19	Orchestra, Chorus, and Soloists	hall
Thursday, 19.03		
11-14	General Rehearsal	stage (Old Opera House)
19	Concert	stage (Old Opera House)

From the start I could tell that this was a very good orchestra, about on a par with that in Wałbrzych, Poland. As time progressed, most of the players worked very hard and ultimately felt more comfortable with the situation. With eighteen hours of rehearsal time that involved the orchestra, one hour with chorus only, and one with just the soloists, I knew that a good performance was within reach. We had about fifty-five players, including thirty strings. One would ask for more on Beethoven's 9th, but the size of the stage in the old opera house would not allow it. Also, a larger orchestra would have overpowered the forty-voice chorus, the size of which was dictated by the fact that they had to fit into a relatively small area on stage in back of the orchestra.

There was one major personnel problem that caught me off guard at that first rehearsal. It didn't deal with those who were in front of me but rather with those who weren't there. The 1st and 4th horns as well as the 1st and 2nd trombones weren't going to make an appearance until the concert itself. This was entirely unacceptable. I was counting on them being there for at least the dress rehearsal. Instead, they were busy playing other orchestral jobs in either Sofia or Plovdiv. A conductor always needs the principal (1st) horn at every rehearsal, to take control of the section in terms of blend, balance, attacks, releases, etc. One could possibly get away with the 4th horn not making rehearsals *except* in the Beethoven 9th, where the 4th horn has an extended solo in the 3rd movement! I asked the 2nd and 3rd horn players if they could change to 1st and 4th, but they didn't have the music! Fortunately, my fears were partially alleviated a as the 1st horn (but not the 4th) was able to appear at the dress rehearsal after all. The situation with the 1st and 2nd trombones was not quite as heart-failure-inducing since they play only in the trio of the Scherzo and in the second half of the fourth movement. Still, the trombones are important, and I had to mark their parts so they wouldn't miss the repeats in the Scherzo.

The remaining rehearsals with the orchestra went reasonably well. I personally have found the third movement to be the most difficult to pull off. Pacing is the key here, particularly as Beethoven provided a number of lead-ups to what turn out to be false endings. My task on this occasion was made even more difficult by trying to accommodate the phantom 1st and 4th horns. Most conductors, however, will tell you that the most difficult part of conducting Beethoven's 9th are the cello and bass (bassi) recitatives in the fourth movement. The orchestra's excellent and exacting concertmaster was very keen on rhythm and, even when I was politely indicating to the bassi what I wanted on the recitatives, she was not afraid of speaking harshly to them. The first violins as a section were very strong, undoubtedly because of her leadership. The woodwinds were outstanding, except for the 2nd flute who displayed a less-than-enthusiastic attitude; afterwards I recommended that she be replaced, though I don't know if that ever happened. The young lady playing timpani was right on task; she *lived* for the Scherzo! She also had a huge assortment of mallets that would have made Boston Symphony Orchestra legend Vic Firth proud.

Mladen had warned me that the chorus was quite chatty, and I found this to be true in the one rehearsal that I had with them by themselves. They did work hard, however, and all went swimmingly well until we got to the one obstacle that I could not have anticipated: the chorus collectively didn't understand the effect that the German umlauts – those two dots above the letters "a," "o," and "u" – have on the basic vowel sounds. Apparently neither Mladen nor his assistant, a very knowledgeable older woman whose specialty was Verdi, were familiar with the German language or else the umlauts were too difficult for the chorus to enunciate. At any rate, the chorus wasn't singing them correctly. When the umlauts appeared in quick passages, it was possible (but not desirable) to ignore them, but when we got to the crux of Schiller's text, *Alle Menschen werden Brüder*, (All People will become Brothers) it was not:

Bruder=brother
Brüder=brothers

They were not singing the umlauts, but rather the German "u," pronounced as the English "oo" in the word "smooth." So, what they were singing translated to "All People will become One Brother," which is incorrect, an aberration of Schiller's intent.

What was I to do? I paused for a moment, then came up with what I thought was a reasonable solution. Using much of my repertoire of hand gestures, I split the chorus into two, pointing to each individual chorister and indicating every other person to sing "ee" (long English "E"). When we tried "ee" and "oo" together, it had the overall effect of something close to "ü." I thought that we were all set, but at the concert, the half singing "ee" could not unlearn what they had been practicing for months and the flat "u" sound came out.

Oh, Brother!

The rehearsal with the vocal soloists was one of those great hours so rarely encountered in the profession. Here were four fully professional soloists – E. Barmova, D. Dkova, N. Mochov, and A. Radev – who were thoroughly engaged in the process of music making and happy to work with me. The time we spent together resulted in a marvelous collaborative effort. The women had wonderful full-bodied but not piercing sounds, rock solid on pitch and on rhythm. The men were from that great Eastern Orthodox tradition of singing and, in a word, magnificent. The bass, especially, filled up the concert hall with his fine renditions in the recitative and solo passages.

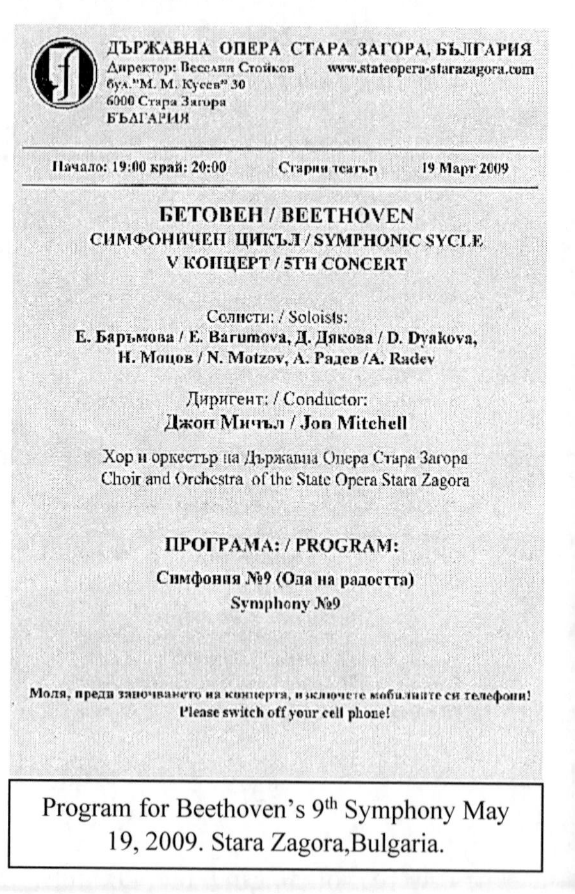

ДЪРЖАВНА ОПЕРА СТАРА ЗАГОРА, БЪЛГАРИЯ
Директор: Веселин Стойков www.stateopera-starazagora.com
бул."М. М. Кусев" 30
6000 Стара Загора
БЪЛГАРИЯ

Начало: 19:00 край: 20:00 Стария театър 19 Март 2009

БЕТОВЕН / BEETHOVEN
СИМФОНИЧЕН ЦИКЪЛ / SYMPHONIC SYCLE
V КОНЦЕРТ / 5TH CONCERT

Солисти: / Soloists:
Е. Баръмова / E. Barumova, Д. Дякова / D. Dyakova,
Н. Моцов / N. Motzov, А. Радев /A. Radev

Диригент: / Conductor:
Джон Мичъл / Jon Mitchell

Хор и оркестър на Държавна Опера Стара Загора
Choir and Orchestra of the State Opera Stara Zagora

ПРОГРАМА: / PROGRAM:
Симфония №9 (Ода на радостта)
Symphony №9

Моля, преди започването на концерта, изключете мобилните си телефони!
Please switch off your cell phone!

Program for Beethoven's 9th Symphony May 19, 2009. Stara Zagora,Bulgaria.

We were fortunate in having the dress rehearsal in the performance venue since the sound was drastically different from that of the rehearsal room. In most performances of the 9th, the soloists and chorus are brought onstage after the second movement, so that the conductor could provide a huge contrast from the serenity of the ending of the third movement by taking the orchestra immediately into the tumult that opens the fourth movement. Because of the tight space, however, it was decided to keep the soloists and chorus off stage until the end of the third movement. The loss of effect was minimal.

The concert came off quite well, though there were a couple of difficult movements caused by the nervousness and excitement of the orchestra performing onstage for the first time in a long while. The audience was sizable, about 250 people in a hall seating 300. The native Bulgarian contingency was enhanced slightly by the presence of about a dozen Peace Corps volunteers whom Ester and I had met in a Chinese restaurant the night before.

Everything went as it should have in the first movement. The orchestra and I were in synchronization throughout, even during the *ritardando* that I put in before Beethoven's terrifying and tyrannical D major recapitulation. It was tremendous. The second movement went nearly as well. The main body of the scherzo and all repeats worked well; the oboe was superb on the trio, though the orchestra got a bit lazy on the recapitulation.

The third movement, however, had its share of problems. The inexperienced 2nd bassoonist came in on my downbeat at the very beginning instead of on the subdivided "and" of the first beat. We must have rehearsed this ten times and she always got it right in rehearsal; I think it was just nerves. The other bassoonist followed her lead while the clarinets followed mine. I briefly thought about starting the movement over, but nobody in the audience would have known the difference and this orchestra, being fully professional, focused in beautifully. The worst part of the movement, however, was the 4th horn player blowing his solo; as mentioned earlier, he was playing it for the first time at the concert. This should never have been allowed to happen. It was totally unacceptable. I was prepared. The orchestra was prepared. He was not. At least the C-flat major scale passage was there. Also, on the second trumpet entrance, one of the trumpets came in early as he misinterpreted my subdivision. This was the only point in the concert where my gesture was misinterpreted, but it passed quickly.

The fourth movement was excellent, except for the 2nd bassoonist, who miscounted at a critical juncture early in the movement. When the 1st bassoonist plays an obbligato part, according to Beethoven's manuscript, the 2nd bassoonist doubles the contrabass line. We tried this a couple of times in rehearsal and it worked. But during the concert, I think that the 2nd bassoonist was still frazzled by her error in the third movement and was thinking about it when she shouldn't have been. Very few people, if any, would have noticed. The excellent violas held the melody very well during this passage and the violins entered as they should have. The cellos and basses played the recitatives superbly, although they had had difficulties in the rehearsals. The vocal soloists were great, and the choir did a very reasonable job – except for the umlauts, of course. Regardless of any of the minor mishaps that may occur, just conducting Beethoven's 9th provides one with an indescribable feeling of exhilaration, that one has somehow been of service to all humanity.

After the concert we had a farewell dinner with Mladen at an old world-type restaurant, one of those perched above a tap room. Following the dinner we headed back to our hotel, totally exhausted, but with that indescribable feeling of satisfaction of having done something truly worthwhile. The next morning, as we walked out of our room, we noticed a yellow plastic sandwich-board sign set up on the floor in front of one of the other rooms. It had a drawing of a vacuum cleaner in a circle, a notice in Bulgarian and, just below it, the following in English:

THE ROOM IS TURNING OUT

But it didn't say just what the room was turning out to be!

XIII. A Duck, a Goose, and a Tunic

During the summer of 2010 IGEB held its 19th Kongress at the place where I had first addressed the society – Oberschützen, Austria. Naturally, Ester and I spent a few days on both ends of the conference in Vienna. We stayed at the Hotel Fürstenhof, where I had stayed about eight years earlier. Our room was a reasonably-sized outer room on the second floor, from which we could see the rooftop of a small church as well as its yard below. It would have been quite pleasant except for one thing: Vienna was in the throes of yet another heat wave.

We figured that we could beat the heat by going to the outskirts of the city, and so set out at 9:00 the next morning for the Zentralfriedhof (Central Cemetery) to pay homage to the great composers. By the time we got there it was 10:00, and it was already sizzling. We had forgotten that the sun rises earlier there in the summer, thus heating things up earlier. After feeling "baked" in the cemetery, we thought we could beat the heat by taking a tour of the catacombs at St. Stephen's. Indeed it was cooler down there by a couple of degrees, but it was musty and more humid, the result being that it made little or no difference. That evening we heard an excellent chamber music concert in the city's oldest church and then had ice cream at Zanoni & Zanoni. Even in the heat, Vienna stirs the senses.

On the second day we headed to the Upper Belvedere Palace to see Gustav Klimt's *The Kiss* among other works of art. While there we were astonished to see a poster that featured Sir Frederick Leighton's romantic masterpiece *Flaming June*, a forty-seven-inch square featuring a woman dressed in an orange gown, curled up – perhaps in sleep, perhaps in despair. The work is one of the focal points of the world-class Ponce Art Museum in Ponce, Puerto Rico. I had seen it many times, and Ester had seen it even more times as she had grown up not far from there. The poster advertised that *Flaming June* and other masterpieces from the Ponce Art Museum were being shown at the Lower Belvedere. We bought the poster instantly: the writing in German featuring an English painting from a museum where the principal language is Spanish!

Things weren't any cooler at Oberschützen, as the presenters and their spouses stayed in hot dormitory rooms. Watching the town's storks moving in and out of their nests atop the buildings at least took our minds off the heat. A couple of days later the heat wave subsided and by the time we returned to Vienna we felt much more comfortable. Bob Grechesky joined us as we toured the Ringstrasse and vicinity. We figured that the best way to do it was by riding the tram that circled around the old city. Our tourist map was very good, although some of the miniscule lettering was a bit difficult to read, the result being that we confused the "O" label with the "D." Consequently, we got on the wrong tram and were surprised to find ourselves back in the neighborhood of the Belvedere palaces instead of circling around the Ringstrasse! We soon realized our mistake and Bob was able to show us the church that he had conducted in many years earlier. After that we went to the Prater where we had an extremely leisurely two-and-one-half-hour lunch. We hadn't planned on the servers being so slow, but at that point we were having such a great time enjoying each other's company that nobody cared.

* * *

Our recording of Anton Rubinstein's 3rd and 4th piano concertos was a success, at least in terms of artistic merit, so it didn't take any convincing for Grigorios (Gregory) Zamparas and me to record the remaining three. It wasn't difficult to determine which of the remaining concertos should be recorded next. Rubinstein's first two concertos were composed relatively early in the composer's career, at ages twenty-one and twenty-two. We figured that we could record those later, if at all; therefore we decided to put our efforts toward the somewhat problematical *Piano Concerto No. 5 in E flat*, Op. 94. This gargantuan concerto was composed in 1874, a full decade after the 4th. Though a stalwart work, it doesn't quite have the brilliance of its predecessor. Rubinstein's 5th is also one of the longest piano concertos of the romantic era; at fifty minutes, it rivals Johannes Brahms' 2nd piano concerto in length, though not in musicality. Rubinstein's 5th, however, does offer some unique compensations. The opening movement in triple meter features a main theme that is pentatonic in nature, perhaps foreshadowing some of the work that Carl Orff and Zoltán Kodály would accomplish a half century later. The second movement is more traditional, but with an ominous walking bass line in its middle section. Most would consider the third movement the most interesting of the three, with a rollicking fox hunt as its centerpiece.

To round out the CD, we chose Rubinstein's *Caprice Russe*, Op. 102, a single movement work composed in the years immediately following the 5th. Rubinstein claimed the work to be based on three Russian folk songs. Even if this were not true (none of the three are familiar to Westerners), this twenty-minute work somehow sounds more overtly Russian than any of his piano concertos. In addition to *Caprice Russe* there was another smaller selection that had interested me; I came across it at the New England Conservatory's Spaulding Library. *Der Thurm zu Babel* (*The Tower of Babel*), Op. 80 (1870), described as a sacred opera in one act, has a short, brooding overture. I figured if there were time, we could record this overture and include it on the CD.

Recalling the problems associated with recording in Sofia, Bulgaria, Gregory and I decided to seek an alternative. The Bohuslav Martinů Philharmonic of Zlin, Czech Republic was available and we jumped at the opportunity. The orchestra had recorded more than two dozen CDs by this time. I had last recorded with them six years earlier and knew from the three experiences that I had with them (two recordings and one concert) that we would be in for a remarkable musical experience and that we would be treated fairly. They had time for recording sessions that November.

The easiest approach to Zlin was through Vienna, and I certainly didn't mind spending my first three days there. It was early November, not an attractive time of the year – the days were already short – but Vienna always has so much to offer. This time I had decided to stay in the city center. So, after taking a train from the airport to Wien Mitte, and then the U3 subway to Stephenplatz (the St. Stephens stop), I walked down the Graben and then somehow stumbled through all sorts of construction to arrive at my destination, the Pertschy Palais Hotel. Totally jet-lagged, I looked forward to making a triumphal entrance only to discover that my reservation had been cancelled by mistake! The hotel's management felt really bad about this and, as a result, put me into a double room at the single price. It was a beautiful room in a great hotel – very old-world Vienna. They offered a superb breakfast too.

That evening, after eating a Wiener schnitzel that extended over the plate at Figmüller's, I walked over to the Wien Kammeroper (Vienna Chamber Opera) to see a performance of Franz Joseph Haydn's 1779 opera *L'Isola Disabitada* (*The Uninhabited Island*). The small palatial theatre seated about 300. I bought the cheapest ticket, which put me on the side of the balcony where there were single-file seats facing the stage. There was no one seated in front, so I moved up; I then had the best seat in the house and could see the entire stage, the conductor, and the orchestra pit. There were four vocal soloists and an orchestra of sixteen players. The overture was Haydn in his best *Sturm und Drang* mood. The hour and a half opera that followed was sung in Italian and had German supertitles, which meant that I could understand about half of what was going on. Nevertheless I knew almost instantly that I wanted to conduct it and, after I returned home, received all of the parts free, courtesy of Thomas Busse, who had prepared a new edition! Two years later my Boston Neo-politan Chamber Orchestra collaborated with Eve Budnick's Opera del West and presented this opera in Cambridge, Massachusetts.

The next morning I walked to Schwedenplatz in search of the Internet Café there, but it was closed as was the model train shop I was hoping to see. I walked some more, taking in some sightseeing (Maria am Gestade, St. Michael's, and a museum with some Roman ruins) before going to the city's oldest square, the Hoher Markt. Arriving there at noon, I was able to see the Ankeruhr Clock in all its glory, with a parade of statues representing historical figures from the Hapsburg dynasty – Prinz Eugen,

Maria Theresa, etc. – accompanied by appropriate music. When Franz Josef Haydn appeared, he was accompanied by his own "The Heavens are Telling" from *The Creation.*

That afternoon I met up with Gregory and his friend Aristea, the daughter of a conductor. Her family was from Greece, though she had grown up in Vienna. We had lunch at the Naschmarkt (great frittatensuppe and wurst!) before heading over to the Wieden district where many of Vienna's greatest musicians had lived. Once there we walked down the Wiednerhauptstrasse (Wieden Main Street) to the Gustave Ignaz Stingl piano store, where Gregory had arranged for the two of us to rehearse. We received a very warm welcome from the store's manager, Mr. Sedlaczek, a man in his fifties with a bow tie, handlebar moustache, and long wavy white hair. He took us to a rather small room that had two grand pianos facing each other. With great glee Gregory immediately took to what was in front of us. He played his solo parts on the Fazioli while I "settled" for the Steinway, thumping out what I could of the orchestral accompaniments. In less than three hours' time we covered the entire 5th concerto and *Caprice Russe*. It was pure delight!

Dinner that evening consisted of goulash at the nearby Café Museum after which Aristea snuck us into the Musikverein, albeit through the players' area to the side. From there we could watch monitors and hear the night's featured soloist with the Vienna Philharmonic play a piece which my orchestra at U Mass Boston had performed three years earlier with Paul d'Angelo as the soloist: Alexander Glazunov's *Saxophone Concerto in E flat*. After the concert, we went our own separate ways to get a good night's sleep.

The following morning I did some additional sightseeing – the winding Schönlanterngasse and the Heiligekreuzhaus, etc. As I walked back through the Graben my thoughts were interrupted by the sound of distant yet approaching drums. I knew what was coming and quickly found a bench that I could stand on, allowing me to take pictures of an army band as it rounded the corner. One never knows what one will find in Vienna.

That afternoon Gregory and I took the U-bahn to the Praterstern station, where we got tickets for the train to Breclav and Otrakovice, Czech Republic, the connecting points for Zlin. The train left on time but was held up along the route, the result being that we missed the connection at Breclav. So, what should have been a three-hour train ride turned into a five-hour one. At least we had a brand-new commuter rail train from Otrakovice to Zlin. Once there we walked over to the Hotel Garni, an inexpensive but really nice place. A single room cost the equivalent of about $40. Later that evening we walked over to the Hotel Moskva (Moscow) and had dinner at the Irish Pub, of all places.

Early the next morning, Gregory and I made the uphill trek to the Dům Umění and met the new orchestra manager, Tomáš Gregůrek. Tomáš, a young man perhaps in his early thirties, was very accommodating, a joy to work with as was Dana Kruyerova who once again served as concertmaster for the recording sessions. The first day's sessions lasted from 9:00 in the morning until 1:00 in the afternoon with two breaks, and things went very well. These were rehearsal sessions and we did not record anything yet. The orchestra's playing had significantly improved since the last time I had conducted them, some six years earlier. The labor problems had been settled, the players were paid better, and a real positive attitude was apparent. And the *harmoniemusik* (woodwinds and horns) was certainly the best that I had conducted up to that point. At the end of these rehearsal sessions, Gregory and I once again headed over to the Hotel Moskva for lunch. This time it was their Greek Restaurant that was open, but they didn't have any Greek food! Gregory was appalled: you can't fool a Greek about Greek food.

With Grigorios Zamparas and Dana Kruyerova at Dům Uméni, Zlin, Czech Republic, 2010.

After practicing and doing some intense score study that afternoon, we decided that we'd better search out another venue for dining. The

Gevitka restaurant, not far from Hotel Garni, was located above a bowling alley. This restaurant offered a nice nocturnal view of Zlin and had really good food – usually. However that particular day, November 12th, was a national holiday in the Czech Republic (St. Martin's Day) and the only choices on the menu were goose and duck. None of the wait staff was fluent in English, so ordering food there was a bit of "hit or miss." I knew the all-important Czech word for beer, *pivo*, but that was about it and when Gregory asked in English what part of the goose we could expect to eat, the perplexed waiter paused for a few seconds, not knowing how to answer. Then a light bulb went off in his head and he responded: "Boobs!"

We just about fell off our chairs, though we knew what he was trying to convey.

There were two recording sessions on the next day, the first being from 10:00 until 13:00 (1:00 p.m.). We started with the third movement of the concerto, since that was the best movement to gain a sense of *espirit du corps*. Everybody was on task from the very beginning. The engineers were from Tonstudio and had set up sixteen microphones on stage. All of the sessions started on time; there was an efficiency here that we hadn't experienced in Sofia.

In the second recording session, from 15:00 to 18:00 (3:00 p.m. to 6:00 p.m.), we turned our attention to *Caprice Russe*. It also went well, although something gnawed at me, telling me that somewhere there was something that was not quite right. Afterward, in checking the score and running around on stage to look at the individual parts, I discovered an error in the printed 2nd Clarinet part. Unfortunately, this wasn't all. Very late in the session the orchestra and I rehearsed the Overture to *Der Thurm zu Babel* (*The Tower of Babel*), which I had just conducted at U Mass Boston. Both the orchestra and I had a difficult time with it, particularly with the opening string cascades, especially since we rehearsed the piece in "concerto position," with me in front of the piano, instead of closer to the edge of the stage where eye contact with those seated on both sides would have been better. We were all very tired, though here too I discovered errors in the 2nd Violin and Violoncello parts; these had been of my own making while extracting the parts from an uncorrected score on my computer at home. Aargh! To add to the frustrations, that evening Gregory and I went once again to eat at Gevitka, but the restaurant was entirely reserved. Since the Hotel Garni's restaurant was open only for breakfast and lunch, we had to settle for the Mexican restaurant in the Hotel Moskva. As expected, it was a disappointment – and overpriced.

The two final recording sessions were held on the following day. I was very tired but quickly recovered. The gargantuan first movement of the concerto was on hand. There were many problems – attacks following the piano cadenzas, hemiolas within the cadenzas themselves that made it difficult for the orchestra to count, myriad themes, rubatos, acoustics, etc. After trying a nit-picking piecemeal approach, one of the engineers suggested that we play the entire movement in one take and then take a break to hear it in the recording room. We did this and it made what followed a whole lot easier. This movement was initially difficult to get into, but after taking time to absorb it as a whole, we did much better.

In the break between the two sessions Tomáš told us that since the time of initial payment (sent in a few months earlier) there was a difference in the currency exchange rate that did not favor the dollar, that we were short 5,000 ČZK (Czech crowns), or about $280. I had anticipated this as the dollar was losing ground against most currencies at that time. During my first trip to the Czech Republic in 1997, the Czech crown was worth about three US cents; this time it was worth about five. So, Gregory and I each withdrew 2,500 ČZK (about $140) from a nearby ATM, thereby avoiding double bank conversion fees. We paid Tomáš on the spot. This was normal business practice, and we did not feel bad about it; we knew that Tomáš wasn't taking advantage of us.

During the final session, we recorded the concerto's second movement. The shortest of the three, it is the least demanding for the orchestra and offered few problems. Following this we rerecorded the part of *Caprice Russe* that had the error in the clarinet part. We also rerecorded *Der Thurm zu Babel* (*The Tower of Babel*). Even though it was at the end of the day and at the end of the final session, the orchestra was fresher and listened well to each other. It was agreed that Tonstudio would mix the recording. They sent me a compilation recording plus all the takes within a month's time and, once again, Toby Mountain's editing wizardry produced an excellent CD product.

* * *

2011 was a year of "European withdrawal." For the first time in nineteen years, I did not go to Europe. Part of the reason was that WASBE (World Association of Symphonic Bands and Ensembles) held its biennial conference at Chiayi, Taiwan, and I was to be one of the featured speakers. I could not pass this up. My topic centered around the 100th anniversary of Gustav Holst's *Second Suite in F for Military Band*, Op. 28 No. 2 [H106]. Ester and I decide to forsake Europe for a year so that we both could go. Shufang Du, who had soloed at different times on both violin and piano with the Boston Neo-politan Chamber Orchestra, was from Chiayi and gave us some pointers of what to see ahead of time.

Taiwan, of course, is a fascinating place, with its temples, bullet trains, and night markets. The one disappointment on this trip was not being able to ride the famous narrow-gauge Alishan Mountain Railway since some of its tracks had been destroyed by Typhoon Morakot. Trains had always been of great interest to me, ever since taking the Norfolk & Western from my home town to go to college. The bad news about the mountain railway, however, did not stop us from walking around the Chiayi's unguarded railway yard with friends Bob and Ann Gifford; Bob and I even got to climb onto one of Alishan's engines.

Of great interest was a tour that Ester and I took to the Fire and Water Spring at Tainan, a natural wonder. On our way back, we stopped at a resort where I was able to sit and enjoy the hot bubbling spa water (about 130 degrees Fahrenheit) all alone. It conjured up thoughts of a hot tub setting maybe from a James Bond movie and was one of the greatest forty-five-minute solo experiences I have ever had. We also had lunch at the resort; we were seated around an immense "lazy Susan," spinning it around to pick and choose the food that we wanted. We tourists were all trying very hard to use chopsticks – but not our Taiwanese guide. She was using a knife and fork and admitted to us that she really hadn't learned to use chopsticks!

Later on Ester and I spent part of one afternoon shopping in downtown Chiayi. I was looking for a conducting tunic. Normally I wear white tie and tails to conduct, but this gets to be uncomfortably hot during the summers. So, I entered a haberdashery and, to my delight, I found a nice black tunic there that fit me. On its price tag was marked the equivalent of $220 US. I indicated to the young woman who was waiting on me that it was too much. Immediately, she smiled and crossed out the price, replacing it with $110. Pleased with that amount, I readily accepted. Thinking that I scored a bargain, I mentioned this to one of the conference hosts. He smiled, shook his head and said that I had been taken, that I should have responded with $55 and bargained from there! Well, at least it's a darn good tunic!

XIV. A Night to Remember and a Pianist in a Hole

2012 saw three trips to Europe; two of them involved conducting.

The first was a solo excursion to Plovdiv, Bulgaria in May, to guest conduct the State Opera – Plovdiv Symphony Orchestra. The title of the ensemble is the result of a 1999 merger between the State Opera of Plovdiv (founded in 1953) and the Plovdiv Philharmonic (founded in 1945). This orchestra, representing the second-largest city in Bulgaria, was a step up from any of the orchestras I had previously conducted. Since the orchestra had recently experienced soloists who had given sub-standard performances, I was told that my concert needed to be entirely orchestral, meaning no soloist. With this in mind, I selected three core works from the orchestral repertoire that met with the orchestra's approval: Carl Maria von Weber's Overture to *Euryanthe*, Johannes Brahms' *Variations on a Theme by Haydn*, Op. 56, and Antonin Dvořák's *Symphony No. 7* in D minor, Op. 70. The orchestra had previously performed the Weber and the Brahms, though not recently, but the Dvořák was entirely new to them.

I spent the first night of the trip in Sofia. There I met up with flutist Natasha Usunova, who had been my tour guide in Vratza in 1998. It had been twelve years since I had seen her, when she and Michael Dejnov, principal clarinetist of the Vratza Philharmonic, had soloed with my U Mass Boston Chamber Orchestra at St. Paul's Episcopal Church, Brookline, MA in 2000. Natasha shared with me some very bad news about Valeri Vatchev. He had brain cancer. I had had mixed feelings about Valeri since his manipulation of my time (and, consequently, money) in my two recording sessions with the Sinfonia Bulgarica. However he was still a conducting colleague and, yes, still a friend; I felt very badly for him. Those in the Vratza Philharmonic, his home orchestra, were meeting regularly to discuss his grave fate and to pray for him. Natasha was optimistic, but my conducting colleague Ricardo Averbach, who had studied alongside Valeri, was not. Unfortunately, Ricardo was correct. Valeri passed away a short time later, just shy of his fiftieth birthday.

I had been to Plovdiv twice before and decided not to stay in Old Plovdiv this time but rather at a modern hotel situated halfway between the bus station and the concert hall. On my way to and from the hall, I walked through the Tsar Simeon Garden, a very nice and peaceful city park. However the first part of the walk, from the hotel to the park, was difficult, particularly in the rain, as many of the pavement stones were either broken or, at the very least, uneven.

The concert hall, located on Plovdiv's central square, was not attractive. It had been constructed by the communists more as a political meeting venue than anything else. The setup of the seating area for the audience was rather strange; about one-fourth of the balcony, on the right side as one looks at it from the stage, sloped downward, ending at the ground floor, but the wooden stage offered reasonable space for the orchestra and the building had good acoustics.

The overall mood among players in all of the Bulgarian orchestras was not good at this time. Positions had been cut and salaries reduced. Still, the music-making continued, and with great respect for the players, I would not have known about this situation had I not been told. Out of necessity many of the players needed to have a second job just so that they could continue to be professional musicians. So, they did what was necessary for the love of music and it showed. The State Opera – Plovdiv Symphony Orchestra was, and continues to be, an orchestra that professional players in other orchestras aspire to – the average age is probably at least forty-five, and for that reason they expect the conductor to be fully professional as well. Musically speaking, conductors coming here to face this orchestra need to have paid their dues.

Viechlav Novak, the concertmaster, and I met a couple of times beforehand, going over bowings, tempi, etc. He and I both felt that the Waltz/Furiant/Scherzo movement of the Dvořák needed a *piu mosso* toward the end, so I inserted it – and the orchestra really came through. Novak was born in Wałbrzych, Poland, of all places, where I had conducted a number of times. He had lived in Bulgaria for most of his life and therefore considered himself a Bulgarian. I found it interesting that on the Cyrillic poster announcing the concert, his name appeared in bold capital letters, but I didn't object. He certainly deserved it as he made my job so much easier.

In general, the rehearsals went very well, with the orchestra attentive to what needed to be done. There was one instance, however, that caught me off guard. I cut the orchestra off at one point during the Dvořák and was about to address something, but before I could open my mouth the principal clarinetist yelled in English: "Shut up!"

He and I had just had lunch together and this was totally unexpected. I looked back at him in shock and he immediately shook his head, motioning that neither he nor I was the problem. I found out later from him that he was angry at two of the second violinists who were discretely discussing the outcome of a local soccer game!

The following dress rehearsal went very well, just touching up on some rough spots. The orchestra's management didn't want me to record the concert, but they did allow for me to videotape this rehearsal.

The concert that evening was fantastic, nearly perfect. The orchestra had been with me in spirit all week, but this evening was something else. I had studied the scores for hundreds of hours, and it paid off. The most difficult part for me was pulling off the Overture to *Euryanthe*. The middle section, featuring eight muted violins, is almost the same as the beginning of Richard Wagner's *Trauermarsch (Trauersinfonie): Funeral Music on Themes of Carl Maria von Weber*, a wind work that he'd arranged to accompany the 1844 transfer of Weber's remains to the Catholic Cemetery at Friedrichstadt, Germany. I had conducted it many times. The hardest part for me was *unlearning* the Wagner and *re-learning* this passage in its orchestral garb. But these eight violinists really played it beautifully. The remainder of the overture was also solid and secure.

Brahms' *Variations on a Theme by Haydn* closed out the first half. Variations V ("Scherzo") and VI (introduced by the horns) were sheer ecstasy. The orchestra even nailed the difficult *pp* scherzo of Variation

VIII. The audience gave me a curtain call after the first half – quite unexpected, but wonderful to experience. But the best thing was when Viechlav Novak, the concertmaster, came up to me, winked, and said, “Pretty good, eh?”

Indeed it was!

The second half went even better. Dan Sommerville, orchestra conductor at Wheaton College Conservatory near Chicago, who recently conducted Dvořák’s *Symphony No. 7 in D minor*, told me that it was a piece that keeps on giving. And so it does – in spades! I am convinced that this work – the first of Dvořák’s final great trilogy – and not the 8th (which I conducted in Prague) or the overplayed 9th (of which I’ve played and conducted the last movement) – is Dvořák’s finest masterpiece. The buildup to the coda of the finale is especially exhilarating, but the whole work builds upon itself – and the orchestra responded to it with real panache.

The audience of 300 (in a hall seating 500), awarded us three curtain calls and more than half the audience gave a standing ovation – and this for a work that the orchestra had never performed before! I’ve had standing ovations before, but it was the force of the music and the orchestra’s devotion to it that really made my day. A good half of the orchestra’s membership thanked me after the concert – I can’t put into words what this meant – and this in Plovdiv, a cultural city that has its own opera company as well as the symphony! Thus, in many ways, what the orchestra accomplished that evening was far greater than some of the New York Philharmonic’s “walk-through” performances. These musicians, from the second largest city in Bulgaria, gave it their all and the result was really impossible to describe. And it came with a bonus – Kat, one of Plovdiv’s bass players who had played for me at Pazardjik back in 2000, gave me a hug and a kiss afterward. Ah, the fringe benefits!

After the concert I found myself ultimately alone, but in a mental state of Nirvana. I wandered through downtown Plovdiv and finally found the bar/restaurant that I had been looking for all week – The Hemingway. Yes, it was inspired by the author. Its decor was mid-twentieth-century

Key West, Florida – sea shells, fishing nets, and the whole bit. I originally sat at an outside table, but when my food arrived – in true Hemingway fashion, I was surrounded by a half dozen cats, so I took my food inside. The piano player there was performing such songs as "All of Me" and "Stardust." It brought back memories of the mid-eighties, when I was a poorly paid assistant professor of music at Hanover College and played piano in a jazz quartet (while enjoying every minute of it) trying to make ends meet in order to support my young family. It then dawned on me how far I had come. The Hemingway's piano player was terrific and I told her so. I was surprised when she told me that she was just a substitute, actually the daughter of the regular piano player! But there was no better way to end my day than spending two hours listening to her play, eating sea bass, and sipping some mellow Spanish wine!

* * *

The second trip to Europe in 2012 occurred in July. It involved no conducting on my part, though I certainly had conducting on my mind; there was much score study to be done for upcoming concerts and the next Rubinstein recording session. The occasion – or excuse for going – was the 20th IGEB Kongress in Coimbra, Portugal, during which I was to speak on English composer Haydn Wood. I had never been to Portugal, and Ester, whose ancestral roots go back to the Iberian Peninsula, very willingly accompanied me.

Getting to Portugal was a nightmare. We took SATA airlines, which showed the same half-hour commercial for the Azores Islands over and over and over again, perhaps eight times during our initial four-hour flight. Brain dead, we couldn't wait to get off the plane. There was a preliminary stop in the Azores first. This would have been a good thing, but we were put into a "holding cell" at the airport while we changed planes and saw nothing of the islands. As we exited the corridor on our way to the second plane, a female flight attendant came up to us, looked me in the eye, and asked very loudly something that sounded like "Leash, boy?"

At first I had no idea what she was saying, and then it dawned on me. She was saying *Lisboa*, the Portuguese (and proper) name for Lisbon. Ester, a native Spanish speaker, and I then realized that, while we could read Portuguese, understanding conversational Portuguese would be a real challenge.

Passing through customs at the Lisbon airport was horrible. When I related to someone at the IGEB conference that it took us an hour and a half just to go through the line, he remarked that we were actually very lucky – it had taken him more than three hours!

Once in Lisbon, we settled into our room at the Hotel Fenix, where many of our IGEB colleagues were staying; it had one of the best breakfast buffets I have ever experienced. Although Lisbon's old town had been destroyed in an eighteenth-century earthquake, there was still much to see – Belém Tower, Jerónimos Monastery, Gulbenkian Museum, National Coach Museum – and this barely scratched the surface. Even the beautiful tiled sidewalks could be considered a tourist attraction.

Coimbra was enchanting. Much of the city is medieval in nature. The University of Coimbra, founded in 1290, is one of the oldest in the world. The university has one of the country's most beautiful azulejos (usually blue tin-glazed ceramic tile artwork) in its chapel. Our bed and breakfast was a short walk from the university as the crow flies, if one wanted to walk down into an urbanized valley and then nearly 100 steps back up again. We usually chose to circumvent this on level ground, walking up to and along the ancient São Sebastian aqueduct.

As always, IGEB had a day trip planned. This time we had a tour of a winery as well as a winery museum which featured hundreds of corkscrews, including many that, for propriety's sake, will not be described here. At another winery we had a dinner and witnessed a presentation of a Portuguese *fado*, a song of lament, accompanied by a number of guitars and a string bass. At the end of the feast, which was late at night, we were rounded up and put back on the bus for the return journey to Coimbra.

Normally, we would have fallen asleep on the bus after such a fun-filled evening, but one thing kept us from doing so: the bus driver was absolutely insane! We passed through the hills in the country at breakneck speed. This was one thing, but when we reached the city, the driver did *not* slow down. We must have been travelling at sixty miles per hour through Coimbra's narrow streets. Ester and I were fortunate in that our bed and breakfast was near the first stop. We were thrilled to exit the bus. Bob Grechesky, who had to ride this bus to the last stop, told us that it got even worse. Was the driver going off duty? Was he paid only up to a certain time? Was he high on something? We never found out, but at least we lived to tell about it.

The day after the conference we rode with Keith Kinder and his wife Susan Smith to the town of Tomar to see the well-preserved remains of the Knights Templar castle. It was very hot, but we still enjoyed our time there, particularly the chapel containing an eight-sided structure with huge arches carved out of each side. Apparently it was constructed so that knights on horseback could enter and be given communion without dismounting.

Ester and I returned to Lisbon and did one more sightseeing trip, this time on our own, to Fatima. The miracle of Our Lady of Fatima is well-known, particularly among Roman Catholics. Ester (Roman Catholic) and I (Protestant) have different takes on this and it remains the source of spirited discussion. One thing we do agree on: Fatima is drowning in commercialization. We even had lunch at the Pope John Paul II Snack Bar!

* * *

In October Grigorios Zamparas and I returned to Zlin, Czech Republic to continue our Rubinstein concertos project with the Bohuslav Martinů Philharmonic Orchestra. The concerto at hand was Rubinstein's *Piano Concerto No. 2 in F*, Op. 35, perhaps the least interesting of the five, though it has its moments. It was composed in 1851, immediately following the success that Rubinstein had achieved with his first concerto. No. 2 has its share of Rubinstein's trademark waltzes, particularly in the outer movements. One such waltz theme occurring in the first movement amusingly turned out to be "Let There Be Peace on Earth," but in a minor key! In all fairness to Rubinstein, that song, by Jill Jackson-Miller and Sy Miller, would not be composed for more than another century.

Everything was set up months in advance – the orchestra, the dates, the finances, etc. – but unlike the Rubinstein piano concertos that we had recorded previously (Nos. 3, 4, and 5), the conductor's score and orchestral parts for No. 2 were not readily available. So, I had to go on an international search to find them. What I found presented both too much information and not enough information:

There were three different publications of the concerto available, yet none was definitive, and none had a full orchestral score. The two-piano score published by August Cranz, Hamburg, bears the dedication to Rubinstein's friend Charles Lewy. The set of parts from C. A. Spina of Vienna, obtained through Duke University, do not contain some of the thematic material indicated in Cranz's piano reduction in certain passages. A third publication, that of the piano condensed orchestra score without the solo part, from Gérard et Cie, varies still further in thematic realization. There were additional melodic fragments with no indication as to orchestration. To add further complexity, all three publications have variances in tempo indications. The third movement, for example, is marked *Moderato* in Cranz, *Allegro giocoso* in Spina, and *Allegro con moto* in Gérard et Cie, with several variances within.

Decisions for the recording of this concerto were based upon a reconciliation of the three publications plus a certain degree of guesswork; in certain cases "wrong" notes were left in where Rubinstein's intent was unclear. The orchestral parts had arrived from Duke less than two months before the recording sessions, so I did not have time to construct a full score of the entire piece. I did have time, however, to edit the parts and make a full score of the four-minute orchestral exposition. For the remainder of the piece, I did the best I could by heavily cueing the Cranz condensed score – writing in many rehearsal letters, dynamic markings, key harmonies, timpani rolls, and countermelodies. By the time we recorded it, I knew this concerto inside out, but the onus involved in the preparation was somewhat overbearing.

The other work chosen for this CD was the *Suite in E flat*, Op. 119, Rubinstein's penultimate work for orchestra, composed during the summer of 1894. The suite was dedicated to the Imperial Russian Music Society (which he had co-founded in 1859). The available publication of the suite, by Bartholf Senff of Leipzig, unfortunately has its share of errors. While the full score and parts were easy to obtain, recordings were not. The work had fallen by the wayside. Its symphonic length and high degree of difficulty may also have played a role in this. Whatever the case, I assumed, probably correctly, that our recording of the *Suite in E flat* would be the world premiere recording.

The suite consists of six separate and unrelated movements. Each is of a decidedly different character and can stand individually. "Prélude" serves as a brief but majestic opener. "Elegie" has a short almost atonal introduction which draws attention to the severity of the funeral music that follows. Tchaikovsky had died the previous year and this movement may have been either a tribute to him or a musical harbinger of Rubinstein's own impending death a few months later. The gregarious "Capriccio" may be the most original of the movements. Scored for smaller instrumentation and marked *Presto*, it shifts its tonal centers with reckless abandon. The lilting "Intermezzo" offers a chance to catch one's breath. The Bruckneresque "Scherzo" in C minor has two trios: the first one featuring the horn quartet and the second, strings. "Finale" features the entire orchestra and is the suite's most formidable movement. It begins with a rather warm introduction that is quickly interrupted by sinister agitation, which exists only to be offset by the sparkling main theme. A contrasting middle section, highlighted by a cello quartet, is followed by an extensive development, recapitulation, and an energetic coda.

Gregory and I had been away from Zlin for only two years, but during that interval the orchestra had moved into their new home, the Congress Centre, a beautiful building on T. G. Masaryka Square, not far from the Hotel Garni. We looked forward to recording in this state-of-the-art facility, not only because of what the hall offered, but also because we didn't have to deal with the strenuous walk up the hill to the Dům Umění.

The orchestra had arranged for the works to be recorded by personnel who were new to us. The producer who essentially ran things was a conductor himself, which was both good and bad – good, in the sense that he knew what to listen for but bad in that he had a difficult time burying his own feeling for the music. There was one time when he wanted to impose himself into the picture. In one of the sessions, he interrupted us and said over the speaker system in English: "Jon, I think that the tempo of the 'Elegie' is too slow."

I responded rather curtly: "No. That is not my interpretation."

That was all it took and he didn't try any more "arm-chair conducting" with me. I quickly glanced over at Gregory who, not involved on the suite, was seated in second row of the auditorium. He was smiling and shook his head. We had many good laughs over this later.

There were two major problems with the suite: difficulty and timing. What looks simple on paper often is not. At this final stage in his career, Rubinstein knew that the *Suite in E flat* would be his "Last Hurrah" for multi-movement works. Therefore he put everything that he could into it – mixed time signatures, hemiolas, abrupt modulations, exposed contrapuntal lines, and something somewhat rare in his piano concertos: a firm command of the orchestral tone color palette. Perhaps it was his way of saying to the Imperial Russian Music Society, "I am still here and still the boss."

Gregory and I usually had lunch with the orchestra manager, Tomáš Gregůrek. During one of these early afternoon meals Tomáš told me that some of the orchestra members had mentioned to him that the suite was "not easy." I knew this, of course, and took it seriously. I also felt pushed for time as I had underestimated the length of the timing for both "Elegie" and "Finale." What I had estimated to be a thirty-five-minute suite was actually a forty-three-minute suite, and since the concerto lasts a good forty minutes, we had too much music to fit onto a single CD. Later, when one of the violists told me that she was quite nervous about a very difficult exposed contrapuntal line in "Intermezzo," I knew what I had to do. "Intermezzo" is perhaps the least interesting of the suite's six movements. We had rehearsed this four-and-a-half-minute movement once but had not yet recorded any of it. So, I cut it. It was the right thing to do; the necessary amount of time that would be required to bring it into an acceptable state could now be spent polishing the other movements. Even with dropping "Intermezzo," we ended up with a CD of seventy-nine minutes and forty-four seconds, just barely fitting onto a single disc. So did I still conduct the world premiere recording of the suite? I like to think so, or at least 5/6 of it.

The music within the concerto was easier to put together, but that didn't matter; there was a perceived extra-musical problem. The recording engineers feared that the overtones produced by the piano would not fit well with those of the orchestra. Now the Congress Centre has a hydraulic lift allowing for a piano (or anything else) to be loaded one story below and then transported up to stage level. The lift itself could also be stopped at intermittent levels.

What the sound engineers first suggested was to have Gregory and the piano situated a good three feet below the level of the orchestra, as if he were condemned to sit in a pit for some awful transgression he had not yet committed. In order to appease the engineers, we tried it their way, but Gregory and I were not able to see each other, let alone hear each other. What we settled for was to have him and the piano situated about ten inches below stage level. This never did make sense to us, but at least we were able to make it work. In later years we recorded two additional CDs in the Congress Centre, but with a different recording team. Neither of those CDs required the piano to be placed lower than the orchestra.

On our return from Zlin to Vienna the trains were on time and we were able to get to the Opera House in time to see Mozart's *Cosi fan Tutte*. Unfortunately it was sold out; all we could get was standing room, which meant leaning forward against a rail. The sightline was good, but after leaning through the long first act, we decided that it would be better not to lean through the remaining second act. It had been a long week.

* * *

Following the flurry of European activity in 2012, 2013 turned out to be a bit of a breather, at least in terms of music-making in Europe. The focus was now on the many other projects that were at hand: doing research for a book (*Transatlantic Passages: Philip Hale on the Boston Symphony Orchestra, 1889-1933*), proofing an article on Haydn Wood for IGEB's *Kongressbericht*, proofing a "Score and Parts" article about Rubinstein's *Piano Concertos No. 3*, Op. 45 *and 4*, Op. 70 for the *Journal of the Conductors Guild*, reviewing the new Bärenreiter edition of the Beethoven *Piano Concerto No. 1 in C*, Op. 15 for the Conductors Guild's "Podium Notes," preparing my presentation of "Abdon Laus and the Boston Saxophone Orchestra" for the upcoming IGEB conference, editing the *CODA Journal*, starting my term as a board member for The Conductors Guild, as well as conducting the Boston Neo-politan Chamber Orchestra at the Goethe Institute and U Mass Boston Chamber Orchestra (UMBCO) concerts. There was plenty to do.

The spring of 2013 marked my final U Mass Boston Sabbatical (with a capital "S"). Most of the time was spent doing research at the Boston Symphony Archives, but I did get to travel to England and Scotland with my son David. Research for *his* book was the reason for the trip, though there was plenty of contact with music.

Our first such encounter was strictly by accident. On our first full day in the UK we were fending off jet lag by having lunch at the "Moon Under Water" pub at London's Leicester Square. We were seated toward the back of the long room, not too far from the men's toilet. As we were eating, we heard the sound of "jingle…jingle…jingle" getting louder as a man approached our table and then getting fainter after he passed us. I thought it unusual but did not look up from the pint of beer that I was nursing. When this happened repeatedly, I glanced up and noticed that the men jingling their way to and from the men's facility were morris dancers, dressed in white, with sashes, jingle bells and all. I immediately walked over to their table and introduced myself as I had conducted Gustav Holst's settings of *Morris Dance Tunes* a number of times. They told me that they enjoyed performing their dances to them and that if David and I waited for ten minutes, they would be dancing outdoors, right in front of the pub. David and I had forgotten that it was May 1st, "May Day," in the UK. The men performed a rather violent "stick" dance and then a more subdued "handkerchief" dance to the accompaniment of an older man playing an accordion and a middle-aged woman dressed like Mozart's "Papagena" playing a concertina. I was so impressed with seeing this first-hand that, two years later, I contacted the Pinewoods Morris Men of Sudbury, MA. They ended up enthusiastically performing their dances to Holst's *Morris Dance Tunes* on my "Fond Farewell" UMBCO retirement concert!

That same night we took the Caledonian Sleeper to Inverness, Scotland, where we saw the Culloden Battlefield; later we were entertained by a pair of Scottish folk singers while eating local pub grub (yes, including haggis). The next day we traveled north by train, bus, and ferry to the Orkney Islands. Late that afternoon we arrived at Kirkwall, the Orkney's largest town, on the island of Mainland, and trekked to the Youth Hostel where we stayed the next five nights.

The Orkneys did not disappoint. There were so many prehistoric landmarks – The Ring of Brodgar (a circle larger than Stonehenge, but without the cross beams), the Stones of Stenness, Maes Howe (a 4,500 year-old tomb with Viking rune graffiti from the ninth century), etc.. Access to all of them required a sufficient amount of hiking in fifty-degree weather that was adorned with thirty-mile-an-hour winds and spitting rain, which only added to the ambience. There were also attractions of a much more recent vintage, including the Italian Chapel on Lamb Island, built by POWs during WWII, and Highland Park Distillery, the farthest north distillery in the world. Of additional interest was the Stromness Hotel, where we witnessed a reading of the Orcadian folk tale "Assipattle and the Stoor Worm" in front of a raging peat fire.

The Orcadians are a fiercely independent people, tracing their ancestries to the Picts, Druids, Norns (Vikings) and Scots. At Highland Park our distillery tour guide summed it up succinctly:

"*Ask* me who I am, I'd say Orcadian.
Twist my arm and I'd say I'm Scottish.
Break my arm and I'd say I'm British."

The Orcadians have their own difficult-to-comprehend sub-dialect of Scots (not Gaelic), itself considered by many to be a dialect of English. Their word for small, for example, is "peedie."

Later on, David and I were fortunate enough to see members of the Orkney Traditional Music Project perform a free concert in Kirkwall's St. Magnus Cathedral. The group consisted of seven fiddlers (one of whom doubled on cello), five accordionists, an announcer/conductor who played violin from the back of the ensemble, and a music director/pianist who doubled on viola. The music consisted largely of strathspeys, reels, marches, and airs taken primarily from *The Orkney Collection*, the organization's publication of fifty-five tunes. The entire group performed on every piece and the combination of fiddles and accordions produced a penetrating sound, even in the cathedral. As I learned from an after-concert discussion with announcer Dianne Hull and music director Freda Burgher, the players we'd heard that day constituted only a small fraction of the group's membership. The Orkney Traditional Music Project was founded in 1998 to renew the art of accordion playing and to foster fiddle playing. Their management team came from three music societies: the Orkney Strathspey and Reel Society, the Orkney Fiddle and Accordion Club, and the West Mainland Strathspey and Reel Society. The project has been very successful and today consists of 120 musicians of all ages.

The Orkney Traditional Music Project is not the only instrumental music happening in the Orkneys. There are also three pipe bands, a brass band, and an orchestra – and this in a "nation" of only 20,000 people!

XV. Waxing Quixotic before a Burleske

The next year, 2014, saw three more trips to Europe; the two bookends involved recording sessions. By the end of my 2013 Sabbatical, I had already started to make plans for my 2015 retirement from the University of Massachusetts Boston. This meant that there was a need for using up grant moneys that had been earmarked for two recording projects. The first of these, in January, was the culmination of the Anton Rubinstein piano concertos project started with Grigorios (Gregory) Zamparas more than five years earlier.

We had one more Rubinstein concerto to record, the *Piano Concerto No. 1 in E minor*, Op. 25. As in the case of its successor, this concerto was not available for purchase. A copy of the full score and parts was available for a handling fee from the Edwin A. Fleischer Collection of the Free Library of Philadelphia, but I would have access to them only for about a four-to-six-week period. In spite of that fact, I put my order in immediately. As fortune has it, I found out that there was another copy of the published full score at the Newberry Library in Chicago. My brother Kurt, who lives in greater Chicago, did me a great favor by going over there and making a photocopy. Though it came out very dark, it still gave me about three months of early score study that I otherwise would not have had.

There is no definitive urtext for this concerto. Among the four sources (full score, orchestral parts, and two different publications of the two-piano condensed scores) there are significant differences in the cadenzas, scoring, articulation, and even in the number of measures! So, Gregory and I did our best to reconcile these. With the presence of a full score, this preliminary work was far less time consuming than what we had to do for the composer's second concerto. The *Piano Concerto No. 1 in E minor* was Rubinstein's fourth attempt at writing a piano concerto (the first two attempts were aborted and the third was turned into an octet), so it appears that he just wanted to get it into circulation, without taking the time to proofread the various publications.

The concerto itself displays the youthfulness of its composer. The first movement, in strict concerto-sonata form, contains a number of repeats, including one of forty-two measures (which we dispensed with). We chuckled a bit at the slightly slower "Midnight in Moscow" ending, though it does work. The second movement features an extended horn solo before breaking into a more intense section, foreshadowing the works of Edvard Grieg and Jean Sibelius. The third movement begins with a woodwind chorale before breaking into a romp that could be described as a Cakewalk precursor to Ragtime had it been composed on the North American continent. Still, this concerto as a whole is a substantial work showing great promise.

The concerto lasts about thirty-eight minutes. This being the last of our Rubinstein CDs, I wanted to balance this early concerto with one of the composer's greatest orchestral works. The *Symphony No. 2 in C major*, Op. 42 "Ocean" was briefly under consideration but it is too long and I had learned from experience not to over-program the CD. So I turned to his symphonic poems and found *Don Quixote: Musical Character Portrait: Humoresque for Orchestra*, Op. 87 (1870), based upon the character from Miguel Cervantes' two-part novel. There was one publication of it available, that by Bartholf Senff of Leipzig; thus there was no problem in reconciling multiple editions. Though *Don Quixote* is one of Rubinstein's finest compositions, it was completely overshadowed a quarter of a century later by Richard Strauss' *Don Quixote: Fantastic Variations on a Theme of Knightly Character*, Op. 35, a tone poem for violoncello, viola, and orchestra.

Rubinstein's work differs from Strauss' in many ways. While Strauss' work is more episodic and somewhat light-hearted, Rubinstein's is more of a psychological study, with three motifs (heroic, sympathetic, and love) used both separately and in combination with each other as Quixote gallantly tackles a herd of sheep, searches for love only to be mocked, and falls victim to pilgrims who turn out to be thieves. The work ends dolefully yet peacefully as Alonso Quixana (Quixote's real name) recovers his senses before passing away. It was a joy discovering this neglected masterpiece and even more of a joy recording it.

As usual, Vienna provided the jumping off place for this trip. By this time I was staying at the Pension Susanna in the center of the city, just around the corner from the Opera House. It is a small hotel which captures the charm of Old-World Vienna, if not perfectly, at least in the eyes of tourists. Gregory stayed out in the suburbs with his friend Aristea and her boyfriend Michael, a puppeteer.

One evening I decided to go to the opera, not at the Opera House, but to Volksoper Vienna, where Bizet's *Carmen* was being performed in German. As in the case of so many European productions of the early twenty-first century, the time was changed – in this particular production from 1875 to World War I. The effect was one of discomfort; it was too close to the Nazi era and the Anschluss; the children marching, not to mention the twentieth-century soldiers' uniforms, gave a foreshadowing of things to come – not what Bizet had in mind. Then there was the final act, with Carmen singing out at the top of her lungs, "Ich liebe dich nicht!" ("I don't love you!")

Absolutely terrifying.

When Gregory and I arrived in Zlin, Tomáš Gregůrek, the Bohuslav Martinů Philharmonic Orchestra manager, was there to greet us. He told us that the orchestra had contracted a new recording team for this CD that was better than any of the ones used previously. Hubert Geschwander, the recording engineer, and Emil Nizmansky, the music supervisor, were easy to work with and helped create a superior product. They would also record our next CD.

The piano concerto came together quite easily. Perhaps it is because No. 1 is the most direct of Rubinstein's concertos or perhaps because Gregory and I had become very accustomed to working with each other; whatever the case, with very few minor bowing, articulation, and instrumentation edits, the concerto almost played itself, so to speak. The same could be said for *Don Quixote*. With instrumentation bolstered by Rubinstein's addition of a piccolo, third and fourth horns, and three trombones, the orchestra responded quickly to the inherent nature of the music, whether in the powerful heroic passages or in the final dissolution of both man and quest. We were all on to something magical.

The end of these recording sessions marked the end of our Rubinstein piano concertos CD project for Centaur. In recording all of them, Gregory and I had accomplished something no pianist-conductor team had ever done and it felt good. Yet, as a team we were not done recording. Later that same year we would record another CD, and with the same orchestra.

* * *

In July of that year, Ester and I attended the 21st IGEB Kongress at Hammelburg, Germany. Though I presented a paper at the conference, most of the trip was of a sightseeing nature. We started in Heidelberg, where we stayed two nights in the old town, took the cog railway up to the castle, where we saw the pharmacy museum, the world's *second-largest* wine vat, and, to top that, the world's *largest* wine vat. Of course we enjoyed the general tourist-oriented gemütlicheit there.

From Heidelberg we took the trolley to Mannheim, where we stayed overnight. I had looked forward to visiting the palace at Mannheim, essentially the birthplace of the classical period in music. The building itself was heavily damaged and partially destroyed in World War II but had been repaired by the time we got there. Its cultural heyday was fairly short, lasting only from 1741, marked by the arrival of Bohemian composer Johann Stamitz, until 1778, when the court was moved to Munich. Stamitz founded the orchestra there in 1743. He was soon followed by his son Carl Stamitz, as well as other composers such as Franz Xavier Richter and Christian Cannabich. These composers of what today is known as the Mannheim School introduced such musical innovations as the Mannheim Rocket (a crescendo paired up with an ascending melodic line), abandonment of the basso continuo, and adoption of a homophonic orchestral blend of woodwinds, horns, and strings.

We naturally took a tour of the palace. The music room turned out to be one of life's great disappointments. It was set up as the royalty and nobility would have enjoyed it in the *nineteenth* century – harp, piano, etc. There was no reference to the eighteenth century, which of course meant no reference to the Mannheim School. Nowhere in the entire palace was there any mention of it, printed or otherwise. When I asked the tour guide about this, she had no idea what I was talking about! They had no idea of their own history and, furthermore, neither would any tourist who was not familiar with the facts beforehand. Ignorance is not bliss!

The IGEB Kongress certainly had its moments. Those of us who grew up watching *Hogan's Heroes* on television were surprised to find out that there really was a Stalag 13 near Hammelburg. The conference itself was held at the Bayerische Musikakademie Hammelburg (Baverian Musical Academy at Hammelburg), about a mile out of town. The performance highlight of the conference was a concert in the courtyard by the German Federated Armed Forces, Music Corps 12. The most notable presentation was by Gunther Joppig, Curator of the Musical Instrument Department at the Munich City Museum. He brought with him several saxophones, including a contrabass saxophone that was seized upon by many in attendance for a photo op. It was twice the height of Ester!

The day out featured a bus ride to the city of Würzburg, where we had a tour of the Würzburg Residence (Palace). A boat ride on the River Main followed, where we were serenaded by a trio of brass players. That was planned, but there was also a group of maybe forty men standing around on the upper deck who were singing some folk tunes from printed music, just for the fun of it, reminding me somewhat of my barbershop chorus music directorship "in a previous life." After the voyage we were bussed over to the small picturesque town of Sommerach, where we had a wine reception at the city hall, as well as lunch in the wine cellar of a Franconian vintner. Ah, IGEB – always the best party in town!

* * *

In November, Grigorios (Gregory) Zamparas and I did another

recording with the Bohuslav Martinů Philharmonic Orchestra in Zlin, Czech Republic. Despite having finished recording the Anton Rubinstein concerto project only ten months earlier, we were ready for something new. I also needed to use up my grant money before retiring. Victor Sachse of Centaur Records, Inc. had long since approved us doing a recording project containing works of the late German romantic composer Richard Strauss (1864-1949). It was a needed break from Rubinstein for both of us. Since many of Strauss' later compositions are still in copyright, I selected three of his early works for this CD: *Burleske*, *Serenade in E flat*, Op. 7, and *Suite in B flat*, Op. 4. The CD itself would bear the title *Young Richard Strauss*. Once again we were fortunate to have Hubert Geschwander and Emil Nizansky as the sound recording team.

Burleske (1886) can be looked upon as essentially a single-movement piano concerto; it is in a truncated concerto-sonata form with a huge coda. The piano part is extremely difficult and well-written but what is unusual about *Burleske* is that the timpani player, not the orchestra nor the pianist, starts the work with a motif that is both rhythmic and melodic. Here Strauss follows Beethoven's lead of eighty years earlier and expands upon it. The motif reappears throughout, sometimes shared between the piano and various instruments. There is significant solo material for clarinet and cello as well, and much of the development showcases the orchestra in a real Straussian tour de force. The coda contains many sections. One contains a hint of Leonard Bernstein's "Somewhere" from *West Side Story*, though that would not be composed for another seventy years. Another is rather melancholic, evoking memories of the Romanian "Anniversary Song." Still another has woodwind attention-grabbing "chirps." When all is done – not surprisingly here, but surprisingly for a piano concerto – the timpani player ends the piece all alone with a solitary note.

Strauss provided *Burleske* with an overall waltz feel, though it is interrupted from time to time. The tempi on available recordings vary greatly, from seventeen minutes to over twenty-three. Gregory and I gave the work a fairly broad performance (clocking in at 20:38) – not one that would drag but, rather, one that would breathe. The recording sessions went well and the timpani player, Grigor Kruyer, played his part so convincingly that we decided to include his name under Grigorios' for the *Burleske* timing entry listed on the back of the CD booklet. He certainly deserved it, but when the CD was finally released four years later, his name, not mine, appears on many of the websites listing the CD for sale! Am I irritated by this? To a degree – *he* did not conduct the CD, *I* did – but I also find a certain amount of humor here in that this situation epitomizes precisely the spread of misinformation that is so rampant on the internet (and in the press) in the early twenty-first century!

The other two works on the CD, the well-known *Serenade in E flat* (1881) and the lesser-known four-movement *Suite in B flat* (1884) are core works in the wind ensemble repertoire. I was after sensorial performances that would capture the romantic feel present in each of these works. The instrumentation for both works is basically the same as for the wind contingency of *Burleske* minus the trumpets and timpani – pairs of flutes, oboes, clarinets, and bassoons, and four horns – plus a contrabass instrument. On the title page of both works, in front of the contrabass line, Strauss indicated "Contrabassoon or Bass Tuba." He probably meant that if a contrabassoon were unavailable, then a tuba could be used as a substitute. However, on the last page of the *Serenade*, all of a sudden there is a separate staff for a string bass line. So there is a certain amount of latitude available (and confusion) as to choice of instrument. To take advantage of the different sonorities available, I stayed with the contrabassoon throughout and doubled it with the tuba in certain passages. I'm glad that I chose to do this; the orchestra's tuba player was one of the best I have ever had the pleasure to work with.

The last movement to be recorded was the *Suite*'s finale, "Introduction and Fugue." The players knew that we had something really special and even with multiple takes of the various sections they gave it all that they had. At the end of the session Gregory, who had been in the recording room, came up to me enthusiastically and exclaimed, "That was exciting!" Oh yes, it was!

This experience marked the end of an almost continuous line of CD recordings stretching over a fourteen-year period. It was not released for a while. At the time of recording, the previous CD, Anton Rubinstein: *Piano Concerto No. 1 in E minor*, Op. 25 and *Don Quixote*, Op. 87, CRC3462, had not yet gone through the final editing process. That one would eventually be released in 2016; this one, *Young Richard Strauss* CRC3574, in 2019. Is this Strauss CD my final one? I have no idea. There is one additional Beethoven CD that has been approved by Centaur though, at the time of this writing, I haven't followed up on it. So, we'll have to see.

* * *

Coda

It has now been five years since my retirement from U Mass Boston, yet life continues to yield many good things. Guest conducting, conference presentations, as well as other pursuits continue to keep me busy.

Although now primarily in the vacation mode, experiences abroad have not diminished. In the year following retirement, Ester and I went to Barcelona and then to the Mediterranean island of Mallorca – riding the Soller mountain train, seeing where Chopin and George Sand spent a winter in Valldemossa, witnessing a Friday evening Lenten procession, and inadvertently making the newspaper by simply attending a performance of Mozart's *Requiem* at the church of Ester's ancestors. Since then we found out through genealogy connections that Ester has a cousin who owns a vineyard there, so we *have* to return. The following summer, in pursuit of my own ancestors, we traveled to Northern Ireland, where we walked the walls of Londonderry, visited an ancestral home near our haunted inn at Carrickfergus, and then continued on to Dunoon, Scotland, where we climbed over the ruins of an ancestral castle. The next summer we traveled to Holland, staying in a B&B run by an Afghan family in Utrecht, then watching the cheese weighing at Gouda, Holland.

The most frightening experience since retirement occurred during 2018 in Israel. While driving a rental car on the road from the Sea of Galilee to Haifa, we got lost. Unfortunately, we had a GPS device hollering at us only in Hebrew. To seek assistance we pulled into an Arab gas station that featured spilled gas, people smoking, and a young child who was pumping gas into the cars. We were more than scared but eventually rescued there by an attendant named Mohammed who showed us the way. Other experiences included serving on a doctoral committee in Luxembourg and searching for fossils with David at Lyme Regis on the south coast of England. These and many more are elements of the spice of life.

University funding may have dried up, but I still have my hearing, my enthusiasm – and my glass remains one-half, maybe even three-quarters, full.

Sincerely,
Jon

Index

Summary

Now You Can Take Off Your Clothes: Vignettes of an American Conductor Lost in Translation chronicles the often hilarious exploits, both on and off the podium, of a conductor and college professor while practicing his craft abroad. Some thirty-nine vignettes – many of them humorous, some more serious – are recounted within a fifteen-chapter framework. Written for the general reader as well as musicians, the book covers a thirty-five-year period and is arranged more-or-less chronologically. Here are many vicissitudes of life, from being awakened by a real gunshot in the next room to being shot at by a chamber maid pretending to kill Al Capone with her imaginary automatic weapon, from being the recipient of lavish praise to being dripped upon while sitting in a Russian Aeroflot plane, from being entertained in a ship's nightclub by a Bulgarian keyboard player who doubled as a tap dancer to cringing while a skirted cymbal player crashed his instruments between his legs. It's all there, and much more – and all of it is true.

Jon Ceander Mitchell holds the title Professor Emeritus of Music at University of Massachusetts Boston, where he served as Conductor of the Chamber Orchestra and Coordinator of Music Education for nearly a quarter of a century. A well-known clinician on Gustav Holst, Ludwig van Beethoven and Anton Rubinstein, he has over one hundred publications, including seven books of which he is sole author and another where he is coauthor. He has guest conducted throughout Europe and the United States and has recorded ten commercial CDs as conductor, including all five of the Anton Rubinstein piano concertos. He was editor of the *CODA (College Orchestra Directors Association) Journal* for over a decade and is the 2019 recipient of the CODA Lifetime Achievement Award. He and his wife Ester live in the Greater Boston metropolitan area.